AMERICAN GOTH

What Reviewers Say About the Author

American Goth

"C.S. Lewis once said that myths 'are lies breathed through silver.' Perhaps, then, we can see fiction, as a golden filigree of words forged by a smith into an ornament that decorates our lives with tales that are not real, but are not lies.

American Goth is such a book—an alchemical reaction of ink, paper and intent, forged in the mind of a writer to tell a tale of a quest, of a destiny, of the life of a woman....J.D. Glass combines the tension of a young woman grasping at her chance to make a life after tragedy and to rebuild herself and her emotional stability with unfamiliar (to her) surroundings, people and rites. Glass's blend of music, ritual and sex forms a bond of its own, as we find ourselves drawn into Samantha's life, her quest and her growth.

Less hard-edged than Glass's previous novel, *Red Light*, this novel is no less edgy. Like a piece of Celtic knotwork, the reader will be following multiple threads through many connections, until the whole resolves itself into a powerful and exquisitely detailed pattern.

This was the book that I was waiting for...I imagine that there are quite a few young, pagan lesbians out there who will be delighted to train with Samantha, to find themselves part of a destiny greater than themselves and most of all, to find love."— Erica Friedman, *Shoujoai ni Bouken: The Adventures of Yuriko*

Punk Like Me

"*Punk Like Me*...is different. It is engaging. It is life-affirming. Frankly, it is genius....This is our future standing tall and, most of the time, alone, and this is the impact of this story. At a minimum it compels us to listen and to remember. Glass wants us to take notice...This is a rare book in that it has a soul; one that is laid bare for all to see. We owe it to ourselves to read this book, but more importantly, we owe it to our future." — *Just About Write*

"Powerfully written by a gifted author in the first person point of view, *Punk Like Me* is an intimate glimpse inside a cool 'dude's' head. ... Glass makes it fresh, makes it real, and gets to the heart of the matter where there is nothing left but truth....Speaks to lesbians of any age but straights will love Nina too. This important novel should be required reading in high schools across the country, especially religious schools, since teaching tolerance should be part of every curriculum. Although adolescents will love it, this is not a young adult novel, but rather a mature account of an admirable woman who stands up for herself. It is truly inspiring." — *Midwest Book Review*

Punk and Zen

"Glass has done a nice job exploring Nina's 'coming of age' story with a timeless quality that will hit a chord with most readers...This is not a lighthearted story but one told with soul that has the right combination of angst and spirit to engage the reader." — *Lambda Book Report*

Red Light

"...Glass constructs a well-researched world around the fierce desires of her damsels....Emotional thrills, medical chills, erotic interludes, and sweet romance: this page-turner has spirit to spare." — *QSyndicate*

"...Glass has created her own formula as a storyteller that is in your face gutsy and down to earth....She knows what she is writing about, and better than that, she communicates it beautifully in novel form.... She tells it to us straight from the gut and heart....Glass continually does what few authors can do well—write in the first person and still let us know what all of the characters are thinking and feeling....*Red Light* is definitely a must read." — *Just About Write*

"Whether you're looking for a sexy book with a plot that holds together, or a good book about a good character, with some romance and passion, then this book will definitely be worth adding to your 'to read' pile." — Erica Friedman, President, ALC Publishing

By the Author

Punk Like Me

Punk and Zen

Red Light

American Goth

Visit us at www.boldstrokesbooks.com

AMERICAN GOTH

by

JD Glass

2008

AMERICAN GOTH

ISBN 10: 1-60282-002-3
ISBN 13: 978-1-60282-002-9

THIS TRADE PAPERBACK ORIGINAL IS PUBLISHED BY
BOLD STROKES BOOKS, INC.,
NEW YORK, USA

FIRST EDITION: JANUARY 2008

CREDITS
EDITORS: RUTH STERNGLANTZ AND STACIA SEAMAN
PRODUCTION DESIGN: STACIA SEAMAN
COVER DESIGN BY SHERI (GRAPHICARTIST2020@HOTMAIL.COM)

Acknowledgments

To the beta readers who rock the world (and one of you who rules it): Paula Tighe, Eva, Jeanine Hoffman, Jan Carr, K. Dellacroix, Cait Cody, Cheryl Craig. Your patience, questions, and encouragement made the story I've always wanted to tell finally get told.

Kathi Isserman for valuable input at a very critical point.

Shelley Thrasher, you've taught me so much about so many things—I'm so glad we've worked together and become friends.

Ruth Sternglantz for holding my hand through the process of making this story a real book—and for being so kind about it.

Radclyffe (aka Len Barot) for once more taking the leap of faith with me. Your continued confidence and support lead me to think that yes, I can, and so, I do. Once more, into the breach.

A deep, and very heartfelt thank you to Arnie Kantrowitz for everything, from the very beginning of this novel-writing adventure.

And Shane? Nothing would happen without you. *Te adoro.*

Dedication

For Marge White: teacher, mentor, guide. Your steady, wry wisdom is missed and I know that wherever you may be now, you go in Light. There is no real way to thank you for shaping and training me. I can only hope to one day live up to the standard you set by example.

Brian, even though you may never read this, once upon a time we spent long, hard nights where we crawled through the muck and slew dragons, all the while knowing the sun would never rise again. We were wrong—it did, buddy, it did. This is what grew from it.

To Smitty, my brother, with all the love I can possibly give, and gratitude to Susan Smith, who guided me to my voice.

Shane, you've lived with Samantha almost as long as I have. Thank you. For believing in both of us.

Sometimes even to live is an act of courage.
—*Lucius Annaeus Seneca*

THE STRANGER—COVENANT

As above, so below; as below, so above.
—*The Kybalion*

I know nothing of the ways of magic, still less of the ways of love except to say this: it leaves. All that loves, leaves. Death, though—death I know, as the face of my father when he told me my mother had gone while I slept the sleep of the very young child; I know it as a visitor, as an unwelcome friend, a friend who rings the doorbell at two a.m. to tell me that my life is gone and I have been again bereft. I know death as a voice on the phone, a sullen, angry voice from over a thousand miles away that hisses into my ear to tell me the last of the light has finally died.

Now, though, death wears my face and uses my hands as I slip the ties that bind me to this earth, to this breath, to this flesh as at last the red ropes fall from my wrists where I've been chained, an endless length and endless flow, the chain of red that falls.

I know how to do this right; I've etched the lines that spell the word to set me free.

I lean back against the wall and close my eyes with a sigh, for at last it ends, and this time I'm the unexpected guest, the sudden voice. The door is open to me and I walk through.

❖

She walked on land, a rolling green field under a late twilight sky. Behind her were the woods, stretched endlessly across the rear horizon, while before her, perhaps two hundred yards away, flowed a river. The ground rolled gently down and, intrigued by the white sheen of the water, she walked toward it.

Indigo sky that faded to a star-studded black spread across its far bank.

"Where am I?" But the question was flat, muted, because she was certain that she knew.

"You know this place," her uncle's voice sounded behind her.

"The Astral," she answered. She wondered with strangely curious detachment at the name that had slipped out, previously unknown, and at her lack of surprise at her guardian's presence.

"Do you remember what's behind you?" he asked, his voice oddly muffled, as if the air were thick and humid though it was neither. In fact, the air smelled fresh, of early spring.

"The Tanglewoods," Samantha answered. She pushed forward, inexorably drawn to the winking shore, and Cort followed behind, his pace unhurried.

As she reached the slope that gave way to the river, she saw it. "Star Bridge!" she gasped in recognition.

Ancient and monolithic, it spanned the widest part of the river and ended under an arch on a shore hazed in indigo light that stretched on forever.

She stopped a moment to stare at the river, the waters that flickered and flashed, a flow of opalescent white that gave the Astral its perpetual haze.

"I can't follow you, Samantha," her uncle's voice said behind her as she stepped onto the first ancient red clay flagstone.

For the first time that she could remember, Samantha felt something—something akin to excitement, an almost delighted anticipation. She knew they waited on the other side, and she hastened forward.

"Samantha—you'll be stopped—it's not your time," Cort called out to her back.

The stone railing was comforting, cool but neither cold nor damp and, oddly restored by the feel of the stone beneath her fingertips, she left the safety of the railing for the center of the broad walkway, her steps quick, certain. She'd walked this path before, crossed the bridge a hundred, perhaps a thousand, times before.

Halfway across, she could walk no farther.

There was no force, no gate, no…anything that she could see or feel. She simply could not move forward.

A figure stood another third of the way across, a figure made of light and shadow, male and female. The gauzy form eddied and billowed, and bits of cloudlike light flowed from it as it spoke, spoke in a voice she instantly recognized and could not name.

"What you seek it is not yet your time to find. This is not your path to the bridge—you must walk a different way."

"But…but it's not—"

"All things in their time, lovey, you'll see," the voice said gently, a voice she longed to hear, and Samantha couldn't help but lean toward it. "You've made a promise—one you must keep."

Right. She knew that, she remembered it, she just couldn't remember why, and as she groped for the memory, a wind came up and tore at her. She tried to protest and she reached toward the figure, the voice. She could anchor herself against the wind, she could wait on the bridge for however long it took to—

"Samantha Cray, choose! Return, or remain stuck between— choose—*now!*" Her uncle called to her and she turned to face him, where he stood in the center of the maelstrom, pulled at by the forces that swirled around him.

She could stay, she could choose to do that, but she knew who she was, who she'd always been—a soul that kept its word—and she stopped resisting and let the wind catch her.

It pulled her backward and she swirled, caught up in a storm of light and shadow and laughter and songs that played in snatches while fear and lust tore through her veins and always, always, those eyes that looked deep within her *as she…fell…down.*

GRAMARYE

The lips of Wisdom are closed, except to the ears of Understanding.
—*The Kybalion*

I could feel the sun. Its brightness cut through my lids, its warmth pierced my skin. And before I opened my eyes, I could feel the tears build in them. I had failed. For the first time in my life, I had failed—failed at ending it.

Ah dammit. It wasn't so much that I'd wanted to die as I wanted... to question, to protest, to understand *why*.

"Don't open your eyes just yet," Uncle Cort's voice cautioned softly from somewhere to my left, "you've been out a while—they'll sting."

Resigned to living for the moment, I sat up and opened them anyway, only to shut them again against the white glare that greeted me.

My arm...my left forearm burned and throbbed, and I felt the scratch of linen wrapped firmly along its length as I heard my uncle draw the curtains.

"That should be much better," he said, and I opened my eyes again, carefully this time. I blinked and found his large form seated in a chair by my bed, his dark eyes somber as they rested on me. He handed me a glass of water. "Here. Do you know where you are?"

He waited while I sipped, the glass thick and heavy in my hands, the water sliding like ice needles past my throat.

My uncle's eyes, set under a broad forehead and a thick shock of deep brown hair that even tied severely back could not be straightened of its natural curl, were eyes I always imagined better suited to a tiger than to a man, and he held them steady on me. My father's eyes, despite their different color, had held a similar glow, though I knew that in fact he and Uncle Cort were not blood-kin, but somehow foster-related.

Although I had faint remembrance of Cort in my childhood, he'd become a permanent fixture in my life, my legal guardian in fact, since my father, a New York City fireman, had been killed in the line of duty when I was fifteen, orphaning me. My mother had died when I was two.

I nodded in answer as the spasm in my throat eased. "Leeds," I managed to croak out past the painful weight that had lodged in my neck—we were in Leeds, England, in the house Cort hadn't seen more than a handful of times since I'd become his responsibility, the house I'd been told my father had summered in as a boy. He'd wanted me to get to know it before we returned to the States.

"Do you know where you were?" he asked, and the air seemed to thicken as he waited for my answer.

I stared at the glass in my hand, at the water that swirled and sloshed, the whirlpool made reality that I'd created. I knew what he asked, knew what he meant.

"Yes," I said and squared my shoulders as I gazed back at him. I knew, with that deep knowing that comes from the very cells of the body, that I had just taken a step in a new direction; my next words would seal that fate. "The Mid-Astral."

"What do you remember?"

I remembered...everything. It left me feeling curiously blank. I sipped some more, destroying the pattern I'd formed, then took a deep breath. How appropriate, I mused, erase one thing to form another. There could be no more stalling.

"I...I made a promise," I said, shocked to hear the airy tone that came from my mouth.

Something flared in his eyes, a lightning strike of power or tears. When he spoke, his voice was gruff, choked, but strong.

"You're ready."

❖

"There are tests, dear heart," Cort explained, "tests for every level, and each with its subsets. Fail in any one and there you must stay—but you cannot be allowed to stay in any level that leaves you—or the Circle of Light Bearers—exposed and unprotected. And so you must resolve to pass all of them. Do you understand this?"

She nodded. She was, as he'd said earlier, ready. It was ironic, she reflected, that in attempting to end her life she'd found a new one, a new path, a new way, even a new name. Ann. That's what she'd decided. It retained the heart of 'Samantha,' but since those whom she'd wanted to hear call her name were no longer alive, it hurt her to hear it spoken by others.

But this…this new path…it felt like her whole life prior to this, including her walk to the Bridge, had led her here. All things considered, perhaps it had.

"Good," Cort continued, unaware of her thoughts as he continued to monitor her with another part of his mind. She would learn how to do that too. "First, there is the Light. Do you remember?"

It was automatic, the correlation in her mind of the Light to Nina, the friend she'd allowed herself to feel so much more for. Light…it had shone out from Nina's eyes in steady blue and silver waves, had eddied from her body and back to Samantha's with every glancing touch, it had enveloped her when they embraced. She had even tasted it in one, perfect, kiss.

Did she remember? How could she forget? She shivered involuntarily in her seat. To think in that direction meant pain, because remembering that loss, the tearing, wrenching knowledge that Nina had returned to the Light that sourced life, had moved beyond this world… it was enough to make her want to follow—and she'd already tried once. She'd honor her promise and not try again. She forcibly shut the memories away. It was not what Cort meant, anyway.

"Yes. Yes, I do," she answered instead. She once more closed her eyes and took another deep, perfectly controlled breath. She focused on the mental image of the perfect white light, a sphere that hung in space, until she could see it without focused concentration. She let the light mass drift, envelop her; then she absorbed it, letting it crawl up from toes to crown until she herself was not only contained in the nimbus, but also made of it. It tingled, a warm and sharp prickle under her skin.

"Are you ready?" Cort's voice sounded gentle, and to her physical ears, slightly faint.

"Um...how will I know?" she asked, uncertain in this new—and yet familiar—space.

Cort chuckled softly. "Because you'll look like a soft white lightbulb."

She felt herself smile even as she drifted further from the physical. "Guess I'm ready, then."

"Good."

Suddenly her awareness, her environment, changed. She stood on the same high plains she'd stood before, Cort beside her. He seemed... different...somehow, his hair longer, even darker, if that were possible, his features sharper.

"You must be able to bridge—walk and balance—between worlds," he told her as she found herself reflexively performing defensive and attack postures, the katas her father had taught her, with her guardian.

"I don't understand," she said as the forms changed, flowed, to push-hand techniques.

"As above, so below, dear heart," her uncle said gravely as push-hands gave way to sparring. "What happens here will manifest in the flesh, the material world. Beings, what you've known before as monsters, demons, and angels, all appear on the Astral in true form, the soul represented and revealed, but they seem as ordinary people on the Material, the Mundane. Events on the Astral, on any of the many Plains, are followed by events in your daily, physical life. This," he warned her as he swept her leg and she stumbled to avoid it, "is one of the many reasons you must learn to see every level, even when you're fully on the Material—this is one small part of how you'll be tested."

She nodded from the ground. So far, she understood. The Aethyr was the energy, the soul or spirit level as some called it, of the Material, the place most minds drifted to in dreams, where haunts "lived." The Astral...was something altogether different, and yet not, since it too had its ties to the physical. But while there was only one Aethyr, the levels of Astral, the Plains of existence, were infinite.

A message from the Aethyr could be delivered to the Material as a vivid dream, the sudden and unexpected fall of a cup from a counter, the coincidental meeting, the unexplained "lucky accident"; but one from the Astral took such energy to send, it might manifest as a flare of flame in a fire, the sudden flight of a bird, or a feeling, a mere sense, of possibility.

"You cannot be forced to battle, not yet," he said, holding a hand out to her, "not before you're ready. Of course," he grinned as he circled her, "they'll try to trick you into it, and they'll try to turn you." He feinted and she successfully dodged.

"Who do you mean, 'they'? What do you mean, 'turn'?" She almost missed the side kick and blocked just in time.

"The Dark, love. They'll want you to be one of them—you've ability, power, and you're linked to the Circle, the perfect entrance to destroy it. That…they want more than anything. To devour, to destroy the Light."

The volley he levied at her was sudden and fast and while she retreated, she held her stance and blocked effectively. "I would never do something like that," she said, horrified at the thought that anything of that nature existed.

She managed it, finally, the first blow that got past his guard.

"Nice," he told her, admiration evident in his tone. "Maybe you'll be ready for your weapon sooner, *rather than later.*"

❖

Dizzy. I felt dizzy and nauseous as I opened my eyes on the floor of the study. *Oh…this…sucks!* I thought as I tried to roll over. One moment, I'd been on the Astral, the next—

"Here." Cort handed me a glass of milk and a nut-studded brioche. "Shut the systems down."

At the first sip, I instantly cleared and after a few ravenous bites, I felt human again.

"Did you say a weapon?" I asked with real curiosity. I'd thought this was all head stuff, ethics and intentions, a new way, almost, of reading the environment.

"Yes," Cort said slowly, "one that will carry, *cut*, as it were, through worlds." He sighed heavily. "For now, its function is mostly ceremonial, but there have been times…well, not before you're ready, anyway."

I laughed at that. Less than three weeks ago I had tried to kill myself, had found myself in the strangest, most familiar place I'd ever known, then had woken back to my body to find that the cuts on my wrist had been overlaid with a brand, an ankh melted into my skin. That had been part of the net, the spell Cort had literally cast to keep me alive, because it was the physical proof of my promise and my choice. That ankh now hung from my neck, above the sword pendant I wore.

"Try me," I said, now fully revived after eating. "Let's find out."

❖

It had been almost a week since our discussion about a sword, and had my plans not changed within the first few days of our arrival, I would have already been back home, back in the States, packing for freshman orientation at Princeton University.

Instead, in addition to the new world my uncle carefully and meticulously guided me through, there was the one we actually lived in: Whitkirk, a suburb of Leeds. Everything was strange, from the brick house that seemed older than the country I'd come from, to the way the town was laid out—groups of houses clustered together, their backs facing rolling greens, highways that suddenly became winding roads that ended in small squares, the pub that seemed to be an old factory in the middle of nowhere, then the sudden heavy bustle of Leeds proper as soon as you crossed into it…

I explored the house itself. The entire first floor was split into three parts: the front half was divided between a sitting room and the kitchen—that took up the front quarter, and while the building was old, the amenities in there were not. I only knew that because Uncle Cort had told me, not because I spent any real time in there. The back half, with a ceiling that rose to the second floor, was filled with carefully placed and arranged items of craft, of large sheets of metal pressed together between huge vises, delicately curved gold wires held with the tiniest of clamps, workbenches with weapons and armor covered in flaking dirt and rust, with brushes, oils, and whatever other mysterious tools would be used to examine and reclaim them.

The walls themselves were mostly exposed stone painted over in the palest apple green with furring strips fitted and wedged to their height to support the sturdy wooden shelves built onto them. These too were filled with more artifacts and weapons in various states of construction or recovery.

My uncle's work had obviously backlogged while he was in the States, taking care of me.

There was a small, perhaps six foot by six foot black iron oven that sat in the back corner, mounded over the top and sides with brick. I never saw it fired up, but Uncle Cort said he had a bigger one in his shop in town and preferred to use that.

When I wasn't watching him and the focused attention he spent on each ancient piece he rescued and carefully restored, I mostly spent time in the study, which took up the entire second floor—books lined every wall except for the one that held the fireplace, and I had a favorite spot, almost a corner really, where the sun would pop in and spend the day over my head. Occasionally, I'd walk up the stairs from the third floor, where all the bedrooms—including mine—were, to exit onto the flat roof and smoke the occasional cigarette while gazing around, either over the town or just up into the sky, watching the clouds or the stars.

Mostly, though, I played my guitar—or, rather, guitars, one acoustic the other electric, but this was an exercise largely in skill maintenance rather than joy; it reminded me of things and people I didn't want to think about—or read any of what seemed like a thousand texts on history, lore, religion. I had *On A History of Symbols* in my hands when Uncle Cort found me in the study.

"You know…there's a bit of work I've got at the shop in town that I need to get to so I thought, well, I'd like you to work with a tutor during the day while I'm out," he said, wasting no time when he walked into the room.

I stared at him in surprise as he set down the small box he'd carried under his arm. "Is this the very nice, polite, British way of telling me I need a babysitter?" I asked and gestured with my arm, revealing the healing lines and brand.

"If I thought you needed that, you'd have a nurse and wouldn't need a scholar, now would you?" he asked dryly.

"I suppose," I agreed reluctantly.

He took a slow and heavy breath. "Annie, can you tell me exactly what went through your head that day?" He studied me carefully as he waited for my answer.

I tried to remember well enough to answer honestly,

"After the…after the phone call," I began, then hesitated. I was unprepared for the rush of pure hurt that raced through me as the preceding events played through my mind.

"After that," he prompted softly, "what happened?"

Anger, disbelief, sorrow, rage had all flowed through me before they turned into something…cold…a disconnect…a chill with a voice that made me want to argue with God, Fate, whatever it was that had ordered my life in this way.

I didn't know, couldn't really say, what had led me to go from cutting myself to digging deeper, only that it had made sense, in that same, frozen, logical way, to do so. It had become an imperative that I obeyed. The hurt was…hot, but the anger…was cold. I tried to explain all of that to him as best I could.

"Thank you for sharing that with me," he said and laid a warm hand on my shoulder.

When I blinked up at him through the tears I hadn't realized had formed, it was to see an echo of them in his eyes as he crouched before me.

"I don't want you to think I don't trust you—I do, I trust you, trust your word. I'd rather you thought of it as a birthday present—a bit late, but a present nonetheless." He gave me a smile.

I rubbed my eyes quickly. "What, no fast-moving convertible?" I asked, trying to joke. Other than the roof or the occasional walk around town with Uncle Cort, who shared the history of the area with me, I barely went outside. I wasn't really interested in wandering about, and I had to keep remembering stupid things, like looking right before left to cross the street. Driving seemed a bit out of reach for the moment, which was too bad, because that was my favorite way to explore as well as to relax.

Besides, my car, a '74 Nova, nestled shiny and safe in a garage three thousand miles away.

"Uh, no. Sorry." He chuckled. "Would you like roller skates?"

"I'm being demoted?"

"Nah," he laughed with me, "but they're great for balance, and speaking of…" He reached into the box he'd set next to him. "This will help."

He handed me four black-canvas-covered rectangles, each about two and a half inches wide and six in length. A cotton band sewn firmly along their central lengths extended another few inches beyond the edge on one end, with two d-rings on the other. They weren't heavy per se, but they had a discernable heft.

"Sand?" I asked as I curiously shook one.

"Yes," he answered as he took it from me, "and you wear it like this." He wrapped it about my wrist, then showed me how to tie the band through the d-ring.

"What's it for?"

"Strength. Endurance. Speed," he said simply. "You'll need to build all of those before we move on to the next phase."

"And this will help how?" I asked, as I moved my arm about. The weight was barely noticeable.

"You'll wear them, wrists and ankles, starting tomorrow. Take them off to play guitar and to bathe," he said with a grin. "You don't have to sleep with them."

I shook my head as I carefully removed the weight from my wrist. "I can't see where such a small weight will do anything." I couldn't. I was used to swimming pools and weight rooms, not little things like this that felt like nothing in comparison.

"You will," he assured me with another wide smile, "you *definitely* will."

❖

"I've someone I'd like you to meet," Cort said later that afternoon when he reentered the study, and he'd brought someone with him. This, I supposed, was the tutor he'd mentioned, my "birthday present."

I marked my page and carefully put the book down to stand as they walked in.

"This is Elizabeth. Elizabeth MacRae. Elizabeth? This…is our Annie. I'll leave you to it, then?" he said and excused himself with a small bow. He closed the study doors as he left.

I stared at the woman before me who stood about five foot three inches, straight steel gray hair pulled back from her face, but loose across her shoulders. Her face seemed familiar as we shook hands, an echo of a memory I couldn't quite place as her palm met mine, and her eyes, a kindly soft amber, seemed to glow with the sincerest of intentions.

"You do know, of course, that Cray is a form of MacRae, don't you?" she said, pronouncing the two vowels of her name discretely and distinctly, as if to illustrate the connection between them. "And that makes us, in fact, distantly related."

I shook my head. "I'm sorry, no. I didn't."

"You know nothing about the MacRae?"

"No." I eyed her regretfully.

"Oh, I can see we've got a *lot* to cover," she said and smiled again. "Let's begin with the Clan crest, shall we?"

❖

There was much more to Elizabeth than was obvious to the first-meeting eye, and there was even more to get used to. The first was that she lived with us.

"I live with Cort when I'm in England," she told me with a smile as I helped my uncle bring her things in from the car, "but when I'm running away," and they shared a grin over my head at that, "I'm fond of Aberdeen."

"Where's that?" I asked. I really didn't know.

And that was apparently the perfect question with which to open my lessons. The next two weeks found my days filled by Elizabeth teaching me things that ranged wildly—and we did indeed start with the Clan crest and motto: Fortitude.

I needed fortitude because both Elizabeth's daily lectures and the now nightly work with Cort focused on the arcane and esoteric, levels of meaning precisely and finely layered. And Cort had been right: the weights, as slight as they may have seemed, did add to the exertion of the physical exercise, but once I got used to wearing them, my body felt light, almost airy, when I removed them.

Still, I had so much work to do that my guitars received little more than friendly tunings and some quick scale exercises. The good thing about this was that it left me little room for emotional transports of any kind—and for the time being, I preferred it that way.

I didn't really know why I had to learn all of these disparate-seeming subjects, but I went along with it—it *was* all fascinating and it kept my mind busy.

But there were things I was a bit curious about. The more I worked with Cort, the more…sensitive…I seemed to become to the environment, to people, or at least, to Cort and Elizabeth. There were times it seemed like I could almost physically see a nimbus, the energy field that both of them assured me was a very real thing. It surrounded each of them and there were times it seemed as if faint threads of that nimbus connected them to one another. That was one part of it. The other was...

"How long have you known my uncle?" I asked Elizabeth one afternoon that had been reserved for free study, time where I picked a specific topic I either liked or wanted to work harder on.

She glanced up at me from her papers. "We've been friends since before you were born. Sometimes, it seems almost before *we* were born, well, before I was, anyway," she corrected herself. "He's a bit older than I am." She gave me a smile and returned her attention to the work before her.

I gathered the books and papers I'd scattered on the rug and came to sit next to the desk. Uncle Cort could be funny, and he could be caring and warm, but other than the fact that I was legally his ward until I was twenty-one, as the court-stamped papers signed by my parents said, and my own sketchy childhood memories, I knew nothing, absolutely nothing, about Cort Peal besides his name, his work, and his seemingly complete knowledge of the Astral. I knew as much of his personality as he let me see, but none of his history, other than he'd known my family forever, it seemed, and was a British national.

He and Elizabeth had been friends for more than two decades... what would it be like to say something like that? To know someone that long? How well did someone get to know a person after ten years, fifteen, twenty? There was one person I could say had been a really good friend since I was about ten, but I was barely nineteen, and of the friends I'd thought would be lifelong...Nina had been seventeen, wouldn't get to see—

"Have you called your friends back in the States since you've been here? Your classmates?" she asked and waited patiently for an answer.

"No." It came out sharper than I'd intended it, partially due to the surprise that she followed my thoughts so clearly—I wasn't used to that yet—and I glanced up at her quickly to see if there was more to what she asked. I sensed a friend and could feel there was intent behind her words, nothing malicious or unkind, but a purpose to her question, deeper than idle curiosity or small talk. "There's no need," I added, tempering my tone. "There's only one person I'd speak with and I'm sure she's…" Triggered automatically by thought, by memory, my heart tightened within me and I couldn't help it, couldn't help but reach out with my mind for—

"Annie, stop," Elizabeth said quietly and laid her hand over mine. "You mustn't reach for her, for any of them, like that."

I shook my head to in an attempt to clear it and the tears that had started to form. "It's just that I can't, I can't—" I grasped the sword charm that hung from my neck. I took a deep breath, then another while Elizabeth kindly busied herself with the papers and books on the desk, pretending not to see when I reached for a tissue and dabbed at eyes that insisted on filling anyway. "I can't find her *anywhere*, not the slightest trace. But when I touch this," and I showed her the pendant, "when it's on my skin, it's as if she were next to me. Nina."

Elizabeth gave me a sharp look. "Did she give that to you?"

I nodded, unable to speak as she leaned over to examine the metal between my fingers. She even held her fingers above it, hovering not more than half an inch away. Her brow creased with her focus. "What a beautiful innocence," she murmured as she straightened. "You shouldn't take that off, you know," she said matter-of-factly and put on her glasses. She began to once more organize the books on the desk.

My hand clenched tighter around the miniature claymore and I could feel the crosspiece of the hilt dig into my fingers.

"I don't intend to," I told her as I tucked it under my shirt so it could warm in its customary spot against my skin.

"Good." Her voice was brisk. She peered at me over her half-lenses. "It was a gift given in and with love," she said gently. "You feel her, because her presence, her *intent*, is in it. The energy she put into finding and choosing it, the feelings and thoughts she had as she handled it interacts with the molecular structure that forms the metal's lattice and—" She stopped as she narrowed her focus and examined me.

I felt like I was about to snap in two because as Elizabeth said the words, I could see it so clearly in my head, could see Nina as if through her own eyes, wandering around with her younger brother during her search, feel the pleased wonder when she finally found it and held it between her fingers, knowing she'd give it to me, considering it the perfect gift. I felt the tremor that had run through her hand when she'd carefully placed it in the box she'd finally wrapped it in, the happy-nervous anticipation when she gave it to me, and that brought a very real memory with it, the memory of the brush of my lips on hers as we stood in the sand by the bay...the kiss in my car after—

"Go," Elizabeth said, her voice still kind as I sat there and struggled against the grief that threatened to overflow. "Enough lecture for one day. I do expect to see you for dinner."

I nodded my thanks as I exited the room, then used all the discipline I had to force myself to move properly dry-eyed through the hall and up the stairs, down the corridor and into my room. Once the door was closed, I sat on my bed. I couldn't look at the guitar that stood forlornly in its rack—it made me think of afternoon jam sessions—and I felt like my knees would bend, my back break, my head implode under the black wave of empty that roared above it, threatening to crush me beneath it.

I paced for a few moments, an agitated circuit around the wood floor before I walked magnetically, inevitably, over to the nightstand and opened the drawer.

They were in there, the little box of blades, sharp, fresh, deadly if used the right way and I curled my fingers around them.

"I trust you," Cort had said, "and even if I didn't, this is not my decision—it's yours," he'd said when we'd finally discussed more about the what and how and why of my first remembered journey to the Mid-Astral.

"I suspect," he said somberly, "that while your feelings were your own, you may have been...pushed."

"What do you mean?" I'd asked. That didn't sound right to me—there had been such a frozen edge to the fire that had blazed through me, a cold fury that acted with what felt like total logic, the words in my head, the dare to the Universe to stop me, to *answer* me. I hadn't expected It would, and especially not in the way It had.

"Hounds," Cort answered simply. "They knew who you were before you did."

I may not have completely understood at the time, but it wasn't hounds that chased me when the wave crashed down, was a swirling force that knocked me off balance, crushed my chest, raced higher with its promise to drown me beneath it.

I don't want *to die*, I promised whatever might listen as the first cut halted the upward rise, *I* have *to live*, I told myself as the slice stilled the whirlpool, reddened unmarked skin, and I felt the flood waters recede. I just…wanted…the hurt…to *stop*. And once the outside bled the way the inside tore, for a single moment? It did.

❖

We were well into August, and while I still rarely left the three-story brick building we lived in, I now hardly saw Uncle Cort at all, except for our evening sessions. "Shop's got me hopping," he'd say, "and we'll get even busier when we get back to London. I've a lot to catch up on and this is my window of time to 'create.'"

He'd then unroll the document tube he carried and show me his designs, sketches made for custom orders. In addition to dealing with verifiably ancient weapons and artifacts, Uncle Cort was an artisan and made custom blades himself, with the metal fired in such a way that it took on multicolored hues, swords with the metal folded so finely that rivers seemed to flow down the edge. Replicas. Originals. Works of art and fancy, works of deadly utility. "I've a very special client who needs something…unique," he added one night, and the smile he gave when he said it matched the great-cat flame of his eyes and made me wonder what exact sort of clients he had. I asked.

"You'll know soon enough, dear heart, and truly, it's not nearly as interesting as an old man makes it sound."

He always said that, but I couldn't really understand why—my father, a rangy fireman who'd lost his life on the job, had been only forty years old when…well, I'd lost him. Cort appeared no older than he had, yet he always spoke as if he'd been around since dirt had been invented. Elizabeth did say he was a bit older than he seemed.

But then he'd ask about my lessons and I knew, whenever he did that, that whatever he hadn't told me yet would probably be interesting at least and more than likely hair-curling and perhaps even slightly terrifying.

"Shall we?" he asked as he got up from the table, and excusing myself to Elizabeth, I exited with him.

"How are your studies?" he asked as we rounded the landing.

I thought about that as I followed him up the stairs. "I'm learning a fair bit, I think. Lizzie"—Cort shot me a grin over his shoulder, because we both knew neither one of us would ever call her that to her face directly—"is giving my Latin a daily workout. She pronounced my French atrocious and said my Spanish is barely tolerable."

Cort chuckled as he opened the sliding pocket doors. "You must sound like a native, then. I understand why you're studying French, given that you've decided to become a European." He smiled at me. "Any particular reason for the Spanish?" he asked, his tiger eyes glinting at me as we moved the furniture to clear a center area.

I shrugged with a casualness I tried to feel. "Studied it in high school." He knew that. He also knew that it was the language—

"Your friend, right?"

I shrugged again.

"It's a nice way to remember her," he said mildly as together we moved the settee. "You may want to take a moment to perhaps remember a few others, as well." I could feel his appraising glance as we set the legs down carefully. "How is everything else coming along?"

"Everything else" covered quite a lot of territory. Elizabeth quizzed me endlessly on each item we read and discussed, from literature to history, including Clan history. Since we were in Leeds, we were far from Scotland, though close enough, in Elizabeth's eyes, to oblige me to learn all about it, from the Jacobite Rebellion (including the death of Duncan MacRae, whose claymore was exhibited for years in the Tower of London as "The Great Highlander's sword") to the dispersion of the MacRaes through the United States. This was accompanied by the promise to visit Eilean Donan Castle—bought and rebuilt by yet another MacRae after it had been in ruins for two hundred years.

Elizabeth herself held two doctorates, one in philosophy and the other in physics, and since I'd already covered more than the mere basics of science and math in high school from taking college-credit classes my senior year, she fed me quantum theory and asked me to hypothesize about ethical evolution as well as to define moral laziness versus cowardice. She also taught me how to recognize different species of what seemed to be entire forests of trees and plants, as well as how to properly care for a sword—not that Uncle Cort hadn't already beaten her to that particular skill.

There were also lessons in manners, always manners, and not the sort that were the simple "please" and "thank you" that everyone was supposed to use, but instead a careful study, an awareness of language and tone, of posture and the messages subconsciously sent that I could in turn consciously decode, things such as observing how a person sat, whether or not they bit their nails and how far down if they did, a sign of passive-aggressiveness, anger not fully resolved, the stark fear that hid behind the most aggressive posturing, the directional shift of eyes that revealed a truth…or a lie.

With Uncle Cort, though, I learned something else entirely.

I shrugged in answer again as I moved into the cleared circle. "I'm not certain. I've not really done anything yet."

"No, not today," he said, shaking his head as I took my accustomed stance and place.

I schooled my face to impassivity and reined in my curiosity.

He walked around me once, inspecting me with a critical eye, checking to see if my stance, my body language, or even the energy field that surrounded my body betrayed any of what I felt or thought. I was almost certain it didn't.

"Nicely done." He smiled, then put a fist on his hip and considered me, deep dark tiger eyes probing mine. "Do you trust me?" he asked finally.

"Yes."

He nodded, satisfied. "Good. Annie, I want you to kneel, straight up, and hold your arms straight out. Close your eyes when you do."

I did as he asked. "Palms up," he directed, and I did that as well. I automatically reached for the Aethyr, the level of essence that was pure energy, and in less than half a second, I was already made of the Light, within and without.

The flat weight in my hands was cool, solid under leather, two and a half, perhaps three inches wide as it covered my palms. It felt very, very familiar.

"This is yours," Cort's voice was low and solemn. "It will carry and cut between worlds. Use it only in the coolness of your mind, *never* in rage. There is a difference between rage and righteous anger—and that difference will burn you."

I swallowed and nodded. It wasn't heavy, yet, but I could feel the beginning, the very start of the pull in my shoulders.

"Your lesson today, and for the days that remain until your initiation, will start and end here. Hold that position as you move between levels. Get used to the weight, Wielder, it's yours by right, by blood, by the promise made before you were born and the one you'll make again in short time. This has a history older than you know, but more importantly, it was once your grandmother's," and his voice thickened, grew hoarse, "before it was Logan's—your father's."

❖

During their initial sessions on the Astral, she had been encouraged, after becoming familiar with certain landmarks, to explore, either with Cort or on her own, the valleys and plains, to meet the beings that inhabited them. Some she recognized, recognitions that came from dreams she'd had since she was a child, others from a life different than the Material one she led. Some were people she had yet to meet, and more than a few were beings who hadn't been incarnate in ages as humans measured time and wouldn't be for ages more to come.

There was a flexibility there that simply did not, could not, exist in the Material world. The fixed form was traded for function—wings that beat with power and strained the muscles of a very physically felt chest, arms that became legs and hands, paws beneath which the ground sped by with satisfying solid thumps, making her eyes sting.

While there were occasions when the actual physical body would be represented, the rigid structures of the flesh could be changed— male, female, human, non, at will. She enjoyed that, the freedom of it, because her body was whatever she wanted it to be, whenever she wanted it, and most of the time all she was aware of was its strength, its capabilities and potential.

Today, tonight, whatever time it was in the eternal twilight, she walked through a grassy field beside Cort. When they had first started working together, if she could have described herself, she would have said that she was slender but strong, not quite finely featured but discernable as female because of the curves that rose on her chest, the hair that flowed halfway down her back, not much different at all than her physical self.

Now, though, as her abilities had progressed, she had lost some of that definition, color; she walked in a body composed of light that became more and more featureless as she grew in her command of craft, in her comfort level outside of the Material.

"Every bit of matter has a frequency, a vibration," Cort told her as they approached a place she'd not seen before. "Flesh, blood, rock, water...they all have energy."

She nodded. She had learned some of this already.

"The higher the vibration, the less muted by interference, static if you will, the purer the energy," he continued as they crossed a ridge. "That higher level of vibration will allow you to cross to other levels of the Astral." He stopped and gazed before him and she followed suit.

They had come to a valley of mixed woods and plains, where even the wind in the twilight carried the scent of near spring.

"Except for Star Bridge?" she asked, remembering her first visit.

He put a hand on her shoulder. "When you are free, completely free of the Material, of the lower vibrations emanating from the flesh, then and only then can you cross that bridge."

Affection flowed from him to her, an affection she returned as she stared down at the valley with him and considered what staying halfway across the span would have meant.

"Are we going there?" she asked, pointing below.

"You are," he told her, "if you can."

She took a few steps forward, then stopped when she realized he didn't walk with her and she looked back at him.

"Go. And if you can enter, remember what you find. I'll come for you when it's time."

She mentally girded herself and strode forward, down through the waist-high grass that tickled under her hands, down until the ground leveled, the first clearing before the stand of trees, and there...she discovered the wolf pack.

They were huge, noble-looking animals, perhaps twenty or so, a range of sizes and musculatures, with fur ranging from the purest white to gold to the inkiest velvet black, and they welcomed her among them in gestures, in sendings, told her she was one of them, a familiar friend, if she chose.

When the cry had risen among them, a joyful cry that called them to chase, the tide rose in her own blood, a heady wilding surge, and, one with her brothers, her sisters, the silken glide of their fur, of skin, of earth and wind and leaves against her, they ran.

"Now," Cort said next to her and—

"Does it always have to be this uncomfortable?" I asked him, my eyes still closed. My head was filled with a wringing nausea that racked through me, while the dull beginning of what felt like a bruise in my lower back spread through my stomach into the top of my thighs.

He already had crouched beside me, glass of water in hand. "That should ease, eventually," he said as I set the sword down and took the glass from him. "Do you want to continue or call it a night?" he asked while I sipped.

I circled one shoulder around and then the other to ease any potential stiffness. The nausea had slipped back to a level I could ignore, and as for the pain that dozed fitfully in my lower back, well, I'd hurt myself worse. "Keep going," I told him and gave him a small grin. I could handle it.

"Good," he said, "this time, bring it with you," he told me, nodding at the sword in my hands as once again I raised my arms, closed my eyes, and was

back to the level of Astral she was familiar with, she stood alone in a circle drawn on the grass, and a glow of light was all that stood between her and them. They were shadows, misshapen humans with wolven heads, vultures with human faces, other similarly repulsive beings she didn't recognize. Membranous wings and skeletal bodies, shapes she'd known previously only in nightmares. They shrieked and cawed at her, called curses and made rending gestures.

The sword was Light in her hand, glowed so brightly she could barely make out its internal structure through the white blaze. Light. White light. That was the energy she worked with, had been taught to seek.

"The energy that comes from the Light is pure, undiluted if you will," Elizabeth had explained, "and the source of energy matters because when you receive it, use it, it filters through your own body, flowing along nerve and muscle channels—and impurities can block those, build within you and cause actual physical harm."

In the exercises she ran through with Cort, she'd learned even more. "It is the stuff of pure potential," he told her as they moved through the same katas and forms they had before, only this time she'd been asked to "carry" the sword through. She had, successfully, and she couldn't resist the sense of satisfaction that filled her even as she blocked and feinted.

"It is what makes you and me, the Aethyr and the Astral, the Material manifest…all of it, and all of it perfect," he said as his weapon hissed in an arc over her head and she countered. "It is not to be used improperly. And here," he signaled to her that they were to stop sparring for the moment, "here is the first place that you will meet those that would do that. Draw the Circle around you," he said and watched as she did.

It was a simple line she drew in the grass with the tip of the blade, a line that glowed with the Light that made it, defined it.

"No matter what you see, no matter what you hear," he began, and gestured about them as she stood within it. A shiver ran through her, setting her teeth on edge even as she controlled it, composed her face, her stance. "Don't engage, and don't leave the Circle."

And then…they came, came as if called. They threw images at her, taunted her, called her by a name she didn't recognize, threatened her, and still she stood in the bright band that surrounded her, guarded her, kept her safe. "You cannot be forced out," Cort's voice sounded in her head, "and you must not allow yourself to be drawn—unless they violate your guard—and that must not happen. This is your first test."

She knew he guarded her body, monitored it with his sense, a floating of hands above her to check her pulse, to ensure the clarity of channels. He heard and watched her heart beat, her blood flow, and if the need arose, he had the ability to envision and affect the very cells of her body. And he'd promised that she'd learn that too. Once she was sworn.

But to get there, she had to pass through the gauntlet, the testing, and this was her first challenge: to maintain her stance in the circle, to resist the temptation to fight. She instinctively understood the necessity of this first basic test. To master fear was to control anger, to allow the higher function of the mind to rule. This was the foundation of discipline, of law and order, of civilization. She could be of no use to the Light if she couldn't first master her own darkness.

Then came the sendings: visions, images, tactile, visceral, filled with smoke and blood and fire and pain…images of lives already lived, of possibilities that could yet become realities, threatened promises. The first image was another life, a mountain, a woman, herself, Nina, older, different…there was a sound like thunder and it ripped through Ann's chest, and cordite stung her nose and eyes even as she felt the hard smack of a wood floor on her back. There was a child taken, another tear of pain that dug deeper than the bullet had. There were men and women in furs with spears, exotic figures with eyes that glowed, emeralds, opals, flashes of nickel silver, beautiful mouths that drank human blood, sucked on human feeling, and she watched it move through their bodies in sluggish eddies of gray light…energy… force…and she recognized them for what they were: soul eaters.

There was more, snatches of bits through time: she was male, female, shifting from one life to another, different times, different bodies, different lives and all of them hers.

She watched her father die, and die again, a blaze of angry orange and billowing black, the smoke choking her with hands that wrapped around her throat, the blistering heat blinding. She heard the raw laughter that followed his death, and it felt like her own body would melt with tears.

The death of her mother: the heart that had stopped, the lungs blocked by blood, her father's heartbreak. And what they, the carrion and the life eaters, wanted her to do was to fail her test, turn her back on the Light, and join them. All it would take was her intent. And they showed her what they would do, should she not fail.

They promised her a violent, painful death, a life that would make her beg to die should she continue through to her sealing.

It wasn't real, it wasn't real, they were just images of a past already done, unchangeable, of a future unknowable, she assured herself, she was in the circle and—

Yes, they howled back, that was true, it wasn't real, at least not for the moment, but as above, so below, they mocked, a high-pitched and windy whine, the scrape of stone on stone, and the muddy, sucking sound of sludge.

These sendings, these images on the Astral weren't just a history of the Material, they promised, they were the future, her future.

More scenes immersed her in their fully dimensioned play, battered at her mind, ripped at her heart. She saw her best friend, Frankie, blue, bloated, dead, her hair shorn and the despairing reek of suicide in the air. Nina, alive again only to walk into school with that beautiful face bruised, and again, Ann watched images of her being beaten, drowned, cutting herself, the same way Ann had.

Cort's robust form broken, lifeless at the bottom of the stairs, Elizabeth, torn, bloody, her eyes, those beautiful eyes—

And then she saw it, no him, no…naked, humanoid, genderless, with black slits for eyes and…were those ears, or horns? She couldn't tell, made as they were of the same gray, almost rubbery-seeming skin, and his voice spoke above the din.

"You can fight, you know—they're no match for you, or the Sword—step forward, and you can banish them," he promised. He held out a hand, no, it was a cleft hoof. "One step, Child of Light, and you'll be free, free of the cycle, the horror, and the pain."

His eyes glittered beetle-black back at her. A tiny pink tongue played about the hole that was his lipless mouth. He, more than any of the other creatures she'd seen, repulsed her. His skin reminded her of a dead rat she'd once seen at the beach near the home she'd grown up in: hairless, bloated, ready to explode into a shower of stinking rot at the slightest touch.

She leveled her gaze on him, refused to answer, refused to move except to hold herself in readiness. She did not know that it was her will, and her will alone, that maintained the barrier that kept her safe.

"Oh, you're scrumptious," he answered her silence, even as the other shapes quieted and drew back. She could feel the avid hunger in their gazes as they watched the exchange. "You have my word." He smiled, and in that moment his mouth yawned impossibly huge with the brief flash of fangs before they were hidden again by the almost ridiculously small opening he spoke through. "I only promise that which can be delivered."

He gestured to the horde that surrounded them. "Look at them— delicate, weak, armed only with their taunts and threats…certainly, what they show you may be true, but what match are they for you, young and strong, armed with a relic of true power on the many worlds?"

It was tempting, tempting to do exactly what he said: she more than likely could defeat them if she were to respond, to step out from the shield she'd surrounded herself with, to strike with the strength that fear and anger granted—and forfeit her place forever, leaving her to become one of them, which is what they really wanted.

She shuddered and almost felt the body she'd left behind twitch in response. It was a certainty that bled from her very core. They would destroy her.

"You lie," she said simply as she faced him.

He held up a hand. "I tried," he told her, shaking his head in seeming resignation. "Have at it," he said to the beasts that surrounded them and dropped his hand, the signal that set them off again.

Creatures made of shadow and darkness, apparitions that stood more than twice her height that she knew to be hounds, circled and hunted in and through the howling, the curses, the threats, and the sendings. Still, she resisted and stood her ground, let the images wash and play before her *as she remained, unmoved.*

❖

It was one thing to willingly place oneself on the Astral.

It was another to visit it like everyone else did, in dreams.

My first test was followed by a series of nightmares, dreams of wolves—not the elegant, noble animals I'd run with on the Astral, had joined and become, but haggard beasts that slavered and snapped with a viciousness that forcibly reminded me that there was such a thing as true, undiluted malice. They shifted and simmered, became what I finally knew were hounds, shadow hounds, ten, twelve feet tall, made of a smoky and oily blackness.

They sniffed and pawed at the doors of my dreams, followed me when I woke, a dark cloud approaching from the periphery when I went out onto the roof to sit by myself and gaze over the town or just stare up into the starry sky, until I realized that I could create in the Material the same ring that guarded me on the Astral.

I centered, focused, walked the Aethyr and cast the warding around the house, the Light manifest within and without until the hounds could only paw and circle the boundary of the yard, track me through Aethyr and Astral in my dreams until there too the barrier I created became reflex, automatic, and their frustrated ululating yowl would wake me in the early morning darkness, the echo ringing between worlds.

I told Cort about it over breakfast the first time I'd done it, to ask if I'd done it right.

"And that's another you've passed," he said with a smile. "You're coming along nicely."

Surprised, I put my fork back down in my eggs. "That was a test?"

"Yes, dear heart," he said as he sugared his tea and Elizabeth smiled at me from her seat.

"Everything you'll ever do from now on is," she said.

"Everything from now on—as in forever?" I asked, and looked to each of them. I was daunted by the prospect—it sounded like a *lot* and I remembered quite clearly what he'd said: I couldn't fail *any* of them.

Uncle Cort's teeth gleamed at me as he put his cup down. "Everyone's life is like that—just not everyone knows it."

Okay, I could go with that, but, "What about all the Astral stuff? Is that different?"

He laughed lightly. "Yes...and no. But you'll know when you've passed those particular tests." He rested his gaze on me as I struggled to understand.

"How will I know when I've passed those?" I asked finally.

"You'll know," he said and picked up his cup again, "because you'll feel it, and you'll know for certain," he grinned at me again, "because I'll tell you."

Elizabeth nodded her chin toward my plate to remind me to eat. "You're not going to like those cold."

She was right, and I allowed myself to be pleased with my progress as I speared my eggs.

❖

It happened almost exactly as I'd been taught: as above, so below. I saw them, haggard and human, lounging in front of Uncle Cort's shop when he finally took me there for the first time. They took off running as we approached the gates that covered the door. But I recognized them for what they were.

"Hounds, right? Human hounds?" I asked him as he passed me a key to unsnap a set of locks.

"Yes," he answered shortly. "They're looking for you. If you can be turned before you're sealed—well, you'd be a very powerful ally. But if they can't turn you," and he faced me, his gaze focused, intense, "they'll try to stop you—any way they can. That's why," he pointed to the ankh that hung from my throat, then motioned for me to precede him through the door, "you wear that. It's older than you think, and it's been charged with more than just your life binding."

"I don't understand." I fingered the charm and its chain and wondered how old it really was as I stopped to put my books down on a clear space on the front counter.

His hand was gentle on my shoulder. "You're marked, dear heart, and for now, until you are safely sealed, you carry a powerful shield with you. It's an announcement, yes, not only of who you are, but also of the Circle you belong to and the energy being focused to protect you. It's safest for you that way."

I still wasn't certain I completely understood, and I let that rattle around in my head as I inspected the display that spread in an arch on the surface. The counter bore athames, ceremonial daggers that were used in ritual that ranged from pure utility—the traditional simple double-edged blade approximately a hand-span in length, the hilt not quite two-thirds that and narrower than the blade—to the downright fantastical—handles wrapped in soft leather, or carved of malachite and onyx and inlaid with opal moons and stars or some of the various symbols I'd learned, blades mirror bright or black with fine filigree patterns, male and female figures, flowers on intricate vines. They were beautiful.

"Damascene," Cort said nonchalantly over my shoulder, noticing which ones I stared at with fascination.

I must have worn a strange expression and he gave me a friendly pat.

"C'mon, let's show you some *real* history," he said jauntily. "I've some things in the back I think you'll enjoy."

❖

Night had fallen on the Astral, and she stood at the edge of the Tanglewoods beside Cort, her aethyric body thrumming with excitement and anxiety. "This time, Ann, we have a target," he told her and pointed down the slope toward the center of the plain where mist rose. It carried a shimmer, a reflection of the starlight above and the river beyond.

In the world of the flesh, the wolf moon, the hunting moon had arrived and in the Aethyr, the Astral tide had changed as the Dark, the hungry nothing, built and swelled to its greatest moment of power in the waning of days. As above, so below: the days grew shorter while the nights became longer, and tied as a particular level of the Astral was to specific regions of the Material world, the changes happened here first.

While she couldn't see all of them clearly through the shifting of forms and function, she could feel the host that surrounded and supported them, some of them beings she knew well. Familiar scents and sensations, here the distinct rub of fur against her arm, the warm press of a flank against her shoulder as another passed, an unmeaning but friendly shove in the jostle and jockeying for position that was more about the relieving of anticipatory tension than anything else. She felt it too, and the jangle of metal on metal sounded through her ears along with the growing mutter, the excited buzz of impatience as she loosened her shoulders, flexed and stretched her back, her legs, in the impatient pound of hooves, the slight brush of her elbows, the backs of her calves as others fought to contain themselves until the time was—

"There!"

The call rang out, the wolf-pack howl, the roar of the great hunting cats that ran with them, the commanding keen of hawks that flew above, and through the center of the mist, a boiling black space that swirled, coalesced, took on form…became a horde, a mass of claws and wings and teeth that charged.

Cort threw her a toothy smile in the half second before thought became action, before the challenge was answered and they were off, the hunt purposeful now: to rout the invading dark force, human adepts and nonincarnate beings who attempted to invade, to twist and remake, this level of the Astral that reflected the Material.

If they could do so, then the Law would be followed: as above, so below, and that part of the Material world would pay the price of their failure to defend now and the Dark would grow, would find it that much easier to further invade other parts of the Astral when the rotation of the planet brought other sections of it to the same vulnerable point.

Ann already knew her position here, Cort had told her clearly. "Don't engage—track, hunt, seek—announce what you find."

"What if I don't know what to do?" she asked. "What if I don't do it right?" *What if we're overrun?* was the question she didn't ask.

"Once we've started, follow the hawks—watch where the lines break, spot for sneak attacks. Learn to see, to fight with your sight. If…" He hesitated. "If the line falls, then you do what you must—but that won't happen," he said and gave her a sharp grin.

"How do you know?"

He looked at her a long moment. "Because it can't," he said, his voice strong, determined. *"It simply can't."*

ANACRUSIS

I see, I forget. I hear, I remember. I do, I understand.
—Chinese proverb

Two weeks later, and my shoulders were so tired they burned with pain that seemed to have voice, a voice that sang high-pitched in my ears; I opened my eyes to find my head had bowed, but I'd held the blade Cort had given me, had held it up and high.

Each physical training session was now followed by an Astral one, and they were both grueling. I repeatedly faced images, realities, possibilities with varying levels of probability above, things that could or would manifest in myriad ways on the Material unless stopped there.

Everything Cort and I did now revolved around the focus of Light, to strike with compassion, understanding, to remember always that every conscious being arose from and was meant to remain a part of the Light, all growing, *evolving*, toward a level of understanding, of being, *existing*, that was beyond my limited human senses and biology to comprehend fully.

Rigid training and discipline—hence, the kneeling position with arms upraised—would ensure that my physical mind and body would act and react from force of habit as opposed to emotion, and in turn, my mind, my intentions, my sense of spirit were etched indelibly upon the metal lattice of the blade's structure due to the constant physical contact, attuning our charges as it were, in the same way that a magnet groomed metal and transformed it. In the process, I became able to perceive the intentions of those who had held it before me, before my father. I could now easily discern the energy, the spirit in which it had been formed, because its essence *lived*, a heart of Light literally buried into the crosspiece from the hilt to the first few inches of the blade.

I felt it every time I held it, and each time I did so a growing sense of comfort with the weapon, with its embedded presence that was fast becoming an extension of myself, grew.

"Let me help you," Cort said as he removed it from my hands, then guided my arms down. "You're pushing too hard," he said gruffly, but his hands were as gentle as they were strong when he rubbed my shoulders against the numb and the ache then carefully removed the weights I still wore.

"I just want to *get* there already, you know?" I told him, and I could hear my voice sounded as tired as I felt. I was so tired, in fact, I skipped our usual friendly argument about the color of the scabbard— we disagreed as to whether it was a deep blue or black—and sat back on my heels. The nausea and headache that accompanied it forced me to use all my will to fight the natural pull of gravity, and the hyperreality of the Astral hunt and chase as well as the images those…things…had thrown at me—anything and everything that could have been or possibly be, all in an attempt to draw me out, to either fight or quit—continued to whirl through my mind.

A burst of friendly cheer that made me smile flared through the room as Elizabeth entered the study, hair bound as always—pulled from the sides and loose at her shoulders, the ends curling over her white blouse.

The wire-rimmed glasses she wore couldn't hide the sparkle of her eyes. "I think you might need this right about now," she said as she smiled at me in return and handed me a heavy, hand-fired mug, glazed in graduated shades that ranged blue to copper, the solidity and warmth of it welcome against my chilled palms.

"Thank you," I told her before I sipped at the milky tea.

She nodded and after making sure I'd neither choke nor drown myself with my almost complete lack of fine motor control, she placed a plate of scones next to me. Cranberry and pecan, I noted. I was a fan of those, and Elizabeth baked them herself in the more than ample kitchen.

"Here," Cort said as he took a throw blanket from the settee and threw it around my shoulders. I tended to feel cold after sessions, and the blanket prevented the chill and stiff from setting into my shoulders.

"I'll take care of the room later," he told me.

I smiled my thanks at him over the mug as the deep blue, almost black wool gently scratched against my neck.

I was almost fully recovered; at least the disorienting nausea had abated, and the throb in my head had faded to manageable annoyance, as he crouched down before me. His gaze matched his tone in solemnity when he spoke.

"Elizabeth and I"—and he glanced up at her for a moment as he took a breath—"we both think you're ready to know, to understand a bit more about the Law. There are things you need to understand, completely, because there are consequences and…" He took a deep breath, then let it out slowly and the lines around his eyes tightened as his face worked. "This is part of who you are, and who you're meant to be, love. It's my job to make certain you're guided to it."

"I'll take it from here," Elizabeth said as he hugged me.

I nodded against his broad shoulder, steadied by the coal-tar soap smell, the same as my father's, which suffused his shirt.

"Okay then," he said as he released me and rose, "and if you've questions, after, please, ask either of us, both of us, however many times you have to, until you understand. Promise me?" he asked as he stood by the doors.

"I will."

He winked at me as he walked to the door. "I'm in the workshop if you need me later," he said, then left.

Elizabeth had already partially set the room to rights and had pulled a seat before the fireplace for me.

"Come, sit with me, Annie," she said and patted the seat.

Refreshed enough, I rolled my shoulders and stretched my back under the blanket I still wore as I crossed the hardwood floor and stepped lightly onto the carpet.

Elizabeth folded her hands on her lap and looked at me expectantly as I sat down.

"There are some things that you know quite clearly by now," she began. "Tell me, what is the first Universal Law, obeyed by default?"

That was easy—we all lived it. "As above, so below."

"Exactly. And the greatest, the gravest possible sin against the Universe is...?" she asked as she peered at me over her glasses and I took a bracing sip from my mug, the warmth and weight now a familiar comfort.

"To control another." I swallowed, then answered, "To abrogate free will, to push your own mind, desire, or will onto another."

"Why?"

"Because..." I hesitated, not certain I could say it, explain it in a way that made sense. "Because it takes someone away from their... their path, from their potential."

"Good enough, for now anyway. Tell me what you know of absolute right and wrong."

I took a moment to think about how to answer this properly. "It's like math," I said finally. "There can only be one right answer to the equation. All the steps you take to get that result may be right, may be wrong, may be circuitous, but the correct answer is just that, the only solution, and it's right, for all time, while the wrong answer, no matter how many correct steps to get there, is also equally incorrect, forever."

"Perfect," she said and smiled. "There are no shades of gray, ever. But what if there are multiple answers?"

Of course. I chewed my lip as I thought hard and focused on the fire Uncle Cort had thoughtfully lit before he'd left the room. There *were* equations that had multiple answers, all of them satisfying the problem. But I knew this, and suddenly, I realized just how well I knew it. I raised my eyes to Elizabeth's and smiled. "It's a solution set," I said, "a grouping of correct answers that satisfy, each of them necessary, and no others permissible and," I said as I thought it through, "it argues for the inevitability of certain outcomes no matter what the decision—absolute inevitabilities. Maybe...parallel universes."

Elizabeth straightened and leaned back against the padded brocade of the settee. "So you're enjoying the physics, I take it?"

I grinned at her, because I did. "Will it help me build a better amplifier?" I asked.

She laughed. "Maybe, but tonight," she said and resettled her seat, "we're focusing on matters...harmonic in a different way."

She had my complete and total attention.

"If the most grievous of crimes is to take another's free will, what would be almost equally wrong? Or, perhaps, even worse?"

As wrong as forcing another's will... "To relinquish your own," I said, my voice almost a whisper because I suddenly realized the full extent of what that meant, and Elizabeth nodded at me as I felt my eyes widen.

"Yes, Ann. *That* is exactly it. You can't get drunk, you can't just go out and get stoned—not that I think you would," she added hastily, correctly guessing that I was about to protest. "But you already know that to choose to give up your conscious ability to decide correctly, given your abilities—"

"—is to permit the probabilities," I finished for her.

"Exactly. You know well enough what might happen. And because of this? You are still responsible for end results—there are no excuses, Ann, about being in any way, manner, or form out of control—you know, full well, what laying down your guard will bring. There are those that would commit the crime of stealing, taking freedom of choice—and thus the energy—from another."

"So," I said as I considered, "they not only remove the person from their path, they also interfere with the plan, the order of the Universe—this is a direct attack against the Light and its manifestations, right?"

"I'm so very glad you understand that," Elizabeth said as her expression became grave, "because it means you know the weight of what happened and what you attempted earlier this summer."

I knew exactly what she meant, and I resisted the urge to rub at the marks on my arm by sipping from my mug in the silence. I stared into the flames as they danced in the grate.

"I don't...I didn't really want to *die*, per se," I said finally. I sat up straight and faced her, to find her eyes as warm as always on me. "I just...I don't know. Even with the grand plans of the Universe or whatever," and I gave her a half-hearted grin, "there's not a lot here for me, you know?"

Elizabeth gave me what I could only describe as a sympathetic glance. "I can understand why you might feel that way," she said quietly.

"Do you?" I asked her as I fought down the surge of hurt and anger that threatened to flood through me and I shrugged the blanket off my shoulders—I was warm enough. "Do you really?"

She leaned forward and gazed at me intently, held my eyes with hers. "I do know what it's like to live with the unchangeable, to love, to lose, to regret," she told me, and I watched the flame dance in her eyes as she said so. "I know what it is to do what you must anyway, to ignore, sometimes to fight, the hounds, to be aware, *always*, of the path. This is what you're learning to deal with—what you must deliberately choose to live with—and," she straightened and sat back again, "this brings us very neatly to our second, but most important topic. Binding."

I raised an eyebrow at her. That was completely unexpected and immediately took me away from the thoughts and the feelings that had started to roil through me. What?

"I know you've just come out of an exercise with Cort, but I'd like you to slip into a monitor state—can you do that?"

Closing my eyes, I agreed to try. First I put myself in the Light, the nimbus and barrier that charged and guarded the body. Once that was quickly accomplished, I forced my awareness back to the Material, carrying the ability to see or, at least, accurately sense the energies that whirled and massed around, through, and in us.

"Got it," I said and opened my eyes to a slightly different world. Hazes, like the waves that drip up off the asphalt and through the air in heat of summer, surrounded different items in the room.

"Can you see the channels?" she asked, waving her hand along her body.

I could, I could see where the energy flowed, the path it took, the centers where it gathered, and the greater areas of exchange. The centers shone brightly, were concentrated masses about the size of a tennis ball that flared in my sight over her head, her heart, slightly below her navel, and if I focused in just the right way, I could see almost through her body to the glowing exchange center that parked almost at the base of her spine.

"What do you remember of overload?" she asked.

God, what I knew I wanted to forget. Not more than a week after the session where I'd had the opportunity to stop but chose to go forward, I learned very painfully what overload was.

A human body couldn't withstand extreme heat, extreme cold, the vacuum of space, radiation—and in the same way, the body could be damaged trying to handle, or channel, too much energy, no matter how pure it was.

It had been a few days, just a few, of slight overload. It had been enough to delay my period. Had that been it, it would have been no big deal, but it also made me cramp like I'd never had before, shot my blood sugar and blood pressure down so low I'd been left unable to do anything but curl up into the fetal position, thrown into a world of mind-numbing pain where all that existed was a world-wrecking nausea that made me heave, a throbbing ache that tore through the center of my spine to my gut, only to pit through the heart of my thighs, and it left me open, wide open to every single thought, being, imprint on the Aethyr, all a chaotic shout in my head and body. Uncle Cort found me on the hallway floor where I'd curled up before I could get to my room.

"I'll monitor," he'd told Elizabeth, the only voice that was clear to me through the haze. "You clear the channels."

The contact of his mind, his energy, on mine, sent the tear of pain into a scud down my body and back up to my throat and suddenly, Elizabeth, her hands, her face, so very clear before me, the concerned expression so *familiar*...It was a combination of physical and mental massage along the lines of my spine and kidneys that discharged the overflow, set the world to right again, and sent the pain and turmoil down to levels that were manageable. I slept for almost twenty-four hours straight afterward.

I may have winced at the memory and Elizabeth nodded.

"I know...I really truly do. That aspect wasn't pleasant. Shut the channels for now," she suggested, "so we can avoid a replay."

It was easily done and I waited with an almost nervous anticipation to hear what would come next.

"There are several ways of avoiding a lot of that, though not all of it. Methods to discharge the extra energy, ground it out," she said, "and the most effective *can* result in a binding."

"Really?" I asked with interest.

"Do you have an idea of what any of those grounding methods might be?" She studied me with interest as I shook my head.

"No clue."

She cocked her head to the side in a way I had come to recognize meant she was considering what to say even as she studied me. "Sex, Ann. Are you a virgin?"

Well that certainly distracted me from whatever I'd been thinking. However, the rather pointed question caught me short, and I choked on my tea as Elizabeth gracefully waited for my answer.

"Um, what exactly do you mean?" I asked in return when I could finally breathe freely without the danger of fluids pouring into my lungs. I was certain that the heat I felt in my neck and head were a very visible shade of red on my face.

"That's what I thought," she sighed as she took off her glasses and rubbed her temples.

"Is that something that matters?"

"In fact, it is. You know how to work on your own Astrally, you know how to work with another, as you've trained with Cort. But," she hesitated briefly, "you don't yet know what it means to be truly bound to someone, and there are some bindings that take tremendous amounts of energy to break and some that can *never* be broken."

I found myself shaking my head again as I tried to understand what Elizabeth meant and she spoke to my confusion. "There are some that can take you from life to life, and there are bindings," she paused and her words were measured, low, "bindings that can steal your heart, your soul, your life essence."

Now I was really confused. "I've no idea what you're talking about," I confessed. "In fact, I don't know what that has to do with *anything* I've been doing. And…" I hesitated; I didn't want her to think I was being sarcastic or disrespectful. "Elizabeth, I've had the 'birds and bees' discussion with my father." There was something, perhaps it was the weight of the knowledge that Elizabeth carried, that projected itself in such a way that I picked it up and read it. It took me past nervous anticipation to downright edgy.

"And he would have had this one with you as well, when you were ready, as you are now. There'll come a time," she said, "when you'll want to be bound to someone, or—" The skeptical glance I gave made her smile. "I know, I know, it doesn't seem like that right now, but eventually, you'll want to—at the very least—exchange the normal human closeness. If you choose to become bound to someone after your sealing, then they too either must be of a level equal to yours, or if they are not, they must become so, and bind themselves to the Light. This is Law, Annie—it cannot be gainsaid."

That made sense in a rather abstract way. "But what in the world does that have to do with sex?" I asked, "Or if I'm a…" That was a little too uncomfortable to think about, never mind say. "What's the connection?"

Elizabeth leaned forward. "Every aspect of the Material has energy—air, water, fire, wood, metal…skin, trees, sweat, blood—they each have a vibration. And then there's the kinetic energy release connected to action—energy will disperse through movement, through sweat, through blood and the final release of sex, the act of—"

I held up an uncomfortable hand. "I know the word," I said.

"Good—I didn't want to have to explain it," she said with a small grin, a grin I returned, relieved to know I wouldn't have to sit through a technical discussion.

"It's very simple, really," she said. "You carry extra energy because of the work you do. Sex is a life energy, and a great way of releasing some of the surplus, and sharing it with someone creates a link. Combine that energy in any way with a life essence—blood, for example—and you create a bond. Depending on what's in your head and heart, your *intent* at the time, that bond can be completely unbreakable."

I couldn't really hear the rest of what she said, couldn't absorb or understand it, because I didn't really want to *think* about sex at all, and the more I tried not to think about it, the more I felt the uncomfortable stir, that long-ignored aspect of my life wake with a churning need that made me choke on my tea again.

That was a good sign, I thought ruefully as I begged off from the rest of the conversation by claiming fatigue. It meant my body, and more, was vibrant, alive.

But still, the arousal was worsened by the intermittent water pressure and the sudden drop in its temperature when I took a shower, and after, the towel I rubbed myself down with felt coarse and rough against my skin. I readied for bed only to strip before I got under the covers. It was too much, much too much. I tossed, I turned, then tossed some more.

I didn't want to think about what I'd just learned, because it took my mind to places I didn't want it to go, an agonizing blank reach I didn't want to make because I didn't want to hurt. Oh I knew, because I'd just been told, that sex—by myself, with another—would literally ground the overload out, but then I'd have to…

What *did* I think about sex? Or rather, what did I *really* know about it, other than the straightforward mechanical realities involved with reproduction?

My first girlfriend, my best friend still, even though we hadn't spoken in a few months, she and I...well, should I, *could* I call what had happened between us sex? We'd met as kids when I'd started swim team with the local club.

Her parents didn't allow her to socialize much with the other kids on the team, but it didn't matter—*we* talked anyway. Between us, we were Frankie and Sammer or even Sammy, even though in front of her parents, and later, in school, it was Fran and Samantha. Then, before either one of us really knew it, closeness became attraction, became a kiss, and then another, until finally kissing became...something different, more intense, a mutual exploration. And then we'd gone from intensity to rivalry, and back to friendship *again*. While Nina...she and I had barely even touched by comparison. There was, there'd *been* one beautiful kiss, many wonderful hugs—the usual physical exchanges made by close friends, by teammates, and I *missed* her, *mourned* her, wanted her still, kicked myself for not going home sooner, wished I'd done something, *anything*, differently... How different was that than being bound, as Elizabeth had put it?

My skin felt hot under my hands. There was no denying that Fran and I had a link, because I'd always known she'd call before the phone rang, could always anticipate her moods, her feelings, because I felt them too, like a haze on my skin... There was magic, magic and power in sex, in the burst of energy that was the end result of—God! I finally kicked the damn sheets off in frustration and leapt out of bed.

I paced, not content with the lack of strain in the muscles of my thighs, unsure of where, how, to hold my hands, wishing like hell that I was running laps, or swimming them, racing them, pushing my body to the limit, while I prowled the wood floors of my room, stepping so deliberately it felt as if the oak gave under my feet.

What the hell am I doing, what the hell am I doing here? I asked myself. My days...they were spent studying with Elizabeth, while my evenings were filled with martial arts and strange meditations. I now knew several dozen ways to disable a living being, spoke of imaginary places as if they were towns another block or so down. And while I was living in a foreign country, thousands of miles from where I'd been born, I hadn't really seen anything but the house, the shop, a few of the local historical sites…and I knew no one, absolutely no one, outside of Elizabeth and Uncle Cort. Oh. And the hounds. Great. That was lovely, simply lovely.

I was old enough, I reminded myself, legally allowed to do all sorts of things in this country, an adult, and…I didn't expect it, the wave that washed over me, the tide of longing that swamped my senses.

I missed my father, though that was now a familiar feeling, but the other pangs were new, surprising almost, in their sharpness. I missed my friends. I missed the guys I'd hung out with in the neighborhood growing up, I missed Fran and even my other classmates. I missed Nina.

I carefully put that thought away because it hurt, oh it hurt to think about her, through the throb that contracted my gut; and Fran…I wondered how she was, what she was doing. I wondered if she missed and hurt in the same way, for the same reasons.

I wondered what it had cost her to call me, to tell me what she had heard from Nina's father, and an awful regret ran through me that I had added insult to injury, accused her of lying.

It had been—what, I mentally reviewed, early July?—when Fran and I had spoken last. The trip with Uncle Cort had really just started, but my plans had already been set: I'd decided to go home a week early, to surprise Nina and Fran, plenty of time to spend with both of them before I had to get ready for the move to the dorm before freshman orientation. Princeton was not only a phenomenal school, but I'd also been offered a scholarship, and it wasn't too far from Staten Island, where Nina lived.

And it had been where she'd planned to go as well…

Fran. Fran was the one who called me to tell me she'd spoken with Nina's father, and it started with a message she left during an afternoon when Uncle Cort and I were touring the countryside. "Hi Samantha, it's Fran. Please call me as soon as you can, okay?"

From the tone of her voice, I'd known it was important, and I missed her on the return call. "Hey, Fran!" I recorded. "How're you doing? I'm coming back in about two weeks—don't tell Nina, I want to surprise her. What say you we all get together and do something?"

We finally connected on her next call. "…and Mr. Boyd asked that we respect the family's grief and privacy—don't call, send nothing."

The words sent a blankness running through me. They made no sense, they were unreal, and I responded with what I thought was logic.

"I'm gonna call."

"Samantha, don't do it," Fran insisted across the miles. "I told you what her father said."

I was silent as I considered. That couldn't be true, it simply made no *sense*, even though a prickling numbness, hot and heavy, crawled up my legs. I said the one thing that did make sense to me, that made the crawling numbness flash over into anger, the words I was now very sorry for. "I don't believe you," I told her flatly. "You're just jealous because we used to date. You want her."

"Sammy, Sammer, I'm just trying to save you some heartache," she protested and I could hear the tears as she spoke. "C'mon Sam, you *know* me—I wouldn't ever try to hurt you or her like that. You guys are my friends. I love you." I heard her breathe, could feel the effort she made to not cry. "God, I *wish* I was lying."

I breathed it in, her words, the emotions so clear to me across an ocean, and knew that whether I wanted to believe or not...

"I'm sorry, Fran, just, don't"—I took another breath—"I didn't mean to make you cry. I can't believe you right now—I have to hear this for myself."

I hung up and dialed another number, and a few rings later I got the confirmation I'd been seeking, though it wasn't what I wanted.

"How many times do I have to tell you fuckin' stupid kids? She's dead—don't ever fuckin' call my house again." He hung up before I even had the chance to ask how or when.

Fran and I hadn't spoken since that call, not since the weight of loss had overwhelmed me, dared me to try to cross the gate, and as my memory once more replayed our last discussion, my body, raw from the shower and hyper from...everything else...remembered her, Fran and the sweet and shy experiments that led to further, more intimate contact until it was done, that first orgasm a revelation of her, of me, the next a response to hunger that had ripped through my stomach and chest the same way the energy did, and the third to ensure we knew what we were doing.

Despite the growth and the changes between us, and perhaps even because of them, I knew we were united. First as friends and teammates, then, for a short while, as girlfriends. But now, any rivalry we'd had left was set aside: we both mourned the one girl neither of us would ever have. I'd loved, still loved, Nina, but so had Fran, and more than that, I owed her, owed *Frankie* for the friendship we'd shared. It was time I called her.

After having paced enough to calm my blood, I pulled out my sadly neglected acoustic guitar, carefully tuned it, and ran through a few scales, then a few finger exercises. It felt good, but it wasn't what I needed; it made me think of things, of people, I didn't want to think about, and the sharp lance of memory, only a few months old, bore hot and heavy through my ribs. For the first time, the strings didn't calm the tangled mess that filled my mind, rode restless and hot under my skin. I put my guitar down and jumped to my feet, only to start prowling the floor again. Okay. I flipped the light, then faced myself in the mirror. Let it never be said, I thought, that I never faced the issues head-on.

My face had thinned, there were smudges above my cheeks just under my eyes, faint purple from exhaustion. *Cobalt blue*, I thought as I looked into my own eyes under hair that had gotten darker since I'd not really been out in the sun. "Moon on the ocean blue," Nina had told me once when we'd sat by the pier on a faraway bay. I closed my eyes for a moment against the remembered glare of the water that burned into my sight and the memory-sting of the wind that blew the hair back off my face as I'd felt her fingers do the same the last time we'd really seen each other, the last real words we'd ever exchanged. I would graduate the next day and leave that continent the day after.

We held each other, close, safe, and silent in the warmth of the sun and the breeze that blew off the water, content for the moment to have this, just this, because I knew, we both knew, we had the rest of our lives to work this out, we had the assurance of tomorrow. If I'd only known then what that tomorrow had held, if I'd had a *clue*…that would have changed everything. If…if…*if*.

There is no "if," I told myself sternly and shut the too-vivid recollection down and away where it wouldn't hurt. I had other things to think about, things to learn, to focus on. I would.

I already knew there wasn't enough motion I could do to make me feel better. Playing guitar was out of the question, and the wave that once more threatened to descend…those little razors were *so* close, I just had to reach for them. I dressed again in sweats and sneakers and went down to the first floor, to the back room where Uncle Cort had said he'd be. The light shone from under the door, and as I opened it I saw him, face screwed in concentration as he sat in front of his workbench, his gloved hands carefully tapping at whatever shone before him.

"Need something, dear heart?" he asked over his shoulder as I entered.

"Do you trust me?" I tried not to shift as I waited for his answer.

"I do," he said solemnly, his gaze steady on me as he gently laid down his tools. "Do you need something?"

"Can I...can I have the sword?"

He got up slowly and crossed the room to the large oven in the corner and opened its door, then pulled the sword and its scabbard from within. He handed it to me and I felt just that much calmer as the hilt fit into my palm.

"Thank you," I told him.

"You're welcome," he answered, his voice quiet, deep, and grave, as if we were trying not to wake the house itself.

"I just want...I want to do an exercise," I said as I turned away and reached for the door.

He nodded. "See you in the morning."

"Yes."

My heart felt heavy in my chest, a burn that climbed into my throat even as I climbed the steps to the study and, once there, kindled a fire in the grate.

I took a centering breath, then drew the blade from its home and let the firelight wink off it before I drew the circle around me, on the Material, in the Aethyr, then took my accustomed position with it—head high, arms straight, posture perfect. It felt so light without the weights on my wrists...

Closing my eyes, I forced my mind to empty and focused on the Light within and without, the swirl of matrices from the sword in my hand, a loop that fed back and forth. I felt it clearly, the current that entered me from the surrounds: it flowed from my hands to the metal and through it, then back to me, the endless circle, the endless Light that sang and pulsed and thrummed and danced. I let it take me away from the ache in my muscles, the burning weight that suffused my shoulders and back. There was no rug beneath my knees, no fire that warmed my face, no air that cooled my back, no breath, no mind, no body, nothing but the Light and my reflection of it...

And that was how Cort found me in the morning just as the sun rose—position perfect and finally, finally, ready to go to sleep.

FRESHMEN

The mind is for seeing, the heart is for hearing
—Arabic Proverb

"Hi, Fran," I said simply when she answered the phone, "it's me—and I owe you a huge apology—I am so very sorry."

She gracefully forgave me, and we caught each other up on everything.

Fran had deferred her freshman start at Columbia until the spring semester, "just putting the last four years into perspective. Adjusting, you know?" she said.

I suspected there was quite a bit more to it, but I let it go—if she wanted to talk about it, she would, and if our reasons were at all similar, I wasn't ready to talk about it yet, either. "Yeah, I get that. Me, too. Kinda why I'm staying in England for now. Oh, I, uh…" I took a deep breath. "I changed my name, by the way—Ann, you know, the middle of Samantha."

She was silent a moment, and I knew her well enough to know she was thinking of all the reasons that might be behind it. "I can understand, I mean, it kinda suits you. Ann," she said finally before falling quiet again. "When do you think you'll come back?"

"I don't think I'll…I'm not certain." I didn't tell her that I was seriously considering "never." I also didn't tell her about anything else I'd been up to.

We changed the subject and as we continued to chat, we realized how much we did miss one another. And since her parents had decided to spend part of the winter in Italy because Fran's older brother and sister (much older, almost ten years older, and twins besides—Gemma and Gianni) ran some sort of art studio in Milan and wouldn't be home for the holidays and Fran was no longer in school…

"Hey," I asked her, suddenly inspired, "why not stay with me for a bit then? Maybe even spend the holidays?"

"That sounds awesome—you're saving my *life* here," she said and I could hear both laughter and relief in her voice. "Think we can pull it off?"

It was easy enough to set up.

Uncle Cort seemed more than appropriately happy to give his okay, and it was decided that when we moved to the London apartment next month, Fran would stay with us there through the holidays, spend two weeks in Italy, then fly back to New York to start school.

"Wouldn't your friend prefer to spend the holidays with her parents?" Elizabeth asked when we discussed the impending visit over dinner.

I chewed thoughtfully over my answer. "Fran…well, her parents, you know, they're nice people—lovely, warm, polite, very, very appropriate, in all ways, at all times," I said, "but it's weird for her too."

"Weird how?" Elizabeth asked. "You should finish that." She pointed to the green things I was trying to avoid on my plate and gave me a quick smile.

My avoidance of vegetables had already become a running joke, and I grinned back at her as I took the smallest possible bite. But she'd asked me a question, and it deserved an answer.

"See, Fran's dad is a politician back on Staten Island, wants to go from county representative to city or, even better, state office, and Fran," I explained as I pushed the green around on my plate to make it look like I was doing something with it, "well, she's…her dad's a conservative and Fran's gay," I said simply. "It doesn't really, uh, *work* well for him."

I felt Uncle Cort's eyes on me, and the warm sense of concern that flowed from him as Elizabeth watched me with interest.

"Do they mistreat her?" she asked, her voice gentle.

"No," I said, the word hard and hurtful as it rose from my throat while I forced myself *not* to think about anything or anyone else who might have had a different experience. "They don't actively mistreat her—they *ignore* her. They named Fran for her mother, then forgot her." Ah, fuck it, I thought, and speared some of the leafy stuff onto my fork. "She'll have a much better time with us," I assured Elizabeth, then focused on swallowing the bitter taste that filled my mouth.

With my uncle's help and guidance, we made arrangements to have the house I'd grown up in appraised by a real-estate company for possible sale, arranged for storage for most of the contents of the house, and the items of importance that had been left behind were shipped to the London address in Soho on Dean Street, a large two-story apartment above a shop, *the* shop, as he said.

When we finally arrived there after a four-hour drive on a late-August afternoon, it was to discover a place that was much less industrial than the part of Leeds proper the other shop was in, and completely unlike the suburb the house was surrounded by. Soho itself was a little seedy: a complex mix of music, art, and sex, though to my eyes and senses it was more of a vibe, a feel to the air, than anything open or advertised. Honestly, it reminded me of Greenwich Village in New York, and I liked it a lot.

The new apartment, even with its two floors, wasn't nearly as large as the house had been, though it was sizeable. It had its own entrance from the street, and a flight of steps led from the front entryway up to another door that led into the apartment proper. My room, a nice-sized sunny space painted in stark white, was on the floor above.

"Now that you're all settled in, you should go out, explore the city," Cort said over breakfast a few mornings later as he passed milk over to me. "Make some friends."

"You need to have a real life, a full one—not everything is about training," Elizabeth added in response to the questioning glance I gave them.

"Uh...okay?" I answered. I wondered just exactly how I was supposed to go about doing that a little while later as I sat on the bed in my room with my guitar.

I hit the tuning fork and let it vibrate against the body, matching the tone to the harmonic as I turned the gear, and in my mind's eye I saw Nina sitting next to me, her complete focus on the note that rang through the air.

I played every harmonic to finish tuning and ran my fingers across the fretboard, reviewing scales I could play with my eyes closed, but as

I did, I watched *her* hands pluck through the same beginning chords, the strain along her forearms as they adjusted to the angle, the pressure, the simple playing… I couldn't, I just couldn't anymore, and those sharp blades I'd used in Leeds still sat in my drawer, but I didn't want to use them, and didn't want to give up music either: it had been such a big part of my life for so long.

I fled my guitar, my temptation, and my room to run straight down the hall, past the spare bedroom to the library. I needed to do something, something different, and it hit me as I sat immersed in a text with some tunes I enjoyed playing in the background. The solution was obvious: if, as Uncle Cort and Elizabeth had said, I was learning to bridge, to walk between worlds, then as above, so below: I'd switch from guitar to bass, the bridge that moved between the melody and the beat, something different than what I'd done before, but still taking advantage of the skills I'd spent years building. I told Uncle Cort.

After picking through some ads in the newspaper and the phone book, then several phone inquiries to discover what various shops carried and what they knew about what they had in stock, one place sounded both reputable and knowledgeable to me. "Electrohill," I told my uncle, "they know what they're about."

"North London it is, then," he agreed, and packed me off with money and a map once I'd written the address and number down.

"Does that watch work?" he asked just as I was about to leave.

I shoved back my sleeve to check my right wrist almost reflexively. Of course it worked, I knew it worked: I wound it every morning before I buckled the tan leather over my skin. "Yes."

"Good, because we'll meet for dinner later, then," and he gave me the address where we'd meet. "It's one of the oldest bars in London, that one on Compton Street," he told me.

In spite of my map, I promptly got lost, confused by Tubes and rails, parks and greens, squares and circuses, and more than once got off at the wrong stop. Finally, though, I found my way to Palmers Green, where I tried, one, two, three, four—and the moment I played it, I knew it was mine: I was in love, smitten with an old Fender Precision bass, complete with traditional tricolor flameburst that followed the contour of the body. I'd held it on my lap when I first tried it, then welcomed the weight of it across my shoulder once I selected a strap, an ox-blood leather that spread to three inches wide. I liked the way it contrasted with my black shirt.

What I loved, really loved, was the way the neck felt in my palm, the thick strings under the pads of my fingertips, the deep, low rumble that echoed through my body when I leaned my ear against the headstock. When I asked the clerk for a patch cord and plugged into an amp, it was even better, and I spent the next hour deciding which amp had the best tone, presented its vibrated voice most accurately.

Affording it wasn't an issue, which it would have been just two years ago, I reflected as I pulled out a credit card that I hardly ever used, and that an accountant Stateside made sure was paid out of the trust fund I'd been left: the insurance paid to me by the City of New York's Fire Department for my father's untimely death in the line of duty.

I'd been left moderately wealthy, but I would have gladly traded it to once more hear my father's voice while we worked on the car he'd bought me in anticipation of my driver's license, traded it twice over for one of his hugs and the smoky smell when he got home, and yet a third to have Nina eat dinner with us, then sit and play guitar on the porch while my Da lit a cigarette and kicked his feet up on the railing and listened. Such were my thoughts as I hefted the dirty-blond tweed hard case in one hand, after arranging for the small, forty-pound Hartke amp I'd settled on along with a gig bag and various electronic accoutrements to be delivered to the shop. I couldn't quite think of it as home yet. But no matter; my instrument I'd carry myself. Everything else could be shipped.

The way back to Soho was quite the adventure as I discovered that New Compton Street was quite far away from Compton, at least on foot. It figured, of course, that neither was near Old Compton Street.

When I did finally get the proper bearings, I met Uncle Cort right outside the door of the pub with fifteen minutes to spare, and it turned out it was on the corner of Dean, which we actually lived on, only a few blocks away from the place I slept.

"You found everything all right, then?" he asked me with a big smile, a clap on the shoulder, and a nod to the case in my hand.

"I take it you expected me to get lost?"

"Yes." He laughed. "Come on, dear heart, let's get some dinner." He opened the door and ushered me in.

The pre-dinner crowd was light as we entered past the sign that announced dancing after dinner, and the smell of old wood, varnish, and spirits over the unmistakable scent of something roasted filled my lungs as a young man—I stopped half a heartbeat—greeted us.

It was automatic, the reach beyond the skin to the aethyric double. Him. The sandy blond hair that curved over the delicate face that perched over a slender neck and slight shoulders said one thing, but the energy signature, the soul the skin wore... I tried not to stare, but I was certain I *knew* him, recognized him on some fundamental level. He led us to a table and handed us our menus, letting us know he'd be back in a moment with the pints Uncle Cort had requested.

"Yet another thing to get used to," I told him with a small grin. The biggest thing had been one of the simplest: crossing the street. A lifetime of checking left, then right had to be reversed and I compensated by truly paying attention to and using the crosswalks. Food-wise, the first thing had been the whiskey in the ketchup. *That* had been an unpleasant surprise. The next had been the unexpected tang of vinegar on my potato chips. Actually, I rather enjoyed that and had gotten into the habit of eating my fries or chips like that, vinegar and salt. But this, the last...

"Warm beer," I said and saluted him with it before I took a sip.

"Don't be a heathen," he returned with a smile, "it's not beer, it's ale, and it's good for your blood this way."

"Sure. Yeah. Right. When did they first get steady current and electrical refrigeration over here?"

He laughed outright. "Logan, your father, said almost the same exact thing to me once."

"Really?" I asked, pleased for some reason. It was the first time anyone had mentioned my father that I didn't automatically want to weep, but instead felt a warm sort of comfort, almost as if he were there and had put invisible arms around me.

"Truly. He insisted the virtues of warm beer were extolled because the people extolling it had no refrigeration." He took a deep pull and smacked his lips. "He may have had a point, but it's still pretty good this way. And besides," he added, "it's warm relative to refrigerated—it's not as if it's heated up like tea."

The waiter came back, introduced himself as Graham, and after he took our order, Uncle Cort took me through the finer points of drinking ale, including a theory about the marketing of cold beer as a plot to destroy the ale industry, since cold beer could be stored for months, and ale for barely a week.

When a woman came up to the table and asked for a dance, I glanced up from my plate toward Uncle Cort and waved him away with my fork. "Go right ahead," I told him, returning my attention to my plate. "I'll be here with my well-done cow and my warm beer."

"Actually, I was asking *you*," she said, her voice friendly and low and I glanced up, first to see my uncle trying not to laugh at me, then to look over into a sparkling pair of light blue eyes, partially obscured by short dark brown hair that fell over in one long lock.

"Well, go on," he said and this time he did laugh. "I'll watch your well-done cow for you."

Flustered, I stood anyway. "And my bass too," I reminded him and pointed to where I'd tucked it under the chair and table, "don't forget."

"It'll all be here," he promised.

Her name was Hannah and as one dance became another and we fell into a real conversation, I learned that not only was I in what was considered to be the oldest bar in London, but also the oldest gay bar. I also learned that she was "taking a bit of a break" from gigging, since she was a studio and session drummer and had just come back from a six-week tour as a drum tech with a semipopular band.

It was a good conversation, and suddenly I realized I'd spent more time chatting with her than with Uncle Cort, who'd invited me.

"Hannah, I don't want to be rude, but my uncle did invite me for dinner."

"Of course," she said and smiled, "and I've kept you. Maybe you'll join me for dinner sometime?" she asked as we approached the table.

I thought about it and grinned. She was all right, but I wasn't up for dating anyone yet, not with all the new…stuff…kicking around my head. Friends, though. Well, Elizabeth and Uncle Cort would certainly encourage that.

"How about…we could meet here sometime during the week and figure it out from there?"

"Sure, then. Here's my number," and she pulled a business card out from her wallet and handed it to me. *Hannah Meyer, Kit and Percussion, Drum Tech and Repair* it read, with her number beneath. *Own Equipment and Transport* it said across the bottom.

"Is that important?" I asked.

"Which?"

I pointed out the last line.

"Well," she said with a little drawl, "it *can* be." The accompanying gleam in her eye let me know I'd stepped into something I hadn't meant to and I felt a rush of heat crawl up my neck.

She let me off the hook. "I'll be here Wednesday, about five-ish—what say I stand you a drink and we can talk about bands, since you're a bass player?"

"All right," I agreed, "I'll see you Wednesday," and I sat back down to dinner with my uncle.

"So," he said brightly, unable to hide his mirth completely in the lift of his brows, "did you have a nice chat? Oh, I think your cow's cold, by the by," he said, indicating my plate with his knife.

❖

The place had begun to fill up by the time we were done, and Hannah waved to me and yelled, "Wednesday, right?" across the room as we made our way through the other patrons and to the door.

"So, the oldest pub, and the oldest gay bar in London," I commented as the cool autumn air blew against our backs and we rounded the corner on Dean. "Any particular reason you picked that, or…" I let that hang in the breeze.

"Simply figured you'd never been, and this one's so very nearby." He shrugged in his thick, brown workman's jacket. "That and you may want to do a bit of socializing there, so you might as well get comfortable with the place, right?"

We walked in companionable silence as I thought on that. I was confused. He was right, I'd never been to a bar before, and especially not a gay bar, but was he trying to help me out, was he trying to tell me something about himself…or both?

"Do you go there a lot?"

He gave me a sidelong glance as we neared the door next to the shop, the door that led directly to the steps into the flat. "No, but often enough. That bother you?"

"No," I shrugged, "but it's, well, it's unexpected, I guess."

He unlocked the door and swung it open, then waved me past him again. I rested my hard shell case on the floor and waited for him at the bottom of the landing. I watched his shoulders work as he took a deep breath and locked the door.

Tiger eyes met mine, deep amber flames in their depths.

"Samantha," he said, the first time he'd called me that since I'd asked him not to, and that, combined with his tone, made something clench in my chest.

"You're making two assumptions, the first one being that I'm straight, and the other being that if I were, I wouldn't be comfortable around people that aren't."

I had assumed exactly that and attributed his comfort level with me to two things: first, he *was* my guardian, and the second—well, I wasn't exactly a "girly" girl, by most standards. Other than biology and appearance, there was nothing I said or did that I could think of that marked me as a girl, and Cort didn't treat me like one either. I guess I'd assumed that he was comfortable with me because he could treat me like, well, a guy.

"I know, I mean, I'm not like *regular* girls," I said, "you know, like besides the gay thing." I stared down a moment at the case that rested against my thigh and took a breath. "I've always sorta hung out with the guys at home and I guess maybe I'm more like them than a girl." I shifted my weight from one foot to the other. "I figure that's why we're, you know, cool."

Uncle Cort laid a gentle hand on my shoulder and gave me an even gentler smile. "First, no one, absolutely *no one*, is completely straight or gay, not me, not you, not anyone, and we'll leave that there for now. As for the rest…" He motioned me up the stairs before him. "I'm not looking at you as a boy, or a girl, as a man, or a woman," he said, his voice firm, an underlying fire behind the words as we trooped up the stairs. "You're here to be a Wielder, and I? I'm the forger, the teacher. There's no room for that nonsense about boys and girls and the inanities about supposed differences. People live, love, bleed, then die. It's that simple, and that short."

He caught my eyes with his when we reached the landing. "Your strengths—and your weaknesses—are completely unique to *you*. That's what I look for, what we have to work with, that's what I help you develop and guard against. So I don't care," he said as we stood on the landing, "who, or *how*, you love, so long as the law of Light is guarded.

Nothing else matters." The flame in his eyes was ablaze as I opened the door at the top of the steps. "Nothing."

My amp had already arrived and sat there in the hallway. "Well, Ann, go ahead and put that where you'd like it," he said in his usual tone, "and no studies tonight—you need to spend time with your new love."

He grinned at me then volunteered to carry the amp upstairs to my room when I said that's where I'd practice. It was a matter of five minutes to discover the perfect floor position for it, and I mulled over our discussion as I experimented.

"No one's completely straight or gay," he'd said. Huh. What did that mean, anyway? And that bit about unique strengths and weaknesses… Did he mean regardless of being a boy or a girl or because of it? And where did that leave me, with my definitely female body and my decidedly nonfemale mindset?

But within seconds, none of that mattered: I found the sweet spot that I was pretty certain would give me back the tone I wanted to hear, and my heart thrumming with anticipation, I tuned up, strapped on, and plugged in. I let the vibrations from the bass flow through me as I plumbed the mysteries of the low end.

I did go to the pub Wednesday and since I was early I sat at the bar, where I met the bartender, Kenny Black.

"So, you're new 'round here, yeah?" he asked as he handed me a pint.

"New to almost everything 'round here," I answered with a grin.

His eyes lit up and he smiled. "Hey, you're an American—I saw you carrying an instrument last night. What're you playin'? You here with a band?"

"Nah." I smiled. "I don't know anyone yet."

His blond and rather curly mohawked hair fell in soft curves over to one side and his eyes, dark and vibrant, were also honest and warm.

"Well, ya know me now, and I sing, play guitar," he said and he held out his hand. "I'm not in a band at the mo', but I've got an eye out, you know?" he told me as we shook.

"Well, I've finally got myself a Fender Precision," I said, "it's what you saw me with last night."

"How long you been playing bass for?" he asked, curiosity sharpening his question.

"Well, if you count the time at the store plus last night," I joked, and glanced at my watch, "about twenty-four hours—but I've been playing guitar for about ten years or so."

A surprised expression crossed his face. "Hey, then you're gonna be good at it. So many of the better bassists played guitar first."

"You think?" I asked, genuinely intrigued.

"Oh sure," he said airily, "you've got all that melody and theory down. You know, there's a couple of all right studios around. Find us a good drummer, and maybe we can rent a few hours, make a little noise sometime, see what we can do?"

"Sounds good," I nodded, warming to the idea. It not only sounded like fun, but I'd never been in a band before and then I could honestly tell Uncle Cort and Elizabeth that I was, in fact, making friends. "Where do you go to find studios around here, anyway?"

As Kenny and I chatted and debated the merits of different guitars, I felt the approach of a familiar energy: our waiter from last night.

"This fellow talking your ear off 'bout his eternal band search?"

I turned to find the same sandy brown hair, now slicked back except for the forelock that fell over bright eyes, and a delicate mouth smiling at me while Kenny laughed. "Ah, Graham, just chatting before you steal yet another bassist for your outfit. He," and Kenny jerked his thumb in Graham's direction, "is a ska-band man, and quite the Rude Boy about town."

I raised my eyebrow at him as I reached for his hand. "Ann," I told him as his palm met mine. That sense of recognition swelled, and I thought perhaps he felt it too from the way he examined my face. "What's ska?" I asked with a grin.

Kenny laughed as he pulled another pint and Graham goggled as if he'd been told that yes, this really was a gag and it was all being filmed for television.

"Not know what ska is?" he spluttered. "And you're a musician? God—*where* have you been? Kenny and I'll have to take you 'round to some of the shows, then." He smiled, perhaps a bit too charmingly for me, and I raised an eyebrow as I looked him over, his black sweater and its turquoise and white diamond blocks, the thin black tie over a narrow-collared shirt, his perfectly creased black pants over thick-soled creepers. I don't know why I thought I knew him, I'd never met him before my first visit to the pub, and certainly never seen anyone that dressed like he did, except, perhaps, in old movies.

"Not that you look like the kind of girl that can be taken, I mean, uh—"

"Graham can't speak to anyone about anything before he's had breakfast, right?" Kenny saved him by handing him his mug.

"Why don't you tell me a bit more about it, then?" I asked as Graham buried his face in the foam.

"Sure, sure," he agreed after a hasty swallow. "Kenny, queue something up, hey?" he asked, pointing to the receiver that sat on a shelf on the wall behind the bar.

Kenny laughed as he moved to comply. "We'll start it easy, then, shall we?" he asked over his shoulder as he flipped and selected through a pile of discs and tapes.

I'd been thoroughly introduced to some of "the best of what's around, I tell you, not that new, Victorian, dark wave stuff," as Graham put it by the time Hannah stepped in to join us.

There was certainly a lot of strong musicianship involved in ska, I mused as I listened to the interplay between the bass and the drum, and the speeding trumpet and horn melodies that danced in my ears. So far, ska sounded quite a bit like super-fast reggae with amazing horn sections arranged not as accompaniment, but as main melody instruments.

I kept listening to the music as a friendly argument ensued between Hannah and Graham about music and genre, the value of the message and whether or not it was diluted by the medium, and by the time I realized that I'd better get back to the shop so I wouldn't miss dinner, we'd all agreed to meet there Sunday morning, then go together to the studio Hannah preferred, see if we could have a bit of fun.

"Well, consider me filler, because you know I'm looking to build a ska band, but we'll give it a shot," Graham said, and just like that, we were set.

❖

With our first rehearsal set for Sunday morning and a second set for the following Tuesday afternoon, I practiced obsessively between lectures and training sessions. My shoulders, with the help of the weights I no longer noticed, had grown immune not only to the weight of the sword, but also to the weight of the bass, and as the calluses on my fingers thickened then smoothed from fretwork, so did the ones on the pads of my hand from the workouts Uncle Cort put me through, first with a practice weapon made of rattan and wrapped in duct tape to give it sufficient heft, and then with live, naked steel.

Somehow I managed to help Elizabeth and Uncle Cort ready one of the two spare rooms for Fran's visit. We chose the one near mine because it received more daylight.

I hadn't seen her since our graduation, and when she emerged from the gate at Heathrow the very first thing I noticed as I moved through the press to greet her was her eyes. They were overlarge and overbright in a face that had thinned since early June, and she'd let her hair, the wavy honey and wheat mane, grow longer. Grief had changed her, I thought as we embraced, the fierce wrap of competitors, the close touch of friends, and if for a few moments I was startled by the familiarity and the strength of the arms around me, the surprise disappeared when I happily returned the hug.

"You made it!" I said finally over the din as we parted slightly to examine each other.

Fran smiled, the beautiful smile that I knew so well, the one that had caught my eye and heart so long ago and, I knew without a doubt, quite a few others as well.

"One piece, no less," she agreed.

Once we released each other, I reintroduced her to Uncle Cort whom she'd met before graduation, and to Elizabeth, which was slightly awkward since she was neither relative nor friend but a bit of each. I finally decided on "close family friend," which worked well enough. I took Fran's hand in mine as we struggled through the crowd to find her luggage at the proper carousel.

It was non-stop chat on the ride back and through lunch. Cort and Elizabeth shooed us out to wander around a bit so Fran could get her bearings, which was funny to me, since I still needed a map. We wandered over to Wardour Street, the London version of Chinatown, and got a neat kick out of hearing the mix of languages and accents, so different from the heavy Staten Island voicing, the Italian lilt, or the occasional Irish accent we'd grown up with. And despite all the familiar enticing smells, it was very different than Chinatown in New York, because it was so sparkling clean.

After, we walked 'round and about back to Soho Green in the middle of Soho Square before calling it a night—even though Fran wanted to go to the famous Ronnie Scott's jazz club.

I laughed and promised we'd go the next day, or maybe the one after—she'd only *just* arrived—and I laughed again when she yawned during her protest.

"You'll be here a few months—we'll get there, I promise."

After she'd settled her things in her room and we had dinner, we wound up talking about everything and nothing all night in my room. I admit to asking more questions than necessary, just to hear her voice, her accent. I was amazed at how much I missed an American tone. And while we avoided touching on anything that might bring up the real reason why either one of us had changed in the ways we had, we spoke until the sun came up before we finally got some sleep.

❖

"Now you've an official excuse to go play tourist for a few days," Uncle Cort said the next morning over breakfast, and both he and Elizabeth made suggestions.

"You must visit Parliament to observe the House of Commons and the House of Lords," he insisted. "Especially if you're certain you want to live here," he told me privately.

The tickets he gave us a few days later took us past the line that waited by Saint Stephen's entrance and directly into the House of Lords. Already disillusioned about politics from the other side of the pond, I grew quickly overwarm and overtired, but I blamed that purely on the lack of real rest and the bit of overload I still carried from the work only a few nights before. I wondered briefly if my uncle was trying to get me to change my mind about staying in England.

Once there, however, when Lord Halsbury tabled a measure he called "an act to refrain local authorities from promoting homosexuality," I was completely awake. The measure seemed to mean that the portrayal of homosexuality—in schools, in media, in anything, in *any* way—as something other than abnormal would be a crime. The ensuing discussion went beyond infuriating and when I stood because I'd had enough and was leaving, Fran understood and left with me.

Fury made her eyes snap, once again overbright and full, and her lashes glinted at me with the spark of tears. "Why is it that if I do this," she asked as she took my hand in hers, "or this," and she kissed my lips softly, a kiss I gently returned, "I'm suddenly less…less human than anyone else?"

I rubbed my thumb lightly over her hand as we walked past the gate and out onto the main sidewalk, back toward the Underground station. "You're not," I said quietly, "you're absolutely not."

Fran stopped and faced me. "Do you know how many laws they have to in fact *break*, then *rewrite*, simply to justify their discrimination?" she asked and we continued walking, anger riding her voice, an anger I could feel too, not only for myself but *from* her directly, a wave of emotion that washed through and over her, a rose blush that suffused her surrounding energy field, coupled with the clear light that backfed through me, shocking me, as it turned into a definite arousal. It was a pierce of physical longing that made my abs contract and my breath catch.

Alarmed, I hastily dropped her hand, but not before I caught the answering flare in her eyes and I dropped my gaze to the cement.

"We should…we should hurry," I mumbled, "I think Elizabeth and my uncle want to have dinner with us tonight."

I was hyperaware of my body, of hers, of how it had felt to touch her, to hold her, to feel the press of her against me and her lips on mine, and while there was no way of knowing short of asking, I suspected she might have had similar thoughts; we couldn't really look at each other, and the uncomfortable silence between us grew, became something thick and heavy as we walked to the station. The discomfort didn't ease until the press of commuters jammed us next to each other and I took her hand again to lead her out through the press of the crowd when we reached our stop.

The silence continued through dinner, nothing hostile, but very, very, self-conscious, and when I glanced up at Fran from across the table, caught her eyes with mine, I could see her cheeks had reddened.

That could have been from the sudden chill that had descended as we'd walked the few blocks from the station back to the shop and the apartment, or possibly the soup—it was on the hot side.

Elizabeth occasionally cast her gaze over at me or at Fran as we both studied our plates and finally saved us from the nearly suffocating silence.

"What did you think of Parliament?" she asked.

"It's amazing about the whole heredity thing," Fran answered animatedly. "One of the Lords asked to table some measure that..."

I was greatly relieved at the lively discussion they got into; it dissipated the tension instantly, and they barely seemed to notice when Cort raised his eyebrows and lifted his chin at me to ask if I was ready for our training session and we excused ourselves from the table.

❖

It was hours later—or at least it felt that way—when I finally made it to my bed. I was exhausted in ways I hadn't felt in quite some time, a combination of tired mind and awakened body. Cort had monitored me briefly before calling it a night and he'd reminded me to continue to monitor for overload, to prevent crisis.

I'd done as he asked, trying not to think, not to *feel* anything, to bear in mind only that I was a tool in the hand of the Lords of Light, as Cort referred to them, just as the sword was a tool in my hand. I focused on my heart rate, on my breath, drawing my awareness inward, concentrating on different areas of my body, tensing and relaxing the muscles as I worked my way up from feet to head, checking the energy flows as I encountered them, trying to ensure they were free and clear, to keep my head the same way. Finally I was done and ready to sleep when a knock sounded. I sighed as I decided that trying to sleep was a wasted effort, and I flipped my nightstand light on before I padded to the door on bare feet that hardly felt the cold wood beneath them.

"Yes?" I asked as I opened it, only to find Fran blinking at me in the darkened hallway.

She bit her lip and shuffled a moment, then asked, "Can I talk with you?"

"Yeah, sure," I told her and let her in.

As she walked past me, not two inches away, it struck like a wave, swamping my senses. To my still-heightened sight and awareness, she appeared to glow, her body lit almost from within, and I could feel, like it was my own skin, the cold of the floor on her feet, the brush of softened cotton against her thigh as she walked past me, the faint soft scratch of her hair against her neck.

And then there was the churn of emotions within.

She sat on the edge by the foot of the bed, drawing her feet up against the chill. "What's really going on with you?" she asked directly.

"I don't...nothing. Why?"

"C'mon, be real with me. You've got a private tutor and you're living half a world away from home. You left your house, you changed your *name*...and you disappear after dinner for hours at a time. What's going on?"

She caught gentle hold of my arm and drew me closer to sit next to her. "You used to say I was your best friend—can't you tell me?"

I gasped when her fingertips ran past the scars on my wrist—they were surprisingly sensitive under her touch, and I'd forgotten they were there, covered as they were by the weights during sessions with Cort, as well as long sleeves and sweaters in the cool days of early autumn. But the sleep shirt I wore offered no such cover or protection, and the light cotton rolled and rode, revealing the original lines, as well as the newer ones.

I was silent as I let her inspect them and, as if conscious of the fact that the fresher ones twinged, she traced the air above them. I felt it anyway. "Did you do this?" she asked finally, her eyes huge in the low light of my room.

I nodded slowly in answer.

"Sammy...why?"

"Ann," I corrected, then shrugged, helpless as I was to really answer, shocked at the tears that stung my eyes, and when she wrapped me in her arms and pulled my head to her shoulder, I let her, let her curl around me as I cried silent tears down the soft skin of her neck.

I didn't know how to explain it, how alone I really was, how my father had filled my world and Nina had brightened it, that my mother was a voice I sometimes heard in dreams and the faintest memory of a touch on my cheek.

The rough affection from Uncle Cort and Elizabeth's caring

tutelage were wonderful and I loved and appreciated them for it, but none of it made the yawning empty go away and now, I knew things, knew things others didn't because I was supposed to, because it was my destiny or some such and it set me even further apart from everything and everyone I'd ever known…even the ones who weren't here anymore.

I would never be certain of exactly how much of this I sobbed out to Fran while she held and rocked me with steady, certain strength.

"You're not alone," she whispered into my ear as her hand soothed down my back and her fingers combed through my hair. "You're not—I swear. You've got me, and I'm not going anywhere."

"Yeah?" I asked, and I tried to grin at her. "Think you'll still say that after I tell what this," I showed her the brand on my arm, "is all about?"

"I know I will," she said solemnly and kissed my head firmly before releasing me and pulled at the thick down quilt that covered my bed. "C'mon. Lie down and tell me all about it."

I did. Beneath the warmth of the almost-cool cotton as the streetlight shone through a crack in the curtains over a window I'd opened slightly for fresh air, under the gentle brush of her fingertips on my arms and face, I told her everything, speaking with her in the same way we had when we'd been younger, closer, before things…changed. And finally, we got to the subject, the source, of that change.

"I don't think it's true, you know?" Fran said as she again played with my hair, twirling a long strand around her finger. Her eyes alternately gleamed and glowed in the uneven light released by the curtain as it moved in the light breeze.

"What do you mean? Her father—"

Her fingertips were soft on my cheek and she brushed her thumb across my lips. "There was nothing, absolutely *nothing* in the newspaper—you know they always print those things, it's like a Staten Island requirement or something." She gave me a small, sad, smile. "My father said either there's something really mistaken about what we heard or…it's worse—because it's something 'ugly,' as he put it."

I shivered involuntarily against her at those words. That had been a fear of mine that I'd shared with no one.

"Shh." She pulled me closer and I snuggled into her gratefully. "I doubt that's it. And when I get time, I'll find out what really happened."

She sighed, a soft sound under my ear and I kissed her neck as she drew delicate patterns on my shoulder and arm while I returned the same feathering touch. "They probably shipped her off to school somewhere or something like that and her parents don't want her to see any of her friends."

I raised myself on an elbow and shook my head. "Her *gay* friends, you mean." The words were harsh and bitter, even to my ears.

"Well, it *is* a possibility. My parents had discussed doing just that when they found out about me," she said quietly, her fingers still stroking along my temples.

"You're kidding!"

"Nope. But since our high school was so prestigious and I was already a senior, my father thought it would create awkward public relations for him and his campaign, the family being such big contributors to the school and all that." Her voice was very matter-of-fact as she spoke.

I gazed down at Fran, who hadn't let me go, who anchored me past and through the pain and the rage that threatened to rip through me, for her, for our friend, at the unfairness of everything.

"That's—that's horrible," I spluttered, not knowing what else to say. I pulled her closer and she nestled her cheek between my shoulder and neck.

"It was, then," she admitted, "because it wasn't as if I didn't know why my father had sent Gianni to art school in Milan, then funded the studio." She tightened her arms around me and I kissed her head. "My mother cried, Gemma refused to be parted from him and now, well, I'm here, right? It's not as if they beat me or anything like that."

I gulped for air as a razor-sharp line of fire lanced across my chest, over my sternum, and I fought down the memory, so fresh, so *real*, and so remembered, now that we had spoken about her, about Nina, so far away, so out of reach and...

Fran's breath was warm across my shoulder, skated over the pulse that beat next to her lips, chilled the tears I didn't know which of us had spilled when she pressed her face to my skin.

"We'll have a great time, it'll be a beautiful Christmas, Fran. Really," I promised, not knowing what else to say as we held one another, aware of each other's hurt and loss, the cloud, the *scent* of it in our faces as we breathed it in, the green apple tart and sweet of it on our lips, and the undeniable reality of the beat of living hearts held close, so very close because we were together, alive and torn in the same ways.

"I know," she whispered reassuringly, and I could feel her lips smile against my neck before she pressed them against the pulse that beat raggedly beneath them. "I just think…that's what happened, they sent her away, and they don't want anyone to know."

The effort not to reach through the Aethyr, to find the blankness where Nina should have been, made my throat close and my eyes sting when my mind touched that blankness anyway. I knew what it meant—she was nowhere I could go, and I shut myself down further against that awareness.

"I can't—I can't afford to think like that." I spoke honestly as I gazed down at her and her eyes gleamed a smoky gold at me. "I can't find her on the Astral, can't feel the, the," I groped for the right word, "the *sense* of her, anywhere, except in this." I tapped the sword that hung low on my throat. "If I even have that hope and then…then it's not true—I don't think I could survive that again."

Hearing that made her put her arms around me and pull me back to her. "I don't want to lose you either," she whispered as I laid my head on her shoulder again and I embraced her in return.

"I didn't really pull myself out of this one," I confessed quietly, "my uncle did. I'm only here because I *have* to be."

The quiet hitch of her breath, the skip in the beat of her heart, sounded in my ears. "So don't, then, don't hold on to something you can't," she said softly, the words a warm brush against my cheek. "I'll hope for you. I'll even make you a deal—you do what you need to do, and if I ever find her, find out what happened, you come back home, okay?"

"You got it," I agreed, because I knew, could tell, the thought gave her comfort. For myself, I already knew that to hold hope for the impossible brought nothing but pain. That was something I'd learned in the days that surrounded my father's funeral.

I shifted and faced her as we clung to each other, cozy and silent. Touch had already changed from reassuring, barely there softness, to the bracing firm press of open hands along the length muscles, and it seemed the most natural thing in the world to kiss the cheek before me, filled as I was with tenderness, vulnerability, and something akin to gratitude for her friendship, the sincerity of her shared hurts, and warmth, a warmth I could feel flow through me, filling places I'd let run dry, knocking on doors to rooms long empty.

When her lips touched me in return, it sent her awareness rushing over me again, and the surge of love and sorrow and an unnamable need that I didn't really recognize or understand crashed over us both with the knowledge that we knew who we were for ourselves, for each other: if she was hope, then I was the heartbeat, and we were held together by flesh.

Her skin was so soft under my hands, softer yet under my lips, as we shifted and shed the clothes we didn't need, too much between us and not yet close enough until… "Fran, this will—" I tried to explain the link we were forging, the bond we'd build between us, despite the urgent flow that pressed my hips between her thighs, her lips to the pulse in my neck, mine to hers again and again, unable to stop noticing anyway how similar, and how different, our bodies were since the last time we'd touched.

"This…it can't be undone, Frankie—it can't be taken back. You'll be tied to me, and," I stumbled for the right words to tell her, so that she'd know, fully understand, "and these things in my life now."

"Sammer," she whispered, and I did not correct her, because I knew she knew *me* in the same way that I knew *her.* I cradled her face in my hands and she reached up to stroke the hair away from my face. "I know that's what you believe—and I," she exhaled, a delicate sound that warmed the air between us, "I told you you're not alone. So let it be."

Her fingers worked a gentle magic through my hair, sent slivers of sensation through my scalp that ran down my neck, my spine, and an electric tang through my thighs and my stomach. "If this…this will bind us, then let it be you and me—I'd rather it was you than anyone else."

"Yeah? Really?" I asked, uncertain that I knew what I was reading, feeling, from her, not wanting to do anything that would hurt her or our recovered friendship.

"Don't you?"

There was no one else, no one living that I could think of or even imagine that I would rather share this with. Fran had been my first girlfriend, my first kiss, my first experiments with sex—and after all was said and done? She was, still, my best friend, and I was hers. We weren't in love with one another, but we loved each other, and that was enough, and more than, because we'd finish what we'd started, and in the end, we were closer to one another than anyone else in the world, because of the things we shared: friendship, rivalry, love, death.

"I'm glad it's you," I told her, and let myself give in to what we both wanted, both needed, to hold each other through the hurt, to prove that we still felt, still lived, still loved.

I let her kiss, the roll of her tongue on mine, carry us where it would and I was consumed with the desire, the absolute wrenching need to touch, to taste her, everywhere.

Her breasts were larger than they'd been last time under my hands, the taste of each nipple as it hardened in my mouth even more gratifying, enlarging the hunger that burned through me, and when I shifted my legs as I eased down her body, I could feel how wet I was.

My fingers sketched invisible lines across her skin, followed the trail my lips and tongue blazed along untracked velvet as she moved and moaned and sighed under me, her hands splaying on, then squeezing my back, my arms, my shoulders with a touch that left me aching to do more as I discovered and explored her, and all the while the siren call of the seat of her arousal drew me on.

My shoulders fit between delicately muscled, beautiful thighs and I touched my lips to the tendon that stretched before me even as I pressed my hand flat against her, short fine hairs pressed under my palm, the hardened point pushing back against my skin, the silky hot wet that I so wanted to taste.

Her fingers stroked through my hair and I could feel more than hear the hesitant, whispered, "Sam…" She was shy, embarrassed, a little afraid, and even a little ashamed, though she had nothing to be ashamed of, not the amazing tone of the body under mine, the heady scent that churned my blood and made me want this even more, or her own desire.

"Please," I asked softly as I glanced up to see her eyes dark upon me, "let me?"

Her fingers played against my temples. "I…you don't have…" She shrugged, helplessly.

"I want to." I took her hand in mine and kissed it. "Frankie, if you…if you don't want to, if you're," I groped for the right words, "uncomfortable, we'll stop, okay?"

Her fingers squeezed mine. "I'm just...you know..."

"I do," I agreed softly because I did know, and I kissed her hand again to reassure her, to let her know I loved her, that we—that *this*—was more than fine, then brushed my lips along the demarcation where delicate skin ended and soft fuzz began. She sighed, a light note that sent a delicious shiver through me and I kissed her again, carefully, tenderly, just that much lower.

I was amazed by the slick, silky softness that felt like her mouth, a taste as warm and sweet with something so plainly, so intensely, purely sexual that if I'd thought I was aroused, this sent me to a state I'd never hit before.

There was so much to taste and kiss and suck, to explore and discover, and I did, everything, while I held her hand tightly with mine and her fingers first skated along my scalp, then pushed and urged and gripped while the gorgeous muscles in her legs flexed and tightened around me, the perfect arch of her foot skimming my ribs until...

God...thick, and smooth, and addictive. I was thrilled by the way her clit grew in my mouth, how it hardened and lengthened until it pulsed on its own, in time to the beat of her body, and then there was the pulse that beat on my tongue, the thickened ring that would bleed and bind us if it tore, no matter how gently, how carefully... As I teased against that beautiful opening with the tip of my tongue she gasped, her hands tightened on me, and her hips pushed up, a gentle body urging that sent the slight tang of blood over the sweet I drank of.

Her body opened, then tightened around me, and the images slammed sharp into my mind, so clear through her eyes. *Fran was five, she was running through the grass, she fell and her tooth came out. She caught it in her fingers and gave it to her father, who swept her up in his arms and told her how brave she was because she didn't cry. Eight and crouched in a racing start, facing the water, scared, unable to explain to anyone how the fear pounded through her until the gun went off and she jumped into the pool, everything forgotten but the swim.*

Her fingers gripped and relaxed compulsively as the rhythm built between us, and I rubbed my palm across her stomach to tell her this was okay, this was unbearably, almost painfully, beautiful, *she* was beautiful as she moved and tensed below me, and when the clutch of her hands became a firm grasp, the pulse became a throb under my lips and my name, the name I'd been born with, was a soft cry from hers. *Ten and I saw myself through her eyes, the wonder and the recognition of a kindred, the...wow...an essential goodness...the same I'd seen in her. Fourteen and there was the sweet warmth of our first kiss and as the heat of her body embraced me I knew,* knew *she saw me, too, saw how I'd cried for my father, then again over the summer, saw the searing hurt and rage, the hounds that drove me until the sharp bite of metal sliced through my skin.*

There were tears, whether hers or mine we couldn't tell and didn't bother to try as her muscles softened, relaxed, beneath me and I covered her body with mine, wrapped my arms around her. She pressed her mouth to mine, linked, bound, the binding done and done again over an astonished "I'm *inside* you" whisper at the revelation of the literal reality, the hot, wet, kiss of being within another, within *my* self, too, a baring of body and mind that joined the pure knowledge of who we were, who we had been, and who we would be. Flashes of a past beyond remembering and a future beyond knowing—mother, daughter, sister, lover, friend, always—immutably bound before and bound once again with her blood on my lips and hands and mine on hers, marked, sigiled and sealed as we were in ways primitive and profound in a deep magic that reached past the oldest of knowledge.

And the empty, the yawning empty eased, filled by her until I knew with the gasping breath I drew into the renewed tightening of my body that held her fast within me that I *wasn't* alone, I *never* would be, and she knew in the answering surge that pushed so close and so tight around me that we lost all sense of separateness, that I would stay, and not merely because I had to but because I wanted to: I would stay for her.

This was our pact, made freely, willingly—bloody, beautiful, and unbreakable—and we would renew and reaffirm it almost every night until she left.

❖

The next morning, when I glanced at Fran over breakfast, she smiled at me in return. Despite her recent shower, her eyes still seemed a bit warm and sleepy, her pretty lips still slightly swollen even as her hair hung over her shoulders in loose, damp waves. I wanted to brush it back with my fingers, kiss the bare skin beneath it, inhale the scent of it.

I could *feel* the return pulse in her neck, in mine, and that pulse flourished into a fevered blush the moment I realized I'd not really understood nor even *heard* a single word Elizabeth had said, until "I'm certain you find each other much more fascinating than whatever suggestions I may have had for you today" broke through in Elizabeth's friendly tone.

The same red tide I felt crawl up my cheeks suffused Fran's face, waved as a discernable heat off her as she sat next to me, and I took her hand in mine under the table to reassure her.

"Do I have to spell it out for you?" Elizabeth asked, hands on her hips and amused exasperation playing across her face. "Go. Back. To. Bed. The both of you."

I didn't even know what to say to that.

"Perhaps I'll leave you to discuss it amongst yourselves?" she asked in that same tone, glancing at each of us.

I nodded and attempted to pick up my cup of tea as nonchalantly as I could manage it.

"It's supposed to be warm out today—I'd recommend a walk over to the Green after lunch," she said casually as she approached the door. "I'll have Francesca's things moved to your room, then."

Silence stretched loud and hard behind the door as it closed, so complete I could hear my heart beat in my head.

I couldn't take it anymore and stood, still holding her hand in mine.

"You know that? I think I'm going to do the unthinkable," I told her and smiled.

"Yeah? What's that?"

I tugged gently on her hand. "I'm gonna go back to bed, get up later, walk over to the Green with you after lunch, and then? We'll go to the pub to meet Kenny, Hannah, and Graham—we're scheduled to have little bit of a jam session."

"That's your big plan for the day?"

"That's it—my big plan."

Fran shook her head, but smiled back at me as she stood. "And you think I should…?" she shrugged her shoulders in question.

On impulse, I kissed the knuckles of the hand I held. "I think…

you should come with me," I said, then kissed her fingers again. "Stay with me—and *you* can decide later whether or not you want your things moved."

I wanted her to have a choice about whether we shared a room or a bed—she didn't have to, she wasn't obligated. I didn't want her to think I expected something from her that she didn't want to give or do, and I wanted her to know that no matter what had happened between us, I fully respected her right to make that choice.

She gazed at me, the tiger in the lady prowling behind her eyes. Despite the difference in color, I was certain mine burned the same way.

The whispered caress across my cheek and the kiss that followed said very clearly that sleep was not the immediate consideration.

"Maybe we'll just make your jam session and dinner," she murmured into my lips as we pulled each other up the stairs.

Right. We'd already had breakfast, we could skip lunch, and I sighed against her in agreement as we fit to each other—we fit perfectly.

The link was already so complete that images were no longer of the distant past but of the night before, what she had enjoyed, what took her beyond, and when her hands and mouth landed exactly where I needed them, I knew she saw the same things too.

❖

The decision to have Fran attend the jam session and then stay for dinner at the pub had seemed a good one at the time. Kenny and Graham had arranged it—with the promise to the manager that they'd work right after, when the "regular" band came.

But as below, so above. I didn't know that a blood bonding would effectively act as the catalyst that would catapult my potential into manifest capabilities. Or rather, it had been part of the things Elizabeth had explained that made me squirm so much I couldn't hear: the opening of new channels from the raw power exchange, the waking of things that hadn't yet been roused—but now I truly understood, or at least, I began to.

I had already been welcomed into the Circle by virtue of my heritage and my training, and warned by my uncle that until my sealing,

I would be its weakest link: I could still be corrupted, taken, the worm in the heart of the rose, even forcibly ridden by another entity and set off, a bomb within the Circle, because I'd not yet made the eternal promise, the promise that meant I'd placed my soul's existence on the line, had yet to receive the literal flood of power that would accompany it and with that, the ability to complete, to close the Circle.

But the blood binding released a trickle of that power, began the Rite of sealing somewhat prematurely. In essence, I was now even more a part of the Circle than I'd been before. But the warding that had surrounded me no longer did since I had breached it, not because I'd connected to someone else, but because the connect was to someone outside of the Circle. It also meant that these new abilities I'd gained were more than partially out of control.

That was below. Above, the power had resonated across the Astral, the white light announcement that a new Wielder had arrived, but it was not the blaze my true sealing would have created, merely the burst of presence. And those that hunted, had hunted for eons beyond imagining, knew it meant a unique vulnerability, a unique opportunity: to turn a Wielder.

I grew tense as we stepped away from the door and began our way to the pub, and suddenly I knew why this neighborhood had been the one Cort had settled in and in which he'd opened his shop.

The environment, the madness of creativity, the overt and covert availability of sex and drugs…this was a hunting ground.

I could almost smell the trails left behind through the Aethyr, and the scent of hounds, and the presence of those they served, filled my awareness. This was what the warding had kept me from seeing, from knowing: the world was full of things that took, things that ate, things that existed only to destroy the Light.

"Hey, you okay?" Fran asked, her fingers warm in mine as we rounded the corner of Old Compton.

"Yeah, I'm fine," I said and smiled at her as I adjusted my gig bag over my shoulder, then thumbed the door latch, "just hungry is all." We'd talk about it later or tomorrow, I thought, as I waved her in before me.

Once everyone was introduced, I could tell that Graham and Kenny really liked Fran while Hannah shot me the occasional mischievous grin, a grin that disappeared when she looked past my shoulder.

But I could *sense* them before they'd even walked in, a tightening in the skin of my neck and the band of muscle across my stomach.

Without even meaning to, because my awareness was so fine-tuned I could feel them, I knew where and who they were before I even turned.

Hounds. And the hounds announced the near proximity, the presence of their masters, eaters of things living, of energy, of essence, of hope and love and goodness until it was gone, dissolved to nothing.

I watched them surreptitiously, and I wondered how it was I'd never really seen them so clearly before.

They may, on some level, have appeared nondescript: gangly, gaunt, thin and pinched with the look of hunger, of the use of too many soft drugs ringing their eyes, a grayish cast to their skin, no matter what its original shading. Nothing shone about them but their eyes, dark, fever bright, almost too wet. They gave sniffing, furtive glances, they jumped at sudden movements. They came out to inspect—whatever—then scurried back into the shadows.

And then *they* came. I watched one feeder, then another, with their thralls, living vessels, and I watched the hounds that looked for fresh food.

It was…interesting. The field that surrounded them seemed to literally draw things to it; energy fields of the inanimate were affected. People seemed to lean in their direction without even knowing, an attunement, pulled to that draw. Few seemed immune besides me, Fran, Hannah, and Graham.

Graham's response intrigued me. He seemed not only unattracted but hostile, a red blush of controlled anger with a touch of fear tightly reined in washed over him as a pair swaggered past the bar to the table the hounds had saved.

I wondered what kept Hannah and Graham clear. Fran, though, I knew, or at least thought I did, since after all, we were bound.

My musings were interrupted as we set up for our session—rearranged amps and the drum kit to the right height for Hannah, then did the same for Kenny's mic stand. It wasn't a real gig in the sense that we wouldn't play long and, really, we were doing it because we hadn't been able to book the studio for the night. That, and I suspected Hannah wanted to see what we could really do in a "live" situation, while Kenny and Graham probably simply wanted to do something more than hear the sounds we made bounce off the four small walls of the studio and us the only audience.

It was a nice little set, took us maybe about half an hour, and the early arrivals didn't seem to mind; in fact, we got a couple of *nice job*s and a couple of enthusiastic *good 'un*s from the pre-dinner crowd that started to trickle in. And while I might have been nervous and edgy for about a whole twenty seconds before Hannah clicked into the first tune, the moment we started playing the nerves not only disappeared, but so did everything else but the groove: I felt pretty darn loose and just plain good way before the time we were done and it was time to unplug and get off the stage. I broke down my setup, then helped set the stage for the real band before I took myself and my bass to the table Fran held for us.

"Sounded good—*and* you look good up there," she told me with a smile as I settled into a seat, and from the sparkle in her eye to the way she smiled, her regard was genuine. The same warmth that had flooded through me in the morning rose under my skin.

"Nah," I demurred, slightly embarrassed as I tucked my bass safely against another chair, "it was just practice—we've a lot of work to do." It was true—we did. We'd covered it pretty well, all things considered, but Kenny was dropping rhythm guitar in parts—although he never dropped the vocal—and whether it was obvious to the listener or not, I heard it, and I was certain Graham and Hannah had heard it too.

Fran leaned over and slid an arm around my waist. "You look and sound like you know what you're doing—and enjoying it as well. Trust me, you look and sound good."

"Thanks," I told her as I put my arm over her shoulder.

Hannah gave me raised-eyebrow glance that I returned with a "what?" look of my own and she tilted her head quizzically, about to speak, when we were interrupted by the supply of food and drink Kenny and Graham managed to send our way.

Hannah, Fran, and I discussed politics and music as the officially scheduled group started their first set.

They weren't bad, not even half, I thought as I sipped at the wine I preferred to the ale while I half listened to the interplay between the bass and the drum. In reality, the rest of me was attuned to the shifting energy dynamics in the room. The level built with the music, released and reflected from different responding bodily energy centers that resonated with the tones that bounced off the walls.

"Hey," Hannah leaned over and spoke in a low voice, "mind if I ask Fran to dance?"

I sat back and cocked my head at her. "Why would I mind?"

Even in the dim light, I could see the slight flush that rose in her cheeks. "Well, I didn't want you to think that I, I mean…" She hesitated as she raised her eyes again to mine, and in that moment I understood.

Hannah and I had flirted a bit during jam sessions, hanging out, and while we'd not decided on that dinner yet, there was an air of *something* between us. It wasn't as if I hadn't spoken about Fran and her visit (it was probably all I'd talked about) with Hannah, with the band, but I *had* disappeared for a week, only to show up with Fran in tow. I knew where Hannah was going with this.

I smiled into her eyes. "We don't own each other, you and I, or Fran and I. Ask her—if she wants to, she will."

"Yeah?"

I chuckled lightly. "Free will, baby. We've all got it."

Fran gave me a quick, questioning glance that I answered with a smile and a wave as she and Hannah made their way to the floor, and I watched them with the same smile as they danced. Fran was having a good time, and that in turn made me feel good.

The presence made itself known as a sudden chill that floated across my shoulders.

"Join you for a drink," the voice asked, low and dry.

"Help yourself," I answered as I turned with my glass in hand.

He sat down, his movements graceful and quick. "You're new here," he observed and stretched back along his seat and lit a cigarette. The smoke rose in lazy waves as he contemplated me.

I returned the cool stare. Black boots. Black pants, fitted at the ankle but blossoming out as they rose. Fingerless black leather gloves. An old marching band jacket that in daylight would be maroon but in the half light of the pub was a bloody red.

"Next you'll ask what's a nice girl doing…?" I asked, then sipped, casually, bored.

He laughed. "Nah, *that* I wouldn't ask." He tapped his cigarette on the arm of his chair, let the ashes fall unheeded to the floor. "I'm sure you've moments where you're not that nice."

I lit one of my own and leaned back in my chair. I stared at him blankly, uncaringly. That seemed to frustrate him and his lip curled into a sneer as he leaned forward. "I know how your father died, *Wielder*." His voice hissed dryly even as he seemed to spit the last word. "I'll live to see you die, too."

Though the words about my father struck deep, deep into a hurt I didn't realize could still ache the way it did, and sent an even colder chill through my bones, I'd already been taught well. Those feelings, and the questions that accompanied them, could be dealt with later. Now, though, the enemy stood declared before me. I took a casual drag from my cigarette and exhaled the smoke slowly.

"I don't know what you're talking about." I stared back into beetle black eyes, black like the bugs that crawled out from under rocks that lie undisturbed through the winter until they're budged in spring for fresh planting. Those eyes glittered at me with malice.

He smiled, somehow managing to show all of his teeth as he did so.

"Of *course* you don't—I'll bet you don't even *know* how he died—and you think you're," and his eyes traveled down my neck to rest pointedly on the ankh that hung just under my throat, "protected. You're not. And you're not the first, though you may be the last. You won't last long."

I sat back like I didn't care; he was telling me nothing I hadn't already learned, and so far nothing I didn't think I'd eventually find out anyway. "What do you have?" he continued. "Maybe twenty, thirty, forty years before you're caught, killed, destroyed? Even if you manage to *breed* and live a mortal life span, I will *still* be here. But," and he leaned across the table, his voice lower now, urgent, full of...full of something I'd learn to recognize in time, "you *could* be one of us. The power sings in your blood, I can *taste* it in the air—I could...teach you...how to avoid your father's fate, to use that power, so that you might never sing the black song and you would be immune to human frailty, suffering." He cut his eyes toward the dance floor where Graham had run away from his duties long enough to whirl around with Hannah and Fran. It was Fran his gaze lingered on. "I can see that you're...connected. I could ensure that's permanent, if you so desire, or," he sat back, a wide smirk on his delicately chiseled face, "I *could* force you because of it, should you refuse." He waved his cigarette. "Tell me, is she even more beautiful when she cries?"

That…that got me, and I tried not to let it show, but I could feel the tendons in my neck tighten, the muscles across my chest grow close around my heart, a fear that snapped into anger. *I bet I could take him.*

And then it hit me: as above, so below. *Don't engage, don't step out of the Circle.* I couldn't be forced, I had to voluntarily step out of the Circle.

I focused and checked my own barrier—it was fine—and it took less than half a second to extend that to the sense of Fran's presence.

"You're not the most pleasant of drinking companions," I informed him as I stood and slung my gig bag, heavy with the weight of my bass, over my shoulder. "I think I've passed my quota on rude for the day. Have a great night."

He was so quick he'd grabbed my arm before I'd taken the next breath, but I was ready.

"We're not done…Wielder," he hissed.

I stared at his hand. "Let go, or lose it." I focused the energy field where his fingers wrapped around my forearm and he released my sleeve as if burned.

"*Je reviens te chercher*," I return to seek you, he whispered.

I caught his eyes, those glittering black pools, with mine. Funny. He wasn't as tall as he'd seemed moments ago and he seemed somehow… familiar. "Good luck with that," I said before I turned my back on him and made my way to the bar.

Fran met me there barely a moment later. "Hey, are you okay?" she asked with a concern I felt even before she cupped my shoulder. "I saw that that guy—was he bothering you? He seemed like a real creep."

"He was," I answered shortly, not knowing if or how to explain. "But yeah, I'm okay." I put my hand on the small of her back and tried to smile reassuringly before I caught Kenny's eye. He nodded back at me when I finally did, then sent two pints over. I handed one to Fran and she watched me as I sipped.

The heightened awareness that invaded me—the proximity of Fran's body, the thoughts and feelings that swirled heavy in the air, thick as the cigarette smoke that surrounded us, filled with the unmistakable sense of hunger, lust—overloaded me, left me feeling heavy and edgy.

She put her mug down and caressed my cheek with her fingertips. She studied my eyes, then leaned in, her lips next to my ear. "Let's go."

"Do you want to?" I asked her in return. All things aside, the weight of minds, the none-too-subtle threat from the…whatever…I didn't want her to worry, wanted her to enjoy herself, the pub, the company I normally kept.

Still, the press of her body and the light whisper of her breath over my face served to remind me of the night before and how we'd spent our day, making my skin tingle with the memory.

Fran curled her hands into the collar of my jacket and tugged me closer. I rubbed my cheek against hers. "Yes."

I kissed the spot I'd just pressed my face to. "All right, then. We'll go."

"Hey, I see Old Ralph Jones made a try at you." Hannah's voice cut through the surround sound atmosphere.

"Jones?" I asked her as Fran threaded her arms under my jacket and around my waist.

"Yeah. Jonesy, our local dealer." Hannah pointed over her shoulder with her thumb and my eyes followed.

There he was still, the brass buttons on his band jacket winking in the stage lights, and sensing my attention, he looked my way and saluted me with his drink. He emanated cold waves in every direction.

I wondered if Cort was aware of him as I cut the contact and returned my attention to Hannah, who'd just swiped my pint.

"It always tastes better from someone else's cup," she said, smirking at my raised eyebrow. Not that it was a big deal, it was now a running gag among us, since everyone's cups, cans, and pints got mixed up in the studio.

"What do you mean, dealer?" I asked as she sipped.

"You know, the usual stuff," Hannah answered after she swallowed. "Soft stuff, pot, acid, that sort of thing, coke if you're into it, some of the more…exotics. If you want it and it's out there, Old Jones will find it."

"For a price, of course," Fran interjected.

"There's always that," Hannah agreed, "and some pay more than others. Ask Graham—I hear they've had some nasty run-ins. Back when he was a girl, I think."

Fran's hold tightened about my waist and I pulled her closer as I shifted, taking her out of Jonesy's line of sight. If he wanted to look, he could stare at my back, but if he wanted Fran? He'd have to go through it.

"Really?" I said to Hannah over Fran's head. "Do you know what it was about?"

I wondered, as I held Fran in my arms and against my body then rubbed my cheek against her hair, what it was Graham and that... thing...had discussed. Had he been threatened or extorted similarly? There was something about Old Ralph Jones. He surely wasn't a hound, he radiated something different, definitely a more...commanding presence, a different sort of energy...and there was a familiarity about him I couldn't quite place.

"Well, not *that* directly. Graham doesn't talk about much, so you'll have to ask her, uh, him," Hannah returned, slipping pronouns for the first time since we'd met. The thought flickered through my mind that perhaps there was a connection between the subject and her slip as I nodded at her.

"Maybe I will sometime. Hey, we're gonna run off," I told Hannah, who rewarded me with yet another smirk.

"So...I suppose we'll see you in the studio Sunday, then? You're welcome to come as well," Hannah told Fran with the same smile.

"Maybe," Fran said nonchalantly, "or maybe I'll take the opportunity to start Christmas shopping."

Hannah and I both stared at her. "But...it's only *just* October!" Hannah observed with obvious surprise. "There's plenty of time."

Fran shrugged, a gesture that brushed the curve of her breast against mine and reminded me that there was more than one reason to be leaving. "It's the only time Ann won't be with me, and I need to find just the right thing. But," she said and lifted her eyes to mine, "I'd be happy to meet you there later."

The half smile that curved her lips got one in return from me and I inclined my head to—

"Right then, Sunday it is. Good, very good." Hannah's voice

sounded more than slightly amused, though it only showed in the sparkle of her eyes when I glanced back at her.

"Yep," I agreed. "So, we're off—tell Graham I wish him luck tonight?" I asked Hannah.

"Sure," she agreed, and returned to my pint, "you too."

I waved to Kenny, who nodded back as we pushed through the crowd to the door.

Once outside, the cool night air made my head feel better even as it raised the hairs on the back of my neck.

For the first time, Fran and I walked back to the apartment with her arm around my waist and mine around her shoulder. I was hyperaware of the sound of our footfalls, the calls of passersby to each other on the streets, and the unique sensation of watching eyes prickled along my spine. I was so alert I was almost twitching and Old Ralph Jones, "Jonesy," as Hannah had called him—his words, his voiced threat to Fran, God, that he could even think to *picture*, to *speak*, such a thing— had me ready to slug anyone that came too near, even though I knew that if his threat were to become more than that, it would more than likely manifest on another level first.

Adrenaline, fear, love all flowed and fought through me and combined with the memories of the sendings I'd endured on the Astral, to blend with tonight's threat.

Once I'd closed and locked the door to the street behind us, Fran waited for me in the circle of light that came from the curtained glass of the door above, the only light in the darkened stairwell and I was relieved, so damned relieved to lock that door. I slid my case off my shoulder and leaned it safely into the corner, then gathered her in my arms to hold her close and breathe.

Jones had scared me, not for myself, not at all—my life was what it was and what it would be, probably brief but fierce and I had no qualms with it—but knowing that Fran's proximity, her closeness to me, brought her into danger, a danger she hadn't asked for, shouldn't be a part of, for no reason other than the fact that it would hurt me, *that* had me terrified. It translated itself into the way I held her, the kisses I laid on her face, and the way I took her mouth with mine.

"Sammy, you're shaking," she murmured into my neck as my hands reached frantically under her coat, her sweater and shirt, to feel the reality, the warm vitality of her skin, the lush fullness of her breasts and the way the tips hardened under my hands, only to drag my fingers down her sides when her back was firmly against the wall.

"It's just adrenaline," I temporized against the fierce pulse in her neck because it was partially true. Oh, I knew we had to speak, knew I'd have to let her go just to keep her safe, even if it meant she thought I didn't care, but now, *right now*, she was everything I wanted her to be: safe, whole, alive, and if I could just know it, I was desperate to know it. "I…yes…" My breath caught hard and fast in my chest when her fingers touched me, palms hard, rough against my skin as they rolled over my now-sensitive breasts.

"Please, Frankie," I begged with my lips against hers, "I need to touch you." I slipped the fingers of one hand under her waistband and used the other to open her pants. "Please."

She answered me by gently circling my wrist and guided my hand past the firm muscle of her stomach. "Hannah asked me," she breathed as my fingers edged over the curve that announced I was almost where we both wanted me to be, "if I was your lover."

"What did you say—God, that's so damned *beautiful*," I groaned as I felt how wet and hard she was under my fingertips.

"Oh," she sighed and rested back against the wall as she released me, "right there." That same hand rounded my ass and pressed hard against me, set up a rhythm that matched the one I played and I leaned heavily against her.

"What'd you tell her?" I asked her again as she spread her thighs just that much more for me so I could enter her.

"I said…I said that," she gasped, then swallowed as I pressed into her, followed the lift of her hips, felt the rush of blood to my clit at the muffled "mph" that escaped her when she lowered them again, settled fully on me with her cunt as tight as my heart as it beat in my chest, as amazingly wonderful as it had been the first time and the ones that followed it, "that we love…each other."

"That's true," I told her, breath tearing past my throat, because the combined sensations of her slick and hot on my fingers, hers that pinched and tugged at the so-hard very tip of my nipple while the others played my clit through my pants, made it so very hard to think of anything other than how very much I needed her. "It's very true."

I had it in my head that somehow, some way, it would be okay, it would all be okay if only we could be together as we were at this moment, the pulse, the proof of her life flowing on my fingers, pushing back against my thumb, the frantic beat of her heart against mine as I swallowed her breath. It would be okay, she would be okay, it *had* to be okay because I wasn't going to lose someone else, not my Frankie, not like that, not—

"I've *got* to touch you." Her voice was as hot as the breath that flew past my ear while her fingers released my breast and left me aching, cold, only to pull at the button of my jeans.

"You are," I assured her and kissed her deeply because I loved the taste, the feel of her mouth on my tongue, soft and slick like her cunt on my hand, and I pressed harder, curled my fingers deeper within. "You *are* touching me."

But I didn't stop her or protest when her fingers eased my zipper down and I was grateful for the wall behind her because the slip of her thumb against the almost painful throb of my clit, the momentary almost-stinging sharpness that disappeared into the intense rush of the sudden fullness in my cunt as she took me, made my knees give.

I had the briefest flash of the friend we both missed, of Nina's face on the day she'd come to school beaten, bruised, and my mind replaced it with Fran's. "No," I said to the picture even as it appeared, "please no." I let myself surrender to the blood that pounded through me, the frantic push of our bodies, the constant give that was the sweet pull of her cunt on my fingers, the pressure of hers as the hand that had held my ass pushed her firmly within.

"Oh, Frankie," I groaned, her name precious in my mouth, and I whispered it again into the delicate skin of her throat, a litany, a petition, a prayer from my lips to whatever would hear against whatever lay out there.

"Let it go," she breathed against my lips, "Sammer, let it go…give it to me."

I didn't have to ask what she meant, because I knew, knew she had felt it, seen it within me and she moved that much harder in my cunt, pulled me that much closer, deeper, as the crushing weight of the veil between us lifted…

"Like that," she said, a throaty whisper that churned my blood with the same ferocity she filled me with. "Give me that, all of it, Sam—everything."

Her touch, her words, the honest desire that surrounded me combined with the unalloyed sincerity of the very real love that washed through us both as we thrust and pushed and kissed against that wall and each other, heedless of the discomfort or the possibility that someone would investigate why the front door had opened but the upstairs one hadn't. The raw black wave of aching roaring empty that threatened to overtake me when I thought for even a second that any harm could come to her…this, this between us, the reality of her body against mine, of my fingers inside her, the fit of hers within me. "Everything, Frankie," I promised as I came, so intense, so good, gasping, crying, the sounds choked in my throat, and she was full and real and deep inside me when I buried my face against her neck, and my fingers inside her.

"Stay," I managed to tell her when her hands shifted, "come inside me."

"Yeah?" she asked, the word strangled as it blew across my lips.

"Please," I asked again as I felt the now-familiar pulse that told me soon, so soon, her cunt would give me, give us, the bare flash of *her*, "I want that."

"I'm glad," she said, then caught her breath while I caught her on me, in me, as she pressed her mouth to my shoulder and her body arched against mine.

"I've got you," I murmured into her hair as I put my free arm around her shoulders, brushed the hair away from her neck, kissed her head as I let the wall hold us both. "I've got you," I told her again as I withdrew carefully to clutch at her hip, missing her instantly when she did the same, her lips so wonderfully tender as she kissed my neck. "I've got you."

"You do," she affirmed between kisses, "you do. And I've got you too."

NADLEEHI

We can only be
what we give ourselves:
the power to be.
—A Cherokee Feast of Days

We both knew we'd make love again once we got upstairs, and we did, sensual and slow, her lips incredible, her tongue another stunning discovery of sensation as she painted exquisite patterns on me, in me, and when we finally snuggled together, close and warm and tight, I lay draped over her, awake, holding her within the confines of my arms and legs as best I could, grateful for the sound of her breath as she slept, the gentle rise and fall, the faint thump under my palm that revealed the beat of her heart.

I can't remember really sleeping at all, and though I left her with a soft kiss that made her sigh and snuggle more, the early morning found me seeking my uncle before Fran woke. Since we were up before everyone else for once, he taught me the secret behind the wonderful sliced and fried potatoes that accompanied most breakfasts.

We spoke as he passed me ingredients and I chopped and sliced, passing them back to him so he could make magic over the burners.

"Have you ever heard of a guy named Jonesy or Old Ralph Jones?" I asked him as I cut through the potatoes I'd just cleaned.

I forced myself to breathe carefully as I moved the knife because adrenaline kicked through me, and I didn't want to carelessly cut myself. I'd known what drug dealers were, I wasn't immune to the news of the day, but it wasn't something I'd ever run into personally—I was an American kid from the 'burbs. But even so, I doubted any of the things I'd heard or read in the news came close to Old Jones.

"Is there something you want to tell me?" he asked me in return.

"Yeah." I nodded as I focused on making slices that weren't too thick. "There is. I met him last night."

"Well, I can tell you that Rafael—Ralph now, is it? He's not as old as he pretends. What did he say?"

I glanced over at him while I scooped the slices and wedges into a neat pile with the edge of the blade, then lifted the board to let them spill into the pan before I carefully put it down. Cort's attention appeared perfectly focused on the hot iron before him, on the alchemy of onions and spices as he flipped and stirred the concoction, but I knew that despite his relaxed tone and posture, he was listening carefully to every word I said.

"He threatened to hurt Frankie—*Fran*—if I didn't, I mean, to make me join his little group or—"

"Have you told her about this?" he asked, his eyes sharp upon me as he shut the burners and set the pan to the side.

"Not yet," I answered honestly, "I wanted to speak with you first. He also said…" I put everything into the sink and ran the faucet over hands that somehow didn't shake, and I thanked the cold water for keeping me focused. "He said he knew how my father died—and that he could tell me more about it."

He took a deep breath and stared at the ground for a moment before looking back at me, his face somber. "Can you finish up here? I don't mean to leave you with everything, but this requires," he sighed lightly, "this requires everyone present before it can be discussed."

"Do you mean Fran too? I don't want her harmed, and I don't want her frightened either," I said. "I'd like to keep her out of this as much as possible."

Cort crossed the tile and put a warm hand on my shoulder. "You did the right thing by waiting, but she made a decision too, the moment she became bound to you."

That didn't seem fair, and as I began to protest, he spoke over me, waving my protests away. "I know there's no way you didn't tell her anything, I know *you* well enough to know you must have told her what it would mean—she made a choice, and that, dear heart, is not something you could or should protect her from. She has the right to make another—respect it, let her," he said and squeezed my shoulder lightly. "And find out if you've made a good one too."

I could accept that, but there was something else, something I thought I needed to know. "Da...my father...he died on the job, under a sustained flashover in a warehouse fire. They gave me his helmet, his badge, and a flag." I held my eyes steady on his. "What don't I know?"

"I promise...I promise to tell you everything, but not right now—this is not the time. You already know the most important things there are to know about Logan. He adored Amanda, your mother, and you were precious to him because you are a part of her. He was brave, he was honest, and he was kind. And you, dear heart," his eyes crinkled at the corners as he favored me with one of his grins, "you are very, very much his daughter."

He left with that, and I wondered about all he'd said as I put everything together.

❖

"So we agree that the actual sealing and consecration to the Circle has to happen sooner rather than later?" Cort asked as we all sat around the table over the remains of breakfast.

"Surely you don't mean for Samhain?" Elizabeth asked, shock on her face and in her voice as she set her cup down and stared at him.

"Sow when?" Fran repeated.

"Close enough," Cort said to her with a smile, "and you know it as Halloween. And yes," he turned his eyes to Elizabeth, "there's no time to wait for the winter Solstice. Let it happen with the Astral tide on traditional New Year. Ann." he turned to me, "the bridge between worlds, a day when the veil between them is thin. Do you understand why then, that day?"

I nodded. "Yes, I do." The bridge between worlds—what was not to understand? In the belief system that had helped form this part of the world, Halloween, or Samhain as the Celts had called it, was the day between the old year and the new. So many minds, so much collective energy, had gone into making that particular day in the planetary cycle on this part of the planet into something extraordinary, that it had become exactly that: as below, so above. The day between the years was the day the normal barricades between worlds were more permeable, and transfer through more accessible.

To perform my Rite on that day carried weight on many levels. I was trained to consciously, purposefully, move between worlds; the easier access to the levels on that day would mean there would be more energy for the ceremony, thereby making my sealing stronger, and there would be the symbolic echo of the day itself—it was *between* and so was I, in so many, many ways.

"How ready are you for this?" Cort asked, but his gaze rested on Fran.

"Wait, why do we need to involve her with this? I'm sorry," I turned to Fran, "I'm not trying to make decisions for you."

She took my hand in hers. "I know," she said, her lips quirking softly.

I gazed back at Cort. "Is that really necessary?"

"But Sammy," she interjected quietly but firmly, "we're already..." She flushed and glanced down at the table before she spoke again. "Bound. So I *am* involved."

Yes, she was right. We *were* bound, but I hadn't thought she'd view it like that. She curled her fingers into my palm even as she straightened her shoulders and focused on Cort.

"Whatever you need from me," she said as their eyes met, flame matched to flame, "I can do it," she told him, her voice steady and strong. She held my hand with the same strength, and I returned the grasp, grateful for the unquestioning support. "Whatever it is."

"I'm glad you feel that strongly," Elizabeth said, giving her the slightest nod of approval. "You're not ready yet, but you *will* be—you'll *have* to be. Part of Annie's future rests on you."

I focused on Elizabeth for a long moment. I wanted to know more about what she meant by that and I would ask, but for now there was something about the way she held her mouth that told me she was either angry or scared; and considering what I'd learned of anger and how much it was rooted in fear, I was guessing fear. "And what's the plan to protect Ann before then, now that you've upped the ante?" she asked Cort point-blank. "I'll make the calls, I'll happily train Francesca, but what will you do to keep Ann safe? I'm sorry," Elizabeth said, redirecting her gaze to mine, "but if you didn't know before, you do now—any testing that is to come your way now will likely be physical, and more than likely will be through the use of deadly force, since they haven't managed to lure you out on the Astral."

"They won't," I said, the words calm as I spoke them, even as Fran's grip on my hand tightened. I wasn't scared, not for myself, not for anything other than Fran's safety and that of this little group I lived with that I supposed was my family for now.

"You're thinking Aberdeen?" Cort asked Elizabeth.

"Wait," I said, wanting to make certain I understood the shorthand conversation between them as he stood. "You want to leave?"

Elizabeth favored me with her favorite quizzing expression. "Do you have another suggestion?" Had I not known better, and perhaps I didn't, I would have thought that this was yet another test.

"I do," I said and gave Fran's hand a quick squeeze before I released it and pushed my chair back. "We stay. I've already left one home and I may still need a map, can't figure out the roads well enough to drive anything other than a roller skate, and don't understand the fascination with warm beer, but I'm not going to leave another." I stood and picked up my tea. "Besides," I said and grinned at her and then at Cort, because this would give me the opportunity to try something I'd always wanted to, "the best place to hide something is in plain sight."

The twinkle that shone at me from Elizabeth's eyes told me that maybe this had been a test of sorts after all—and I was certain that if it had been, I'd passed it.

❖

It would be a few days before I'd be able to speak with Graham, ask the questions I had in mind, and while I continued at an accelerated pace with Cort after dinner, Fran now had her own work with Elizabeth while I trained.

The schooling was so intense there was barely time to answer my question of why, and Cort explained it to me through the furious clash of steel in the study. This time, there were no weights involved.

"You," he began as we paced one another, searching for openings, "are connected to the Circle through your heritage, your training, and through me."

The attack went left and I parried, followed it with a single beat—the smart smack of my weapon on his—to change the direction of the sturdy practice blade he used, then a direct attack that went for the inner shoulder joint. The quick flick of his wrist deflected the strike and I blocked the blow aimed for my gut. We parted, only to circle again.

"I understand that," I said, recovering from the ballestra lunge that he nimbly avoided even as I instantly followed it with an upward rip.

"Nice!" he enthused as he tossed it aside.

"But why does Fran have to be so fully involved?" I asked and went for the outer crescent kick—he sidestepped it and we both went for the same overhand strike, the deadly scissoring of metal. Close, too close. There could be no stepping back, that would leave my entire torso vulnerable, and to step forward would be to bring the scissors closer to my own head and neck.

I had to think quickly and act in miliseconds—a double beat and riposte wouldn't work; I could never match his upper body strength and reach. But my own biology provided me a different advantage: my push kick was strong enough to break the fatal blade lock and with that gone, a single beat and lunge brought, for the first time, the tip of my sword to the delicate spot just under the center of his sternum.

"Beautiful!" he said admiringly as he gazed down at the point that hovered before him. He grinned at me, a grin I couldn't help but return.

"Good work," he said, "take a break," and pointed over to the desk where a pitcher of water stood next to the food we kept there during our sessions.

After carefully placing my weapon in its stand and pouring myself a glass of water, I realized he hadn't fully answered my question.

"So why does Fran have to train with Elizabeth?" I asked after I swallowed. I was grateful for the brief rest—we hadn't even begun to do Astral work yet for the night and already I was sweaty, tired, and hungry. Still, I'd managed to not only not be "killed" during this practice, I'd actually managed to land a kill strike, and I was not only pleased with myself, it also gave me a new sort of confidence as I waited for his answer.

Cort grabbed a bowl from the desk and quickly popped a few raisins into his mouth. "Fran is bound to you," he said simply, "and untrained. She has no barriers, no protections. Anyone can reach through her, to you, to the Circle—and destroy it. We eliminate that threat if she too becomes sworn to the Light."

He handed me the bowl and I squinted at him as I picked through for the almonds I preferred. "So it's sort of like an ungrounded circuit?"

"More than 'sort of,'" he said as I chewed, "more like *exactly*."

❖

Fran and I met after our respective personal study sessions in what had become our room, too mentally tired to take the time to discuss the direction our lessons were going in or what we were learning, and too roused from the work, too heightened by the energies we channeled, to do anything other than to wrap around and sink into each other, let the bare hot slide and the slick wet rhythm of the urgent give and receive shove it all into the background until there was nothing left but the breath and the beat, the bodily reality of existence as the overload threat dissipated in a raised cheer to the triumph of life, of my own binding to the Material through Fran and her to me in a gasped and choked expansion and explosion into the Aethyr.

That's not to say I didn't try, albeit very briefly, to discuss some of my ideas for hiding in plain sight with her, on an afternoon we got caught out in a rainstorm.

Fran hadn't been to Carnaby Street yet, an area filled with interesting shops and stands, and it was purely for the eye candy that we went. Well, that, and I wondered what would catch her eye, perhaps give me a hint as to what she might want for Christmas or her birthday which came right before it.

I took her there on Friday and let her drape different shirts and jackets across my shoulders as we went through the different shops. We found some T-shirts with funny sayings—my favorite pictured a shepherd standing in the midst of his flock wearing an evil grin and the caption "I Fuck Sheep"; Fran picked one that said, "God's coming: look busy"—and while she teased me a bit on my monochromatic choices, since with the exception of a navy blue wool peacoat, everything else I'd chosen was black (although Fran insisted the coat was too), I made sure on the way back that we stopped over on Regent Street so she could visit Hamley's, London's answer to New York's FAO Schwarz. It was over five stories of toys for kids of all ages, where the good lighting, the cheery music, and the bright multihues made it seem like the CandyLand game had come to life.

The weather changed abruptly as we walked back to Dean Street. "Oh, man!" I complained when the skies opened up to pour viciously down and force cold wet drops beneath my collar and down my neck.

"C'mon—we'll wait it out here," Fran suggested and I grabbed the door handle for the shop we happened to be in front of, one whose window posters advertised comic books, music, and other novelties. I quickly ushered her in before me.

As the bell tinkled behind us and the door closed, it took about an entire thirty seconds to realize that gag items were not exactly the sort of novelties the store sold.

There were two, maybe three standing racks of comic books, a low shelf filled with magazines of all sorts, and a section of wall behind the counter that was covered with films, the most innocent of which had a title along the lines of "The Uncut Boys of Brazil." A clerk glanced up at us with a bored expression beneath the green strand of that hair hung down to his chin, the fluorescent light a quick wink on the ring that pierced his lip, before he dismissed us and continued to flip through a magazine. Rain slapped unceasingly, the sound of hundreds of pebbles being thrown against the glass windows.

At least we were drier than we would have been otherwise, and since we were there… "So," I turned to Fran and said brightly as I shuddered off the last bit of chill, "wanna look around? Might as well make the best of it, right?" I grinned at her and she shook her head at me with an amused smile. We headed down the aisles.

The blow-up dolls *were* pretty funny, as were the packages labeled "Prisoner of Love" with the pictures of a black plastic eye mask, purple feather, and fuzzy purple handcuffs, and I managed to get a giggle out of Fran with the line-up of flavored and sensation-inducing lotions and their caricatured labels. But it was the harnesses and the assortment of multisized, shaped, and hued phallic replicas—there were *bins* of them—that made her snatch at my sleeve.

"We should leave," she said rather tersely and I glanced at her in surprise.

"It's *pouring* out," I said unnecessarily as thunder crashed down and shook the worn wood floor we stood on, and in that moment, the light rapport, the connection that had existed between us snapped, a recoil into my own head that resounded through my body like a physical blow and left me equally confused.

"It's only water—it won't hurt me," she said, her eyes dark on me and her face somber and still. "I'll meet you back at the apartment if you want to stay."

I stared at her, unable to speak for a moment, because the sharp disconnect wasn't only from her, but also from the world that surrounded us. It was horrible: I felt the heavy layers of my skin, the barrier between me and the environment. *How can people live like this?* I wondered. *How do they live, unable to feel, to connect, to measure, mark, and map the environment in its entirety?*

But even without the extra senses that made me feel comfortable in the world as I knew it, I could *still* tell Fran was upset, because the last clear sense I'd received from her had been an almost crawling discomfort in her skin, and that was what mattered.

"No, we'll go if you want," I told her, "but your jacket's not warm enough. Here," I said as I fumbled through one of the packages I carried until I found what I wanted. "Put this on—it'll keep you warmer and dryer than that." I draped the wool peacoat over the shoulders of the corduroy jacket she'd worn. My own jacket was much warmer, a black wool and fleece bomber I'd found on a trip with Hannah and Kenny only a few weeks before.

She shook her head again. "You *just* got this—it's gonna get wrecked," she said, protesting even as she let me settle it on her.

"It looks better on you, anyway," I told her honestly and when her eyes met mine, some of the warmth had returned, as did just the slightest touch of our connection. I brushed my thumb against her cheek. "This is bugging you, huh?" I asked softly.

Her lips tightened a moment. I didn't understand why, but I didn't have to—it was more important to me that she feel all right—and I squeezed her shoulder briefly as we walked back through the store and out into the rain.

Both the thunder and the lightning had settled even as I made sure to raise my collar about my neck and we sloshed our way across the street. I let Fran walk ahead of me for a bit and tried to read what I could from her posture: shoulders and head gathered because of the rain, a bag tucked under her arm and her hands shoved deep into the pockets of the wool coat that did an admirable job of letting the water bead off and run down.

Finally, she stopped and waited for me on the corner, and she let me take her arm. I tucked her hand into my pocket for warmth as we walked on in silence through the downpour until we reached the corner of Dean.

"You know, my parents, they're not happy that I'm gay," she said finally, turning the same dark eyes she'd had in the store on me.

My father once told me he didn't care who I dated, so long as I chose a decent person. He'd emphasized the genderless "person" and "decent"; he knew, and he, *we*, were fine. Fran, other than what she had shared recently, had never before discussed her experience with her parents so I simply listened and let her continue. "My dad, he said, 'Well, at least you're normal looking, you're not one of *those* kinds of dykes.'"

"What do you mean?" I asked her as I pulled the keys from my pocket and fit them to the lock. I opened the door and waved her in before me. The cold of the wet had gone bone deep and made me shiver as we took off our coats to hang them on the hooks, there just for that purpose. I caught her eyes as I eased one of my boots off. "What's one of 'those' kinds of dykes?" Water dripped in fits and starts from my coat onto the mat over the well-preserved tile.

"You know what I mean," she answered and shrugged, "the whole 'want to be a man' thing, the penis obsession, all of that."

I stared at her in shock—did she really feel, think that way? Now, I'd spent a lot of my free time before she'd arrived with Graham, Hannah, and Kenny, and there were a few things I'd come to understand: Kenny was bisexual, he made no bones about it, and neither did anyone else. "Pretty" was more or less good enough for him, and since he declaimed, loudly and proudly, "I'm not getting' soddin' married," he paid attention to condoms and that was about it.

Hannah was, as she liked to say, "your garden variety dyke," which I supposed meant that she was a lot into girls, a little into sports, and left it at that. She'd recently cut her hair to match the current popular look: short back and sides, long on top.

All things considered, it was honestly a little hard to tell the boys from the girls just from a quick glance. Even Graham barely edged over to the "guy" side, and it was mostly because of the hats he occasionally wore, as well as the almost-forties-style clothes he preferred as a ska man and Rude Boy, with the sharp suit jackets and super thin ties, though he did every now and again sport the shadow scrub that so many of the guys favored.

But the point was that there had been more than one occasion during rehearsals where a conversation evolved, or devolved, into a comparison of dick size and use, and the impression I'd been left with was that it wasn't about the dick so much (well, not all the time, anyway) as it was about sex, its enjoyment, and occasionally, the expression of something that maybe couldn't be expressed another way.

And…I had my own curiosities about, well, everything. But still, I said nothing as I closed the door.

"My mother, of course, is very grateful I don't 'look' that way."

I kicked off my other boot, all the while very aware of the raw rub of my jeans on my thighs, the harsh scrape of the seams, the chill that had set into the skin of my neck. I made sure my boots were set properly below my coat in such a way they wouldn't be dripped on or in. Done and set, I took a breath before I faced her, my friend, my lover, and the strange disconnect that had grown between me and the world, between us. If that was really how she felt, she wasn't going to like what I had planned.

"Fran," I said finally, "I think it doesn't matter what you look like. People, your parents, they're still gonna judge you, still gonna criticize. And you know what? If that's what you think, if that's how you feel, it's gonna be harder for you—because you look like one of *them*, and wait till they find out you're not."

Her face worked a moment as she stared back at me. "Hey," she said softly and reached for my shoulder. "I didn't, I mean, I wasn't trying to offend you."

I shrugged away and turned to the stairs, but she caught my chin in her hand. Bound as we were, connected as we were even if I couldn't feel it at the moment, perhaps she still did. "Sammy, did I hurt your feelings?"

"Ann," I corrected stonily, my mind churning, hurt, in ways I couldn't describe, dismayed at the chasm that yawned between us, "and I'm fine." I tossed my head free of her grasp. "We both have work to do after dinner, we shouldn't be late." I went up the stairs, and Fran followed moments later.

❖

"The Mid-Astral is a center, a nexus, to the other plains. We exist, are manifest, in the Material, while the Tanglewoods border the Elemental Plain where live the kings and queens of Fire, Earth, Water, and Air," he explained as they jogged across the broad field toward the trees. "This, your form as you see it, your simulacrum, is a projection of how you see yourself, but look closely," he said, and pointed to her waist, then to his. "Do you see that?"

She did. A faint white light, a rope, that led from navel to... She peered carefully through and shifted her awareness.

"It's your tie to your life, to your body," he said. "It can stretch, bend, go through, go as far as you can ever possibly need it to, but now you must know this: it can be severed, and that severing will end your physical life."

She nodded, unsurprised by the knowledge.

"This...this is why this work must happen with a monitor, at least during this stage," he continued. "You can guard your aethyric self, but who will guard the body?"

"But...if you're here with me now, then who does that?" she asked, confused.

He smiled at her, then pointed to the almost indiscernible ring of light that glowed through the trees in the first copse they approached. This was the next step in their journey. "I do," he answered, "and the warding circle that was built before we started. I can hold my awareness in both places simultaneously. You'll be able to as well, after the Rite, after you've been consecrated to the Light. And then you'll have full control of your abilities. But first, for now," he said, and he took her hand in his as they stood before the glow, "you must meet the Lords of the Elements."

She stepped through the portal with him.

❖

I barely remember the shower I took before I went to bed, earlier than Fran for once, and after pulling on a T-shirt to guard against the morning cold, I collapsed on the mattress, embracing my pillow as my head reeled with the import of what had happened this night.

I had come out of the trance with the directive and the ability to hold the deeper vision, to see the underlying energy structure of the Material. I had seen for myself the salamanders that danced in the fire, the undines that sang in the smallest drop of water, the gnomes whose very steps could shake the earth, and the sylphs of air. The shock of feeling that tiny hand on my face, of witnessing a curtain shift, then flap with definite gusty enthusiasm in an airless room after a polite and carefully phrased invitation... It wasn't that I had anything resembling control of the elements, it was merely that they responded to my well-worded request, and *that* had me wondering for my sanity.

I let the disjointed thoughts roll through my mind. As I mastered my weapon and the bass, both seemed to respond not only to my hands but almost to my thoughts, my *intent*, actions completed almost before they'd been fully considered, a swing, a block, a strike, already in motion before I was fully aware of it. Notes fretted and sounding through the air that were the perfect blend, the bridge that walked between melody and rhythm, a driving counterpoint of its own that gave the music its muscle, the blood and the breath beneath the surface that made it live, forced its way through the air and into Hannah, who'd lock into a sync with me that would take the drive, double it, send it out, where Graham would pick it up, dig in, and pass it on to Kenny, who'd sing and sway with reinforced enthusiasm, even if he didn't always play guitar perfectly. The balance of parts perfect, a fusion of elements into something vibrant, vital...

Oh but those Lords, the Kings of the Elements... I shivered as I hugged the pillow closer to my face. They'd presented as pillars of pure force, of intellect, of power and knowledge, of experience not even remotely human, Material, incarnate—they never had been or would be. They spoke in image, in emotion, and made me more aware than ever that I *was* human, I was frail, I was mortal, and very, very ignorant of the reality of the world that surrounded us all.

How petty and so very small it all seemed, the discomfort of rain, the ache of the physical, lust, want, greed, when there were forces that ran through the very structure of Universe, *were* its very makeup, and our understanding and harmony with it was so limited.

Such were my thoughts as I fell asleep, a combination of the images and messages I'd gleaned over the muscle ache brought on by the physical workout and its accompanying lecture on the manifestations of intention and forces into the forms of deities. Some deities were thought-forms, the collection of projected energy sent by worshippers until a godhead was...*created*...by what amounted to group wishful thinking; while others, like the Elemental Lords, were actual entities with true presences. The shocks of above, below, and within all rolled and roiled with the extra energy through my body.

I awoke to feel the sensual stirring of Fran against my back, and as her fingers skimmed my T-shirt up, her body warmed the skin she bared. Her legs made my skin feel alive where they caressed mine.

The feel, the warm, satin weight of her pressed along my spine, the sensual drawl in my ear, and the breath that blew on my shoulder created a perfectly satisfying, satiating intensity, and strangely enough a safe zone of sensation.

"God, you've got the most amazing ass," she murmured as she laid a line of kisses across my shoulders and ground against me. Her hands clutched firmly at my hips and pulled me closer to her.

I wasn't even close to fully awake, but I was definitely aroused, suffused with a sleepy sensuality that hummed through me. The disconnect that had existed between us earlier was gone, replaced by a wave of pure incandescence and the energies the work had stirred that flowed from her, mixed with a desire so palpably for me and for the body she eased against that I couldn't stop the sound that came from my mouth or the lift of my hips that brought her into closer contact where I needed her.

Her hands, her body, left mine for a moment only to reconnect with hot, wet demand that made me gasp, and her fingers trailed along my back, my sides, to reach around and cup my breasts before she tweaked the hardened points in her hands.

"I love the way this feels...you feel," she said, her voice a harsh whisper on my spine before she kissed it. "You like it?"

Whatever I might have wanted to say became a choked groan of her name, because the slick feel of her pressed to my cunt robbed me of air, while the fingers that shifted from tits to slip along my folds took me away from thought of anything other than Fran and what she was doing to my body. Yes—I liked it, a lot.

"Or do you want a cock inside you, filling you?" she asked in the same throaty tone. "I can just feel your cunt on me, pulling at me. Or would you rather," and she spread me apart and began to tug on my hard-on, slowly, deliberately, firmly, forcing me still between the combined sensations she drove into me, "would you rather do that to me?"

"God…Fran…" I managed to croak out, shocked at her words especially considering our earlier discussion, shocked further still at how vivid the images those words created, because I could see it, I could *feel* it, and I covered her hand with mine, the hand that worked my clit so fucking good, as the pressure changed from the buildup of steady and slow to the frantic please-make-me-come stroke that made me throb beneath her.

"I can come like this," she said in a fevered breath along my back. "I'm gonna come like this, with my cunt against yours all slick and hot."

"God…yes!" I sobbed into the pillow that prevented me from smashing my head into the wall, one hand partially knotted and tangled into the T-shirt we'd somehow managed to get mostly off, wanting nothing more than to feel her do just that, because she was taking me with her. The wet grind, the strong slip of her fingers, the heat against my back, and I was, God, so close and she was…*please*… The link, the connect, was absolute as I felt the power gather within her, sluice through me, ohmygod we were going to come together and I was…she was…there, right *there*…

I gasped for air beneath her as she held me closely, and it took every bit of strength I had left to reach for her hand, to entwine her fingers with mine as she slid along my back and we lay there, curled together as she touched tender lips to my shoulder.

Fire still blazed in my belly, a comfortable pulse of flame that flared every few seconds as she rubbed her face along the sweat slick of my neck and cheek and I turned to face her, entwine my legs with hers.

"I thought…I thought you were upset," I murmured sleepily as I kissed the warm skin before me.

She released my hand to wrap her arms around me. "I was," she said as I rested my head against her chest, the beat of her heart steady under my ear, "but it's my issue, Sammy Blade, not yours. You…" and she kissed my head then pulled the comforter over us, "you can be, you can do whatever you want. We'll work it out."

I chuckled lightly, hearing my high school nickname from her lips, because it was ironic, because even though I wasn't certain what she meant, the familiarity of it was as comforting as the hands that smoothed along my ribs, and I snuggled against her.

As I drifted off to sleep, two thoughts ran through my mind. First, the whole dick thing that had upset her earlier had probably been because she had her own curiosities, things she thought she couldn't— or shouldn't—explore. God, even with the normal heightening of sensation, of desire, with the work I did and that I knew she was learning, she had never before been so demanding, so open, either in how we made love or the way she spoke. I didn't know what surprised me more: that it had happened or that I'd found it so hot. The second thing to run through my mind was a question: What in the world was Elizabeth teaching her?

I must have mumbled the second part aloud, because her voice was low and husky while her fingers traced light patterns across my skin. "You work with the white light—I'm learning what she calls 'the green ray.' Today," she continued, "she taught me the 'Charge of the Goddess.' *Let My worship be in the heart that rejoices, for behold, all acts of love and pleasure are My rituals.*"

I rubbed my face against her chest and tightened my arms about her, ready to drift once more back to sleep. "Are all the rituals like that?"

She gave a low chuckle. "Only the important ones," she said as she settled beneath me, then kissed my head once more. "Only the important ones."

Sam-I-Am

*As I walk the trail of life in the fear of the wind and rain,
grant O Great Spirit that I may always walk like a man.*
—Cherokee Prayer

If Kenny's getting the hang of playing his guitar at the same time as he sang could be considered progress, then one could definitely say rehearsals were going well, especially now that we'd evolved from "let's hang out and have a bit of fun" to "let's try to play some music."

But since we were serious, we needed a serious rehearsal space, one that we didn't have to schedule hours for.

Since it seemed that even with Graham's constant "I'm just temporary" reminders, we were all more than a bit committed to making something happen, Hannah found a building with a bunch of bedsits—one-room apartments with a kitchenette and a bathroom—that were let for studio space. The landlord had signs posted everywhere that said "no living," and if we got there by nine-ish or so weekend mornings, we tried to be done by six, so as not to hear that accusation. Our Tuesdays were the same, though, and I usually ate dinner those nights with the band, or grabbed something quick at home before bed.

We celebrated our new space with a switch in caffeine sources, from tea to coffee.

"So," Hannah drawled as she draped a casual arm across my shoulders, "how far are you *really* getting?"

But the feel of her words wasn't casual at all, the real meaning behind them as manifest to me as if she'd asked outright, and I could also read from her, whether she knew it or not, that her feelings were very mixed: she liked me, she also found Fran attractive—that I could easily understand—and wasn't certain what to do with any of it. As much as I sincerely liked Hannah, I was at the moment in no mood to either help or add to her confusion. I had enough of my own.

Making love with Fran had been amazing, gut-stirringly sensual, loving, friendly, fulfilling, but it had raised issues for me.

The new images she'd painted in my mind had so stirred me, played through my body with such a visceral reality that an already incredible and intense experience had been heightened, sharpened—and those images had opened new questions.

No different than most, I supposed, I'd always wondered what it would be like to be a boy; an only child, I'd played with neighborhood kids and grammar school classmates, as well as the children of other firefighters at the family events and barbecues my father had taken me to. There had been occasions, not too many, certainly, but enough for me to remember, where well-meaning moms and dads of other tots and tykes had told me I couldn't climb a tree, or wrestle with the boys, or do some other activity because I was wearing a skirt, because I was a girl. And girls didn't do that.

The first time that had happened, I might have been about five or so, but I remembered the day clearly. Bruce and Mario, two of the boys I played with regularly (we didn't like to play with Mario's sister, Theresa, because she always wanted to play with her Barbies and after you took their clothes off, then lost their shoes, there was nothing else to do with them besides bend them into crazy inhuman positions or switch their heads around) had brought their knapsacks just like I had.

We'd fill them up as heavy as we could, sling them over a shoulder, and then go climb trees, because we knew firemen had to climb ladders carrying heavy hoses, and one day, that would be us—we wanted to be ready.

"Come here, Samantha," Bruce's mom called as she came walking over. "Let me see that pretty dress."

It was my favorite, a royal blue that my father, my Da, had picked for me because he said it matched my eyes, and it had a bunny with a red baseball cap on his head and a ready-to-swing bat over its shoulder appliquéd to the front. The cap I wore matched the bunny's and I liked it—a lot.

"But we have to practice," I protested as she had snatched my resisting body.

"Yeah, practice," Bruce echoed behind me.

"For the fireman's test," another little boy added.

Bruce's mom laughed. "You and Mario go," she said to her son. "Samantha needs to sit here and play nice with Theresa. You don't want to ruin that pretty dress," she said to me with a smile.

"It washes, my Da said so," I informed her and turned to run away with the boys—they were gonna get there first!

She reeled me in by my knapsack. "You can't climb trees with a skirt on," she told me in no-nonsense tones, "and you're not going to grow up to be a fireman." She bodily lifted me and placed me on the bench next to Theresa where she'd spread her dolls out along the table. "Girls can't be firemen," she said.

She was wrong, I *knew* she was wrong, and I stared back up at her as I spoke. "I'm gonna be a fireman like my Da."

The smile fell from her face. "No. You're not—you *can't*—you're a girl. Sit here and learn to play nice."

Play nice? Play nice? Theresa was *boring*, her dolls were *boring*, and her mother's words had just ruined my world.

I slid under the table and cried.

"Come out from under there, Samantha," she cajoled. "Do you want a hot dog?"

Nothing answered her but my sob. "Here, honey, you can have Theresa's favorite doll," she offered under the table.

That made me cry harder and just as I drew in enough breath to think, "I want my Da," he climbed under with me.

"What's the matter, Sam-Sam?" he asked softly, his head crouched under the table.

I crawled into his lap and snuggled my face into the coal-tar smell of his shirt, staining it with my tears. "Da, I don't *want* to be a girl," I cried onto his chest. "I don't want to play nice, I want to be a boy so I can climb trees and be a fireman."

Later that night when Da had tucked me into bed and I said my nightly prayers, that woman's words, the tone and the meaning, echoed through my mind. I didn't know any other girls like me, I didn't like *any* girls at all; maybe I wasn't one. For the first time when I spoke to

God, I asked for something new: to wake up the next morning a boy. I would ask this every night for the next eight years, and I never wore that dress again.

The next week, in kindergarten, I cut my own hair with the duck-handled construction paper scissors. My father shook his head at me when he picked me up from the principal's office, then drove me down to his barber, Moretti's on the corner of New Dorp Lane and Railroad.

I liked going to Moretti's with Da, and we went at least once every three weeks. I liked the smell of talc, the bottles of blue water, the striped glass pole by the door and the overstuffed red-brown leather and metal chairs. And then there was Mr. Moretti himself, with his thick jet black hair and even thicker mustache, the soda he always had for me (in a glass bottle with a top he had to open), and the warm, indulgent smile he threw my way while I watched his hands as he worked.

"Logan!" he exclaimed as we walked in, and he slapped the towel he carried over his shoulder. "You're at least a week early. What are you—oh…" he said as he looked at me. "I think someone needs a seat."

Da sighed as he patted my shoulder. "Jump up, Sam-Sam," he said. "Vinny, cut it any way she wants."

I was thrilled—I wanted it short, really, really short. As Mr. Moretti clipped, trimmed, then buzzed the back of my neck, I felt delight sneak through me like warmth from the sun after a cloudy day. Maybe if I looked like a boy, no one would tell me I couldn't be a fireman anymore.

"I don't like girls," I explained to my Da over my slice of pizza as we drove home. "They like cats—and cats bite and scratch and are sneaky and mean. I like boys, boys like dogs, and dogs are nice." I'd watched a lot of Disney movies; I knew what I was talking about. "And they play in mud," I added, "and girls don't."

He nodded as he drove. "Well, you know, Sam-Sam, your mommy was a girl, and she wasn't like that."

That was a revelation. Mommy was a girl? Mommy was, well, *Mommy*, and while I didn't remember much, I did remember that she liked to play, that she'd liked to laugh, and that she'd never scolded over dirt.

"Mommy can't be a girl," I said finally. "Mommy was nice."

Bruce and Mario knew the score, though, and because we lived in the same neighborhood, we ignored Bruce's mom and did whatever we wanted to anyway, from playing soldier in the dunes of the beach a few blocks away, to pick-up games of baseball (softball was for *girls*), or just riding our bikes as fast as we could, everywhere they'd take us. And everyone we met, from the teenagers that drove the ice-cream trucks that trolled our streets, to Old Man Joe who owned the candy shop on the corner, called me Sam. No one questioned whether I was a boy or a girl, and I had too much fun to think about it.

Until I was about ten. Every year, the members of Rescue Five would get a bunch of cabins someplace up in the Pennsylvania Poconos and make the trek, either every weekend or for two weeks or so depending on their schedule, to what we kids simply called Firemen's Camp.

It was great—we'd run the trails, swim in the lake, boat, fish, and generally get as dirty as we could without any parental supervision so long as everyone made it back on time to the central picnic area for lunch and the nightly barbecues, and me and the boys, we had our routine down pat.

This particular year promised to be no different, and my excitement grew as Da went over the checklist with me before we made the annual pilgrimage.

He laughed when I jumped out of the car on arrival, knowing the first place I'd run to was Mario's cabin and we'd go together from there to collect Bruce, and then on to Dave's, who was a little older than all of us, until the four of us were gathered and we'd head down to our favorite spot by the lake.

There was the usual friendly squabbling and shoving, the "you're such a dickhead" joking around until Dave dropped his pants.

"Yeah? Well, mine's growing," he announced, and showed us.

We all stared a moment, then Bruce unzipped and did the same. "Mine looks nicer than yours," he said. "You've got that weird skin thing."

Mario dropped next. "I don't have that skin stuff," he said.

They looked at me expectantly, and I could feel my neck turn as red as my canvas sneakers. We all knew I didn't have one of those. But if I didn't do it, I'd be a wuss, a sissy, and couldn't hang with them, relegated like Tim and couple of others, like the Scanlon kids, to play with Theresa and the other babies. I was one of the guys, so I unzipped my pants. "I don't have one," I muttered, the burn in my neck now blazing through my face.

"That's a pussy," Dave said, "because you're a girl."

I stared at the ground as I redressed. I knew that, but I'd never felt quite so ashamed of it before, or so angry about it, either.

"Hey, maybe Sam's dick is different, you know? Like eye color or something," Bruce offered.

I looked at him with gratitude. Maybe I *was* just different—that could happen, right?

Dave guffawed. "Yeah, it's on the *inside*, 'cuz that's where dicks go—in *pussies*."

Mario smacked his head. "What are you, a faggot or something? You can't stick a dick in Sam, she's, you know, like a boy."

I could feel the blush grow even worse at that and the guys looked away. I didn't know how to explain it either.

"Hey, at least I don't have that weird skin thing," I told Dave as everyone else zipped up and we dropped the subject to discuss whether we wanted to fish from the dock or from a boat the next morning.

Still, confusion, resentment at the unfairness, and the strange sense of shame still roiled through my head, and I went for a walk by myself after dinner, just because I could. I wasn't going too far, I knew we were supposed to watch out for bears and all of that, but I wanted to get away from everything, from everyone, smell the deep scent of the pine and the moldy leaves, the water off the lake, and the smoke that floated in the cool breeze. I wore my favorite denim jacket under the summer night sky.

"Hey," Bruce said as he fell into step behind me.

"Hey," I said back and kept walking.

"You know," he said after we'd gone about another dozen yards or so, "maybe yours is just stuck inside or something, you know?"

"Huh?"

"Well, my big brother, Johnny, he said his gets bigger when his girlfriend sucks on it—maybe you just need to suck it out or something."

I stopped so suddenly my sneakers dug into the trail dirt. "You think that would work?"

"Can't hurt."

Just as quickly as hope rose, a bright burning that thumped in my chest, it grew cold and fell. "I can't do that," I said. "Can't reach."

Bruce shrugged. "I could help you, I mean…you're my friend."

Yeah. We were friends, good friends. And just like that, with the burning smoke smell from the fire pit, the slight breeze through my hair, and the occasional sound of crickets in the high grass, I got my first blow job.

❖

That was the year my father did two new things when we got home: he registered us with the swim club and put me on the team, and I was given my first guitar, with twice weekly lessons with Mr. Dobson at Lane Music, on New Dorp Lane.

It turned out that not only were these two things I was good at, they also effectively curtailed a lot of my neighborhood hanging out—and that's where I first met Frankie. But still, when I tried out for swim team right before the semester started at the all-girls high school Da insisted I go to, I was miserable; it sounded to me like it would be four years without my friends, four years without the guys to pal around with, four years surrounded by bitchy, nasty, catty girls, with their lies and their meanness and their talk about makeup and boys. Not a brain in the entire bunch. For the life of me I couldn't figure out why, why, *why* my Da was sending me there of all places when there were co-ed schools I could go to as well, and I protested and complained daily until he sat me down at dinner and explained.

"Sam, I know how important your grades are to you, and you want to go to college. You passed an entrance exam to a school famous for its academic program—a ninety-two percent or better scholarship rate!" His eyes shone with genuine enthusiasm. "The girls there? I'll bet they care as much about that as you do—you'll make friends, I promise."

I eyed him doubtfully over the dinner we'd ordered. "I'll also bet," he said as he cut into the food on his plate, "you even meet a few girls you like."

As much as I didn't believe it, my Da had been right. For the first time ever, I met girls I *could* actually like, girls who cared about academics, girls who cared about sports, and even music, girls who weren't solely into boys and makeup, and to make it that much easier for me, Frankie was there too, with her beautiful smile. She loved the hair I'd allowed to grow a bit too long, and she made me think maybe, just maybe, this "girl" thing wouldn't be so bad after all. And because Frankie—Fran, now—liked to run her fingers through my hair, for the first time since I was five, I *really* let it grow.

I still wasn't thrilled about my body, the twin swellings on my chest that needed to be supported and the accompanying monthly inconveniences, but I learned to ignore all of that as I made friends and devoted my attention to my studies, my instrument, and my sport.

It wasn't until I realized that Fran and I liked each other (another bit of knowledge imparted to me by my Da with his casual, "That there Fran, she likes you now, huh?" after a swim meet), and then, a few weeks later, the feel of her hands as they caressed me with real enjoyment over my curves that I thought that my body might have some redeeming qualities after all.

But then there was Nina, someone I'd wanted to be strong for, someone I wanted to do things, amazing things, *any*thing, for—and I'd failed, failed in all of it. I wasn't able to keep her safe, I wasn't able to keep her alive, and I wasn't able to bring her back.

I couldn't help but think that if I'd been a guy maybe I could have made a difference. Of course, the fact that the girl I was obsessed with would probably not have been interested in me at all if I was male made no difference.

Guys had strength, power, absolute ownership—of *everything*. They strode through the world, back straight, legs wide, and stared it unblinkingly in the eye, daring it to strike, ready to strike back with the muscle to back it up.

No one, *no one*, questioned their right to do so, and people got out of the way for those that flexed their muscle, even if it just looked like they might. Guys wanted, guys got, and asked or apologized to no one.

I wanted that—the respect, the *untouchableness*, the sense of invulnerability that guys carried with them all the time. There were times I'd had that sense of strength, of purposeful power, moments where I'd felt strong and untouchable, undefeatable…and in none of those instances was I aware of anything other than my mind and body working at the best possible level. I wasn't aware in *any* way of being "male" or "female" in thought or deed—but simply of *being*, of being *whole*. On those occasions there were no questions at all, just a steady surety. I'd had it during swim practices and competitions, band rehearsals, sessions with Cort that left my muscles aching while my mind spun, and when Fran and I were alone together.

Did that make me "that" kind of dyke, as Fran had put it? Did I really want to be a man? The feel of her breasts, full and supple in my hands, the pebbled hardness under my fingertips or my tongue was something I really enjoyed. I even liked just looking at them, the way those curves pushed out her shirt and rounded under a sweater, or just the rise of them above her skin... I loved watching her walk, the perfect sweeping lines that defined her, unmistakably feminine and equally unmistakably strong, *proud* in a way that so, so flattened me with sheer desire until I was almost on the bare edge of insane with the need to make her come. I *loved* doing that. Loved the sexy, hot taste, the warm and wet embrace, the hard push, the slick pace, wherever on me, my mouth, my hands, my cunt, oh my God, she'd get *so* hard, *so* wet, the way her clit would grow and her body open under my hands, only to tighten around me again. And when she touched me—*any* way she touched me—it felt so damn good: the way she stroked my clit with her body, her tongue, her hands. And when she was inside me in any way...oh the *intense* of it...

But that was confusing too, because if I was "that" kind of a dyke, then wouldn't I not like that? Or maybe...maybe I was straight, because wasn't that something straight girls were into? The guys I'd pretty much lost contact with since the middle of high school thought so, and God, Fran's words had so turned me on. And now I was hard, so fucking hard, and I didn't know if it was because I wanted her touch me like that or because I wanted to fuck her with a dick I didn't have. Even that troubled me, because "fucking" seemed so disrespectful, as if I didn't care, as if I was one of the guys I'd hung around with.

Ah hell...what did I know about being gay anyway? I still didn't like girls—but women, there was a *definite* difference. Women with their fine steel strength flashing over and under an almost delicate softness, intelligence bare and proud, hard muscle or yielding tenderness...I was attracted, turned on, *into* that. I wanted to shield that and in turn be covered by it. It was what drew me to Fran, what I had seen blaze from Nina, what I so admired and respected about Elizabeth. Hannah had that too.

Bruce and I had tried once, just once, to go on a date when we were both freshman, and it had gone terribly, from my not noticing his attempts to hold my hand and the awkward reach of his arm over my shoulder, to both of us trying to flirt with the counter girl at the popcorn stand. There wasn't even an attempt at a kiss; by the time the movie was over and we'd just relaxed into being buddies again, it wasn't even a consideration. We'd mutually, mutely, decided to forget it was a date.

I already knew I was different from most girls, and then I'd met Fran and eventually we'd dated, but then we'd drifted because we'd both been into… Dammit, this was all so much simpler when I was back at the apartment, curled up next to Fran after we made love because I didn't have to *think* about anything at all, I could just *be*, but when I hung out with the band at the pub there seemed to be so many rules about all sorts of things that I just didn't know.

❖

"Earth to Ann," Hannah said, waving her hand in my face. "So? How far?" she repeated, breaking me from my mental gymnastics.

"I've got the new pieces down, I can try putting in a harmony line or two if you'd like," I told her, deliberately ignoring both the knowing grin she wore and the subtext of her question as I pushed my thoughts down and we walked through the archway into the kitchenette.

She laughed as I poured a cup of coffee from the maker we'd collectively bought, and I raised an unamused eyebrow at her as she passed me the cream.

"I'm so very certain that harmony is *exactly* what Hannah's after," Graham said with a wink and the quickest flash of a wicked grin at me. "The question is whether she wants it as one, two, or three part?"

"Let's settle on getting a lead vocal down, and worry about the numbers after," Kenny said as he walked in and grabbed a mug for himself.

I heartily agreed and we sat around the little table to discuss which sections of which song were stronger than others and which needed much more work.

Another grueling couple of hours, by which time I wanted to take the guitar from Kenny and demonstrate to him how to breathe over the passage as he played it to find the body rhythm within it (and I finally did, privately, when we took another break), the sun had gone down, and I was, as Hannah put it, knackered. But I still wanted to speak with Graham and since both Elizabeth and Cort had asked me to please, please, stay away from the pub for a few days, until they enacted whatever it was they were thinking of, this was the only opportunity I had.

"Hey, Graham?" I asked as we buttoned our coats and shut the lights.

"Hmm?" He shifted his gig bag with its guitar over his shoulder.

"Join me for a quick bite of something?"

"Sure," he said, "there's a great spot not too far from your place, fabulous desserts, even better cappuccino. Want to go there?"

"Sounds good," I said as I set the last lock—it was my turn to hold the keys, since we rotated the responsibility—and off we went.

"So...what's on your mind?" he asked as we crossed the sidewalk.

"Not much. Why?"

He turned his grin on me. "I've got a *feel* for these sorts of things. Now give—what's up?"

I gave him a crooked grin of my own. Well, he had been right. "I...I wanted to ask you how you do it."

"Do what?" He eyed me with friendly curiosity and I fidgeted a bit with the strap of my gig bag.

"The guy thing," I said finally. "How do you do that?"

His grin grew into a wide smile and he tucked my hand in his arm. "Forget cappuccino, sweetling, I'm going to take you to meet Uncle Billie and Aunt Sheila."

"Uncle Billie?" I repeated to make sure I'd heard correctly as I let him lead the way.

"Yes, and Aunt Sheila," he affirmed. "C'mon, you'll see."

❖

Twenty minutes and one quick Tube ride later we were warmly
ensconced in an old railroad-style flat in a part of London I'd never
visited before, and seated around an old Formica table in the kitchen.

Graham hurriedly explained as we walked up the stairs that Uncle
Billie was a drag king and Aunt Sheila was his wife. The act was "a grand
thing," Graham said, but Billie was a "regular guy," too: he worked as a
lorry driver during the day and did a steady show nighttimes, at a club
I hadn't been to yet. "We'll go, you and Fran and I, if you'd like, next
Thursday," he offered as he knocked on the door, and I wondered what
in the world a drag king was. I was about to find out.

"Wotcher, Graham!" floated out the door as did a pair of hands,
their wrists bearing perhaps fifty or sixty assorted beaded and bangle
bracelets combined.

Graham was almost suffocated between two of the largest breasts
I'd ever seen with genuine affection that he obviously returned.

"'lo Aunt Sheila," he said finally and gave her a hearty peck.
"Uncle Billie still about?"

"All right, china! How's it going, then?" came a low voice from
behind her and Sheila released Graham, so he and who I supposed was
Uncle Billie himself could enfold one another in great big slapping
hugs, accompanied by a rush of talk that I think was supposed to be
English but made no sense to me at all.

"Ignore them and give me your coat, dear," Aunt Sheila said, her
hand already outstretched for my things. "They like to pretend they're
still in Liverpool. I humor my boys as much as possible." She gave me
a wink as I unshouldered my bass, then handed her the same fleece and
wool jacket I'd worn a few days ago.

In seconds I was in a seat, given a cup of hot tea, then asked to
stand again and turn while Uncle Billie inspected me with chin in hand
and a critical eye.

"You'll do," he said finally. "You're not too big on top, you don't
have any bad walking habits, and you're a little stringy, but you've a
nice bit o' muscle to your thread."

I dropped my arms with relief, knowing his opinion carried weight
with Graham and that it should with me as well.

"Well, I suppose the most important part is your tackle, then,"
Uncle Billie said as he played with his mug, "and you'll need a bunch

of these." He reached into his back pocket and tossed a handful of multicolored square envelopes onto the table before he took a chair.

"Now, you needn't waste your money on going out and buying something just yet—though it's not like the old days," Uncle Billie said with a grin and a twinkle in his eye. "Will ya hand me a bog roll, Sheil?" he asked, turning to his wife.

"What, no stealing the tops off of crutches for you now?" Sheila teased with a smile as she left the room.

"That required some imagination, a little derring-do," Uncle Billie said to me, his smile even wider as she returned and handed him a roll of toilet paper. "Quite serviceable too," he said to Sheila, with a sly grin and a raised eyebrow as he looked at her. "Always an encore."

I threw Graham a questioning glance. Did he mean what I thought he meant? Graham nodded and winked at me.

"Stop showing off," Sheila chided and slapped his shoulder lightly, "and show the boy what he needs to know. What are we going to call you?" she asked, directing her attention to me. Her eyes shone a friendly green.

I thought about it for all of two seconds. "Sam," I said finally. "Call me Sam."

Graham nodded in approval. "Suits you."

That at least I knew, and I grinned at him.

Uncle Billie wore a plain butter yellow work shirt, a black patch over the left chest pocket that read *B. Dwyer* in matching yellow letters. He wore the sleeves neatly rolled to the elbows, and it was fascinating to watch the strings and cords of muscle work in his arms as he made a quick assemblage of the condoms and paper before him.

"Now this," he said and he pushed the new construction across the table toward me, "is something you can walk about in. It'll hold its shape, sit nicely in your shorts, and look pretty much the way you want it to—but it's just for show, nothing you can get down to business with. For that," he said as he cleared the space before him and set himself up, "you'll want something like this."

I watched, fascinated, as he carefully measured then tightly rolled some longer segments into tight cylinders, then slowly, patiently, wound over them, layer by layer, paying painstaking attention to the tension in the wind until he had achieved the diameter he wanted.

The diligent care he took reminded me of Uncle Cort when he worked, his focus completely on the task before him, as Billie rounded off an end with a satisfied breath and tucked the loose end under another wind.

"These are your bog-standard choices," he said as his fingers neatly tore open the condom envelopes. He slipped one, then the others, over the cylinders he'd built, and they looked for all the world exactly like some of the toys Fran and I had seen in the store.

"This isn't necessarily something you'd want to pack, unless you're careful about the sort of shorts and pants you wear," he said as he hefted the first one, then held it out to me, "but you can slide it into your harness and it will do the job admirably."

The pale blue rubber was cool under my fingertips, and I could feel the slight slip of the membrane against the paper that filled it out to its slightly flared end. I was surprised at how solid it felt, then thought I shouldn't be, considering how it had been created. I felt as bizarrely self-conscious as I had when I'd dropped my pants in front of the guys all those years ago.

"If you're a bit of a 'tweener'—no shame in that, you like what you like," Billie added hastily as I put the first one down, "then this will be what you're looking for." And he passed me the other one, done in pink on one end and yellow on the other. "You can always test it out, see what you like, see what the girl you've copped off with likes, and then either adjust it, or when you've found what works, save your scratch and buy whatever matches."

I didn't know what to say as I held it in my hands, my palms measuring the length, spanning the firm girth, trying to appear nonchalant as my brain attempted to grasp the import of what he was telling me through the shorthand words I didn't fully understand, to make sense of the confused excitement and fear that surged through me. I found myself doing my best not to think about *exactly* how either of these was supposed to be used, even as the very clear image of— I mentally shook my head to erase the thought. I wondered if I was doing the right thing. Cort and Elizabeth had wanted to take me some place they thought would be safer until the "big day," and I'd wanted to stay. I didn't want to run from anything, not anymore.

But…if I had to take precautions, I thought hiding in plain sight would work—especially since what people were looking for was a girl.

I'd learned in the last few days how to walk invisibly, leaving barely a trace in the Aethyr. The only way I could be found was directly, either through a link, or physically—but whoever was searching would have to know what I looked like, and I was about to change that, all of that.

"You can pull your hair back like so many of the boys are doing now, that straight and pasted-to-the-skull thing, or do you want to cut it?" Sheila asked.

I glanced at her, grateful for the interruption, and handed the dick over to Graham, who inspected it as critically as Uncle Billie had inspected me. I could see his nod of approval from the corner of my eye as I answered Sheila. "If I pull it back, I'll still look like me now, only with a ponytail."

"Nah, not at all," Graham corrected with a smile. "Show 'im the trick, Unc."

He flashed warm brown eyes on me before turning to Sheila, who was already leaving the room. "Would you…?"

"On my way already—I know just what shade!" she answered and returned seconds later with a small pink tube, scissors, a comb, and hair clippers in her hand.

Graham rubbed his hands together and leaned forward. "Look, I know, it's girls' makeup and all, but the trick, see, is that it's waterproof, which means it won't come off, and it'll look and feel right—nice and scrubby—I'll show you."

Uncle Billie explained as Graham pulled out the little wand from the tube and Sheila started to fuss with my hair. "You've just as much hair on your face as anyone else—it's called vellus or some such. This will make it stand out, nice and visible like, and it'll look like you've trimmed it neatly as well."

As I watched the scrub shadow grow on Graham's cheeks, Sheila patted my shoulder. "So you want to cut it, then, right? Do you want what all the kids are doing now, a bit more of an Elvis sort of thing, or altogether gone?"

I thought about it, about the current looks that were so popular, about the classic ones only a few wore. I remembered Mr. Moretti and his thick black hair, the glossy wave over his forehead, my Da's salt-and-copper he'd kept neatly trimmed unless we were on vacation; even brushed back, it was soft as it feathered across his head. Finally, I thought about the boys I'd hung out with, of Mario and his thick, thick hair that would curl unless he kept it short, of Dave's flat-tops, and Bruce's regular cut with the severe side part his mom would plaster in place with a very wet comb. And then...I thought about the one guy even I found good looking. "James Dean," I answered finally. "Can you cut it like that?"

We'd collectively decided that the scrub look didn't work for me. I had areas on my face that had no hair at all, and what made Graham look good made me look like a fifteen-year-old trying to stretch the peach fuzz out, although I could do sort of a mutton-chop thing if I wanted. But that wasn't me, and I cold-creamed the rest of it off as Sheila put the finishing touches on my hair by applying some stuff, then played with it a bit. "Run your fingers through a few times," she told me, "that'll make it a damn sight sexy."

Billie shifted in his seat and pointed a stern finger at Graham.

"Now I know how you young boys are—you like to go tommin' about, so I hope you're wearing a jimmy hat and all that," he said.

"Every time," Graham nodded and said reassuringly, "no worries there."

"And you, even though you might be foolin' with one of these," he said, nailing me directly with his gaze as his hand indicated the constructions on the table, "best to use more," he ordered, pointing to the remaining packets on the table. "You don't want to be getting something you don't want to give," he said and snatched one up, "and there's a lot of things out there now that a shot in the ass won't cure."

He tossed it at me, then gave a low whistle as he checked my new look. "Nice job, Sheila," he said and smiled. "Go take a look, Sam— loo's to your left down the corridor."

I thanked Sheila as I stood and went through the apartment, a jagged electricity filling my head as I felt the firm round edge of the little square I held between my thumb and fingers. I was nervous when I jammed it into my front pocket, and took a breath before flipping the light on in the bathroom, not certain what, or who, I'd see. I stared at myself in the mirror, amazed at who gazed back at me, then I thought the same thing that would be the first words my uncle would say to me when I got home, after the color returned to his face.

"Christ!" he swore quietly. "You look just like your father."

❖

Elizabeth smiled when I came upstairs. "It suits your face," she said, "and now you *really* look like you're in a band."

I gave her a grateful smile of my own, pleased that she liked it. Strictly speaking, it wasn't purely James Dean, though it may have been James Dean inspired. It was a touch longer and stood up a bit more as well, only to fall with a short, soft edge. Sheila thought it shouldn't be too old-fashioned, and while I didn't look truly punk (which was fine, because I didn't think I could pull it off), it looked, like Graham had said, like a wolf's ruff or even a lion's mane.

When Fran came in and joined us at the table, I could tell she was torn between staring and trying too hard not to, and other than a quick hello before dinner, she'd glance over at me, and seem like she was about to speak, but then wouldn't.

Fran's bemusement had me grinning to myself as I followed Cort into the study after dinner.

"So…back to Sam, is it?" he asked as we set up.

I shrugged. "Maybe, sometimes, I guess."

He nodded before he looked at me again. "How far do you plan on going with this?"

"What do you mean?"

"I mean, how far does this go for you? Hair can be cut and grown again, you can always change how you stand, your dress, but other things…they're more permanent. Are you thinking in that direction?"

That was news to me—I hadn't known there could be anything done permanently, and that gave me something new to think about. But still, he'd thought farther ahead than I had, in directions I hadn't gone. I answered as honestly as I could. "I'm just…just trying some stuff," I told him. "Hiding in plain sight. I figure if I'm not recognized as the girl everyone's looking for, then so much the better, right? As for the rest…" I shrugged again.

He clapped my shoulder. "Just…just talk to me before you make any decisions, will you?" he asked. "I don't mean to jump on you, but your physical, corporeal makeup is as important to this work as your mental and emotional states."

I nodded. I knew that—it had been stressed to me to the point where I occasionally felt like my skin was chafed raw by all the restrictions.

"You do know your gift"—and I knew he meant both the skills I was developing as well as the sword that was my family legacy—"is blood bound. Genetic," he said into the silence.

"I thought...I thought that these were things anyone with the right training, temperament, and patience could learn."

Cort nodded. "Some of them, yes. But not even the forger, the original blacksmith and arms master of that sword, could touch it barehanded once it was done—in fact, it couldn't be handled barehanded during its creation."

"Yeah, but...you handle it all the time—"

"I hand it to you in its scabbard, or wrap a cloth around the hilt."

I stared, momentarily stunned. He was right. I'd noticed that, but I'd thought he was merely being careful not to mar the steel.

Cort continued to speak, and what he said next brought me to open-mouthed shock. "Under normal circumstances, only those that came before you, you, and your children, will ever be able to wield it. And right now? You're the last—the last of your line. Do you know what an avatar is?"

That was a strange segue, but I went with it. "Yes, of course," I answered and shrugged casually. "A highly evolved being of the Light that's chosen to incarnate—live a human life."

Cort nodded. "And how powerful do you think anything that touched that incarnation would be?"

"Well, it would depend on the item, the type of contact, the intent surrounding the act as well as the resonance in the Aethyr, all that sort of thing."

"Exactly. Before this metal was forged into this blade, it was used to...wound...an avatar. Because of this, the lattice structure is keyed to that blood, to its descendants—the relic is the heart of the blade. You'll need to leave an heir someday."

Shock ruled me as I reached for the scabbarded weapon he held, but the next thing he did surprised me, in a good way. He reached out and mussed my head. "You do look tough." He smiled, and I smiled back.

"Okay, let's get started, then."

The night's lesson consisted of working in and with the monitor state, of visualizing and manipulating systemic body functions such as heart rate, breath rate, and energy flows, starting with my own.

This work was even more exhausting than strict Astral work, and

Cort not only cut the physical portion short, he accompanied me to the kitchen to make sure I had a bit more to eat than just the usual after-study snack before I went up to bed.

Fran and I ran into each other at the landing by the stairs and she flushed a bright red when she saw me.

"What, you don't like my haircut?" I teased and took a step closer. From the shine in her eyes to the flame she radiated, I knew no matter what she said, that wasn't what she felt and she shook her head.

"You just…you're so…" she stammered, and I closed the distance between us and with a surety that made my head buzz, I put my arm around her waist.

"So…what?" I asked, knowing that my mouth against her ear was distracting her, "So turned on?" I pulled her closer to me, and she ran a hand through my shorn hair, scratched her fingers under the short hair that skirted the base of my head. "So into you?" Her lips welcomed my tongue between them and she gasped when I pressed my hips against her, when she could feel what nestled between my thighs.

When Graham and I had left Uncle Billie's, he'd steered me across the street to the chemist's. "Well, go on, go get some," he said with a broad grin.

"What?"

"Eel-skins…rubbers, mate!" He clapped me on the back. "It's a man's rite of passage. Go—I'll wait for you out here."

Dammit but he was serious, and while I could have said I had one stuffed in my front pocket, the challenge in his eyes wasn't one I'd back down from. I squared my shoulders, resettled my bass, and opened the door.

The bright light was shocking after the darkness outside, but I probably wouldn't have noticed it quite so much if I hadn't been on a mission. I found them at the back of the store, a shelf range of a handful of brands. Ribbed. Lubricated. With or without spermicide. That I didn't need. Lambskin. Out of the question—I knew that much from high school sex-ed, anyway. Latex. Colors. Flavored. I decided I didn't need that either.

And then I saw them. Royal blue, foil pack, about the size of an American fifty-cent piece, the coin with Kennedy on it. Considering his reported personal history, that made me laugh, and I thought it appropriate.

I took them off the shelf and walked up to the cash register. That was the easy part. The placing them on the counter before an older woman who gave me a squinty-eyed glare and a disapproving twist to her mouth followed by the "hmph" as I handed her a couple of bills—*that* was hard. I kept my eyes on the fake black-eyed-Susan blossom pinned to her pocket, the bright orange plastic petals nestled against the pebbled coffee-brown center.

"Well, aren't you a young one," she commented as she handed me my change.

I said nothing other than the briefest of thank-yous as I pocketed the coins and my prize. I felt her eyes on my back as I walked out the door.

"So...you got 'em?" Graham asked immediately.

I handed him the three-pack box.

"Good." He opened it and took one out. "Did you have to ask for them?"

I shook my head. "Nope. They were on a shelf and I picked something out."

"You got off easy, then," he said. "Next time, try a place where you've got to ask at the counter—now *that's* an experience." He grinned and handed me one of the foil coins. "Put one in your back pocket—just in case, like, and you can leave the rest at home." He tucked the box into my gig bag.

I nodded, wordless because my face still burned and I hadn't quite gotten the hang of breathing normally again. As I slipped the rubber into my right back pocket, I didn't know I was starting a habit that would mark every pair of jeans I owned with a distinctive raised brand.

"And how're you feeling?" Graham asked as we walked back to the Tube. He bounced next to me like an excited puppy, and my nerves aside, his joy was contagious.

"I'm feeling a little...reckless," I told him as I shifted my gig bag over my shoulder. "I'm feeling like...shopping."

He quirked an eyebrow at me and I gave him a smile. If I was in for a penny, I might as well be in for a pound, and the hair I'd grown for the last several years was already floating beneath the London streets. I felt daring, and alive, and good, and for the first time in a long time, even though the road before me was unknown, I had the sense of control: I didn't know where I was going, but it felt like I knew what I was doing.

This was an adventure, a "follow the leader" straight line exploration like I'd done as a kid: what would we walk through? Woods or dunes? Yards or streets? Would we have to climb over logs or fences? Would we be stopped by angry dogs, railroad tracks, or hunger? How far could this go, how far could *I* go? I wanted to find out—and now was the perfect time. I could feel the smile I wore grow wider. "Accessories," I told him. "Why wait?"

He raised an eyebrow at me. "You've got enough cash for that?"

"No," I answered, then grinned. "But I've got plastic."

"What a *great* reason to go into debt," he said with a laugh. "I'm sure that Uncle Billie won't mind that you prefer store-bought over something a bit more...custom. Lucky *you*, I know just the place."

"Lucky me is right," I agreed. "Great. I just need to make a phone call." We found a pay phone, one of the famous London red boxes, and I dropped some coins into the box. Elizabeth answered and after the exchange of greetings and the friendly "How are things going?" I told her I'd be later than expected, probably just in time for dinner.

"Fran's out with your uncle," she informed me, "so dinner will be late anyway."

That was surprising, but under the excitement of the adventure I was undertaking, I didn't think about it much—we'd cancelled our plans to meet after rehearsal, and I knew she'd wanted to start her own holiday gift hunt. I assumed that was what it was all about.

"Are you by yourself?" Elizabeth asked. Despite the friendliness of her tone, I knew she held real concerns for my welfare and I took the time to reassure her.

"I'm with Graham, safe as houses," I told her, "and only two"—Graham tapped the glass of the booth and held up three fingers—"three stops away."

"Wonderful, then. Well, don't let me keep you—have fun, and call if you think you'll be later?" she asked.

"Will do."

We hung up and I clapped Graham on the shoulder as I stepped out of the booth. "Lead on, MacDuff," I told him, and off we went.

On our journey, Graham told me that most of these stores, stores that basically sold sex toys, were illegal, which was why their windows

were covered in huge flyers that advertised comic books and novelties—
they weren't allowed to advertise anything else. This explained why it
seemed like almost every second store on Compton had its windows
blocked out in posters.

"This one's a bit more popular among our crowd," Graham told
me as we approached the brick-faced building with its door a few feet
below sidewalk level. "It's a nice little shop, everything all legal-like,
friendly. The people are helpful if you need—ah, here we are," he said
as he strode down the steps and I trailed behind him. "After you." He
grinned and held the door for me.

I agreed with his description as I looked about. The lighting
wasn't as harsh as the only other place I'd been in, the layout a bit
smaller, but neater somehow, even a bit cozy. *Fran would be all right
with this*, I thought, remembering her discomfort—and all things
considered, including the environment and the clerk with the pierced
face, I supposed I didn't really blame her. But this place was different;
the atmosphere was similar to that of any boutique-style clothing store.
Heck, there were even clothes here, too, complete with a sign for a
dressing room, except they also sold—

"What about this?" Graham asked, handing me something the size
of a small missile.

"Are you *insane*?"

He laughed. "Just thought you might be ambitious."

I shook my head at him. I already wasn't certain how well this
would go over at home; I didn't think showing up wearing a killer
whale in my pants would endear me to Fran—or to anyone else.

"I'm not looking to scare horses into submission," I told him as I
handed it back. "Let's just stick to the basics."

Graham agreed.

By the time we were done, I was more than set. Graham had given
me advice on fit and placement.

"Mind if I show you something?" he'd asked before I stepped into
the dressing room.

I shrugged as he approached.

"Most make the mistake of wearing it up here," he said and placed
the edge of his palm against my pubic bone, "but you'll want to wear
that nice and low," and barely touching my fly, he shifted his hand at
just about my clit. It was clinical, advice, talk between friends, not at all

sexual. "Get the center right about there and I guarantee you'll like that better when you're gettin' down to business—and you'll have much better control. Hey…what sort of underpants have you got on?"

I had to think for a second. "Nothing special. Nylon brief—girl stuff."

To my surprise, he nodded approvingly. "As authentic as boxers or Y-fronts are, they won't hold you good and snug and if you want to go out, you'll need to either wear something altogether different or show everyone your hard-on. But with a well-fitted bikini brief, or girls' underwear," he grinned, "all you've got to do is tuck yourself right, and you'll be right as rain and ready to rock."

That jagged electric pulse that had filled my head back at Uncle Billie's kicked in again as I closed the door behind me and tried to figure out what to do next. Once I had proper blood flow and sensation in my hands again, it took a little while to figure out which strap went where, sizing the black leather up right so nothing would slip, and then…it was the strangest feeling I'd ever felt. I stood there with my jeans about my thighs and my cock in my hands, and as I slipped it through the ring, I experienced a moment of surreal disconnect: this was my body, the body I'd always seen, with this "thing" sticking out. But something about it *felt* right, *looked* right; the arrogant bounce between my legs— insensate as it might be—*worked*, and I made one final adjustment on the strap that made it snug up hard against me. It was a matter of a few more minutes to make certain it didn't look like I was ready to shoot someone with my crotch, and between my underwear and my jeans which weren't terribly loose, I managed it.

All set and tucked and with my jacket on, I looked at myself in the mirror. Billie had been right, I was a little…stringy…like he'd said: long arms and legs like my Da, and my hair… I grinned at my reflection. Even with the stuff in it that made it stick up a bit, the short angle got rid of the shadows, revealed bits of honey in the brown, wasn't quite long enough to fall over bright blue eyes in a face not quite as sharp as it had been a few months ago. I decided I liked the slight square to my chin, the smile I couldn't help when I felt the soft, short hair and rubbed the bare skin of my neck, its length sensitive, exposed. I even liked my ears now that I could see them. Maybe…I considered as I looked, I'd pierce one, maybe both, put a hoop in, or a cool stud of some sort…and maybe not.

I shrugged my shoulders, which had a decent breadth to them from years of swimming, shifted my stance until everything settled comfortably, and reset my jacket. I looked like my own brother, if I'd had one, and if he was sixteen. Right then and there, I felt and understood something new: I'd known what it was to desire, to lust, the combination of affection and attraction, but this feeling was different. It was similar to the one I'd get when I'd strolled out to the deck of the pool as a competitor, strong, confident, unbeatable, and *everyone* knew it. But there was something else mixed with that. I liked what I saw, and the pressure in my pants against my body felt good, as good as the silhouette looked right. For the first time, I felt like I *myself* was sensual, desirable. Sexy, that was the word I was looking for, I felt sexy, and that feeling sent wilding sparks under my skin.

"Smashing!" Graham said when I walked out, now also wearing a dumb grin I couldn't turn off and could literally feel tug at the corner of my mouth. "If Fran doesn't jump on that, Hannah will."

Yeah. I already knew Hannah was interested. For less than a nanosecond I wondered what one particular someone else would have thought, but I clamped down on that—I couldn't afford to go there. "It's not about that," I said. "It's—"

"Whatever," he said waving a hand in negation. "It's *always* about that in the end."

Considering the way things were progressing on the stairs just a few short hours later, I mentally gave a brief, grudging admission that he was right.

"Hot," Fran said, the same heat in her voice with her tongue and teeth on my neck. "It's fucking hot!"

While Graham had told me I'd like this position, he hadn't really told me why, and the pressure of Fran's body against my dick pressed it back against me in a way that sent a lick of fire from my clit up my stomach and down my thighs. It made me lean into her that much more.

God, it was insane, as insane as it had been that time by the front door, only without the fear, without the anxiety and as we ground against each other, held up by the door frame to the room, I tore my mouth from hers just long enough to ask, "Are you sure you want to do this?"

She ran strong, strong hands under my shirt, the skin on skin, the precision of her thumbs rounding hard tips she made harder, driving me as wild as the driving of our bodies, her waist, her hips, a perfect fit in my hands. From the tension I felt growing in my belly to the frantic breath of air we shared, one or both of us was gonna come and soon, and God—we were wearing too many clothes… My hands shook—I didn't know whether it was nerves or anticipation—as I kicked the door closed behind us and snapped open the button of her jeans.

I wasn't certain if I knew what I was doing, if I'd like it, if *she'd* like it, if I'd be any good… "I love you a lot, you know," I whispered against her lips as we fell onto the bed.

"Me, too," she answered and kissed me with a hunger that matched my own as she pulled me to her. My pants were only halfway down when she hooked her leg over mine and the heat of her body against me, the silk feel of her thighs on my hips as we rocked together with my cock between her pretty pussy lips drove all the doubts out of my head, lost in the swirl and churn of heat and blood and the magic sensation that flowed through me, through *us*, and the desperate, desperate need to—

"Yeah?" I asked her again as I wrapped my hand around my cock. I wanted to, God, I was *dying* to—but I wanted to control this, guide it, make this as good for her as it already was for me, and I didn't think a blind wild plunge would do that. I was caught as I gazed into her eyes, a smoky amber glow in the streetlight that shone in through the window, suspended with the knowledge that in that moment, she was the whole world, she was the *only* world to me, and struck as I was, I could only stare while I stroked the high angle of her cheek with my thumb.

She caught my face in her hands, then kissed me, her tongue achingly sweet in my mouth as I stroked along her cunt with my head. She was so…beautifully…wet.

"Can I…can I do you later?" she asked gracefully, haltingly, a mix of desire and vulnerability in her voice.

I said what I felt, the only thing I could, in the face of that. "Yes," I answered as my cock nudged at her entrance. "Yes," I whispered again as I closed my eyes and pressed my lips to her neck. I felt the frantic flutter of her chest against mine, the same pressured cadence that ran through me as our bodies came together.

"Yes," she gasped into my ear and she fully embraced me.

❖

Work. No one ever, anywhere, had ever described the traditional missionary position as work, but it was. The first time had been pretty easy: we were both so high, so revved, had already been so close to coming from everything else, that it seemed like scant seconds before her hands dug, fucking good and fucking *hard*, into my back as she arched under me, with my lips drinking the sweat from the skin on her throat while the proud jut of her breast, the swollen and contracted point, rolled under my palm.

The pure, primal way she groaned into my ear made me respond with a frantic breathlessness. The need to hear that sound again and again pounded through me, was a bodily pulse that focused through my clit to my cock and drove the thrust to what it was, slick and hot, heavy, fast, and hard.

God that turned me on...the body-to-body so close, the ardent press...to know Fran was coming with my dick inside her, to know she came *because* of it...that I *could* make her come with my cock...and as my abs contracted with the effort of building to that final release, all I could think of was the way her cunt would suck on my fingers when she came and I knew she'd milk my dick the same way.

She meant so much to me.

We held each other close, and I stroked the hair away from her face, off her forehead, then lay soft kisses on her brow, on her cheeks as she nestled her lips into my neck.

"You okay, Frankie?" I asked finally as the blood tide receded and she pulled the quilt over us. Somewhere in the middle we'd managed to get my pants the rest of the way off.

"Mm-hmm," she answered, trailing silky fingertips along my spine. "You?"

"Great," I told her and kissed her softly. I shifted carefully, not wanting to hurt her or cause discomfort.

"Stay," she asked, and she held my hip for emphasis.

"You sure?"

She kissed me in answer and as the kiss deepened, her mouth once again sweet and warm and so, so soft around my tongue, the comfort of our contact changed, evolved, from easy glide to crawling need. Once hadn't been enough for either of us—what with finding the right angle and staying there, to making sure there were no accidental exits—this was about making certain that *this* time was even better for her than the last.

When her ankles locked behind mine, we'd found the right groove, the rhythm and stroke that worked for both of us, wrapping into a sync that made me reach and hold her tighter even as I moved on her, in her. And as the thought flitted through my head that this was something I could do forever, for the first time since I'd phoned the States in the summer, Nina's face floated through my mind and I felt a twin-touch of sorrow stab at my chest.

Forever was not something that could ever be, not on any level, not for me. Nina was a world, an ocean, and six feet of dirt away, and while I loved my Frankie, loved her unreservedly and in ways I hadn't known it was possible to love anyone, I didn't love her that way, nor she me.

And besides, even if I'd had, or wanted to, for her own safety and, beyond that, for the betterment, the enrichment of her own life, she would leave at the beginning of January, right after New Year's Day. She would leave just after the holidays and I would be alone again. I tightened my arms around her, kissed her desperately.

"Easy, lover," she whispered, "you're okay, I'm right here, right here with you."

The beautiful grasp she held on my shoulders eased and she pressed one hand against my chest while the other trailed down, grabbed my ass, and held me firmly.

"Look at me, Sam," she asked as her fingers played against the charm I wore and pushed it against my skin. "Sammer…she's right here." She touched her own chest, right above her heart. "Right here, and between us? Between you and me?"

Her palm pressed back against my sternum, while the fingers that held my ass eased under the strap that ran so tight, pressed and swirled in ways that made my breath catch again, because it pulled my cock even harder against me, because I wanted her inside me.

"We can touch her." The words were an almost airless sigh as she filled me and I knew, knew this was okay, knew that as we sank in and against each other, I had never before loved my Frankie more than I did at that moment. This, between us, it was all we had, everything we could give, and we gave each other all of it. For a moment, just before I came with my cock buried inside my best friend while she teased and pleased and played me with urgent strokes in my cunt and the frantically choked declaration that she was coming, the thought ran through my head that maybe, just maybe, we were something more than friends too.

Pretty Boy

And he who Love touches walks not in darkness.
—Plato

The next morning, and the mornings that followed, I woke up feeling strong, loose in my limbs, with a sense of true joy I hadn't felt since I was a kid pedaling like mad down the street.

There were days I snuggled in with Fran, content to wait until the last minute before we had to run downstairs and work on matters of the intellect with Elizabeth, while on others, I'd join Uncle Cort in the kitchen and work—on breakfast.

I didn't feel the need to walk around with a dick on all the time to complete my disguise, as it were. Besides the fact that it really just made me too sensitive and distracted me from everything, I didn't need to. Maybe it was cutting my hair and maybe there'd been a slight shift in body language, or maybe it was simply in the way I thought about myself, but whatever it was, it was enough.

Things were different, at least with Uncle Cort. He lifted my traveling restrictions enough that I was once again allowed to wander about the neighborhood freely, and he didn't wait too long to let me know it.

"Hey, why don't you and Fran take today and tonight off—get out for a bit, go and do something fun?"

I turned from the skillet on the stove to stare at him, surprised. It had been well impressed upon me, and Fran as well, how important progressing my training had been—where did fun fit in with that?

"Watch, kid," he said, nodding at the stove, and I quickly returned my attention to the task before me. This was the first time he'd trusted me solo with his secret mix and I didn't want to muff it up.

He came to peer over my shoulder and roughed up my hair. "Doing good," he said, approval obvious in his voice. "You can finish that, then seriously, it's been a stressful few days—you need a break. Why don't you guys get out of here after breakfast, okay?"

"Sure," I agreed. A break sounded good to me, and there were a bunch of spots neither Fran nor I had gone to yet. I thought maybe we could do something extra-weird and touristy like visit the Tower of London.

He carried a tray with the rest of breakfast in his hands. "Stop by the shop before you go, will you?" he said, then left for the dining room.

When Fran came downstairs and entered, she greeted everyone with the usual good morning.

"Hey, Frankie." I smiled up at her as she neared.

"Hey, Sammer." She leaned over and kissed me, a kiss I returned with genuine affection, before she sat. It wasn't until I caught the smile Elizabeth cast upon us, or the warm spark from Uncle Cort, that I realized anything different had happened.

"This is something I've been thinking about for a bit," he said as Fran and I walked into the shop. A set of athames glittered on the counter, while artifacts were hung carefully from the walls. We followed him to the back, through the boxes of raw materials and past his workbench the light shimmered on through watery glass, and Fran gave my hand a quick squeeze.

There was a door for the back room—it led out to a small courtyard that could be reached from an alleyway from the sidewalk. We kept it gated, and I never went there, but out to the yard was where we headed. I felt the excitement jump from Fran's skin as Cort waved us out the door.

"Been on my mind," he said as he gathered us around a black-cloth-covered pile on the center of the cement. "Seems a shame your car's in storage back in the States and you can't drive around. A young"— he hesitated —"person needs a little freedom, needs to get around, so…" He fished into his pocket and tossed something to me. I caught it reflexively.

"This is for you."

A key, it was a key that winked from my hand in the early morning light, and Fran grinned at me as I palmed it.

"Go ahead—what are you waiting for?" he asked, and gave me one end of the black tarp.

I'd always been the sort of person who carefully unwrapped things—I untied ribbons, delicately slit tape, unfolded corners only to fold paper back with perfect precision. It was odd, I supposed, but I suspected it was part of what made me a musician, part of what made me enjoy other things I cared about as well, the savoring of discovery, the collection of clues and hints until all was revealed.

This was no different, and I could hear Fran sigh impatiently—that made me smile to myself, because I knew she was equally meticulous—as I gathered the corners and walked forward, uncovering a chrome metal basket that jutted out with a small luggage holder that held a thick tire. I uncovered the rear wheel and its side compartments, excitement and disbelief warring in my throat. One black helmet, then another, perched on two leather seats, and by the time I'd uncovered the handlebars, the front leg shield with mounted glove box, the perfectly restored dial indicators, and the front tire, I was speechless, the canvas knotted in my hands as I stared at the onyx and chrome shine.

"Sixty-six Vespa," Cort said. "It's got—"

I knew what a Vespa was; I loved old cars and old bikes. "By Piaggio," I almost whispered. "This…is a VBC Super 150." I handed him the canvas as he smiled widely, then popped the key I'd squeezed in my hand into the ignition. I'd missed that: the sound, the pop in the lock, the unmistakable click, the resistance of the key against my fingertips and my palm as it snugged in and hit home.

"It's been kitted out a bit," he said offhandedly as I scooped up a helmet and handed it back to Fran, then grabbed the other one. Lightweight but solid, and it felt good under my arm.

"Electronic ignition," I commented, observing the new work. "Single-cylinder engine?" I asked as I stroked the handlebar.

"Yeah, and automatic transmission. Tweaked your speed a bit too, you'll get over," he frowned as he thought, "seventy mph if you treat it nice."

"That's a little over one hundred twelve kilometers," Fran told me, and I gave her a smile before I checked out the seats then popped the glove box. I laughed at the map he'd already put in it for me, wrapped about with a rubber band and a small clear plastic bag with almost three pounds' worth of change, and a compass.

Mine? This was mine? I could go anywhere, I could, I could… "I don't know what to say," I told him honestly, "I just—"

He messed my hair again. "Seats are new, gas is full. All it needs is someone to ride it."

Still I stared, unable to convey how much it meant, how much I appreciated it. "Go on," he said and patted my shoulder, "you two, get out of here." And he turned back to the door of the shop. "Oh, by the way," he said as put his hand to the knob, "take a ride over to the local Green, that'll give you a feel for the streets before you head out—use your American license if you get stopped, and we'll get you a regular one next week sometime. Oh, and skip the visit to London Bridge—go by Tower instead. They've a tour and all that, and then you can go on to visit the Tower proper, if you're still of a mind."

He grinned at us both before he closed the door.

"Did you know about this?" I turned and asked Fran.

Her eyes shone a pure gold and her smile beamed at me. "Yes—and this is yours too," she told me and reached into her coat, "because I know you never button up."

She put a scarf about my neck, one of those wide, long ones that would fold and wrap properly, done in the MacRae tartan. "Besides," she said as she tucked its ends into my coat, accidentally-on-purpose smoothing over my breasts to ensure it lay right, "since your haircut, your neck is almost bare."

I put an arm around her waist and pulled her to me. "Thank you," I said quietly, then kissed her as her fingers caressed my cheeks.

"Do you want to drive?" I asked her.

She bit her lip and smiled at me in a way that only gave one message. "Maybe…later. Let's go."

After about twenty minutes of zipping around the neighborhood, we were off, and we had more fun getting there and back than doing the actual tour. The Tower of London, other than the crown jewels, was a rather grim place, from the legend of the ravens—when the last ravens left the Tower, the Empire would end—to its often violent history: there was a heavy cast, a weight in the air of the past, proof that events did indeed embed themselves for all time in the Aethyr.

"Hey, can you feel things?" I asked Fran. Even though we might not have been learning exactly the same things, I was sure there had to be some similarities, especially if as Cort said, she would be bound to the Circle, and to the Light as well.

"What do you mean?"

"You know," I shrugged, then waved a hand about to take in everything, "pick up on the traces left, that sort of thing."

She gave me a slow grin. "Can you?"

The spark of friendly challenge in her eyes and the angle of her chin made me smile. "Let's see."

We went through the halls and galleries, extending that extra sense, allowing the memories imprinted on the walls to form images in our minds that could be described. We'd narrate what we "saw" to one another before we'd look up the history; we were both surprisingly accurate. Maybe that shouldn't have been a surprise.

It was more than enough after a while, tiring as well as depressing given what we were picking up on, so we cheered ourselves after by taking a detour over to the dockyards, where we found the tiniest chip shop along the harbor, a small newsstand-like construction, and after I insisted on paying for the well-battered and deliciously fried fish and chips, wrapped in newspaper and soaking through a paper bag, we amused ourselves by warming our fingers as we ate them, bumping against each other while we walked along one of the piers.

"Hey," I asked with sudden inspiration, "there's this new club the band keeps telling me is great—wanna go?"

"Sounds cool. Do you know how to get there?" she teased, her eyes and smile bright under the lamplight in the twilight.

Her smile was killer, and I couldn't help but respond to it. I crumpled what was left of the paper bag in my hand and shoved it in my coat pocket as I leaned closer to her. "I'm well supplied for these things, you know," I told her, then wrapped my fingers into the thick wool of the peacoat. "*I*...have a map." I gently pulled her to me as her hand came up and cupped my neck, while the other eased under my jacket, over my hip.

"That's not all you've got," she murmured against my lips as her fingers slipped against my back pocket, traced the projection of what they found, and kissed me.

From the sure way our lips moved and the sensual haze that clouded around us, even if I wasn't completely sure of where we were going, map or no, I knew where we'd end up.

❖

We eventually found a phone so I could call and let my uncle and Elizabeth know that we intended to stay out a bit later than originally planned—I didn't want them to worry too much—and after promising both of them that I'd call if there was a problem, we were set and on our way.

Hannah, Kenny, and Graham had described it well. It was an old factory, and a little placard right next to the door claimed it as a one-time refuge during the— The rest was pasted over with a bit of laminated cardboard that read: "The original scoundrel who owned this place was mad as a hatter, a dashing dresser, a scoffer of parking laws, a lover of wine, and a master of the tango, both long and short forms. In short, a legend. We liked him—lots. Welcome to SPIT."

A faint hum, a hint of beat, of rhythm, came through the door itself, which was spray-painted with a large, black message: "You don't know SPIT." I gave Fran a quick smile over my shoulder, then opened the door.

Even without knowing that the building had survived the industrial revolution, the moment we walked through the door and onto the worn, broad brick steps that flowed down in huge half circles to the main level, there was no hiding the age of the place. There was no missing the blast of sound either, the low sensual throb that pulsed under the electric buzz of people and the pattern of emotions, muted by the brick, that came wafting through the air.

I handed the bouncer a few bills, then asked where the bar was.

"First time, huh?" he asked with a wide grin as he handed me back my change.

"Here, yes," I agreed.

"Well, don't miss the show—or the house drink."

I wasn't certain I wanted to drink anything called "spit," and he smiled at my expression.

"It's not spit, really," he assured me. "It smells like a suntan and it's a real treat. Get one for your girl," he said, nodding at Fran next to me. "She'll like it."

Down the steps we went, through another corridor, following the beat that became a buzz under our feet until we passed through a darkened archway and there...

I hadn't known how thick the walls were, how effectively the combination of layers of brick and iron could contain the thoughts, the feelings, the nonsubtle sendings of intent, but because there was nowhere for them to flow, they gathered, concentrated, a thick soup of sensation, accentuated by the music that poured through the speakers, the press of bodies that moved to it under the lightning strikes of color and the illuminated panels that played a variety of images, only to darken as others lit up. Somewhere, farther in through the cavern, was an unlit stage, hinted and highlighted by the occasional glancing strobe.

I stood still for a moment, letting it all run through me as I peered through the dimness for the promised bar. I felt the lift under my skin, the rise of my blood, the automatic body response to the call that sounded out across worlds, and the heady, reckless feeling that accompanied the unmistakable, unavoidable sense of hunger.

I shut down the extension of myself that echoed through the Aethyr, shut out the sense of others as well until all I felt directly was Fran's presence, the barrier that surrounded us both, and the remains of the tide the wild call had roused through me. When Fran's thumb brushed along the column of my neck while her fingers tickled under my collar, we exchanged a glance, and I knew she'd felt it too.

It figured. It simply figured. Soho may have been a hunting ground, but Spit? Was a lair.

❖

"Dance or drink first?"

"Hmm?"

"Dance or drink first?" Fran repeated as we came to stand near one of the many steel columns, the bare supports for the floor above us, and she gave me a smile.

I glanced around and decided there was no time like the present to know for certain whether or not my "hide in plain sight" plan would work.

"Drink," I said and could feel the tiniest quirk of a grin work my mouth.

"Wait here, then," she asked, "otherwise you won't let me pay for them."

I rolled my eyes at her and was about to argue the point when she curled her fingers into the edges of my jacket and tugged me to her. The kiss she gave me was purely sensual—and she didn't merely slide her tongue between my very willing lips, she pressed her body to mine and kissed my mouth with intent, an intent I answered even as it made my knees loosen, made me force a hand around her waist and the other to the nape of her neck, everything forgotten but the race of blood through me, through her, the very real need to—

"Wait," she whispered into my ear, and leaving me with another small kiss, she strode through the crowd to the bar.

With my heart rate and my knees unwilling to let me move very far, I leaned my back against the steel column and fumbled into my pocket for a cigarette and a light as I watched her, the set to her shoulders, the toss of her head, the pure "don't fuck with me" confidence she radiated as she moved. She was beautiful, on every level, inside and out, and I knew it.

Fran, I thought, was every inch, every bit, the golden champion everyone had so admired in high school.

It had been...interesting, I reflected.

When we finally had "switched," since I'd promised we would, it had been a little awkward at first, and as I caressed her hips, untwisted the strap that had gotten caught up and smoothed it along the silken skin, I realized something: she was afraid, afraid of her own strength, her own power, and as much as she'd helped me find and explore myself, she hadn't done that for herself, not really.

Something had changed, between us, within me. She accepted me, welcomed me, let me be whatever I was, without reservation, without hesitation, from the embrace of my cock within her to the deepest hurt of my heart, a hurt we shared honestly. And it was the sharing, the sincere and accepting acknowledgment, that somehow set yet another part of me free, a part even I didn't know was there; it allowed me to love her with an ease I hadn't had before.

As her friend, I wanted to help, wanted her to know herself; as her lover, I wanted to see that, to feel it, because I saw it so clearly in her. Her bravery awed me, left me humbly honored knowing that she would dare so much, face so much, test herself so deeply, with me, for me.

I watched the muscles play in her back as she took another step away from the bed, and she adjusted whatever she needed to. I took in and admired the fall of her head, the drape of her hair as she set her hands on her hips, then glanced down her own body. And then, suddenly, something shifted for her, in her—I not only witnessed it, I could *feel* the switch.

She squared her shoulders and tossed her head, and as she turned to me with the light from the window glancing from her eyes, the tiger no longer prowled behind them, trapped within. From the bronze cast that lit her skin in that same light, the jut of her jaw, the proud, proud set of her body, she *was* the great hunting cat, the lion unleashed.

She really was. That beautiful body, the muscles that built her shoulders, stretched across her chest, the lush breasts I couldn't fill my hands enough with, nipples dark, hard, tight…the taper of her ribs to her waist and the split, the narrow channel that led down her stomach to her navel, down to the lovely curve, the demarcation sharply heightened by the dark leather that skimmed skin over skin on compact hips. She wore that cock nice and low, good and proud. She wore it perfectly.

I *wanted* that, wanted *her*, all of her, and I did my best to let her know it. "God, how I want you," I told her, the words barely audible above the beat of my heart. "You…that…you're just so fucking hot!"

"You think so," she stated more than asked, her voice silky and low as she neared.

I glanced up at her eyes, the bright flame in them. "Yeah," I breathed against her lips and I wrapped my arms around her and drew her down, the warm fit and weight of her on me very welcome as I covered us against the chill of autumn.

Fran sucked the tip of my tongue, drawing it between her lips and into her mouth the same way she did my clit as her legs fit along, then became a velvet slide between mine.

"Sammy," she whispered when she took her mouth from mine, "is it really okay for me to *want* you like this, to want to do this?"

A wayward lock fell down over her face, tickled against my neck, and I carefully stroked it behind her ear, reading the desire, uncertainty, and fear that swam in her eyes. I brushed my thumb against her cheek. "Yes," I assured her, then pressed my lips against her neck to confirm it with the taste of her on my tongue. I reached down between us and guided her cock to me. "I want you," I told her and gently bit the delicate skin under her jaw. "I want you to."

She drew in a slight shuddering breath before her body closed over mine, then caught my mouth with hers. She kissed me with a deliberate intensity she'd never shown before, a commanding thoroughness that delivered her intent, a sending of riotous sparks that flared under my skin while her cock slid between my thighs.

Her fingers covered mine and I let go so I could smooth my hands along her face, her neck, the span of her shoulders and the muscles of her arms, to feel for myself the contained power and the strength of the woman above me, the tremor that moved through her, the result of her restraint as she played her cock against my pussy, and the pounding in my chest was painful, savage. My breath caught, became a solid weight in my throat, and in that one very naked second, I realized why: I was scared.

"Sammer," Fran groaned into my neck as her cock pressed with contained urgency against my entrance, "do we love each other?"

"We do," I assured her and myself. Still, I couldn't help the shiver that ran through me.

"But...but we're not in love, right?" Her eyes searched mine and I searched deep for the answer, in me, in her.

There was no denying we loved each other in ways so profound I had no way of defining them, and I knew she couldn't either. But there was something... In these conscious moments, where there was time to reflect, to analyze, it was almost as if there was one last step, one last barrier held in place only by the fact that it seemed that if we said it out loud, put it into actual words and admitted this...this indefinable thing, it would plunge us both into something neither one of us could handle.

"I think..." I began as I stared up into her eyes, caught once more by what I saw in them while I reached to skim my fingertips against her face, to loosely twine them in her hair over and over again. What I read, what I felt, from her, for her....it wasn't something we could say, *I* could say, only show. "I don't know."

She shifted her weight and caressed my cheek, traced my lips with her fingertip. "That's okay," she said and smiled so gently it pierced my

5

AERICA TH*

heart, made my eyes sting. It made the fear recede and it completely disappeared when she lowered her mouth to mine. "I think I don't know either."

If there was a kiss that could convey everything someone felt and meant, even with the meld we already shared, this was that kiss: honest love and muted longing, real friendship and unmistakably deep desire. It was the melody that played over the deeper, anchor notes of pain, linked in perfect harmony and timing to the rhythm of life.

As strange as it may seem, there was a safety in that, a security in knowing that while I couldn't, or perhaps, wouldn't, name what we shared, we *did* share it, and we loved each other.

We held each other carefully, tenderly. "I do know that I love you," she whispered as she moved against me, erasing everything in the building need that made me burn, burn with a flame that licked along my legs as I skated my fingers down her spine, then fanned them across the toned and tight flex of her ass.

"Me too," I murmured against her lips, "I love you too." It was such a relief to finally say it, to say it and know that she knew what I meant, the way I meant it, how much I meant it. And then I couldn't speak, couldn't breathe, all I could do was hold her tight, cling to her with everything I was, everything I could be as finally, finally…she filled me.

There was the initial slow breaching of entrance that was a combination of thrill and bruise and I was surprised, the shock a lurch in my chest, that it actually hurt. But she pushed past that and farther into me, replacing the discomfort with the absofuckinglutely incredible slide of her cock fully within me, stretching me, and I couldn't help but bear down on that.

"Oh…" It was a soft and beautiful sound in my ear as once again she rested her body on mine and wrapped her arms around me. "This… feels *really* good."

"It does—*you* do," I told her, reveling in the way we moved together, the profound sense of satiety at the complete body contact. Even my skin felt full.

It wasn't at all the same as other ways we'd shared love, but ultimately it wasn't very different, either, and it was more than really good, the effort and strain of muscles that shifted under my hands, the glaze of her belly as her breasts grazed against me, and the clear, clear knowledge—beyond the hurts, the loss, the past—that I loved her, I really, truly loved Fran, my Frankie, for herself. It blazed through me, a heat that moved into my chest as she took my mouth with hers again, and I knew, I *knew*, she felt it too.

Soon. It was too soon to end the sheer beauty of our embrace as my body tensed below hers and Fran herself was a sexy, sweet encouragement, in my ear with every hitch of her breath and the low song in her throat, the taste of her tongue on mine, the deliberate drive of her dick deep inside me, the heavy wet thrust. Her hands...her hands touched me everywhere with a love and longing that made me ache with her desire.

"Don't stop," I begged her, speaking to the moment between us, what she was doing, to the pure clarity of how completely she loved me. It made me desperate to be even closer to her, to reach through until her very heart touched mine through the skin that slicked over hot, working muscles, the breasts that now pressed firmly against mine with the sublime ache of coalescence as we held each other in the ultimate connect, through the air and the Aethyr.

I gripped and slid my hands along her back, to her waist, her gorgeous ass, wrapping my fingers around the leather that fit so snugly against her, then unable to stop running my fingers through the beautiful hot wet that lay beneath it.

"Baby...please...don't stop."

"I won't." She caught my face in her hands and as she stared into my eyes, I saw the glint of tears in hers. "Sweetheart, I promise—I won't."

There was so much she meant in that, so much she was telling me, the rapport between us once again perfect, the sending of emotion and intent so clear that I let my body speak the words I couldn't say any other way as I thrust my fingers into the open softness of her cunt and I came, wrapped around the lion that roared in my heart.

And still, that wasn't enough for her as she covered me with kisses stained with sweat and tears, a burning trail until she had me in her mouth, and I understood, I so very much understood her need to do that, to touch and taste the place her cock had been, because I had done that, had needed it too. But I also understood something else: I might not speak my pain, but she wouldn't voice her desire—and what she wanted, what she *really* wanted was so very easy for me to give.

"Frankie…" I spoke past the eloquent way she sucked on my renewed hard-on, dipped her tongue inside me with a precision that was about to make speech or even thought impossible as I stroked my fingers through her hair. "Baby, come here," I asked and held my hands out to her.

She raised her eyes, then folded her fingers around mine, and once more she covered me with her body, her cock dancing between us.

"I'm sorry," she said softly. "Do you—"

"Shh." I hushed her with a kiss, explored her mouth with my tongue. I let my hands, let my body guide her until I was where I knew she wanted me, and she had what she needed.

"I'm gonna come, baby…" Her voice was a hot breath behind my ear that flowed down my neck, her arm wrapped tight around my waist as she jerked me off, the hard muscles of her belly working smooth along my spine as her fingers clutched through mine.

"Oh yeah," I groaned out, "come just like this, just like this inside me." She felt so fucking good, and she felt so fucking right and I could feel how good she felt for herself, in herself, in me, and then there was no room for words, no room for air, no room for anything but Fran, my Frankie, beautiful and beloved, filling me exquisitely while her fingers were frantic on my clit, and over and under was the beat, always the beat, of my heart, of her heart through me as she came taking me with her, to her, her lips so wondrously soft on the nape of my neck, her body a beautiful warm weight on my back until we rested, amazed, sated, overwhelmed by the exchange.

We lay awake for what seemed like hours afterward, reassuring each other of the naked power in touch, of the very real enjoyment of our bodies as they were, and we finally slept to the whisper touch of kisses and the incredible clutch upon the flutter of fingers within which in the end we both preferred.

So with that on my mind and her kiss still fresh on my lips, the flame that flared before my eyes surprised me as a voice I recognized said, "You're the prettiest boy I've seen in a while." And as I recovered and accepted the light for my cig, I looked up into Kenny's eyes.

"Kenny, it's me," I told him and laughed at the searching look he gave me before he righted himself and grinned.

"Bloody hell, mate," he chuckled, then clapped my arm, "you look *just* like my kind of boy, and if we weren't in a band together, I'd definitely do you anyway." He grinned broadly. "Unless of course, that doesn't trouble you?"

"And what *exactly* is it that shouldn't trouble her?" Fran asked as she stepped up with a pint for me and one for herself. She smiled sweetly at Kenny, but her tone was exactly like Elizabeth's: silk over steel.

I took the mug from her and she casually draped her now-free hand across my shoulder.

"Nothing at all," Kenny answered hastily.

It didn't require any extra sense of anything, or even the connection between us, to know that Fran had not only heard the earlier exchange, but was less than pleased about it.

"I'm not sleeping with you, Kenny," I told him very deliberately and I smiled at him as I eased my arm around Fran's waist to reassure her. I slipped my fingers beneath her waistband, scrunching her tee out of the way a bit so I could smooth them against her satiny skin.

"Right-o. No touchy, then," Kenny agreed and saluted us both with his drink. "But still, you'll make a boy turn his head, that's for sure. Oh hey, Hannah and Graham will be here in," he peered at his watch through the ambient flicker, "about fifteen minutes. And what're you doing out and about anyway? Isn't this a school night for you or something like that?"

Fran took a sip from her mug, then snuggled closer and brushed her lips against my ear before leaning against me.

"Night off," I answered shortly, because suddenly the skin on the back of my neck prickled, sending a cold shiver through me that I covered by shifting my stance along the column, but then two things happened that took those thoughts out of my head.

"Wotcher," Graham greeted with a grin that turned into a wide smile as he caught sight of Fran's head on my shoulder.

"Hey." I couldn't help smiling back; I was the one with Fran, after all.

"Hi," she said and I could hear her smile as I felt her slide her thumb into my waistband.

"Can't *believe* you're out tonight—great band's coming on!" he said enthusiastically.

"Yeah?" I may have sounded a bit more distracted than I'd meant to because Fran was skimming her fingers—a light little stroke that fit exactly to the circumference in my back pocket—teasing against the denim in the same way she would before she entered me, and it sent bolts of arousal flaring through me. I kissed her temple, let my fingers slide over the ridge of her hip, and pulled her that much closer to me, pressing and massaging against the warm skin, an unconscious imitation of how I'd move within her, until I suddenly realized what I was doing. I didn't stop, though.

"Absolutely smashing—they're playing under a different name, of course, trying out new stuff, and"—he turned as a hand grabbed his arm and resolved into Hannah's face above his shoulder through the flicker—"perfect timing!"

"Of course—I'm a drummer," she teased, before she saw me. "Ann, is that you or your brother?"

I laughed. "It's me—and I'm my brother," I joked.

"Looks fantastic," she said and Fran's grip shifted slightly as Hannah's gaze seemed to almost automatically travel down past my waist. But in the next moment all was forgotten, because the lights went out for half a second and the most amazing sound flew through the air before the stage lit up.

Graham, I decided, knew a lot about dicks, but less about music. If this was the new "dark-wave" stuff he'd decried weeks and weeks ago, then he didn't know what he was talking about. Then again, he *had* said this was a fantastic band—maybe this was the exception to his rule, because Floorshow played the most amazing music I'd ever heard—and if it was dark, it spoke to me, and when it moved, it was with a sensual thrum that needed no translation. For the first time in my *life*, I was completely transported by the live performance of music, and I got it, I really got it. That was the music I wanted to play, to write, to breathe, to *be* to, and I listened and stared, rapt, lost in rhythm and melody, carried by the muscular pulse of the bass as they played.

When Fran wasn't next to me, people kept grabbing my rear end. Correction—men kept grabbing my rear. One particular guy I'd bumped into, or more accurately, was bumped into by on the way back from the bathroom was a bit more aggressive with his come-on.

"Nice ankh," he said after he'd jostled me. He pointed at the charm that hung over my shirt with his glass.

I gave him a quick glance. He was pretty enough, several inches taller than me, with dark hair swept to one side and curving to his jaw, dark, dark eyes under full lashes that made his face look delicate. He wore the requisite black long-sleeve tee that hugged his frame and the single hoop earring that so many favored. *Kenny's sort*, I thought as I gave him a brief nod in acknowledgment.

I turned to make my way through the press back to the group and he followed me through the crowd.

"You're pretty, I'm pretty—let's cut the bullshit and get out of here," he said almost in my ear.

Startled he'd gotten so close so quickly, I almost stopped, but didn't. "You're not my type," I told him and kept walking. I considered opening my awareness a bit, but decided against it. If I could see "them," they could see me, and that...that's what I was trying to avoid. In the meantime though, there everyone was, exactly where I'd left them.

"Oh, what, you're straight? So we'll get a girl too, if you want—I can do that, it'd be pretty hot."

Later I'd realize that he, like Kenny, had thought I was a guy and I'd be happy about it for several reasons, not the least of which was that it meant my idea worked, but this had to stop and I turned to tell him exactly what he could do with his suggestion.

"Paolo—you made it!"

The smirk he surveyed me with changed to a friendly smile as we both looked over my shoulder. "Hannah."

She stepped next to me and reached out to shake his hand. "I see you've met our bassist," she said with a smile. "Since Graham's sure he's taking that singing gig with the Waves or whatever, Paolo will audition with us next Sunday," she told me.

Well, that was certainly news, but I'd been schooled well enough not to let my surprise show. *Good for Graham*, I thought as Hannah officially introduced us. He'd said all along that was what he preferred; I was glad he'd gotten what he wanted.

"Ah," Paolo said after the ritual exchange of names, "my apologies. I know band rules quite well." He smiled as he shook my hand and was pleasant enough for the rest of the night.

I got nothing from him, not a read, not a pulse, just the faint flicker of energy that surrounded every human being; he was completely closed to me, not even the attraction or whatever it was he'd professed evident. I dismissed it as my being too closed, too guarded to get the usual read that the brief contact could have given me. But I should have known then not to trust him.

"That's right," Kenny said as he shook his hand next, "Ms. Anarchy here follows the no-touchy tradition."

Paolo raised an eyebrow at the "Ms." part and gave me a searching glance that I returned with a blank stare.

Someone told me, and I don't remember if it was Paolo himself or Hannah, that he'd played guitar semiprofessionally for the last six years and that he was the son of the Brazilian ambassador to France, or his cultural attaché, or something like that.

It meant nothing to me. If he played well, great, if he didn't…there were plenty of guitar players around, I was certain. Meanwhile, the music was too good, the dancing lively, and the combination blanketed out quite a bit of any other sense. Here and there, I'd catch the trace of hounds, the circling search, the occasional flash of triumph as they found potentials to play with. But there were also moments, the random send that I'd catch, not from Fran herself but nearby, the very edge of a dark cloud that would surround her. But when she'd catch my eye, she'd throw me an amazing smile, and it would all disappear.

When it really was way too late and time to leave, I finally managed to realize that Fran had perhaps had a bit more to drink than I had. That was her prerogative—she wasn't under the same restrictions I was, or so I assumed.

"I think…you're driving," she said with a smile after we said our various good-byes and I retrieved our things from the coat check.

"Am I, now?" I drawled at her, and drawn by the bright sparkle in her eyes, the slight flush to her cheeks, I leaned over and kissed her. God, I loved kissing her, and I learned a few things in the embrace of her lips. The first was that any natural barrier she'd had seemed gone, her feelings were on the surface and perfectly readable, and I understood exactly why I'd been asked not to get drunk: Fran was wide open and vulnerable.

The other thing I learned was not only that she loved me, I knew that already, but that she held images of us, a future she was thinking about and—there, I saw it, the dark cloud edge and it reached over her and toward me.

That caught me cold. I hadn't even come close to being recognized, and I was rather certain I'd left no aethyric trace, but my energy, the unique signature that marked me as an individual was bound to and threaded through Fran's—and if she'd been read, it was inevitable that I'd been sensed as well. And once I was found—and I had some idea what kind of damage it might do to Fran to accomplish that—it was a direct line through me to Cort, to Elizabeth, to the yet-unknown others that were the Circle. It would take less than the half second of realization before whoever was doing the sending actually found me.

Not wanting to startle or scare her, I gently ended our kiss. It took no effort on my part to break the connecting reach, to bolster her barrier with mine, and it was the work of less than another five seconds to seek the source.

About fifteen feet away, a knot of about a dozen or so people tramped up the stairs, Kenny and Paolo within it. Somewhere in that crowd was an adept hound.

I didn't have time to search further—I wanted Fran safely out of there—and besides, I'd caught a unique signature. I'd find whoever it was on the Astral and deal with it there.

As we rode home, Fran's arms snugly around my waist and her head on my back with a warmth that reached through my coat and made me feel equally warm within, a sinking feeling filled me anyway. I knew I had made a huge mistake: I'd let myself forget this had to end.

❖

The chill of the ride home had driven whatever effects the few beers Fran had had from her system, and once inside, upstairs and in our room, we went slowly, prolonging the exploration and the dance, to love with a tenderness that made me want to weep because I knew what we shared was rare and precious, and too soon it would be gone.

She was still so amazingly wide open to me, her love for me so clearly distinct from her love for Nina, a difference she laid bare before me as she let me see myself through her eyes. And I let her do the same, to see for herself what I saw, what I felt.

I held her in my arms so she could sleep with her head pillowed under my chin and it hit me so hard it made my head reel: of course I couldn't love Fran "that way," how could I? They were different people. I loved Fran *her* way, the way I was supposed to, distinctly and completely. She was my Frankie.

That shook me, shook me in so many ways. There was no one I could name that I loved who wasn't gone. I cared, so very deeply cared, for Cort, for Elizabeth, but I hadn't—I *couldn't*—allow myself the luxury of more than that. I had more than allowed that here. I had done the thing I'd promised myself I wouldn't do after my father had died; I had allowed grief to open the door for familiarity and comfort, and then not only permitted, but encouraged and welcomed it to become so much, so very much more. And now, having allowed it, I couldn't pretend it wasn't what it was, or deny what I felt, even if I couldn't ever actually *tell* her.

I had been completely selfish in allowing it to happen—and at what cost? I wasn't concerned that I could be read and tracked through Fran; I could take care of myself. What scared me all over again was that in using her to reach me—and that in and of itself *infuriated* me almost past the point of rationality—she could be, she *would* be hurt, and not in mere physical ways either. She'd be hunted on the Astral, haunted by dreams, her mind clouded, her heart used against her, to her own pain, to her own regret, and she didn't deserve that, my golden champion didn't deserve that.

Some of my thoughts and feelings undoubtedly translated to her as I held her even closer.

"Love you, Sammer," she whispered and kissed the skin that lay beneath her lips, over my heart, and she tightened her hold a moment before falling peacefully back to sleep.

"I love you too," I whispered into the waves and curls of the wheaten gold of her hair and kissed the top of her head. "God, Frankie, I love you so much—I just can't keep you."

I allowed myself a small scatter of tears before I swallowed them down. It was an indulgence I couldn't afford: I had plans to make, things to learn, and little time to do it. First things first. I had to speak with my uncle in the morning—there were other things that had been left in storage back in the States, including my father's footlocker; I wanted it. And I wanted to finally learn how and why my father had been killed, because I had more than the niggling suspicion it would hold clues for me.

I would spend however many hours or days it took to track that hound—fuck my work with Elizabeth for the day, this was more important. I wondered for half a moment if this was a test like so many other things had been, then decided it didn't matter—I knew what I had to do.

I'd been very well trained, and while I might not have my full strength yet, I knew what to do and I knew I could do it. Oh, it wouldn't be a full-on hunt, just a small one, small enough for me to find the hound, then trace it back to the Material. I was still furious over the attempted breach of Fran, and until that cooled or until matters warranted it, I would do nothing else. But I wanted a good look at the enemy because as above, so below, and if things had moved on this level, something else had already progressed even further on another. I knew enough to know that something major was headed my way; I needed to know where it would come from. And as for Fran, well, I'd talk with Elizabeth. I needed to know more about what she could and couldn't do, then create both the shields and the distance that needed to be there, to keep her safe, or at least, as safe as I could.

I *hated* that, hated to think about it, hated knowing I had to do it, hated even more the hurt I would cause her and I felt something inside me tear and break just imagining it.

For a moment, I wondered if there was a choice, if perhaps I could share any of this with Fran, discuss it with her, but as her breath warmed my chest, I remembered how determined she had been when she'd been asked if she was ready, the fire in her eyes when she said she'd do whatever it took. It was the same fire that burned from her heart through her eyes when she looked at me, blazed from her when we touched…God, she loved me, and I knew just how much she loved me, but I loved her too, and I'd already risked her enough. Fran might be willing to go with me to hell, but there was no way in this world or any other that I would lead her there. There was no other choice.

This time, I did weep.

SCION

also ci·on:
A detached shoot or twig containing buds from a woody plant, used in grafting.
A descendant or heir.

"I'd like to know more about Fran's training," I announced casually at breakfast. "Last night a hound tried to track me through her—why hasn't she been taught to block that?" I asked point blank as I reached for the salt.

"And I think it's time I know whatever it is you haven't told me about my Da," I told my uncle, who gazed at me somberly. "That, and I want his footlocker sent here. Can we make that happen today?"

Fran stared in shock, Elizabeth in surprise, and my uncle nodded at me.

"We can do all of that."

"Good." I picked up my tea. "And I'm sorry," I said to Elizabeth and to Fran, "you'll have to excuse me from our plans today—there's something I need to do." I glanced over at my uncle. "Would you monitor?"

This time, he seemed surprised. "What do you want to do?"

I put my cup down and pushed my chair back. I took a moment to think about what I wanted to say as I stood. I said what I thought, I said what I felt. "I want to find the son of a bitch from last night, and I want to know what Old Jones has to do with my father."

❖

"This is *your* hunt," Cort told me once we were in the study. "Handle it however you want."

I nodded. There were any number of ways this could go wrong, from sheer ineptness on my part and failing to make even the slightest of transitions, to bringing something unpleasant back with me that didn't belong here, or even creating a massive backflow of energy, of power, that would rebound through me and overload not only my own system, but that of every "sensitive" in the vicinity, blowing open gates that should remain closed. Not to mention the literal headaches.

I could accept that, the responsibility for it. I was absolutely certain of my ability to do this and to do it well, and before I did anything else, for the first time, I pulled off my shirt, then reached for the robe that was presented to me. I'd do this the way I was meant to: sky-clad.

❖

The first part was easy: I drew in energy from the earth, from the air, from the surrounding Aethyr and created the white light simulacrum. The next part wasn't hard either, to travel through the Aethyr, find the track and print of the night before, to once more seek and see the dark signature that had reached out for Fran and to grab hold of it.

The trick was to maintain the hold, then transfer it with me to the nexus of the Astral. At first, it was a bit of fog, like gray cotton-candy in my hand, and as we moved through Aethyr to Astral, to the higher level only those invited, brought directly, or trained could reach, it thickened, grew heavy, oily and sticky, like an ugly black putty or the tar that was used to repair cracks in the street, and it fought and twisted in my hands, unable to stand my grip, the pure energy of the Light I carried, as we rapidly approached the Mid-Astral proper.

I had only a moment to see what it had resolved into when we arrived, before it tore from my grasp and the simulacrum ran, a frantic, beetlelike scuttle of skeletal legs and arms, while its oily cape billowed behind it.

What a waste of energy, the creation of the aethyric double that was meant to frighten, to intimidate, I thought. I could feel the smile that crossed my face echo on the body that lay inert on the Material as the sheer joy of the hunt sluiced through me, and I flew forward in pursuit.

I was gaining as we ran across the terrain and not twenty yards ahead of us winked a small hole in the ground, a burrow my quarry aimed for. I lunged, reaching for and rewarded with a good hold of the black, viscous cloak, which writhed around my fist, a cold and slimy feel, and together, we fell through.

We tumbled through dirt and water and clouds, a collage of energy and elements until we came to a halt and I maintained a firm grip as I looked around.

We were in the Material, but not exactly. I stared around as I realized we were in the Aethyr itself, the literal energy double of the world we inhabited, and we were in London, not far from St. Katharine dockyards.

"Who do you answer to?" I asked the hound I held in my hands, and as he opened his mouth to speak, a look of horror crossed his face as he choked and clutched frantically at his stomach. The robe was rapidly dissolving and I looked down as he did. There, dangling from his navel like live wire, was the torn end of the lifeline that had kept his soul tethered to his body. And as his now-human eyes met mine, we both knew what had happened: he'd been murdered in the Material to prevent him from speaking to me here.

He mewled in terror and clawed at the robe that was the waste of the resources he had left, shrinking and changing before my astonished eyes until a vaguely human figure, round and childlike, perhaps six inches tall, stood, cowering and crying before me.

"I won't hurt you," I promised and it shook in fear as I reached for it.

It trembled as I caressed its small round head and I caught it up in my hand.

No longer tied to a body, it couldn't speak in words, in language, but it could send pure thought and emotion and it clearly broadcast its remorse and regret.

"I'll bring you to the River, and you can start again."

A burst of pure joy, followed by doubt.

"Yes, you can, you really can—would you like that?"

Another burst of joy mixed with gratitude waved forth as it threw itself on my neck. I turned once and was instantly back where I needed to be, the Mid-Astral, and it rode my shoulder as we approached the glowing banks of the River.

A shadow of fear crossed its little body and I understood. "No," I said, "your Master can't follow you now." I carefully set the body of light on the grass of the bank.

It took one hesitant step, then another, and another, glowing brighter and brighter until it leapt with pure joy and glee into the opalescent glow. It took a moment to look back and wave at me as the current carried it past a curve in the bank *and out of sight.*

❖

I slapped my hand hard on the wood beyond the rug I lay on, before I even opened my eyes, to ground out what energy I could.

"We have a problem," I announced to the serious brown eyes that greeted me as I sat up and Cort put the food and drink that would help shut the channels into my shaking hands.

He covered me against the chill and after I sipped and swallowed what was now tasteless in my mouth, I was able to speak. "This one's a killer." I told him everything I'd seen, and his face grew grim.

"Can you wait here a few moments?" he asked me.

"I'm not in a hurry to move," I said and gave him a small grin. I was still a bit shaky and unsteady from the work, and I wanted at least a second or two for myself to reflect on what I'd seen and what had happened.

"I'll be back," he said as he strode to the door. "Shall I send Fran up?"

"Yes, please," I answered as I picked at the nuts and raisins in the bowl I held. I had been shocked by the callous murder I'd witnessed, disembodied, to be certain, but murder nonetheless. I wondered which of the many crimes reported on the news and in the papers it would be, or if it would go unnoticed.

And after…what had happened after, I had known what it was, the little soul that stood before me, had known what to do, as if I'd done it a thousand times before, would do it a thousand times again. How…*why* did I know that?

It had happened despite the fury of hunt that had ridden me. Faced with that living Light, my anger had disappeared, to be replaced instead with an overwhelming… What was it I had felt, anyway? Care? Not a strong enough word. Compassion wasn't exactly right either. I glanced up to see Fran enter the room and as her eyes met mine, I knew what it was. Love. I had felt love for that creature that in the Material had tried to do such damage, had hurt and willfully hurt others out of fear, out of pain.

So small, so young in the Universe, and I had seen it in its pure essence, brought it by its own choice back to the Light, to begin again.

I couldn't control the shudder that ran through me as I pondered what it meant.

"God, Sam—you're freezing!" Fran said as she knelt next to me and vigorously rubbed my shoulders. I was unresisting and let her wrap around me until my head rested against her collar.

"Are you all right?" she asked as she stroked her fingers through the hair that feathered against my ear.

"I'm fine," I said, then kissed the hollow of her throat and sat up straight to gaze into her face. Her eyes reflected the concern that waved off her.

"Did you have lunch yet?" I asked, not ready at the moment to discuss anything.

"It's almost dinnertime," she said softly, "you've been here all day."

I had known it would take some time, I just hadn't known how much, and that explained the cold and the stiffness I felt in my limbs. I stood and stretched until I felt my back loosen.

"I think they might actually be arguing," Fran said and passed me my tea from her perch on the floor.

"Who?"

"Cort and Elizabeth—no one's yelling or anything like that, but…" She shrugged, then stood herself and handed me the rest of my clothes.

She was right. I let my senses extend and felt not anger but fear and frustration roil through the household.

What was between Fran and me could wait. This had to be taken care of *now* and I took her hand in mine to go downstairs, but we heard their discussion in the hallway as they approached.

"She's mastered movement through the Aethyr and the levels of Astral on her own. You're certain?" Elizabeth's voice said.

"Yes."

"Guide for the willing return to the River—you didn't teach her that?"

"No."

"Then she's more than Wielder."

"More *what* than Wielder?" I asked. Fran's fingers were warm and steady in mine as Cort and Elizabeth stepped into the room. They'd each brought a tray.

They stared at us in apparent surprise.

Given the look they shared, it wasn't difficult to guess what they were thinking.

"I'm not avatar."

"How do you know?" Elizabeth asked as Cort set a tray down on the desk, then took hers, placing it next to the first.

I shook my head. "I'm not. We're all..." I cast about for the right words. "We're all a part of that, all of the same Light, and if I was avatar, I think...I'm certain I'd know it. I'd think differently, see and feel things differently."

They all looked at me curiously and I shook my head in an attempt to clarify my thoughts. "Every avatar I've learned about—they've each had a sense of mission, of message. Most of them seem to have been born with it—even if they didn't know what they'd do or who they were while on the Material."

That, I realized, was it, the real difference. Avatars incarnated knowing they had a mission and it was the guiding force in their lives, whether they recognized their true self or not. Me though, I'd had no such self-knowledge of my role in life—I'd been born into it and stumbled upon it, unknowing.

Elizabeth smiled at me. "Well, you might not know if you were, but you do know that you're not—and at this point, we have to decide what to do. Right now, you need something a bit more substantial than that," she said, nodding at the bowl I'd left on the table, "so tonight, we'll eat up here."

The covered bowls and plates revealed a simple but hearty meal: a thick potato soup, with no sprigs of green on top because I hated the superfluity of garnishes (which Elizabeth took a moment to tease me about), several steaks (Cort promised me the "raw" one was mine), and string beans, which, as far as vegetables went, were the most innocuous so far as I was concerned, which meant I'd actually eat them.

"Please eat," Elizabeth requested, "and then let's discuss this."

Cort built a fire, and it wasn't until after we had finished dinner and the plates had been cleared, when I was comfortable on the sofa with Fran curled at my side and a blanket over both of us because I was still a bit chilled, even with the merry sound of crackling in the grate and the occasional pop of wood, that I felt functionally human again, or that anyone spoke.

My uncle went first. "You've so much yet to learn, but your abilities outstrip my training. In fact, you've gone out of the sphere I'd normally teach within. We still don't really know," and he began to tick off the points on his hand, "what your natural gifts will be once you've been sealed, or what your blind spots will be. We know the threat to you is physical, but I suspect…" And he glanced over to the fire.

For a moment, I saw the salamanders dance in the flames, an urgent jump as they tried to convey a message, or merely a greeting, before the world righted itself again.

Once it did, his eyes were steady on mine, the same flame within them. "This one is very close, and will not stop, even after, *especially* after, you've been sealed to the Circle. That he…eliminated one of his own adepts proves it."

I knew that. I knew that, had expected it, and even as the quick rise in Fran's heartbeat was as audible to me as the quick catch of her breath she tried to quiet, part of me relished the challenge.

"Ann, you've changed all the rules," Elizabeth said into the silence that greeted the last statement.

"How?" That puzzled me. I'd been certain I'd been almost rigid in my adherence.

She smiled at me again. "We didn't know what would happen— how you'd face your training, your testing. You've done things no one has done before—you've managed to change the whole game, and you didn't even know you were playing."

I stared, fully confused.

"Your abilities, your senses—they're still somewhat intermittent, are they not?"

"Yes, sometimes," I answered.

"We call that being head blind, or mind blind. And when you have been stripped, as it were, blinded, you were tested—you've had to make decisions. What were they based on? What you wanted, or what was needed?"

I thought about the times I'd found myself trapped in my skin, forced to act based solely on the information the usual five senses gave me.

"Always what's needed," Fran said and put an arm around my waist.

I gave her a grateful smile and wrapped my arm around her shoulder. "I try."

"When faced with your first real threat, there would have been no wrong, none, in taking you to a safer place, yet you chose to stay—and then? And then you teach yourself how to change your own projection."

Elizabeth got up and poured a cup of tea, then offered me one, but I declined, fine as I was for the moment. It was bizarre, because she spoke as casually as if this were one of our normal discussions about history or literature. Perhaps we'd discuss Blake, or Joyce, or Hemingway in a few moments.

"Now, you've faced several of the deeper trials, passed those tests, and on your hunt, your *first* solo hunt—no small milestone—you decide to track using the Aethyr, and then? You're not only successful, you moved through at least three different levels of the Astral, all while attached to another. Do you have any *idea* of how..." She paused to shake her head, and her eyes were lambent as they gazed at me.

"Of all the things you could have done, from pursuing your curiosity to your own revenge, you instead gave someone something precious. You gave them back their free will."

At that moment, the doorbell rang and Cort stood. "Anyone expecting anything?" he asked. "No?" he said to our negative expressions. "Back in a moment, then." His footsteps echoed across the floor, then faded down the steps to the door.

"I owe you an apology," Fran said softly as she stirred next to me, and I twisted my head around to see her clearly. "I haven't told you much of anything that I've been doing."

"At my request," Elizabeth clarified as she drew her seat closer, "at my very specific request. It was necessary at the time—it would have distracted you." Her eyes still flickered with their own flame in the firelight as she neared.

Touch was a rare thing in this household. At first, I'd assumed it to be the normal formality that existed between people forced together who were still more strangers than friends, but as the weeks had flown by and my own knowledge had grown, I'd come to realize this was not the only reason for the physical distance.

There was no one in this group that was not a sensitive of some sort, and touch, the bare of skin on skin, could forge an instant connect, not merely the recognition of general mood or condition, but of mind-view, a peek into the inner thoughts and feelings. It was brief, certainly, but it was also intrusive and potentially uncomfortable unless one's barriers were perfect or the sense of the person's self was so familiar as to be comfortable, a normal part of the background noise, so to speak.

That Fran and I could sustain such continued contact was due to many things: we'd been teammates and friends for years, were linked because of the contact we'd shared when we'd dated, and now we were bound to each other because we were lovers, though that in and of itself made our rapport almost constant, to the point where we were almost extensions of each other.

So when Elizabeth briefly skimmed her fingers across the back of my hand as it lay resting on the arm of the settee, I was happily surprised by the level of affection it meant she held for me, that she *let* me see, and for a moment, I *remembered* her. I had a very clear image of her face reflected above mine in a mirror as her hands gently parted then plaited my hair…and then the image blanked.

And while I already knew she and Fran had a special bond by virtue of the learning they shared, I was stunned but pleased to discover the deeper, nurturing aspect of it: Elizabeth cared for Fran as if she'd been born to her. Perhaps, in another life, she had been.

"Francesca…is adept," Elizabeth said softly. "She is very easily made priestess, High Priestess."

"What do you mean?" I knew, of course, that there were different religions, pantheons, schools of theory and of belief, and each of them had their representations, their godheads. Some were historical figures, real, "living" incarnations of an archetype that had its root in the beginnings of the Universe, some of them were actually highly evolved and advanced beings, and a few, like the Elemental Lords, were the existence, the ultimate manifestation of a principal force, but most of them were constructs, the projections created from the combined energies of worshippers—and I adhered to none of them. However, it didn't surprise me that Fran might or that Elizabeth had trained her in a specific Rite. Fran had told me about the "green ray"—and being a priestess, or, more specifically, High Priestess, was something unique within that school of thought.

Fran, with her essential…I didn't know what to call it, couldn't quite name it, but it was something akin to buoyancy, an unshakeable part of her core makeup. It was that part of her, I was certain, that responded so well to that philosophy. I had no doubt that it was her innate talent that made her adept, and the combination of her own personality, ethics, and intelligence that enabled her to advance, take on a larger role.

"It means…" Fran said in a low and throaty drawl, and she gently caught my chin in her hand and turned my face to hers. I couldn't help the skip in the beat of my heart when I read her expression, caught the shape of her deeper desire. "It means that before you can have your sealing, you have to go through mine."

I struggled to understand even as she kissed me, and I glimpsed a very clear image of part of the role I would play. This was not what I thought would happen; this would wreak havoc on my plans, on the path I had intended to take.

"There are some decisions that are not yours alone," Fran murmured against my lips.

"But Fran," I tried to explain, "you've already been threatened twice and approached—*attacked*—once. This hasn't even started yet, and it's only going to get worse. You heard what Cort said—it's *not* going to stop."

Fran leaned back, her eyes blazing, body radiating heat. "Do you really think I don't *know* that? Do you really think I'd let you go through that—alone?" She gestured vehemently. "You've lost your mind if you—"

I caught her hands in mine and spoke over her. "I don't want you to get *hurt*—or worse. I couldn't—I didn't—do anything for Nina, and she's gone." I didn't know I was going to say that and it hurt, oh God it hurt, a churning lump of aching sorrow and anger that I thought I'd forgotten. I was wrong. I felt worse than ever, and it was because I now knew what it was I felt. Guilt. I felt guilty. I should have done something, *anything*, differently than I had. "Let me do what I can," I said quietly. "This I can at least do something about."

Fran stared at me, eyes wide. "What in the *world* could you have possibly had to do with that? Sam, you don't *know* what happened. All either one of us knows is what her father told us."

It was my turn to stare as I realized Fran didn't know, had no idea about the conflict that had existed between our friend and her parents, the very real physical threat she had dealt with at least once at their hands and survived.

I don't know why I had assumed Fran had known; thought she'd have been told. How much should I tell her? It wasn't my story, it was Nina's, but if she was gone, then shouldn't someone besides me know it? That story was a part of who I was now, of who Fran was, whether she knew it or not and Fran...had loved her, still loved her too. And like it or not, for better or worse, Nina was also a part of how Fran and I loved each other.

"I know enough," I said finally, "I know that..." We spoke as if we were alone, as if Elizabeth wasn't there, and I started by holding Fran in my arms. I told her what I finally realized Nina hadn't wanted to tell *anyone*—not even me—but had been forced to by circumstance at the time. I told Fran what I could.

"...and you think her parents or—or she herself...?" Her voice choked with the shock that so clearly suffused her, and though she couldn't complete the sentence, I could complete her thought.

"Yes," I said finally, the word spitting through my teeth, "and I still can't tell which one I think is worse."

"Oh, Sammer," she whispered, her head tucked tightly against mine. I could feel her heart break within her, the equal echo of mine, the not-so-old hurt doubly renewed with the fresh cut of new knowledge, and I tore again, knowing I'd hurt her. "I wish I'd known—maybe we could have done *something*. My dad, I mean, maybe he—but it's not your fault—I swear it's not."

I couldn't help but laugh at the irony of what she said. "You just found out," I said, raising my head from her shoulder and wiping my eyes, "just now, and even *you* think something could have been done."

I touched her face gently, and my thumb wiped away tears that still streamed hot and wild from her eyes. "Frankie...I can barely live with that, I wouldn't, if I didn't have to. Do you think, even if you know what you're doing—even if you accept responsibility for it—that I can live sanely with something happening to you? Especially if it's something I can prevent in *any* way?"

She caught my fingers against her cheek, then turned her head to gently kiss my palm. "I hear you, Sammy, I really do. But this doesn't have to happen now. Can we talk about this again after we both know more about what happens next for you?"

"I recommend that," Elizabeth broke in, startling us both out of the little private world we'd just been in.

"By courier, today, as you asked," Cort said, having just entered the room. He carried something large in his arms and I stared as he set it down before the hearth.

The skin on my scalp went numb as I recognized it: the footlocker. My Da's footlocker. I got up on frozen feet to open it.

I hadn't seen it, set eyes on it, since it had been sent to me from his station right after the funeral a few years before. I couldn't bear to see it, to even begin to look within it, but I wasn't going to get rid of it either—it was my Da's, and I'd had it left in storage with other things.

But it was time, more than time, and I needed to find out if my Da had left me something besides the mixed blessing that was the blood I carried.

"Shall we leave you to it?" Elizabeth asked as I knelt before the first puzzle: a tubular combination lock that held the brass clasp firmly shut. She briefly laid a warm hand on my shoulder, a firm gesture of support, a lending of strength and affection I was grateful for.

"I'll be in the workroom back of the shop, if you need me," Cort said.

I didn't even look up as I nodded and once more heard the tread of his retreating step as Fran knelt next to me and I faced her.

Lit by the fire that still burned happily away, her eyes carried the same flicker and I was struck sharply by how beautiful she was, by how much I wanted to forget the tasks that lay before me, forget everything to touch the delicate curves and planes of her face, to taste the honey-sweet soft of her mouth, the feel of her body yielding to mine, and for a brief instant, I did. I reached for her, folded her to me, let myself feel the beat of her heart against mine.

"I'll wait for you," she said quietly into my ear before we

disentangled ourselves. She paused to give me a smile before she left the room, to leave me to my discoveries in the half-light.

The lock shimmered before me and I hesitated. My father, my Da, had been the last person to open and close it, and in my mind's eye I could see his hands setting the clasp, then setting the bar through, giving the tumblers a final twist to scramble them before letting it loose to bounce back against the hasp. How could I disturb what his hands had wrought, who knew how long before he'd been taken from me?

Then again, whatever was in there was mine, was what I had left of him and maybe, just maybe, would provide me some insight into who I was and what I was doing.

I inhaled slowly before I took the lock into my hand, half expecting it to move, or be warm, or perhaps shock me in some way. Instead, the brass was cool, and I received a very clear image, hands firmly set upon the trunk, and a sense of finality, of resignation, before the tumblers were spun for the last time.

What would he have set as the combination? The two most important things in his life, or so I'd been told, had been me and my mother, and I smiled as I remembered how he'd joked more than once as I'd gotten older that they ordered me the moment they'd gotten married, they'd wanted me so much.

I'd never doubted the love, but now I wondered how much of what I'd thought was a joke had been true. I did a quick calculation; my birthday marked the beginning of the last week of July. Maybe...

I dialed in the numbers that signified my parents' anniversary, a day of delight for many American children. First the ten, then the thirty-one, then finally the last two numbers of the year before my birth. I tugged the lock. Nothing. Damn.

No, I was doing this wrong. Perhaps...I reversed the order. Thirty one first, then ten, then the next—there was an audible click as the last number fell into place, the lock popped open in my hand, and I knew my father had told me a partial truth: I hadn't been ordered, but I'd been planned.

I let out the breath I hadn't realized I'd been holding and took another as I laid my hand on the latch. This was it, the moment of decision. Forward to perhaps a dead end, or leave it forever unknown. My hands were steady as I shifted the brass, then opened the footlocker.

The first thing to greet me was the scent, the familiar coal-tar and smoke scent, and right on top of everything lay his bunker boots, neatly laid over an FDNY sweatshirt that covered most of what was beneath it.

I carefully lifted the boots out and set them on the side, then took out the sweatshirt, the slightly faded navy blue fleece with its worn patch. It was soft against my face and I let myself miss him as the scent washed through me bringing memory upon memory, things I'd thought forgotten: his laugh, his smile, the pride he couldn't hide when he came to my swim meets, first at the community club, then when I was in high school.

I missed him, I missed my *father*, his comforting solidity when I was small and snuggled into him on the sofa where we'd watch Disney movies or karate flicks on a rainy afternoon; later, sitting side by side, shoulder to shoulder, we'd sit out on the deck in back of the house and talk, about everything: school, girls, cars, and even—sometimes, not too often, but occasionally—my mother.

Enough of that, I told myself and sighed as I folded the sweatshirt then placed it behind me. Inside the trunk itself there were two well-packed and distinct piles. To the left were a few more articles of clothing, the first a T-shirt of mine that I'd outgrown at about the ripe old age of six. It still proclaimed "Fireman's Kid," and the sharp lines of the folds indicated that it was wrapped around something—in fact, it seemed like several shirts had been used in exactly that way, considering the stack that lay beneath it. I picked it up, felt the weight and solidity under my fingertips and, removing the shirt, stared. My mother, her hair loose and tossing about her, sunlight streaming over her in the park I'd played in, twirling me about by the hands and caught in the act of laughing. We had the same smile, and I traced hers with a fingertip through the glass.

I put that down too and picked up the first book on the other side. Bound in leather the color of blood, it too had a lock, a hinged flap of leather with a brass button, the sort that you push to the side and release and lock with a little key in the center. I tried to shift it with my thumb, first left, then right, and when it wouldn't budge, I put it down, frustrated. There had to be a key somewhere.

There were three more volumes like it underneath, then below them photo albums and scrapbooks, filled with old school reports and cards I'd made for him and photos my father had taken of us, of his friends from work and their families, and a few of him as well. I glanced quickly through those; many of his coworkers I'd seen last in full dress uniform, their wives in black and their children similarly dressed at my father's funeral.

I sat back on my heels. The key. Where was the key for all of these books? The very fact that they were locked convinced me more than ever there had to be something in them that could shed some light on the current situation.

Frustrated, I pulled all the albums and scrapbooks out in a heap, and as I lifted them over the edge, an envelope fell out.

Hope thrilled through me and as I unfolded the legal-sized flap that hadn't been glued shut. But it quickly dissipated when no key materialized as I unfolded the papers within.

They were documents. My parents' original marriage license—and when I read it again, I realized it was dated five years before I'd been born. Behind that was a copy of my mother's death certificate. It listed the usual information, such as her name and dates of birth and, of course, death. I read quickly through the primary cause, pulmonary embolism. I'd known, of course, what had killed her, from the initial "Mommy had something in her lungs" explanation to the fuller one I'd received when I was old enough to understand. But it was the contributing, or secondary, factor that caught my attention: spontaneous abortion.

That rocked me so hard I almost dropped the paper. I'd almost had a brother or a sister and instead, I'd lost my mother. I wondered that my father had never told me, then thought better of it. My poor Da; he'd lost his wife and a child—how could he have told me? What would he have said?

Maybe he would have told me sometime, I thought as I separated that paper from the ones behind it, then folded it back into the envelope. He'd obviously taken care to make certain it was preserved.

The slip between my fingers told me there were two more documents left. The first was my birth certificate, or a copy of it at least, a black background and white type. It contained all of the information I'd expected, female infant, 7.5 lbs, 22 inches, the time, the date, father's name, mother's name, and mine: Samantha Joan Cray.

Everything was in order and after I'd put it away with the others, I read the last. The paper was as old as the rest, printed with a coral-colored ink. *Certified Copy of an Entry of Birth*, it read in the upper left hand corner. There was a shield in the center, and *Given at the GENERAL REGISTER OFFICE* on the right.

Another birth certificate. *Also* made for Samantha Joan Cray, for the same date and year, except for the glaring differences: the hospital Saint James, not more than a quarter mile from the shop in Leeds, and the unmistakable seal in the bottom right corner, two lions rampant surrounding a shield, encircled by the words "X General Register Office X England."

My mind reeled as I placed everything—save the sweatshirt, which I put on—back into the trunk, then closed it up again. The fire was almost gone and the chill of fall was once more creeping through the room despite the hum that said the heat was on.

Answers. I'd been looking for answers, but as I went downstairs, heart full with the new information I had, hurting again for my father, I grabbed my jacket to walk outside to the shop and to Cort's workshop. I now had more questions than when I'd started.

By the time I trudged back up the stairs to my room I was numb, overloaded from the work, slammed on all sides with new information that conflicted with so much I'd thought I'd known, and gnawed at from within by questions still unanswered. Fran was already in bed, but she sat up and switched on the light by the nightstand as I opened the door.

"C'mere," she said and opened her arms to me.

I kicked off my shoes and went right to her. Her body was all sleepy warm, even under the tee she'd worn to bed, and I rubbed my face against the satin of her neck.

"Did you find what you were looking for?" she asked. Her fingers drew comforting lines against my spine.

"No." I shook my head and sat up straight. "I didn't even go through the whole thing. I found—" I shivered and Fran drew me back to her. I didn't know what to say, I didn't know what to make of the welter of questions and news that squirmed in my head.

"I found out that I have dual citizenship," I said finally, attempting to smile, "and that my parents were married longer than I'd thought."

Her eyebrows raised at the first part and stayed that way for the second as she studied my face. "And?" she prompted. "What does that mean?"

"Well, there are two very legitimate birth certificates, one from Richmond County, New York, and the other... Well, according to Uncle Cort, I was actually born in Leeds, in Saint James Hospital, and didn't actually hit American soil until I was about six weeks old."

Fran started at that. "Are you serious?"

I nodded, unable to speak because my throat tightened around the lump of grief that rose with that admission, because it brought to my mind not only the loss of my mother, but of the second loss my father hadn't shared with me. There were other losses as well—Cort told me of grandparents I'd vaguely known about, childhood events I had no memory of. I'd lived for two years, from the time of my mother's death until I was four, in the same house I'd just summered in, with Cort and Elizabeth—why didn't I remember that? And he told me my father had thought there had been hints, signs, of a gathering...darkness, for lack of a better term...that seemed to be growing, had been gaining strength for some years now. But *why*?

Fran stroked my cheek and caught the tear that had fallen. "What's this mean for you now?" I knew she was aware that there was more, but that I wasn't ready to discuss it yet, and I was warmed by both the touch and her readiness to let me speak when I would be better emotionally equipped for it.

"It means..." I said, then caught her hand with mine to kiss her fingers. "It means that I'm not the one who really changed the rules. Somehow, during the time between our move and my Da's...murder..." I almost choked on the word, the first time I'd consciously used it. "Someone found out...something."

I slammed my free hand down onto the bed. "I wish I knew what it was." I was frustrated, frustrated and torn between wanting a moment to absorb, to reflect, and to properly mourn losses that were new and refreshed for me, wishing I'd never known, and the gut-level certainty that there was something vital I was missing. But through all of that, there was one thing that was clear: I'd been very right in thinking Fran's proximity to me brought her into more than mortal danger. Beneath my thoughts anger smoldered, the beginnings of a rage at the unfairness of it all, and for the first time in my life, I doubted how wonderful my Da had been, because if what I understood was right, my mother's death as well as that of my potential sibling had in all likelihood had some connection to him. And there was no way he wouldn't have recognized that possibility.

Fran stroked my hair back from my face. "You're overloaded," she said quietly, "on every imaginable level."

"You understand, don't you?" I asked, latching onto the one thing I could fully comprehend, desperate to convince her for her own sake as well as mine. "This…this between us…it can't, it just *can't* continue— not if—"

She quieted me with her lips on mine and gently pushed me down beneath her. "I understand," she said, "I understand that there are things you don't know, things out of your control."

I wasn't going to, hadn't meant to let her kiss me again, or help her hands undress me as they licked along my sides.

"Let it wait right now, let the Circle complete," she whispered. "Nothing, but nothing, can be done till then." Her energy weaved through me, sweeping mine with it, her body silken warmth as her thighs embraced mine. She ground against me in a way that took my breath from me when her knees met my ribs and she reached between us, spreading us both, the contact shifting from subtle to sublime, her cunt on mine as amazing as her tongue.

The expression on her face as she settled that incredible body over me, the mask of the day gone, replaced with the love and desire that shone from her eyes, curved her lips even as she licked them was enough to— "You need me, right here, right now."

And she needed me too, needed me to remind her that I loved her, that we were still here, that there were things that existed beyond what we'd known and learned, that as deeply as we could hurt we could love as well and not only in spite of it, but also because of it.

I felt the embrace of her body and filled my hands with her curves, her breasts rolling under my palms, in my mouth, hips gripped and marked by my fingers because I pulled her closer, tighter, ground back into her, glanced down to see the working muscles of her stomach as her breath blew hot past my cheek, and that just so fucking set me off I could only sink my lips against her neck, then wrap my arms around her, filled with need, filled with blood and fire and once more the tearing knowledge that all I had, all *we* had was *now* and now was all that mattered as I lifted her and set her on her back.

"Oh God," she groaned as her spine hit the mattress, her own shock and heightened arousal at my having done that an echoing wave through me and into the slick glide that resulted. The rock of Fran's cunt under mine found us with her hands tight on my ass, shifting me, holding me, pulling me even harder against her when I grabbed her hips, eased my hands around the perfect globes of her ass, let my fingers wrap around and spread her further beneath me. I loved her, loved the way she felt, the blazing pure power that flowed between us, intense, so, so intense it drove me out of my head and I couldn't resist playing my thumbs against that gorgeous entrance.

"Please," she gasped, her hips a smooth wave under me, pushing against me, drawing me further in until... "Oh yes."

I couldn't pretend for one moment that being inside her didn't turn me on even more, because it did, it so did, and the fit was so close, so very, very close, and even better when she bore down on me. "So... fucking...tight," I breathed out, my heart pounding as hard as my clit. "I *love* that—I love *you*," I whispered against the tendon that strained in her neck, then traced it with my lips, my tongue, as I moved within her, filled her, stretched her, let her scratch deep lines into the muscles of my back and loving it even as she grew tighter around me, and I felt the tension build in her, in her cunt, in her stomach and the way it heaved under me, the toss of her head and the way she bit back on her lip when I gazed down at her face.

"Say it," I asked, knowing there was something, something deep, something desperate, she needed to let out.

She shook her head once and her hips lifted as she worked with me, shoving me harder within her.

"Please," I asked again. "I want to hear it, I *need* to hear it." And it was true, I did, I wanted and I needed her to be free, as free as she could possibly be with me, it meant so much to me—it meant everything.

"Ah, fuck, Sam," she groaned out. "*Fuck* me—just fuck me."

That. Was. Hot. It was so fucking hot I felt it everywhere, my clit, my toes, my chest, my fucking head that felt like it could come too as I thrust deeper, harder, able to move only because she was so beautifully wet, she held me so snugly.

"Oh my God," I managed to grind out between teeth set in muscles that had locked, with air that almost didn't exist, "you're gonna make me come."

"Good," she managed to gasp, "because I'm gonna…just…just—Sam…"

I felt it when she came, the pulse of her body, the wish that came from her heart, from mine, to stay in this eternal now, and I came too, a deeper burst that started in my chest and spilt colors before my eyes before I was blinded by the flood of Light, floating in it, until I came to rest, back in the skin, back to earth, and cushioned from it by Fran, who smiled and laughed even as tears streamed from her eyes.

We held each other closely, with loving, soothing strokes, with the most gentle of kisses, and as we finally settled in to sleep, Fran securely over me with her head on my shoulder, and her breath across the hollow of my throat, she nuzzled my neck and whispered, "It will all work out—you'll see. Have faith, Sammy Blade, have faith."

I kissed her head, drew her to me just that much more, and resettled the comforter firmly over us. I closed my eyes to drift, the rapport between us so easy and clear, and something I hadn't understood earlier about Fran became suddenly transparent: she had faith, and I loved her for it, wanted her to keep that. It was part of what made her soul, her spirit, so beautiful. It made her innocent in so many, many ways.

My mind played with that, stretched it farther. If Fran had faith, it was because she had hope. I, on the other hand, I knew that in my world hope was a dangerous, perhaps even fatal luxury, and ultimately a fool's errand. I shivered as I realized what it meant: I would do what I had to for no other reason than because there was no one else to do it, or at least, that's what everything I'd been taught implied. Hell, hadn't I been told it outright—otherwise, why would there be a need to leave a blood heir?

But before that happened, part of what I had to do was to keep that fool's errand called hope alive for others. And I couldn't help but think in some small part of me that this… Really. Sucked.

THE FIRST CUT

Those things that nature denied to human sight,
she revealed to the eyes of the soul.
—Ovid

I brought my Da's trunk from the library to my room so I could thoroughly investigate it, and I searched everything. There was no key to be found anywhere. I suppose it would have been easy enough to get a razor and slice through the covers to open them, but I couldn't do that: they had been my Da's and he'd taken good care of them—I couldn't so blatantly disrespect that. Instead, I discovered framed photos I hadn't seen in years. These included two of my Da, one in his dress uniform with his graduating class on his Day of Assignment. He looked happy and proud and I had to admit Uncle Cort had been right: my father was so young in that photo, and without the length of hair framing my face, I very much favored him.

The other photo I suspected had been taken by Mr. Moretti, not too long after my first "official" haircut. I stood next to my father with my head no higher than his waist. We had the same stance, our hair had been parted and brushed similarly, and our matching navy blue polo shirts made our eyes a deeper shade of blue.

The last picture I found was one I remembered. My Da had taken it after a swim meet the winter before he'd died, and it was strange to see that, the girls I'd known, Nina and Fran, myself, in such a different context. I stared at those happy smiles, the innocent affection and pride on those tiny faces frozen in time. God, the things we didn't *know* then… My head filled with a strange buzz as I arranged the frames on my dresser.

"It's finally starting to look like you actually *live* here," Fran commented with a smile when she came up for a break later that morning. She touched my shoulder lightly as she went over to investigate, and I grew a little nervous, wondering what she would think, what she would feel, when she really saw them.

I watched as she looked through them, pausing a moment at the group shot, and I watched as she reached, then changed her mind to select a different one to examine. I understood her reasons. She took the one with me and my Da.

"You were adorable!" she said then grinned at me. "You have his eyes." She set it carefully back in the place I'd originally put it, then reached for another.

"That's my mom," I told her quietly. "Mom and me."

She held her breath and let it out slowly as she scrutinized the photo. "You have the same smile," she observed, and I couldn't help but smile myself. That I knew.

"I kinda guessed," I said and came to peer over her shoulder as she stared.

Fran touched the glass lightly with a finger tip. "You have her hands too," she told me. "See?" She pointed to the photo where my mother's hands caught mine.

"Really?" I edged around her as she turned to hand it to me, and it bumped into my stomach, jarring the wooden frame.

At that moment, the back popped off and Fran reacted automatically—she tried to catch whatever she could with her free hand, gashing her palm wide open on the glass as it sliced its way down.

"Christ!" I didn't think—I tossed the frame onto the bed and clutched her hand to my stomach, heedless of the blood that spattered as I tried to put some pressure on it.

"I'm all right," she said as I used my other hand to pull my tee over my head, slip it down my arm, then wrap her hand as best I could.

"No—you're not," I told her, part of me incredulous that we were arguing as her blood soaked through the gray material.

I held the drenched cotton over her hand as tightly as I could, hoping that it was at least doing some good as I led her down the stairs.

Her pain and my alarm must have reverberated through the house, because even though I didn't call for anyone, Elizabeth met us at the landing.

"What happened?" she asked, her face as calm as always, but there was a fierce concern she couldn't completely hide in her voice.

I explained as between us we got Fran seated in a chair in the dining room, her hand wrapped, raised, and still held firmly against me. Elizabeth took a towel out of the sideboard and tore it into wide strips to place over the soaked shirt.

The bleeding seemed to slow or at least didn't come through the additional makeshift bandages, but it wasn't until Uncle Cort burst into the room and I caught the expression he wore that I had any idea of what this looked like.

I hovered over Fran in my bra and jeans, my skin streaked with her blood, while she sat there composed and pale, occasionally protesting that she was fine. There was a visible trail of droplets that led out the entry, and I was certain there was more on the steps.

"Let me take a look at that," Cort asked, his voice slightly gruff as he reached for her hand. He focused as he held it, then slowly unwrapped the bandage.

The glass had sliced across the pads of her palm, just under her fingers, leaving a line that gaped then filled red as he pulled something out of his pocket. "It's nasty looking, but it's not truly deep," he said quietly as he squeezed a small tube along the opening of her skin, then gently pushed the edges together, where they stayed closed.

"Crazy Glue," he said nonchalantly as the bleeding stopped. "Liquid stitches—I've cut myself a time or two, and it's a great trick."

"Thank you," Fran said quietly.

I couldn't help myself, I hugged her head to me and kissed its crown as a flood of relief washed through me, cooling nerves I only now realized had kicked into overdrive.

"You'll want to be careful for a few days—but it should heal up nicely, not even scar," Cort continued and I understood why he knew that.

I'd completely forgotten what he and Elizabeth had taught me, that it was possible to monitor and evaluate another's bodily functions. What if it had been worse and those moments had been critical?

I shook my head, angry with myself for forgetting something so basic.

"Rest here a moment, let's make sure you're steady before you go charging off," Elizabeth said to Fran, who nodded in quiet agreement. "Why don't you go wash up and get a fresh shirt?" she then suggested to me.

"Yeah, yeah. Good idea," I agreed, my brain still numb.

I felt Uncle Cort's eyes on me as I left the room, and the question he wanted to ask followed me as I walked past the dark red drops that had fallen on the floors, to the larger ones on the stairs, and finally to the spatter in my room.

Blood had sheeted over the glass that had cracked in the corner when it hit the floor, still covering the photo, while the backing had twisted to an odd angle when it fell. I squatted down near the pile; all the right edges of everything were painted in drying blood. I edged the cover glass carefully over with a fingertip, not wanting the pieces to scatter, or to cut myself—again.

That cut, my first cut...driven by anger, by a voice that told me I could dare to question everything, had been a vicious slash that had first run a heavy thick red, then eased, the sting and burn a mockery of what ripped through my chest. How could it be possible to hurt so much and *not* bleed?

I couldn't, I didn't understand it, and the surface pain had taunted me with its pale comparison. It had been the second cut, and the third behind it, the ones that had gone beyond exterior—they'd hurt with a grim satisfaction even as the world had flickered before my eyes in hazy shades of red. It had been fury, fury as cold as my blood was hot, that had driven the final cut. Even now I felt the beginnings of an icy flame lick at my edges as I contemplated the dark spots on the floor and the glass, blood on my things, Fran's—that stopped me cold. Fran.

It was my Frankie who hurt for the reasons I did, who'd willingly bound herself to me, unhesitatingly had become a part of this strange mess I called my life, who even now sat downstairs with Uncle Cort and Elizabeth, her hand gashed open due to my clumsiness.

I shook my head, trying to physically dispel the cold burn as I picked the picture up by a corner. *That's strange*, I thought.

Behind it lay a thin sheet of white corrugated cardboard, and it had a faint line beveled outward, as if something had pushed it from the back. I reached for it and heard a faint scratching noise as I drew it to me. I turned it over, and taped behind it was an envelope, a light blue one such as used for airmail. It was overstuffed and had been addressed in a handwriting I recognized instantly. It was my Da's, and it was addressed to Samantha.

My heart hammered against my ribs almost painfully as I shook it lightly and I knew, before I carefully slit the fold with my finger and unfolded the pages and pages covered in his handwriting, what I would find at the center even as it slid out into my bloody palm: it was a key.

I held it carefully and smoothed the top page out.

My Samantha, I read, *I'm sorry, so sorry I'm not there with you. You're probably in England, safely in Cort's and Elizabeth's hands, and wondering what the hell kind of a guy your Da is that he didn't tell you so many things.*

I could hear his voice, almost feel his hands on my shoulders as I continued, unable to stop smiling here and there where he'd written something that showed how very well he'd known me.

I learned that it had taken a few years before my parents managed to have me, and that it had been the very specific result of ritual. I read about the car accident—and I wasn't surprised to discover it had been a hit-and-run—that had cost my family the sister my mother had been certain she carried, then my mother herself perhaps forty-eight hours later. I'd been in the car too, and no one knew what I'd seen or remembered because apparently I'd said "Mommy" at the scene of the accident itself, then didn't speak another word for two years.

My Da wrote about how my mother was adept in her own right, as was Law, as was required of those sworn, to be bound in spirit and body only to those of equal stature, to those equally bound to the Light and the Law, and that her gift was an affinity for metal. She could pick up traces left in the structural matrices and, depending on their strength, discern thoughts, emotions, even clear pictures, and link through to the person who'd left them.

He told of his own gift, what he referred to as "reading the threads." He could see potentials, flashes of what could and what would be. *But remember, Sam-Sam,* he cautioned, *if this is your gift, there are infinite possibilities, controlled by the very real limitation of varied levels of probability, and in this world or any other—it's the probabilities that count.*

I suspect, though, he continued, *that you'll either take after Amanda, because you've no idea how like her you are, or inherit a variant of my gift, perhaps a purer version. Who knows, maybe you'll get your grandmother's—ask Cort about that sometime.*

I wondered about that and put the pages down to finger the charms that hung from my neck. I focused more on the ankh, and it gave such a burst of mixed thoughts and images that I felt the beginnings of a headache between my eyes. It would take me hours to concentrate on any one sense long enough to see if my father's suspicions were correct.

I shifted my attentions to the miniature claymore, and as I ran my fingertips across it, I braced myself for the razor-cut pain that always, always accompanied my deliberate playing with it. I tried, I really tried, to move past that, to open beyond the crystal pure burst of light, the icy sense of loss, the warmth of communion I'd had the one time her lips had touched mine. I tried until I didn't know which would burst, my head or my chest, and I was forced to stop. I could hear my blood pounding in my ears from the effort. I took a centering breath, released it slowly, then read some more.

Now let's talk about you, the next line read, *because there are things you have to know, the things I've learned that I don't think anyone else knows yet. So much of what we in the Circle do is aimed at preventing things from becoming manifest in the Material, but I think that's all about to change.*

But first, and this is from me as your Da, because I want you to be happy, as happy as you can. It is possible.

Your friends are important, Sam. You need to keep a bond to the Material, and you've always had pretty good judgment. Trust your gut, trust your senses, and trust me, even though I'm not beside you. Fran… what did I tell you? I was right, she did like you, and she's got a heart like a lion. I hope you're still friends. And hey, did you ever tell that other girl you liked her? Nina, right? She's something special, that's for sure. Well, I hope you did, because Sam? You can't turn back time, and there's so little of it. Don't waste it.

My eyes pricked and stung, but I didn't want to cry, refused to, because I wanted to read the rest and there wasn't much left, these words, from my Da to me, written because he knew he wouldn't be there to say them.

I love you, Samantha. No matter what happens, no matter what grows and stops and changes, that never will. Even in the multiplicity of Universes, even in the uncertainty of ever meeting again in this life or any other, my love for you is a constant. It's the one thing no one leaves behind.

Remember that, and remember this: we die, Samantha. We all die, but it's what we do while we're here and how we face that fact that counts. It's not enough to be "good," we must be good for something, and as strange as this may sound right now? You're lucky in many ways—you were born to your "something," you don't have to struggle like so many others to figure out what it is.

I'll bet you've got that key held so tightly in your hand it's probably imprinted in your skin by now. Start from the bottom. Everything's dated, I've left notes on what I've done and you'll need them to make sense of what I think is to come. There are patterns everywhere, nothing is ever an accident. Pay attention to the signs, there are more around than you know.

Two things, Samantha.

I think an avatar has arrived, perhaps more than one. There have been hints that it would happen and given what I think I've discovered…well, I don't know who it is—you'll be the one to discover that. And I know, because you are Wielder, that you will find them, and you will protect them.

Use my notes, and make Cort tell you the legend of the mark of Judas if he hasn't already.

I think the cult has been revived and maybe tonight, if I'm lucky, I'll be able to prove it. The tides are all wrong, we've hit the moon's nadir, but I have to try, I have to find out, because if I'm right, the game's been changed for some time now, but no one knows yet.

I'm out of time. A few hours ago you came home from school. We ate dinner, we watched a movie, and I kissed you good night before I left for the station. I'm off duty, but Joe Scanlon's a good man, he knows where I'm going. You can turn to him in an emergency, if Cort's not around. He knows. Not everything, but enough.

I hope you never have to read this, but the threads as I read them say you will. Trust Cort, trust Elizabeth, but most of all? Trust you—I do.

Go. Read. Put the pieces together, find what I missed—I know you can.

Love you always,
Da

❖

I smoothed the pages out on the ground next to me and sat, staring at nothing for I don't know how long, the key gripped so tightly it had gone beyond imprinting to embedding in my palm, and I felt her before she entered the room.

"Are you all right?" Fran laid gentle fingers on my bare shoulder. The bandage around her hand scratched lightly on the skin.

I twisted my head and kissed her fingers. "Fine. How're you?"

She knelt beside me, and let her arm rest across my shoulders. "I'm okay. Sam, aren't you cold?"

"No." I shook my head. "Careful!" I cautioned, perhaps a bit too sharply as I saw her hand near the raw edges of glass that still lay on the floor. My mind replayed the slashing fall of it, the spurt of red through the air.

"I'm not going to touch it," she assured me.

"I should clean that up," I said half under my breath and I gently plucked her hand off my shoulder, holding it in mine as I stood.

"You should clean that up first," Fran said, nodding at my waist.

She was right. It looked a bit macabre, I supposed as I looked down, the clear lines of her fingers, the larger section where I'd pressed her hand to me, the trail that dripped down my waistband.

There was more than one thing I had to straighten out and I grabbed the waste pail from its corner, then hunkered down next to Fran. I picked up the first few shards and tipped them carefully into the bag that lined the bin.

"Is the picture of your mom okay?" she asked.

"Frankie, it's fine, that's not important." I stared down at my own hands a moment. "I got scared for you," I admitted quietly. "And as weird as it sounds, your," and I gestured at her hand, "turned out to be a good thing."

"*Felix casus?*" she asked with a small grin as I took her uninjured hand in mine.

"Mm-hmm, a lucky accident," I agreed as she let me open it, revealing her palm to me. I placed the key on her skin, then closed her fingers over it. I held her fist in my hands.

"Who knows how long it would have been before I found this, if ever? So thank you." I kissed her cheek and as I did, a chill ran down my spine. My father had told me to watch for signs, that there were many of them, and it struck me that the way I'd found that key hadn't been a sign at all, but an omen.

I picked the pages of the letter back up from the floor where I'd left them, and handed them to her. "You can read this if you'd like," I told her quietly.

She held them carefully and let out a slow breath. "Sam…this is yours. You don't—"

"—have to?" I finished for her and gazed into her eyes, melted honey warm on mine, and I gave her a tiny smile. "I found it because of you. Yes, I do."

"All right," she agreed, and I left her sitting on the bed to do exactly that.

I cleaned the glass, I cleaned the floors, I cleaned myself, and despite the curious and concerned thoughts and questions thrown in my direction, I shrugged them all off as politely as I could before I clattered down the stairs and out to the yard to get my Vespa.

In the aftermath of everything, the reliving of things that were almost too much to bear, the anxiety over Fran's safety, and the need for my mind to make sense of everything I'd learned, my head felt like it had been stuffed with cotton, then dipped in peppermint or something similar.

I didn't know where I was headed, really, or how long I'd be. I just wanted to let the throb behind my eyes dull before I tackled the task my father had laid before me. Images and thoughts chased each other like bright goldfish. My Da thought an avatar had returned. What in the world was the Judas myth, or its cult? What would my gifts be after my sealing? Could I keep Fran safe? Could I protect anyone, really? Where did Old Jones fit into all of this? My mother? I wish I'd known her… What purpose had it served in not telling me what had really happened to her sooner? My poor Da…were he and my mother together somewhere? Was that even possible? What happened, where was the potential new being that had left the Material just before my mother did? These things and more darted and dipped around my mind, chasing one after the other, each nipping at the heels of the next, and I didn't see Fran by the gate until I almost knocked right into her.

"Let me go with you."

I squirmed inside, not knowing how to say I wanted to be alone, alone in my mind, alone in my skin, away from all the thoughts and the emotions that rode down so hard on me they made me feel sluggish, heavy, trapped.

She stood there, her hand in her pocket, eyes calmly considering me, observing the play of emotion through mine.

"You don't have to talk, you don't have to say a thing. I can ignore you if you want, but you shouldn't be alone right now and I'm not about to let you do something you'll regret."

I gaped at her. I didn't know what to say, and this time, she touched gentle fingers to my cheek. "Sammer, you can't do this on your own." Her voice matched her touch.

"Frankie…" Her eyes were clear, her intent so pure, I could only shake my head and sigh. "Fine." I unclipped the other helmet from the seat and passed it to her. "Let's go."

She settled around me and we were off. The vibration that raced through me, the cold on my face even as her hands were warm on my stomach while we roared around the corner, made me feel a little better, gave me a little distance from the weight that pounded in my head.

We rode aimlessly, down streets we'd never visited, got stuck for a bit in the eternal traffic around Piccadilly. Once back in the swing again, I kept riding, stopping long enough for gas only to ride off again, back to the dockyards, and then, almost as if irresistibly drawn, I headed back toward Spit.

Fran's unspoken curiosity combined with puzzlement was an electric haze around her as we walked back over to the door, so different now in the half-light of early dusk. It was quiet, still, like something sleeping, not the peaceful sleep of restorative dreams and untroubled calm, but the fitful slumber of hot and heavy fevers, the vivid kaleidoscope of colors and sounds interrupted by the dizzying endless drop into black that might mercifully end in abrupt awareness, the sort that sits up suddenly, ravening.

I traced the plaque with my fingertips, felt the hum of industry, of purposeful labor and toil, some with cheer, some with a muted resignation, bleed from it into my hand.

"What are you looking for?" Fran asked quietly, the first words she'd spoken the entire ride.

"I don't know," I answered honestly, turning from the plaque to the main doors to do the same. The construction was newer, despite its almost abused appearance, but the read was completely different. There was the white welding arc the doors were forged in, the same industrial pound of its installation and then…a flash of blood, of fire and fear, sex and despair. I caught the scent of burning tar and plastic, and a vision, a flicker of light, surrounded, devoured, by creatures similar to the one I'd hunted on the Astral.

I dropped my hand and faced her. She looked pale. "What are *you* getting?" I asked her.

She pursed her lips, then shook her head, loosening her hair from its confines under the collar of her jacket as she stared at some vague point on the ground. "Do you remember…schoolyard fights?"

"You mean, like, fighting itself?"

"No, I mean…do you remember how the other kids would watch? Cheer?"

"Yeah."

She raised her eyes to mine. "There were always a few who would watch that…and liked to, enjoyed it. That's feeling I get."

I nodded and suddenly, I was clear of the haze in my head, human again, a snap back to the skin and I was standing outside the empty club, freezing my ass off with Fran, who I'd been really rude to for no reason other than I'd felt hazy and crummy. I was a jerk.

"Hey, this…this is stupid. You want to go back?" I asked her and took her hand. Her fingers were cold and I chafed them between mine. "I'm sorry," I said softly. "I'm being a jerk."

She grinned, her eyes sparking at me. "Just a little," she agreed. "But," and she kissed my cheek, "it's been a rough couple of days for you—well, for you and me both." The bandage on her hand scraped gently against my chin. "You're not ready to go back yet, are you?"

"No. Would you mind…" I hesitated a moment, because I knew I wasn't really being fair, but it was a gut feeling I had to follow. "Do you mind if we stop by the studio?"

A sudden chill ran through her and she shivered, then went still. "Why there?"

I shrugged. I had no answer. "Dunno," I said finally. I kissed the hand that had finally warmed in mine. "Just a thought."

I didn't know how to explain it, that in the rush of images, there had been a scent, a sound, a thread that led there. I didn't understand, couldn't quite place the connection, but I had to follow it.

She dropped my hand. "Let's go."

❖

This time, I made sure to rub her hand, hold it against my waist, before we took off. The one thing about riding with someone, even at slower speeds, was that conversation was difficult and it wasn't until we pulled up to the block that I finally said, "You've haven't been here yet."

"No, not yet," she answered as I cut the engine.

"C'mon." I took her hand, careful of the wound, a momentary stab of guilt at how it happened jabbing through me as I keyed the lock.

"It's not much, but it's—" I stopped as I opened the door to find the lights on and Paolo and Kenny comfortably ensconced on the beat-up blue tweed sofa, apparently in deep conversation.

"Well, if it isn't Ms. Anarchy herself," Kenny drawled with a smile.

Paolo smirked at me.

"I thought there was only one key," I said as we moved into the room.

Paolo's smirk widened. "There's only one key, but there's more than one way into anything."

"Well, we're done here, anyway," Kenny said, slapping the cushion as he jumped up to stand. "You've got the place to yourselves…" He winked at me, then smiled, "I'm sure you're eager to show your friend the drum kit and the coffee maker—fresh pot, by the by." He pointed toward the kitchenette. He seemed edgy; his hands moved almost frenetically, and he kept working his jaw. It was a marked contrast to Paolo's languid pose.

"Yes, energy and rhythm—I'm sure you've plenty of both," Paolo drawled, his gaze arrogant as he looked me up and down, and I shifted slightly so Fran was behind my shoulder. I didn't like his look, I didn't like his tone, and I didn't like the gleam in his eyes on me or when he shifted to her.

I hope he plays like shit, I thought vehemently, *even if it means another month or more of finding a replacement for Graham*.

Fran put a hand on my shoulder and moved to stand next to me. "More than most, less than some, I'd say." Her tone was friendly, joking even, but what waved off her was heat, a liquid blush of anger, and threaded through it was the faintest hint of fear. That fear was the source of anger came as no surprise—I knew that from what I'd learned, ingrained in me as part of my very first test on the Astral—but what did surprise was the direction of the fear: she was afraid not for herself, but for me.

Paolo rose to his feet so suddenly it was alarming, but I stood my ground as he gave me an enigmatic smile. "A man among men and a woman among..." He licked his teeth. "Well, I'm sure you have your moments. Let's go, Kenny," he turned and said. "Leave them to their...discoveries."

It was the way he said it, so like Old Jones, that made my blood turn to ice and my mixed impressions coalesced into dislike.

"I'm here to check my amp," I said finally, and that wasn't a lie—I'd blown a fuse in our last session, and while I'd replaced it then, it wouldn't be unusual for me to want to fiddle with it. "Why are you guys here?"

"Just thought he'd like to see what sort of setup we have, not be unprepared Sunday," Kenny answered as they brushed by us, Paolo before him. "Ta!" He waved and Paolo threw one last look over his shoulder before they shut the door behind them.

"What the hell...?" Fran asked as I took off my jacket.

"I don't know," I said, and stared at the sofa, as if it could give a clue. Of course, it gave nothing, and I waved Fran over to the kitchen. "Well, at least there's coffee—want some?" I asked as I moved to the counter. "You can use my mug."

"Stop." Fran caught my hand as I reached for the pot. "Don't. I don't like him, I don't trust him, and I wouldn't drink anything he had anything to do with—you shouldn't either. Look."

She pointed with my hand still held in hers at the counter. It could have been sugar, it could have been salt, it could have been the powdered creamer that Kenny was so fond of, but the color and texture was off for all of those things and Fran wrapped an arm around my waist, pulled me back to her, even as I stared.

"Paolo wants something from you—and he can't have it." The words were said into the light hairs on my neck and the guarding pull became a possessive hold that sent a flash of flame through me as her lips touched down onto the skin beneath them.

Fran proved how well she knew me, knew my body, as one hand unerringly found the button of my pants while the other slid beneath it so her fingers could spread me, and found me hard.

"Baby," I breathed as she pulled me to her and I craned my head for her lips. My back jarred against her as she leaned against the wall and when my tongue skated over hers, she jerked me off with the same slow strength.

"This...is not his," she vehemently whispered before she filled me, hard and fast, full and good, all while the firm, slipping grip on my clit as she pushed the hood back and played with my head made me feel like I was fucking her.

"No...it's not...oh God—I-want-to-fuck-you," I gasped out, meaning every word of it, the vision of her impaled on my cock so real my fingers wrapped around her wrists, urged her on as she slipped another finger into me, stretching me so fucking good, so...fucking...

"I love that," she growled into my ear, my hand pushing on hers, pushing her deeper.

When we got home, her tits swayed over my head as we both watched her cunt lower onto my cock, the deep drive that only touched the surface of satisfaction, the weight of her body centered perfectly over my clit as I thrust, she rode, and when she parted her pussy lips so I could see more, the vision of her clit sliding down my dick as it filled her made my own feel like it would explode and I couldn't help but sit up and reach for her, wedge her fat clit between my fingers, exposing her head so it could ride my shaft.

The sound of her cunt as it sucked on my dick, the clench of her stomach, the hug on my hips, the grip on my shoulders, the curl of her lips…it all combined when I tangled my fingers into the hair against her neck to pull her closer, to reach for the kiss that made everything so complete. It created a haze, a suspended moment of time, the forever hang where the Universe centered, coalesced, became *us*.

I saw things, felt things, knew she caught them too, and when, once again, a face floated through my mind, she gasped, released my hip long enough to press the charms I wore back into my skin, forcing the image bigger, brighter, until it was almost real and I loved them both, knowing it was okay, that this had its own reality, if not in this Universe, then perhaps another.

When she came all I could do was hold her close, tight, kiss her with the all love I had for her and the love I carried with me. The love we shared had part of its root there; we both held someone, the *same* someone, in us, between us, and here or not, we both loved her dearly. And I knew that in loving each other, in a very real way, we honored that too.

Still, deep within her, within me, was the knowledge that as united as we were, I simply could not do what I needed to so long as we were so close to one another. I'd forgotten something basic in my concern for her, something I should have not only thought of, but done immediately. There was no doubt in my mind that Fran was instrumental to who I was, who I would be, and the finding of the key proved it. That she had shed blood for it, even accidentally, Jones's threat, Paolo's gaze, all told me quite clearly that she would constantly be in danger, for me, and from me. And…there were no accidents.

I kissed her again as she cried, silent tears that shook her shoulders, even while she still moved on me.

"I don't—I don't want…"

I hushed her with a kiss. "I know," I whispered into her lips, "I know. Me either. But we don't end Frankie, we don't," I assured her as I wrapped my arms around her, shifted us, laid her gently beneath me. "This will always be between us, this you and me, this time…" I didn't know what I wanted to say, or how to say it, just that I suddenly needed to feel her, all of her, show her in ways that were unmistakable what I knew, that when we said good-bye, it wouldn't be to what we felt or meant to each other—it was to what we *could* be, together.

It was that possibility, that probability, we would let go of, mutually, with love, understanding fully what we would give up, because there were things in this world larger than both of us, hungry things, needful things, dark and sad things that looked at love and sacrifice as toys, as food. I would not submit her spark or her life to that.

I carefully eased my cock from her and fumbled with the harness, removing it to replace the hardness of my cock with the slick ride of my cunt against hers.

We slipped against each other again, my fingers within her, soothed, comforted, loved by the deep, wet embrace and the pulse under my thumb, the return feel of her within me as she stroked my shaft, the sighs and the kisses, the "I love you" whispered through tears, hers, mine, it didn't matter through the pound of my heart, the return beat of hers that matched it as she once again roared through me.

In gentle caresses, in careful negotiation, in full awareness of how much we would hurt ourselves and each other, we compromised: we'd be lovers until she returned to the States, but when she did, this aspect of us would end. Of course, we would still be close—we loved each other, and we were bound—but we would be *friends*: we would walk away from the rest of it. We had to. Her distance from me would at least partially ensure her safety and even if she didn't fully believe that, or wasn't as concerned about it, she *did* understand me: there were moments I could barely *breathe* when I thought about what could happen. And I now had a very good idea of what already had.

❖

In the mornings that followed, I pored through every single one of my father's books, passed them to Fran when I was done, brought them and my notes to my meetings with Elizabeth, showed them to Cort, made them each sit and tease it apart with me.

There were answers in there, dammit, a puzzle that spanned almost thirty years, and I wanted all eyes on it.

Patterns started to emerge, repeated places, names; unexplained fires, mysterious suicides, unanticipated drug overdoses, and seemingly random disappearances, all tied to certain geographic locations, like the neighborhood around Saint James Hospital in Leeds, or the borough of Brooklyn in New York, or Newark, New Jersey. There were a few other places as well, and in all of them there were spurts of crime, very specific types, that came into fashion, then went out again, ebbing and flowing like the tides.

Two things added to my frustration level as the days went by and my Da's meticulous notes allowed us to slowly peek into how well the web had been spun.

The first was that Paolo turned out to be an excellent guitarist, and since both Hannah and Kenny liked him, he was in. I bit my tongue on that; perhaps I'd been wrong, perhaps he wouldn't be so bad after all—even I had to grudgingly admit he did have talent.

The second occurred that night. Fran had crawled down my body, nipping, tasting, teasing, and the promise in her eyes was as stirring as her touch.

"I want to suck on your cock," she said, her gaze heavy and hot on me, her breath warm on my belly as she fit her shoulders between my legs.

I stretched an arm over to the nightstand, fumbled within, and as I brought everything down by my waist, she caught my hand and what was in them.

"Not that," she told me with a smile, taking the harness and the toy from me. She placed them to the side, then gently spread my cunt before her. "This…" She blew softly on my exposed clit, and teased me with the very tip of her tongue in a way that made my eyes close even as I couldn't help the whispered sigh she drew from me—I *loved* the way she did that.

"Watch," she asked and I forced my eyes open as I sat up on my elbows.

The sight of her tongue as it swirled around my clit, the dip of it inside me, the feel and fit of it that made me groan only to make me do so again when she drew back out to show me how wet I was, turned me on as much as what she was doing.

Fran smiled at me with sensual knowing, a carnal regard that glowed from her eyes when we both watched my clit jump under her skillful mouth. I felt her *everywhere* as the sheets slipped under my fingers and the heat rose through my skin, the intoxicating rush a thrilling flood through me. But when she gently pushed the hood back to expose more than just the head of my hard-on…

"You're so…fucking…*hard*," she whispered, then stroked her

tongue against the sensitive underside, "I want your cock in my mouth." She took me between her lips.

"That is so…fucking…*good*…" I managed to choke out as I gulped for air while she licked and sucked and I couldn't help the surge of my hips against her, the pressure just that much better.

Every now and again I would glance to see the way her mouth moved my cunt, shifted my lips, and when I felt a hand leave my thigh, her body twist between my legs, I knew what she had in mind, what she was going to do when I felt her press the hardness she'd retrieved against me, toying just at the very entrance.

"Oh yes…*please*…" I breathed, the word a drawn-out hiss in the air, wanting that, wanting her to do it to me. "Please…fuck me."

She did, brilliantly, beautifully, sucking me off, letting me fuck her face as she played the head, just the head, deep enough in me to pop past that point that felt oh-so-fucking good, only to pull back out and repeat the move over and over. It slid so easily in and never fully out in a rhythm that stepped and paced until I was so damn close, so damn hard, so damn ready, wanted her deep and hard.

Holyfucking*everything*… Fran blew my mind with my cock between her lips and mine deep in me when I came, came so hard in her mouth, under her hands and the way she worked the cock inside me. I couldn't breathe, I couldn't see, I could barely hear anything as she crawled back up to hold me, kiss me, let me savor the taste of my cunt on her tongue as I sucked it.

"You like that, baby?" she asked in that low drawl I loved to hear as she teased her lips against my chin, my throat, my whole body so sensitive I could only take either the lightest of feather strokes or a firm grip on skin because anything else made me jump.

"That was incredible," I answered when I finally had enough breath to speak and the firm weight of her breast in my hand, her nipple wonderfully hard and edible between my fingers. "I…just…thank you."

"I'm glad you liked it," she murmured against my mouth before I claimed hers again, eased my leg between hers, felt along the contours of her ribs, the hard muscle under soft flesh of her stomach and the hollow inside her hip where I held her when she rode me, however she rode me, and the soft rise and the fine hairs that were right above—

"We're going to have to not do this for a few days," she said, the words a soft sigh as I flit my fingers along the lovely wetness that waited for me.

"What? Why?" That stopped me short "Did I—" In the entire time we'd been together, since we'd started making love, the only thing that had ever, ever, curtailed us from being together was the one night that Fran had suffered through really bad cramps, and the only thing that made her feel better was to feel me snug against her back, my hand warm and light on her belly. Otherwise, we hadn't—

Fran put her hand over mine, urging me to continue. "No, it's not you," she said, her eyes slightly hazy from the light swirl of my fingers on her clit as she moved beneath me, "it's the ceremony—several days of building the right energy."

"How many?" I asked, dreading the answer because I didn't want to lose any of the time we had together. The countdown in my head never stopped and just because I knew it was something we had to do didn't mean I looked forward to it.

"Seven," she answered as she wrapped an arm around my shoulders and drew me down for a kiss that left me light-headed, "and then my initiation, and then we're fine."

"Well," I growled against her lips, and teased my fingers against her, barely inside her, then just a little more, making her breath catch and her fingers dig into my shoulder. "It's gonna be a long night, then."

❖

Fran was the first to note that the crime clusters preceded my birth by about three years and lasted for about three after.

"Look," she said, when we sat in the library after another hours-long session of meticulously combing through the notes my Da had left.

I was reviewing the observations he'd made, she was creating a graph with the newspaper clippings he'd included as reference points.

There had been a tremendous rise in drug use, not just in the States, but in Europe as well, along with an increase in crimes involving pregnant women and infants—young women murdered, newborns poisoned in hospitals, babies being stolen from their prams on the streets by desperate addicts.

When arrests were made, some didn't know who'd paid them to

do the deed, they just wanted the money for the fix; others had heard that such and such person or group would pay for a young child. A few arrests had led back to cultlike family-structured units with drug ties.

I noted as well that this period coincided with my mother's death, and that it wasn't until a year after these sorts of crimes seemed to disappear that I'd been brought back to the States.

Cort whistled low under his breath when I drew the pattern out for him. "Oh shit," he said softly, "I thought...I thought he was paranoid, grieving. These things have happened before, rises in certain crimes, certain events. There was no reason to think—"

"What?" I interrupted and looked at him sharply. He met my gaze. "That there might be a link? Other than the obvious, of course, that as Wielder, he and his family were vulnerable to begin with?"

"I'm sorry. He'd lost his wife and child, and the one child he'd left was an ocean away for safekeeping."

"With you."

He nodded. "Yes."

"I don't remember," I told him, my eyes steady on his. "I remember *you*, here and there, but it's vague." I thought back to that flash I'd had the night of my first hunt, when Elizabeth had laid her hand over mine. Perhaps that *was* a memory. "I'm not entirely certain I remember Elizabeth, or anything else."

He dropped his eyes to the table and pulled the notebook to him. "You're not supposed to remember anything at all," he said quietly, then sighed.

"Why?" I was irrationally angry. Rage flowed through me, hot and heavy in my blood, and I swallowed it, choked on it, even as it tried to suffocate me. I felt played with, used, and some of that was directed at the man who sat before me, my appointed guardian.

"The last known avatar," he said heavily as he scanned along a page with his finger. "No one is completely certain of who she was, her real name, her birthdate—the Romani don't keep records—and she'd been lucky enough to avoid all but the last sweep. Your grandmother died, was killed, August of 1944 in France, just outside of Drancy. Her body was found by a member of the Circle, hers and that of the girl, the avatar, maybe ten or eleven years old." He laughed, a harsh barking sound, and in that laugh I heard the same rage that burned under my skin.

"Your father was barely a year old. One bullet—one bullet that drove through Wielder to avatar. That's all it took."

When he looked at me again, the flame in his eyes wasn't as bright, and for a moment, his face seemed to sag. He seemed old, immeasurably, impossibly old, with eyes that I suddenly realized had seen and suffered through much, too much. My anger drained away as I understood what I saw.

"Forgive me...forgive us all. We failed her, we failed the avatar, and I failed your father."

"That's...that's not possible," I said through the churn of images and thoughts in my head. "You were a child."

He stood and turned away from me. "I was *there*—I raised your father." He walked over to the fire in the grate, poked and played with it until it burned brightly. "Well," he said heavily, "the Lords of Light will not make the same mistake twice—we're done for tonight."

I stared at his back, his shoulders as they worked under his shirt, stunned at what he was asking me to believe. "How can you tell me something like that and then tell me we're done?"

He shrugged as I rose and walked toward him. "You already know more than you should." He kept his focus on the flames that danced before him. "You know more than all but a very few ever have."

"And you've told me I can do things you haven't even taught me. So tell me more, and I'll tell you what I think about the avatar." I crouched down next to him. "Fran found a six-year window, so let's say ten to give it room, someone as much as five years older or five years younger than I am. That's what all those crazy murders and baby stealings were about—finding the avatar. But if the pattern is holding, and something new is brewing, they never found him or her. No one has, and they're looking even harder."

He was so quiet, so still, it was only the fact that I could feel his focus on me that let me know he was listening.

"You just said," I continued quietly, "that the Lords of Light will not make the same mistake twice. What if *this* avatar doesn't even know who they are yet—not all of them do—and that keeps them safe for now? It makes it crucial for Dark to find them before they find themself, hence the stepped-up activity, the new cult, my father's"—I swallowed, then finished—"murder."

He craned his head up at me, the gleam back in his gaze. "I

think…I think you might be right." He put a hand on his knee, then straightened to tower above me. "And I think it's time you met some of the others. Let's go."

I followed him down the stairs and out the door, and he spoke over his shoulder. "This'll keep your mind off the enforced celibacy, anyway," he said, then grinned at me, a quick gleam of white over his shoulder.

I couldn't believe he'd just said that to me, but I had to laugh as I grabbed my jacket off the hook and followed him out into the night.

❖

We took my Vespa and went to crummy little dives, to tiny little offices in warehouses off the docks, we visited churches and schools. I met policemen, retired teachers and professors, truck drivers and laborers, old reverends and gardeners, housewives and bank tellers, and in the flat of one those in the East End, I met Graham, because as it turned out, he lived with his aunt Lydia, or Lyddie, as she invited me to call her. She was reed slender, but her handshake was solid and strong, the hair that skirted her collar was as unruly as Graham's could be, and she had the same bright eyes.

"How're you swinging?" Graham asked with a cheery smile after we gave each other a hug and smacked each other up a bit. Our affection for one another was rough, but it was palpably genuine. Literally.

I smiled just as widely back. "To the left, to the right, you know how it goes."

He laughed. "Knowing you, you're swingin' it in one direction—Fran's a good woman."

"She is, I know," I answered shortly. I did know and I didn't want to think about how much I missed her now, never mind how much I'd miss her in a few weeks' time.

It was at that moment Cort turned around and said, "Well, since everyone's so well acquainted, and Lyddie and I need to catch up, why don't you show Graham your new mode of transport?"

"Yeah, c'mon," I told him, "let's go."

"Would ya look at that?" he said as I unclipped the helmets and passed him one. He ran his hand over the chrome of the rack, the seats, stroked the handlebars. "How'd you afford it?"

I shrugged, more than slightly embarrassed. I knew my friends worked and worked hard for everything they had, and I'd grown up like that myself, had expected that I would live paycheck to paycheck too, after college. The way I lived now, I didn't do laundry, or clean things, or any of the million daily tasks that had once made up my life; someone else, someone I barely even saw, did all of it. I didn't even have to cook if I didn't want to; all I had to focus on were Fran, my studies, my investigations, and my instrument, in any order I preferred.

It was something I couldn't help but feel guilty about; maybe when things calmed down a bit, I could do something, work with my uncle maybe, or teach music, anything to feel…useful, normal, maybe. Not so different.

"Uncle Cort," I said finally, "he rebuilt it for me. C'mon," I said and slapped the seat. "Where to?" I popped on my helmet.

"Well, since you're driving, let's go…" and he named a spot I'd not been to yet, known for "bad attitude, good coffee, better eats."

I didn't ride terribly fast, but at one point, we did have to take a rather tight turn and Graham held on to me for balance.

"Nice hips!" he said as we pulled out of it.

"What?" I asked, not certain I'd heard him. We'd only a block more to go, and as I found a spot, then cut the engine, Graham finally let go.

"You've very nice hips," he said, removing his helmet and running his hands through his hair to make certain it sat right. "Not that I'm, well, you know." He gave me an embarrassed grin, then hit me with his elbow.

"Thanks," I said dryly, returning the shove. "Fran likes them fine."

"I'm certain," he agreed as we walked into the little eatery with its orange curtains trimmed in tiny brown puffs in the windows.

I enjoyed hanging out with Graham; it was so much like hanging out with the guys back in the neighborhood, and I felt relaxed, my uncertainties and even some of my fears gone because I didn't have to hide them, didn't have to be anything other than myself.

That's what it was. I didn't know what I was or even *who* I was sometimes, but with Graham, I didn't have to be anything I wasn't, I could just kick back and be; there were no testing questions, no mysteries to be solved, no heartbreak waiting to happen, ready to pounce and eat me. I could sit, say, do anything I wanted, and he was all right with that. In fact, he encouraged it—there was something, I dunno, akin to a likeness, a core that we shared, where we were the same. It wasn't simply that we were musicians… I couldn't put my finger on it, but it didn't matter. What mattered was that it *was*.

We ordered coffee because tea was what we drank at home, and got cress sandwiches to go with it. They weren't nearly as good as the ones Elizabeth made, although they were decent, but the coffee was better than decent and the conversation even better.

Graham agreed that Paolo was a cipher, but he was enjoying the new band he was working with and in fact they were hoping to start performing within the next month or so. He grew concerned when I told him about my stop in the studio and the run-in with Kenny and Paolo. I even told him about the stuff on the counter in the studio kitchen.

"I'd hate to think Kenny was going back to that shit," Graham shook his head and muttered almost to himself.

"What do you mean?"

"Kenny…well, he used to be a cokehead," Graham explained. "I'd hate to see him getting back into that."

I didn't know how to respond to that—it wasn't anything I had any familiarity with. "I don't know what to say. I wouldn't know the first thing about it."

Graham nodded sagely over his cup. "I wouldn't think so. But," he picked up his sandwich, "get used to it. You're in the music scene, you'll see it a lot. See it a lot most places, in quite a few of the gay bars, to be honest. Best not to let yourself get tripped up with it if you can avoid it."

I thought that went without saying, and we were quiet as we ate our food.

"So," Graham asked into the silence, "how *is* Fran? She'll be leaving after the year end, right? How're you doing with that?"

I swallowed my last bite hastily because the taste had gone flat in my mouth, and toyed with the rim of my cup.

"I'm doing," I answered finally, then gave him a small grin over my mug, "I'm doing."

"Uh-huh," he answered, "I can see that. What exactly is it that you're doing?"

I measured him, his face, his eyes, the energy that surrounded him, the acceptance and comfort he radiated. Graham had guided me, brought me by the hand almost literally, to a place he thought would be comfortable and appropriate for me, just so I could find the dick I used with my girlfriend, had introduced me to people he cared about, had given me advice about something so intimate, so personal, and he'd asked for absolutely nothing in return. It was a pleasant little jolt to realize I not only liked Graham, I trusted him, instinctively, completely—he had a very generous heart.

"We'll be friends, then, that's all, that's what I'm—we're doing. That's what we're doing." I couldn't completely hide the way I felt from my voice despite the bland expression I was almost positive I wore, and would have been angrier at myself for it had it not been for the expression on Graham's face.

"Tell me you're joking," he set his mug down with a thump and demanded. "You must be. I've seen you together—you can't *possibly* or seriously want to do that." He shifted in his seat and called for a waitress as he reached into his back pocket. "Bill, please," he asked as she passed. He pulled out his wallet, threw a few bills on the table, then jumped to his feet. "On me," he said, "no arguments, and we're going for a drink. We'll call my aunt Lyddie, let your uncle know you'll be a bit. I'll even talk with him," he said over my protests that I was my uncle's ride home.

"C'mon," he said and gave me a friendly thump on my shoulder, "man can't go through that and not talk about it with his mates. Do you play billiards, pool, darts?" he asked as he snapped on the helmet.

"Choice d—none of the above. Why?"

"Tonight you're going to learn. Let's go."

❖

Once I spoke with Uncle Cort, he not only approved, he insisted I spend some time out.

"I'll get back perfectly fine," he told me, "so just go hang out with Graham. Oh, and take care, all right?"

"Are you certain?" I asked.

He chuckled. "Just drop a coin into a phone somewhere if you think you won't be home before morning."

I was a little surprised, both at the permission and its latitude, but Fran was home, and I had no intention of staying out all night. "I'm sure I'll be back way before that," I said, "and thank you."

"You're welcome. Later, then."

And Graham and I were off.

Fact was, Graham was better than his word, and as the night wore on, I found myself telling him, between rounds of darts and turns at the pool table, coins stacked high on the ledge to declare the next player, about how Fran and I had started years ago, about the girl that came between but then united us, how much I loved them both, and that it was okay, it was all okay, because Fran knew how I felt, because she did too, and even with that, what we felt for each other was ours, between us, its own living, breathing entity.

"Listen, mate," he said, his hand heavy on my shoulder after a few rounds, "if Cort's come 'round to Aunt Lyddie's, then it means one of two things. Either the Circle is being called—well, actually, the Circle *is* being called—but this close to Samhain? Who's being initiated? Or is someone being brought into the inner Circle, the Light Bearers?"

I put my pint down so sharply it splashed a bit over the sides, and goggled at him in pure shock. "What do you...I mean, how do you know any of that?" I spluttered.

Graham's gaze was kind. "Sam, my aunt's part of the inner Circle—'course I know."

I'd been much slower to understand than I normally was, but when I got it, I smiled at him. It definitely explained some of the recognition we had between us.

I felt his smile disappear when a cold breeze floated against the back of my neck and Graham stiffened.

"Let's get out of here—I've got your back."

"And me yours," I told him as we stood.

I didn't need to ask why we were leaving. In that clammy chill I'd read the signature of Old Jones, and I wasn't ready to face him yet, to ask the questions and get the answers he might have. He didn't even see us when we walked right by him.

The air was as cold outside as the freeze Jonesy brought with him.

"If Cort's brought you around, then *you* must be the one for the inner Circle," Graham mused aloud as we walked to the scooter, "but then, who'll be…oh…"

"Who'll be what?" I asked him as we readied to take off.

"Nothing, just some thinking aloud," he answered before he was drowned out by the engine.

"Come in for a cuppa 'fore you go," Graham offered as we pulled in front of his building, "and feel free to stay if you're tired—my aunt won't mind. Bring your scooter in—it'll be fine here just inside the door."

"I'll join you for the tea, but I'll leave after," I told him as we went up the stairs. "I don't want Fran to think I've stayed away because—" I caught myself and felt my face burn as I'd realized what I'd been about to say.

Graham opened the door and we entered the kitchen. "Don't want her to think what because why?" Graham's glance was puzzled over his shoulder as he set the pot for tea.

"Tell me more about the Rite, about your Tradition," I said, changing the subject when I could speak calmly. I was proud of the even tone I heard in my voice. "Tell me about the green ray—start with the Goddess."

Graham told me more about the Rite and the tradition the outer Circle worked with than anyone yet. While the inner Circle worked with the undiluted energies of the Universe, the outer one worked with energies just as pure, but eased down into the Material.

"Think of it as the difference between what comes out of a generator plant and what comes through the wall," Graham suggested. "Powerful, useful, even the same in many ways, since one is sourced from the other."

It had rained a bit while I'd been talking with Graham, and I considered as I rode, the streets shining back up at me as I made my way back over to Compton and Dean. I, who had been given so many more answers, proofs, of things unknowable and unknown, had so many more questions. There was the heady esoteric, the onion-layering of the Astral and power, but there was also the starkly Material: searching for the avatar, and for my father's murderer and perhaps my mother's as well, the connection between the seemingly disparate elements of old news and new enemies. And then the Rites, mine and Fran's, and what they would mean, to us, through the Astral, for all time.

I covered the scooter up with the tarpaulin and decided to enter the building through the shop. I was less than surprised to find my uncle seated at his workbench, the sword I'd held so many times during our lessons before him. He wore the leather work gloves I'd seen him wear before when he worked, and the blade rested on two supports as he examined it under the bright light with the magnifying glass that was bolted to the table.

"Are you all right?" he asked, peeking up at me from under his brow for a second before he squinted down the edge of the blade. "Did you have fun with Graham?"

"Well, I managed to play a game or two of darts and not seriously maim anyone," I answered, "and we've discovered I'm much better at pool than billiards. I find it a little confusing, but Graham promises to teach me yet."

He grinned up at me briefly. "Sounds like you've made a solid start."

"We ran into Old Jones."

There was silence as he stared up at me. "Did you seek him?"

"No. Of course not," I answered. "He didn't even see us and we walked right by him."

"Well, that's a relief at least. Then what's on your mind? I can feel the question burning right through you."

"Not now, not tonight, because I want to go upstairs—I don't want Fran to think I've disappeared because, well, you know," I told him, and he gave me a faint smile. "But tomorrow? I want to learn more about two things. No one has ever really told me what exactly it is Fran's learning, and *I* need to know what she can and can't do, and why this specific Rite for her. And…" I took a breath and let my eyes be drawn down to the sword on the table, the play of light on its edge winking at me with a brightness that seemed to come from it as opposed to merely reflect off it. I faced my guardian again. "I want to know everything you can tell me about the legend and the cult of Judas. My father thought it was important. So do I."

He nodded at me. "There's quite a bit to cover."

"I'm okay with that. And…thank you."

"You're welcome," he said gravely.

We wished each other a good night and as I reached for the door that would take me through the shop, he spoke again.

"I'm proud of you," he said quietly. "I know what you and Fran plan on doing, she told Elizabeth, who is, by the way, *very* upset with the two of you about it, but I'm proud of you, proud of you both."

My back stiffened as the tears I'd so successfully kept at bay the entire evening threatened again, and I couldn't look at him for fear they might finally fall. It took me a second or two before I could speak the one mangled word I could manage past the lump that grew in my throat. "Why?"

"You do it because you care about her safety, she does it because she cares about you, what you would suffer in your concern." The words were soft, and behind them was his genuine regard for me. "We do things because they are *right*, not because they are easy, and I'm proud of you because you know—you *both* know—something that has nothing to do with your body, and everything to do with who you *are*."

The tears had gone, receded and I turned to face him, my uncle, my guardian, my teacher. We rarely spoke like this, and when we did, it was special because he was sharing with me not just what he thought, but also how he *felt*. He deserved my full attention, and I gave it to him.

"On this level, in this world, this Material world with its coded rules and physical strictures, you've managed to do something few people ever do, male or female. You know how to stand up and be a man."

I knew what he meant, something beyond chromosomes and biology and gender, so much more than who and how I loved or didn't. It was about honor, nobility, sacrifice. It was about the grace of strength, not only in body, but in mind, to face fear and forge forward anyway, to offer compassion when one could overwhelm with force, to nurture with one hand and protect with the other.

"Thank you," I said simply. I understood.

"You're welcome." We watched each other a second or two longer, and when he smiled at me, it was his warm smile, and I thought maybe, just maybe, a touch sad too. I wondered what he saw, what he felt, what he remembered as he looked at me, but those were things I would never ask. "Go to bed," he said, his voice low and gentle, "Fran's probably still awake and you'll be busy tomorrow."

"I look forward to it," I told him with a grin of my own. "Looking forward."

"Good. Good night."

"You too."

I curled up around Fran minutes later and nuzzled my lips into her head as she snuggled back into me. The perfect peace of it, the trust, the warmth and fit, the kiss she laid on my hand when I laced my fingers through hers, all of it flooded through me, filled me, made my body feel like it expanded past its own barriers with an emotion I couldn't contain. What would it be like to live without that? I had no idea, but I as I fell asleep, I was glad I had it.

PAGAN POETRY

And before my face, beloved of gods and of men,
let thine innermost divine self be enfolded,
in the rapture of the infinite.
—*The Charge of the Goddess*

Cort was in no way exaggerating when he'd told me there was a lot to cover—in fact, I was beginning to suspect that understatement was part of his sense of humor.

"Do I really need to know this?" I asked, and stared aghast at the three-page list of titles he'd compiled for me.

"Okay, I understand the books on symbols, the Brit history books, and even these compilations of legends, but do I really have to read *this*?" I pointed to the listing.

My uncle peered over my shoulder where I sat in the library, then chuckled. "What?" he asked lightly, "not a horoscope fan?"

I glanced up at him and met the light that danced in his eyes. "You're kidding about the astrology, right?"

He laughed in answer. "Leave it for last if you'd like, but it's not what you think. Come on, grab the first thing"— he pointed to the exact shelf—"and let's get started."

We went through history: Paleolithic cave drawings and the Venus of Willendorf, the Romanization of the tribes that had inhabited this part of Europe, and the martial history hidden in mythology—most especially the mythos that surrounded the *dux bellorum*, the War Duke, the leader of troops.

"Don't take that part too seriously," Cort said offhandedly when we moved from history to period literature.

"Which part?" I asked with a grin, "The fairies, the witches, or the quest for the—"

"Any of it," he interrupted. "You just need to know how it relates to the history, forms the mindset that has since become part of the green ray. All of that other…" His forehead creased as he measured his words. "What's real is so hidden under metaphor, I'd rather you ignored it for now—it'll confuse things otherwise."

I chewed on my lip as I thought about that. There were things he'd teach me outright, but others, he liked for me to reach my own conclusions, and I suspected this might be one of them.

But I did learn, and what I came to understand was exactly what Graham had meant by the difference between a generator and an electrical outlet.

That, and there were fascinating things on the Material, including the first level of Aethyr, the nonphysical dimension of our very physical world. The interactions were intricate, and astrology, the science I had much maligned, played a real role. Not in the "you'll find some money today" or "beware of a black dog rounding your corner" sort of way, but in a measurable physical one.

As I struggled to understand the effects of one form of energy on another, I surfaced from the charts I was immersed in, just so I could watch Fran across the room, her head bent over the texts she studied. Every now and again, she'd toss her head and her hair would shift, then settle on her shoulder. She wore an expression of such intense concentration. I found myself staring at the way her brow would furrow or her lips purse as she pounced on the right answer and wrote it down.

"What?" she asked, her lips quirked with the smile she couldn't quite repress as she raised an eyebrow at me.

I put down my book and swallowed. There was a very good reason we sat so far away from each other—we weren't forbidden to touch, it was simply that once we did, there seemed to be almost no boundary, no marking point between loving touch and making love; the last few nights we'd held each other so tightly, bodies rigid with the effort to not cross that line, to relax, soften, entwine…

"What?" she asked again, and this time, she did smile.

"The moon," I said finally when I found my voice and the subject I was supposed to be focused on. "How can an orbiting lump of rock be so important to anything?"

"Sam. It pulls the *oceans* from one side of the planet to the other. How can it not be important, not affect you?" She shook her head and returned her attention to the equations spread before her. "Two days," she said softly.

"What?" I knew it was an echo of her earlier question, but Fran didn't mind.

"Today, and tomorrow, and then…" She let that hang there as her glance told me everything she thought, she wanted. We wanted the same things.

"And then?"

"If you keep looking at me like that, we won't find out."

I was warm, I was restless; I couldn't take it anymore. I closed the book, shoved away the charts, and got out of my chair. "Look like what?" I asked when I stood next to her. Even six inches away, it was almost too much to bear, the shimmer of energy that radiated from her that reached toward me, not in a hungry, seeking sense, but as part of its natural flow, part of our connection.

I rested my hand on the table next to her notes. "Look like what?" I repeated softly as I leaned over to catch the scent of her hair.

She placed her hand over mine. "Stop, please." She looked up at me. "I can barely *breathe*, never mind read, with you this close. You know this is hard on me too."

"Yeah?" I couldn't help myself anymore; I so wanted to kiss her, a simple, little kiss on the cheek. "Is it very hard?" I hadn't meant to speak in double entendres, but once it was said, it was the question she answered.

"Very," she whispered across my lips. "It's *very*, very hard." And then her mouth was next to mine as I kneeled next to her chair, her hand held tight in mine and our fingers almost crushing as we told each other as directly as we could how we felt.

"Would the two of you prefer lunch here or in the dining room?" Elizabeth's voice broke through to my consciousness and it was with great regret that I ended our kiss.

Fran's nostrils flared, her hair was slightly mussed, and the glimpse of golden primal wild that flashed in her eyes as they held mine told me

I probably looked no different. The sweet of her tongue lingered on my lower lip as I tasted it.

"Whatever's easiest," I answered, unable to tear my eyes away from Fran's. I could barely hear myself through the rhythm that beat in my head, and completely lost whatever it was Fran said as I stood with her hand still in mine.

"I'm sorry," I said to her and finally, to Elizabeth. "I wasn't, I mean, we weren't—"

"I know, I wasn't worried about that," she smiled and answered. "I've an idea, though. Lunch up here since you're both studying, but Ann, would you mind spending a moment with me? I'd like for us to talk."

"Sure," I agreed and Fran gave my fingers a quick squeeze before she let me go. "I'll go down with you, then."

"Thank you."

I bent to give Fran the original kiss I'd planned. "Hurry up," she said and grinned. "It's hard *and* I'm hungry."

That made me laugh, and I kept the smile until I walked into the kitchen to help Elizabeth with the food and the trays. Everything was already laid out, soup, sandwich fillers, it merely had to be arranged and served.

I knew what she wanted to discuss and I preempted her as we worked together on the counter. "Elizabeth…Fran and I, it's what we have to do. Surely you understand that."

"I do," she agreed. "I understand why you would think and feel that way, as well as why she does. But, Ann, she's not weak, she's not less than you. If anything, she's your match in so many ways."

"But the threats, and that hound, the one that almost—"

This time Elizabeth interrupted me. "It wasn't because she was unable to defend herself. You, you're under her barrier, all the time, within it, as much as she's within yours. What that…" And her lips tightened even as I could feel the wave of anger and disgust that came from her. "What that *thing* attempted to do was to breach it, to force the rapport, mental rape, if that explains it for you, gives you a better idea, and that can happen to anyone, for any reason." Her voice gentled as she continued. "It's what happened to you, when you were so very small."

I felt the blood drain out of my face as I tried not to spill tomato soup anywhere but into the bowls, and a flare of quickly muted fury that anyone would try to do such a thing, to anyone, and *especially* to Fran. "I didn't know that."

"No, you wouldn't," Elizabeth agreed. She paused as she sliced perfect forty-five degree angles into the bread before her. "I'm afraid that…" She sighed, then began again. "You're hurting yourself, hurting each other unnecessarily. I think you're making a tremendous mistake based on gaps in your knowledge, and until they're filled and corrected, you'll make others."

"I expect that I will make some mistakes," I said, "as this is not something I was born knowing. But," I added quietly, "Cort thinks I'm doing the right thing."

For the first time since I'd known her, I felt as much as heard something as close to a snap as I'd ever seen from Elizabeth.

"Of *course* he does—he trains Wielders, the Light Bearers, and *nothing* comes before that."

Wielders. Plural. My father counted as one and I as another. But the way she'd said it… Was there another he'd trained besides the ones I knew about? "Wielders…as in more than two?" I asked.

Elizabeth didn't answer that as she took a tray and I another to follow her back out of the kitchen. "Just remember," she said, stopping to face me as we stood before the landing. Her very being almost vibrated with her intent as she searched my face. "There is more to you than the sword and the Light. You…your very self, are a living soul, and you too are meant to find the happiness you can, as much as any other."

❖

It turned out that we were all encouraged to eat as much as we wanted since the next day would be a fast day until after the Rite.

"We have to do this starving on every level," Fran joked and I agreed. But we were well behaved, as well behaved as we'd been for the prior six long nights even as we lay skin to skin in a careful embrace that satisfied only the most surface need to touch and nothing else.

"You don't have to go through this with me, you know," Fran had said one night when the connect and the skin and the kiss had left us both with a longing that was a physical ache.

"You could let me just…" And she skimmed her hand along my side, over my hip, and I caught it in mine.

"No," I countered as I linked my fingers through hers, "if you have to, I have to." That just didn't seem fair, and besides, once she touched me, I had to touch her, not for any other reason than I needed to, I wanted to, I simply had to. The compulsion was as irresistible as it was undeniable.

"I love you," she sighed as she kissed me and we pulled each other closer, let our legs tangle together.

"And I love you." I kissed her nose and we lay together, simply staring into one another's eyes, reading the world in them, the world that was us, letting the energy and intensity grow and build.

"Turn around, let me hold you," she asked quietly. "We're never going to sleep like this."

"If I do that," I whispered back, "you have roving hands and we still won't sleep."

"Guilty as charged," she allowed with a tiny smirk, "but we'll feel better."

I smiled back at her. "Close your eyes. We'll sleep fine, I think." I did as I suggested.

"Are you asleep?" I asked less than a minute later.

I knew the answer, though, even before I opened my eyes to find hers still on me, and I chuckled.

"You giggle?" she teased. "Can you do that again?"

"Don't tickle me," I warned, "things might happen." Her fingertips played up and down my arms anyway.

"Oh yeah? What sort of things?" God, the way she spoke was so sensual even as she teased me.

"This!" I surged against her, pressed her beneath me, and she welcomed my tongue between her lips.

"So…" I said almost breathlessly as I stared down at her. I held her hands over her head in mine. "No tickling."

"You're evil."

I thought about that for a moment as I released one of her hands and her legs slid against mine. "I might be," I agreed and circled her nipple with my thumb. It was so beautifully hard and Fran sighed under me.

"Okay, you've made your…point," she said, glancing down at

my hand and I stopped, only to kiss her again, but this really had to stop before we couldn't, and we fit around each other, her back curved against my belly, my hand firmly on hers.

"You owe me," she said into the almost-sleep silence.

"Hmm?"

"When all of this is done, I'm gonna tickle you."

"Ha. I'll remember that," I promised as I tightened my arm around her waist and tucked my head behind hers.

"No, you won't," she teased, "and then? I'll get you, you'll see."

"Uh-huh, sure, if *that's* the first thing you want to do when you can," I teased back.

She turned in my arms and I could see the slow, sexy smile she gave me in the near dark. "That's not the only thing I want to do."

"Really?" I asked, the words soft and muted as I spoke them so close to her lips. "What else do you have in mind?"

I kissed her and the ardent return of her lips gave me the answer even as she eased her leg between mine and she slipped a hand down to my hip to clutch me to her.

I knew what she wanted to do, and I wanted her to do it. The quiet, sensual little moan that escaped when I felt her breasts against mine—*wehavetostop, wehavetostop, wehavetostop*—"What makes you think," I gasped out raggedly against the pounding in my head and chest, the feel of her heart wild against mine, the muscles of her back under my fingertips and the desperate way hers dug into my hip, "that I'm gonna let you?"

She gave a small chuckle, and I knew she recognized my tactic for the diversion it was. "Because," she said and kissed the sensitive skin just under my ear, "you like the way I do it."

Of course I did—and we both knew it. "I don't," I said anyway, just to play.

"Really? You don't?" she drawled, knowing I was playing as I drew my fingers up her back, along her shoulders, then up her neck until I could catch her face in my hands.

"You know I don't *like* it," I said softly as I gazed into eyes that gleamed at me in the intermittent light from the window and drew my thumb against her cheek. "I love it," I told her and kissed her gently, "I love you, love what you do."

The urgent need hadn't abated, but the frantic pull eased back to a manageable sensuality. "Love you too," she murmured against my lips, "love what you do."

Entwined as closely as if we'd just made love (and maybe we had in a way), we once more settled in. "Shh now. Sleep," I whispered.

"You're still gonna owe me," she whispered back, then kissed my neck.

I did, and knew I always would. She gave me everything and I owed her everything—and the only way I had right now of paying her back was to do everything I could to keep her safe.

❖

That rode through my mind as we separately took the long drive, me with Cort, Fran with Elizabeth, to wherever it was that this whole thing was supposed to take place. With almost every suburb ending in "ham" or "shire," they tended to blur in my mind, in much the same way that the three different versions of Compton had when we first got to London, and I was not as surprised as I'd thought I'd be to discover that most of the ceremony would happen outdoors.

"Won't everyone get cold?" I asked Cort.

He clapped a hand on my shoulder. "Between the ritual, the fires, and the energy, no one will notice. You'll see."

As we walked along a side path that led to the yard, the carefully tended shrubs gave way to vines, all obviously painstakingly trained to grow along a canopy so that at the far end, a scene from ages past was set in a yard that seemed to roll on until it met yet another field bounded by a stonework fence, that yawed from there to a mountain.

I didn't know what I'd expected, but this… People, perhaps sixty or more, some in regular dress while others were in robes, all rushed about in an organized chaos, moving tables, setting torches along a set path, groups clustered to light not one, not two, but four well-contained fires that were about six feet or so in diameter and were maintained to a height of about two feet.

"They're getting ready to meet the first star of the evening," Cort said into my ear as I gaped about.

Someone pressed a mug into my hand, glazed warm clay that was smooth under my fingers. "It's okay, you know—it's part of the whole Rite," he told me after he sipped from his own mug.

I took a tentative sip. It was sweet, almost overwhelmingly so, and the taste made me think of pears.

The sense of excitement and expectation grew, was a palpable haze in the neoprimitive scene that blossomed before my eyes.

"C'mon," Graham said, appearing at my shoulder out of seemingly nowhere, "we have to wait here." His eyes danced with reflected flame, with his own energy. His outline hazed, shifted and glowed, and I glanced over to Cort, who nodded.

"Go on," he said and grinned at me, "go join the other young bucks."

I glanced at Graham, who smiled widely. "It's a traditional...test," he said. "C'mon!" and he pulled on my elbow.

"Good luck!" Cort called and waved at me.

Bemused, I walked with Graham, careful not to spill my drink as we crossed the yard, and he took me downfield where a knot of people gathered. "Here," he said, "we wait here. Have another sip," he said kindly. "You'll *see*."

I hesitated a moment as I looked about me, the energy thick as it swirled around us with the heavy, edgy bite of expectation. "You feel it already," Graham said quietly into my ear, "because you walk between worlds. This," and he hefted the drink he carried in his own hand, "is to help open the gates, and you," he examined me closely, "well, you're already walking through them, aren't you."

Following his example, I lifted the mug to drink. The sweet taste of herbs and pears flowed past my lips, my tongue, was a soothing, syrupy river down my throat. A gong sounded deep and clear, ringing in a tone that seemed to echo across the Worlds.

Voices called from different corners, the Convocation, the formation of the Circle, the welcome of the Elements and their respective directions. The air shimmered as they were called and came, and the Circle grew almost visible, a gauzy light curtain I could see so long as I didn't look at it directly.

From behind us came the answering call that rang with its own crystalline purity as the note hung, swelled. It filled the Circle as they came, the procession.

A woman led them, her carriage strong, proud, and graceful, her hair a glow of white as they entered the cleared center. They were six in all, dressed in white that flowed with the currents of air and fire, flowed with the grace of water, meeting the earth only to flow back up, the cycle over and over and over.

Elizabeth, it was Elizabeth, I realized even as I sipped again, and when she stopped, a new, smaller, Circle formed: one stood within and she without.

It wasn't so much that I couldn't hear the words spoken from the inside, nor the responses the crowd made, so much as I couldn't translate them, but it didn't matter; I *understood* them in a deep way. This was familiar, this was something I'd done a thousand times. This was the way *home*.

"What's the test?" I asked Graham quietly as the excitement I'd felt before grew in the hearts that surrounded me and in my own, an impatient wilding surge of energy that powered my limbs, sharpened my senses, made my chest beat with the same pounding rhythm that echoed through the Circle.

Graham's fingers tapped with nervous energy on my hand and when I glanced at him, his smile seemed to grow. I *knew* him, recognized his soul clearly, and put my arm around his shoulders in welcome. I kissed his cheek. He was my brother, my friend, my kith and kin, and his fingers drummed on mine in return.

"Who will be the Champion for the Goddess," he whispered and held me closer. "Consort, defender, willing sacrifice—all of it. As above, so below."

The shuffle and the mutter grew around us, an agitated jostle of bodies, the restive twitch and flex of muscle. We were waiting, waiting…oxen caged and penned, dogs given scent straining against the leash, a pack, an army about to charge, the arrow nocked against the bow, waiting on the word, waiting for—

"No worries, my brother," Graham said into my ear and I couldn't help but notice his lips were soft along its edge, "you'll win, I know it."

Brother. Yes, we were, had always been…

My blood sang, sang a fiery high praise through me as it rose with the stars, with the voices that called all around us, my body flowed with the rhythm of the tide, filled with the strength of the earth that pounded with the drums beneath my feet, the scent of smoke and herbs and cut grasses the counterpoint that swirled around my head and…

She was out there, in the center of that smaller Circle, shining like ice, like fire, like crystal, the nimbus around Her the borealis, a flame into the sky.

The question blew out into the Circle, the clear call of challenge that I moved forward to answer, forging my way through the bodies that blocked me, the impeding arms and legs, Graham encouraging and solid at my back. No one else had the right, not the way I did, and I knew it as I pushed and wrestled through, using my shoulders to advance, to open my path. I could feel them around me, the ones who struggled through as well, saw them with my peripheral vision as the very physical challenge continued, the gauntlet we struggled through. There were five, then four, then two. This was my place and I knew it, knew that I was the one to do it—*no one* else had the right, or the claim, I had. Then my forward progress was arrested as someone solidly stopped me.

Completely halted, I looked at the large bare chest before me, the arms that bulged with muscle and strength ending in firm large fists that curled on hips perched over solidly planted legs. He. Was. Huge.

His head was shaved and the firelight glistened on the light sheen of sweat that covered his face, his shoulders, highlighting the muscles in his chest. "Let the Champion be tested," called the Guardian of the Goddess. "By what right would you defend?" His lip curled at me with scorn.

His eyes caught the bonfire, blazing with contempt as everyone seemed to fall back and away, Graham too, after a reassuring press on my shoulder. They left us to stand alone, the Guardian between me and my goal. I could feel Her eyes on me from behind him as I squared my shoulders, felt the line of force flow through my spine as it straightened.

The energies became intersecting lines, the Elementals jumped and jigged about me as my bones, my blood, my soul remembered the answer, then spoke it for me.

"I claim by right of blood," I said as he swung at me, his feet planted in the earth as I floated away like air. "I claim in the face of death." He burned, moved with living flame, and I flowed around him like water. "I claim it for life." The leg came up for the aerial move and I hit the ground, let it sweep, a sharp gust over me and I *saw* it as I straightened, the opening in the nexus of force and I reached out to tap his chest with my finger as my own fire burned within. "I claim it with love." He overbalanced and fell hard, and the earth gnomes danced around him as the salamanders of fire lit my way.

She was the Goddess before me and I fell as the rain to my knees. "I claim it for you," I whispered. Undines sang and the sylphs brushed my hair away from my face as She took my hand in Hers. She raised me to stand before Her as the world shifted and shook, the Light that surrounded Her almost blinding as the voices sang in my ears, *"Isis, Astarte, Diana—Hecate, Demeter, Kali—Inanna!"* loud enough to match the heart I suddenly felt beat within me, the painful lurch of life.

"And I lay claim to *you*," the Goddess said, and She crowned me as Consort with Her kiss.

"The Challenge has been answered," the voice of the man I'd just seen fall to earth cried. "The Goddess will be served!"

"Isis, Astarte, Diana—Hecate, Demeter, Kali—Inanna!"

Elizabeth stood before us when the kiss ended and I saw her as she held the chalice before me. I took it from her hands and pulled deeply, the words she spoke a buzz in my ears as the syrupy mix raced under my skin, her meaning clear as the inner Circle closed around us. Quick, careful hands stripped me, then covered us both with a soft blanket.

It was impossible to tell if we were guided or carried to the pavilion-tent-grove-room— whatever it was—because Her skin played against me, wrapped under that smooth cloth and around each other as we moved. Fingers fed me as hands stroked my hips, my ribs, the catch of my body on Hers. I don't know what I ate, only that there was the taste of grapes and the soft lips perfect on mine. Somehow we lay together, and everything everywhere was the touch of silk, of satin, soft and cushioned against my back with my nerves alive and tingling.

"Isis, Astarte, Diana—Hecate, Demeter, Kali—Inanna!"

The chorus sang over and over, the call and cry of strength, of triumph, to the beat of blood and drums, a pulse of life and love and lust that the rhythmic pound focused in me, and even as I hardened and swelled, my vision splintered further, now the world, now the energies that intersected it, and She towered above me, *"Isis, Astarte, Diana— Hecate, Demeter, Kali—Inanna!"* the Great Huntress and Healer, the Mother and Reaver, the essential primitive perfect warrior, the consummate nurturer. Golden fingertips placed a ruby of fire between my lips that I sucked and swallowed.

The elements and energies swirled and coiled, focused, filling the air, thick enough to swim through. *"Isis, Astarte, Diana—Hecate, Demeter, Kali—Inanna!"* She smiled down at me even as She rose again to part Herself, Her body, to receive mine.

I was Her Champion, by right, by contest, by choice—I was Her *chosen* Consort. *"Isis, Astarte, Diana—Hecate, Demeter, Kali—Inanna!"* I gasped at the connect through it all, the snap of the intense physical that married us on every level as She claimed Her prize.

❖

"I so rarely get to see you like this," Fran's voice tickled against my ear as her fingertip traced a light path along my face.

"Hmm? Like what?" I asked as I stretched, enjoying the strength I could feel in my own body, the warmth of the sun that shone in through the window on us, and the completing and satisfying pressure of Fran next to me.

We had two days, two whole days to do nothing but enjoy one another before we were back to our routines, the lectures and studies, the research, and of course, rehearsals for me, but for now…we had one another and the time to relax. I supposed everyone needed to recover from the Rite.

"Like this," she said and slid over me. She caught my hands in hers then spread her palms against mine, and I looked up into eyes that still hadn't lost the extra spark they'd carried since she was the Goddess before me. "Warm and relaxed." She smiled, then kissed me softly. "Soft…open…peaceful." She kissed me again between each word.

"Do you have anything in mind for today?" I asked quietly. "We haven't gone to Ronnie Scott's yet, and there's…mph." Her lips had found the sensitive spot of my throat and tugged gently.

"Nothing I can think of or want," she said against my ear, "involves leaving this room." Her entire body eased along mine and I returned the slide of her hands before I wrapped my arms around her.

"I *love* the way you think," I told her as the warmth from the sun became the warmth from her skin and suffused me, made me liquid sunshine next to her.

"You just love me for my mind," she murmured as I ran my hands down her back, gently kneading the muscles on the way until the beautiful curve of her backside was under my palms and I pulled her closer to me.

"I do," I answered, then kissed her. "And I love your spirit." I shifted my hips and held her closely so I could roll her beneath me. "I love your heart," I told her and kissed her again. "I love your soul," I murmured against her breast, her nipple hard between my teeth, the taste sweet under my tongue. "I love the body that holds them," I said as I let my hands go where they wanted, "the way you look," she parted her thighs for me, "the way you feel, taste…" And I gazed for a hot and hungry moment upon her cunt, the fine dark gold hairs, the proud jut of her clit that hardened for me and the sheen of her arousal as it pooled at her entrance, the entrance that had welcomed my tongue, my clit, my cock and my fingers.

I loved to look, but I couldn't wait anymore. "This…" I whispered as I felt the shiver of anticipation that ran through her echo through me. "This is how I show you," I said and I gratefully took her into my mouth, knowing I had the rest of this day and the next to show her just how much.

❖

It was probably the shortest forty-eight hours I'd ever known, and when we did finally emerge from our cocoon to the world, it was to discover that everything and nothing had changed.

The rapport between us was so absolute that if she was hungry, I felt it; if I was sore from an evening session with my uncle, she would absentmindedly rub her own shoulder. When we wanted one another there was no way of knowing with whom the desire had originated.

And…I noticed that the flame that danced and beckoned in Fran's eyes was the same added shine that both my guardian and my teacher bore; it was part of Graham too, if I took the time to think about it.

We hardly parted, choosing instead to maintain a physical connection in addition to the emotional and psychic, partially because being apart actually hurt, was a clearly discernable lack. And while we never spoke of it, we both knew our time was running down—so we were making the most of every moment.

What hadn't changed was that I still couldn't connect all the dots, and learning the myth that formed the background of the cult of Judas didn't help.

"They say," Cort began after a session that had further developed my ability to monitor and to affect small changes in metabolism, "that Judas had thought to escape his fate, his karma, his wyrd," and he grinned at Elizabeth and Fran when he said it, knowing that was the preferred word in their tradition, "by hanging himself. But he did not. In fact, the legend says that while he seemed dead, the Lords of Light had sentenced him to walk the earth until he could save as many as his actions had betrayed. And in greedy zest for mortal life, he learned how to steal, to drink, to trade in the essences of life for youth of the body, of the mind.

"In time, a cult grew around this, believing that to steal another's essence was to increase one's own. They each wear a token—and since they're all *about* power, the placement of the token varies with position in the hierarchy."

Fran curled her fingers into mine on my lap and snuggled closer into my shoulder. "Well, what is it?"

Cort gave a grim little smile. "Since he hanged himself, the token is a piece of rope, usually hemp of some sort. Hounds who are not vessels—do you understand what vessels are?" he broke off to ask, his gaze resting on each of us in turn.

I took a wild guess. "Voluntary servants or something?"

The twist on his lips tightened further. "They voluntarily give their services, their minds, and their energies, to a dark Master and their hounds."

Cort nodded into the silence that greeted that. I couldn't think of anything more horrifying. To knowingly, *willingly*, give oneself up like that? But why? Why would anyone choose such a thing?

But there was something even more important to know for now. "So the hounds have tokens too?"

"They tend to wear them about their wrist or ankle. Vessels and those chosen to advance will wear one about the neck, and those fully fledged…well…" He stared into the fire. "They bear a mark," he said softly. "They wear a rope around their bodies in ritual, and are marked by a brand, an incised brand, where they say the heart used to be. Those chosen to be devoured are marked similarly, with an iron cross."

"Are they right?" Fran asked.

"In what way?"

"Can they actually extend their lives?"

"Legend says so."

I shifted in my seat. Maybe there was something here after all. "How long?"

His eyes rested on mine with serious intent. "No one knows for certain—nor how they die either."

I nodded as I absorbed that. "Ignoring the live-forever thing," I said, "what does that do? Stealing essence, I mean?"

"It can extend their abilities through the Aethyr, and they can share some of their abilities with their hounds and vessels," Elizabeth said.

I twisted my head to see her clearly. "What do you mean? What abilities?"

She answered quietly and her face bore such quiet anger I almost knew what she'd say before she spoke it. "The ability to track and follow, to reach through one to touch another, and the breach of the natural shield—the forced rapport."

I didn't know if it was Fran or I who shivered at that, and I held her tighter even as her hand closed with strength around mine.

"If the cult's been revived, then how do we stop them?" That's what my father had thought, and if his theories were as sound as his notes...

Cort stared into the flames and they reflected back into his eyes, making them burn from without as well as within when he faced me.

"There are two ways," he said. "You can strip them of their abilities—bind and contain them on the Astral or," he took a deep breath, "your sword, yours specifically."

"So, if we find them and contain them, we can eliminate the threat?" I asked, puzzling it out aloud.

"No." His answer was curt, abrupt. "If Judas still walks, they look for him. Every incarnation of the cult has sought to find and put him into temporal power."

"But this is a legend," I interrupted. It was confusing because he'd began as if he was sharing a story, but now, it seemed as if he considered it more than that.

"All legends have a root in truth," Fran said quietly.

"Well then," I asked, "what if we find and contain *him*?"

The tiger that I saw so often in Cort's eyes came roaring to life as he gazed at me. "He cannot be contained—only destroyed."

"Then the real question is," I said as I thought it, "*who* is Judas?"

Cort shook his head. "No one knows—but then, no one is certain that it's *that* much more than legend either."

His jaw set as he stared once more into the flames and I felt the anticipation that waved from him, from Elizabeth, become something thick and heavy in the air as everything suddenly clicked, a definitive lock in my head as pieces fell together.

"What's the relic?" I asked into pregnant silence broken only by the occasional pop in the grate. "What's the heart of the blade?" I'd held it so often, had felt its vibrations and carried its extension through the Aethyr, the Astral, on the Plains, and now it had a connection to a legend that my Da had died to prove had been brought to life.

I didn't know if I was afraid of the answer, didn't know if it would make sense, might fit into the puzzle in a way that would give a hint of the larger picture, but if it was worth my father's life to find out, then it was worth my discomfort to ask.

When my guardian and teacher faced me again, his eyes seemed haunted.

"A nail," he said finally, "a very old nail."

❖

In the week before Samhain, Cort and I spent the first three days traveling. It would have been a few hours' ride, he told me, but there were more people to see and speak with on the way—the Inner Circle was being called and told the location as close to the time as possible.

As he explained to me on our way in a car he'd rented for that very purpose, any member about to be inducted to the Inner Circle faced, as he'd put it, "certain mortal peril," which meant no riding about on my Vespa, no wandering around town without him, and pretty much no *anything* outside the apartment that was not under his very watchful gaze.

Thankfully, our very first stop would be Lyddie and Graham's, and as we rode along through the traffic-congested streets, Cort explained some of the details of the Rite to come. I'd be asked to maintain a three-day vigil, a trance that he would monitor throughout, to face for the first time, truly alone, whatever waited out there on the Plain and to confront it as best I could, armed only with what I knew. I would be given breaks, small ones for essential food and water.

I nodded grimly, wondering if I'd be able to endure it and determined to no matter what. My Da had done it, and so had his mother, my grandmother, the woman neither of us had ever known.

"You'll need a second," Cort said.

"What's a second?"

"Someone to follow you on your journey, to be the living recorder of what happens. And since I'm certain you'll be nervous," he cut his eyes toward me and gave me a grin, "to make sure you've been properly prepared, haven't forgotten to tie a shoelace or some such, once the Rite begins."

He answered my question before I spoke it. "No, it can't be Fran— she has her own part to play."

I wondered about that as we stepped into the building.

"The time and place have been decided," Cort said when Lyddie opened the door.

She took my hands in hers and bowed her head over them. "I welcome the youngest of the Inner Circle to my home," she said.

The words had the force of ritual behind them and I didn't know how to respond.

At that moment, Graham stepped up and Cort clapped a hand on my shoulder.

"Well, ask him, then," he said, and I could hear the humor in his tone. I glanced back up at him to see the briefest twinkle of amusement in his eyes.

I took a breath, not certain if I felt anything other than numb. "Graham...I need a second. Will you be mine?"

"To work with the Light Bearers," he whispered reverently, eyes shining. "To be your second, your shield bearer? Yes, of course," he answered and we shook hands to agree.

He pulled me into a strong hug which I returned. "I won't let you down, brother," he promised solemnly.

"I know you won't."

My second. With everything else that was about to happen, it was reassuring to have Graham with me.

Since Graham would stay with us for the next few days, we stayed long enough for him to pack the things he needed while Cort and Lyddie covered whatever details they had to, then he continued the journey with us as Cort took me through the rounds. They all greeted me in the same way Lyddie had.

"This isn't everyone," Cort said as we pulled back to the apartment. "There are a few—not all of them part of the Circle, but certainly part of the plan—you'll meet the night of your sealing."

I felt light-headed as we trooped up the stairs after we'd hung up our coats by the door, and even with the almost festive air during dinner after Graham had been shown his room, as well as the very real joy Fran and I shared later, I couldn't help but lie awake even as I tried to force myself to sleep, not because I didn't know what tomorrow would be, but because I did.

Everything I'd learned would be tested, would bring what had previously been practice, lecture, and exercise into a very visceral reality—a reality where my Da had been killed, not because he was a fireman in the line of duty, but because of this, the pursuit of a legend, a reality where innocents had been hurt, maimed, murdered, for sport, with greed—in fear for the protection of a secret I now knew only the most surface part of, a secret that put people I loved in danger.

The days that followed the Sealing would bring the search for the truth my father died for and the identity of whoever had killed the hound I'd hunted what seemed like ages ago on the Astral. Tomorrow would bring me closer still to the coming separation from Fran, from *everything* in so many ways. The future carried the sword I still wasn't sure I could use or how, and the very real confidence that Cort and Elizabeth seemed to have that I could live up to whatever it *really* was that was expected of me. And the very real probability of a particularly violent death.

My Da had died to find a truth, my grandmother in a failed defense. I didn't know how I could do or face *any* of that, and accomplish what they couldn't. That…scared me.

Blood Line

I am the Hunter and Hunted,
I am the Wolf and the Shepherd,
I am the Vine and the Grain.
—The Charge of the God

Three days. Three days on my knees, maintaining the trance that would bring me through to the Astral, to the Plain. I traveled through the Aethyr, found spots of darkness that hid among the brighter lights that shone from healthy human life, ran with wolves through the Plain, was forced to wrestle something that looked like a bear only it had no fur. And throughout, the bright spark that was Graham was never too far in the distance.

Twice I came out of the trance with my nose bleeding freely while I ate blankly, drank enough water to maintain my system, then went back under.

I traveled through memories older than myself, fought and died with my family when they were attacked by Northmen who announced their presence by releasing herds of hogs to rampage through small towns and villages before they would strike, butchering all, letting the hogs root through the remains before they burned the rest; died and died again, shot through with a black and yellow feathered bolt that flew from an unseen hand rather than let my brother, recently handfasted and awaiting his first child, take it in his own body; shot again by my own hand in yet another land when I thought someone I'd dearly loved had died.

I saw them, saw them all, my family, my friends, my loves,

different names and faces, different bodies and relationships, and saw clearly the connections through space and time, the inevitability of the past and how I'd come to my present. I understood the ancient word *wyrd*, the concept of karma, Fate, and when I grounded back to the Material, Cort's voice sounded in the room.

"It's time."

My sealing was to be held in a semiabandoned warehouse off the docks, an ancient brick building still scarred from an explosion almost a generation ago.

I'd been dressed in white and waited by a fire that had been set in a large clay bowl as the Circle formed around me. All wore robes and three were hooded, shrouded from my sight. Somewhere far above my head and hidden in darkness, pigeons roosted and complained about their interrupted sleep.

I was handed a chalice that I passed to everyone else before I sipped. This wasn't the same drink that had been given at Fran's sealing. This was thick, spicy, and not quite as sweet, and I felt light, almost gauzy as the Circle closed around me.

"Let her summon the Elementals, complete the Circle," a bass voice commanded.

When I turned to the directions the elements corresponded to, I made the request, not to the elements but to their Kings, as I'd been taught. As they manifested to the Material, they brought their attendants. The fire leapt with greater brightness, a gust of air blew the robes about, a spatter of rain struck the windows, and the stone vibrated under our feet.

Four columns of indeterminate shadow now guarded the Circle.

Unlike the last Rite, the first one I'd been to, I no longer needed the mix of herbs and wine to open the channels for me; I had mastered them. I hefted the chalice in salute to all those that surrounded me, then offered it to the fire.

It hissed as the first figure stepped forward and I recognized Lyddie, her eyes bright and her gaze solemn. "You have been called to the Gate," she said. "To what purpose?"

"To guard," I answered. "To defend."

"I accept your call," she said and nodded, satisfied, then returned to her position.

I felt a surge run through me, a heat race through my skin as the fire snapped and flared. One of the faint pillars that guarded the Circle shimmered faintly.

Another stepped forward. His face was lined, his shoulder-length hair cloud white, and his eyes were a shocking blue, even in the firelight. There was unmistakable strength in his gaze, and he emanated presence, knowledge, sureness. He was old, older than anyone I could ever remember meeting.

"Called to the Gate, to guard and defend," he said, "but for how long? We are but a moment on the Material in the sight of the Universe. Do you chose the moment, or do you pledge for the greater Challenge?"

The wind rose up in a howl around the building, blowing through the chinks and cracks in the doors and windows as I answered truthfully from the deepest part of me.

"The greater Challenge—life to life."

The wind ruffled the very hairs on my arms as it swirled around us, then calmed, and another pillar shimmered.

"Let the living Dark Lord issue his Challenge as is right in the balance," a voice hissed dryly, a voice I knew, and I looked among those that ringed me to discover from whom it had issued. My eyes found the figure, shrouded in a gray cloak before he threw back his hood, and it was somehow unsurprising to recognize Old Jones, only here, now, with my vision open to the different levels, he held a form, one I had by now seen many times before: nonhuman, but humanoid, a slender figure made of gray skin, with a face that looked more like a mask and two black slits that shone like oil for eyes. I still couldn't tell if those were ears or horns that rose from his head, the same color and texture as the rest of his aethyric body.

Cort stepped forward. "Rafael has called for the Challenge, his right as Examiner," he said to the others. "Do any deny him?" He looked about the crowd and no one answered.

"The Challenge has been accepted," he said, and returned to his original position.

The next figure that approached me was cloaked in a black that seemed to absorb the light around it. He was taller even than Cort, and the hood he did not remove added to his height. He radiated strength, power, menace, as if he meant to frighten me. I stood my ground anyway as he advanced.

"Called to the Gate," his voice echoed as he circled me, "to guard and defend. Called to the Gate, through each life that ends. Will you honor the pact, the natural flow? Will you honor the balance that existed before time began, back when the Dark and the Light were equals and sang the same harmonic song?"

I saw the faint gleam of his eyes under the shadow of the hood and I focused on them. "I swear to honor the balance, to do all in my power to restore the flow where it has been damaged, to sing the same harmony."

He threw back his hood, the living Dark Lord who operated, too, by the Law, in service to the Balance, revealing long dark hair that disappeared beneath his cloak and a mouth framed by a sleekly trimmed beard. He smiled at me before he turned to rest. "The Challenge has been called and answered—the Dark recognizes your youngest Champion."

The wind howled once more as rain beat upon the roof and windows, the sound of a thousand hammers smacking down on slate while cool electric lines descended from my head to my feet, a shock of sensation through my spine, my arms, my legs, as it joined the other energies that had begun to coil through me, and in my peripheral vision, yet another pillar shimmered.

With each question and answer, they seemed a bit brighter, and as my very human body struggled to contain the flows that ran through me, I began to feel the shimmering, dizzying approach of overload as another came to me.

The robe did nothing to hide the lush form beneath it and she emanated jovial warmth. The flame was reflected in the copper of her hair, and the smile she beamed at me was sincere as she took my hands in hers.

The touch of her fingers to mine felt like a hundred different caresses, the press of skin to skin all over, and my mind wavered as she opened her mouth to speak.

"And what would you take in return, Child? Would you bind yourself to the Material, not seeking to shirk the life that awaits you? Your gifts are manifest within you, your path set before you, your life, your death, your return to the elements. Do you accept it in its entirety, or would you seek more? It is much to bear and unfair to ask without your complete acceptance."

My body began to tremble under the onslaught but I held my voice steady, firm, as I gave my answer.

"I accept that which is mine within the natural order, I accept the choices I've made in the past that have led me to this place. I will walk the path before me."

"Take your gifts, Child of Light, Child of Fire and Air, of Water and Earth," she said, then leaned up and kissed me. Her mouth met mine with an electric tingle, and as her tongue eased between my lips, I felt the swift twirl of the planet beneath my feet as the final flood of power churned within me. The pillars seemed to blaze before my eyes, and as I gazed about the Circle I saw their aethyric forms clearly, read the secrets of their bodies and knew their healths and ailments, so clear, so very visible to my eyes…smiled at the crowded gnomes and sylphs as they jostled one another, wrestling and pinching each other to get the better view, saw Graham just beyond the Circle and the beauty of his true self, the pure body of Light that was male, female, both, neither… The salamanders jumped and played like dolphins in the sea of flame that held them as the undines sang their liquid song.

Once again the aethyric and the Material merged, crystalline lines and patterns that danced and twisted, and the minds before me were so very, very visible.

"You are not only to be Wielder," Cort's voice spoke clearly into the swirl that jigged before me, "but you have mastered the Aethyr. More than guardian, you are guide. Will you honor the heritage that rides in your blood? Will you carry Linea Sanguen, the thread, the line of blood, to maintain the balance and guard the Gate?"

His gloved hands held, half pulled from its new black scabbard, the sword I'd seen so many times, but it had never looked like this before. It had been buffed and polished to newness, the hilt redone in the same inky black as the scabbard. It reflected and refracted the flames and seemed to glow with its own inner light.

I carefully took the hilt in my right hand and removed it. "I will," I swore and drew the diamond edge across my palm, cutting a line from the pad just under my index finger to the outer edge by the pinkie, right above my wrist.

I held my hand up and let the blood drip onto the floor. "I bind myself to it."

"Called to the Gate," he said, his voice echoing in my head, "to guard and defend. Called to the Gate, through each life that ends. Called to the Gate, so swear and so bind, not the cup, nor the spear, but the sword and the mind."

A knock of thunder shook the very walls around us.

"The Lords of Light have accepted the new Wielder!" he called out as he bound the scabbard about my waist.

I was almost blind, reeling as the world revealed itself and the power, the energy I would use and control unleashed within me. Every mind was wide open; I could walk through any at will, pick a thought or memory, plant one if I chose, create or negate will. The sword sung in my hand, a myriad of images and emotions, each one readable, touchable, and as I looked through the nexus lines that blossomed before me, I could see where each possibility led, the higher and lower probabilities of outcome.

It was Elizabeth, her energy and aethyric double I recognized through the blaze that took away normal sight, who put her hands on my shoulders when I'd sheathed the blade, the weapon with a name I now knew: Blood Line.

"You are bound to the Light," she said as she bandaged my hand, "Wielder, and Master of Aethyr besides, but you must work on this world, in the Material. Would you be equally bound to it, to its hopes and fears, its loves and sorrows as well?"

I nodded, unable to speak, and suddenly Fran was before me, not the Fran I'd known before, and not the Goddess, but *her*, the essential her, fierce, proud, and golden, infinitely beautiful and blazing with an emotion that went beyond words, what she felt for me. I could see the bond we shared that stretched from this life to the ones that preceded it, to the ones that followed. And I knew I could do anything I wanted, anything at all: I could take her mind and remake it any way I saw fit, I could take her on floor before the fire and none would stop me as the power ravened through me.

But I couldn't do that because I *wouldn't* do that… I grabbed the ankh around my neck and let the force flow to it, charging it—it now not only had the net of my life, but its strength, my energy and essence.

As I channeled the overload into the matrix of metal I squeezed in my hand, I knew with an unshakeable surety that this had been yet another test: to be part of the Circle, fully empowered, and fully able to turn on it, to impose my will upon and destroy it, yet deliberately choose not to… And as the world began to right itself once more I witnessed the mantle of the Goddess, the distinct nimbus of power, descend upon my lover, my friend, transforming her once more.

"Do you acknowledge the power of the Goddess over your life and your death, so long as you take breath on this world, live in this structured form?"

"I do and will," I answered through the pounding rush in my body, the energies given to and unleashed within me a mad swirl barely under my control, the tilt and spin a force that beat with my heart and through my chest, a throb that pressed and pulled at my body, filled me with an ache. On the many levels of existence, I was Hers: Champion and Consort, the willing sacrifice, the one who would shed blood so that others might not, a means, a weapon, a tool, no more but certainly no less in the hands of the Light.

She closed the distance between us and Her fingertips brushed against my neck, opened my collar, opened the robe I wore and pressed against my chest, pushing me down before her. I felt more than saw with my peripheral vision the backs that turned to us, the approach of Graham, of Elizabeth, of Cort, as they surrounded us.

Her hands skated down my sides, and She kissed me as she carefully undressed me. "Will you accept the Goddess?"

I saw the curtain that surrounded us, thick enough to block direct vision, thin enough to permit the light of the flame to glow within.

I gazed into Her eyes, the lambent glow from within and without, breathless from the visions that swam before me and the flow within me. "Yes," I whispered, and She murmured ritual blessings against my skin as She kissed the points of energy exchange and collection, painting a line of incandescence down my body. The robe She wore was silken against my skin, the feel of the cool flow of water as She breathed against me, the stone solid beneath my back.

"This," She said as She fit her shoulders between my thighs, "is the Gift of the Goddess."

The Gate opened before my dazzled eyes, and I found my voice when she took me into her mouth.

There were no barriers between Worlds, the living and the newly dead mixed freely, one mostly unaware of the other, except for those that wandered in their sleep, and I saw them in their multitudes, the hopes and dreams, the fears and despairs of the world, and the monsters and saviors that moved among them. And as I yielded to the kiss of the Goddess, I slowly grounded as She restructured and settled the energies that flowed within me. I opened my eyes as Her lips caressed the tendon of my thigh.

She kissed me again, enough to make certain that I was fully in the body, then flowed up me, Her robe open, covering us both as She hovered over me.

"You have accepted the Goddess," she murmured, then kissed me, briefly but thoroughly, allowing me to taste myself on her lips.

"Then accept, too," She said, and Her aura shimmered, shifted, a reflection of graceful strength, of power with form, of the Light, focused, directed, active, "the God." He plunged His cock, heavy and thick, hot and hard, in me.

"Yes," I agreed as the Gate slammed shut with me within it, and as my body lifted to meet His my life flowed back, back, I saw my friends, my father, my childhood, my mother. I felt my first breath, the explosion that was my creation, and the wheel of the planet gave way before me, threw me into the Great Void.

And then it was us, me and Fran, close, closer, immutably bound, and I flew, a downward rush, a speeding spiraling path through the Universe, the branching reaching touches through worlds, the fast-forward play of my life to this very moment until again I burst forward, past the now, past the future that played before me in a white haze, past the body and into the Light.

There, I saw the pattern, the entire Tapestry in its beautiful unfinished completeness, understood the limits of the Material, the full possibilities of the rest not similarly contained, and even as I saw, it slipped away to be replaced only with the assurance that there was a meaning, an order, a reason.

I had the full, cell deep knowledge that I was promised, sealed, this life, and the next, for however many would be, to these people and to the ones I'd known before, to the woman who bore the power of the Goddess and the God as she moved within me, bringing me to my knees before the one Great Truth. She brought me back to the Material, to the body that slipped urgently beneath hers, and as we came together once more, the power became mine.

ME AND MY CHARMS

There are some whose bravery increases At the sight of their own blood...
...And so I'll scorn all injury, And hardships I will disregard.
—Shantideva, *The Way of the Boddhisattva*, Padmakara, tr.

The constant tick-tock and the flipping calendar ensured the days flew, and as mid-November approached, the West End lit up for the holidays.

Not only was it my first Christmas in London, I also didn't want Fran to miss a thing, and I enlisted everyone's help in finding out what all those things were, from choir performances to newly lit trees to little skating rinks that popped up in different neighborhoods.

"Christmas seems to be the ultimate Victorian art form," Fran observed one evening as we returned from our wanderings.

"True," I agreed, and caught her about the waist, "but I'm certain they were willfully ignorant of the true meaning behind mistletoe."

The smile she wore seemed to match the way mine felt, and her eyes shone up at me before she glanced over my head to the sprig that hung over the door. "Well," she said as she put her arms around my neck, "you know I'm not about to forget."

I wasn't about to, either.

But still, Fran grew tense as time wound down, and while I was concerned as well, I didn't quite have the same frantic approach. Then again, she was facing a late start to her freshman year at Columbia, back in New York, and I was rather certain I'd be staying in England. We didn't talk about it, but she knew, and *I* knew it upset her.

I didn't tell her to relax or anything like that—that would have been dismissive of her very real concerns. Instead, I distracted her by taking her to places she hadn't been to yet, and I teased her about her birthday and Christmas, both of which were fast coming.

The tension she carried, the will to succeed, translated into everything she did, and coalesced between her shoulder blades. "Oh yeah...that, right there..."

I refocused my fingertips on the knot beneath her skin. If I let my sight drift, I could see the neural netways, the paths and channels, the blocks and flows as they ran through her, and I worked on clearing them, soothing the muscles that had stretched and tightened during the day.

"Thank you," she sighed, then settled her head on her hands. "I suppose it would be nice if I decided on a major before heading back," she observed, and gave me a wry grin over her shoulder.

"Study whatever you want. You'll go to grad school anyway," I said as I molded her shoulder blade under my hands. I *really* liked the way that looked—my hands on her body.

Fran shifted, her legs grazing the inside of my thighs as she turned and gazed up at me with eyes a mellow caramel in the lamplight. "Why don't you come with me?"

"What do you mean?"

She sat up on her elbows. "You got comped to Princeton—Columbia would easily give you a scholarship, academic or athletic. Come with me. My father's paid for an apartment so we've already got a place, everything here's quieted down, and you can do your research just as easily there as here, maybe even faster because you can speak to some of those people in your notes, visit those places."

"Hmm..." I stroked the strong lines of her shoulders as I considered. "Maybe I can look into it for next fall."

She was right, nothing, absolutely nothing earth-shattering had happened; life seemed to simply be. Her idea did have possibilities, and they seemed much more appealing when she took my hands in hers and placed them firmly on her chest. God, I loved the way her breasts felt in my hands, and as I leaned down to kiss her, her words were throaty as she spoke and she lifted her hips beneath me.

"You've never been on top of me like *this* before," she said against my lips, and her fingers undid the knot that held up my pants.

In seconds we'd skinned each other of the little clothes we'd had left and I let Fran guide me on her. First I felt incredible warmth, but as my body settled on hers…Oh. My. God.

I don't know who gasped first or which of us let out the shuddered breath. I knew and knew well exactly how and why I enjoyed Fran riding me, how amazing it felt to feel her cunt play over and swallow mine; now I knew why she enjoyed it too, because the horizontal length of her engorged clit wedged into me and with every slide of my hips, my clit licked against her pubic mound.

It was good, it was really fucking good, and as good as it felt in my body, it felt even better to watch Fran's eyes first flutter shut, then open with surprise. I loved watching her chest heave as she fought for enough air to fuck me, loved too the tilt of her pelvis to increase the grind, the way the fingers of one hand dug into my hip while the others threaded through my hair, cupped the back of my neck, her tongue a line of fire up my chest before she pulled me in for a kiss that deepened the connect.

For the first time, or for the first time in a long time, we loved one another without the weight of the past, without the presence of power, without fear for the future. We simply were, and we followed our rhythms and desires, free to simply be us, because for once, finally, we had tomorrow. And even that didn't matter as she fit to me, back pressed firmly to my chest as I filled her, the gratifying solidity of her a constant brush on my thighs when she craned her head around and strained to kiss me while I touched her everywhere I could reach and hold, soft, silk, hard, wet…everything…she was everything, we were everything, one pulse, one song, one blood, one living cadenced beat.

When we fell asleep curled around and still holding each other wherever we could, it was to sleep with a sense of sureness I'd never felt before.

❖

I'll never really know what it was that woke me. All I can say for certain is that I'd gone from one of the most peaceful slumbers I'd ever had to full alertness, a sudden knowing that my attention was required. My eyes were open even before the knock on the door.

"Annie, Francesca. My apologies, but it's urgent," Elizabeth's voice said through the wood.

I could feel Fran snap to wakefulness perhaps a second after I did, and I gave her fingers a quick squeeze before I jumped out of bed.

"Just a moment," I called back. I grabbed the discarded sweats from the floor and tossed a pair back to Fran, then quickly rummaged about for some T-shirts.

I wiggled into my clothes and after quickly checking over my shoulder to be certain she was dressed, I crossed the floor to the door, Fran right behind me, her fingers laced through mine.

Elizabeth wore a grim expression as she faced us from the hallway. "Francesca," she began quietly, "your father is on the phone—pick it up in the library."

Fran hurried down the hallway and I would have followed, but Elizabeth gently restrained me.

"I'm sorry, Annie. You were right," she said in the same serious tone.

I shook my head in confusion. "What do you mean?"

She patted my shoulder gently through the sleeve of my shirt, and for just a second, between the emotion that waved from her and that which flashed through the overbright eyes she shone on me, I thought she might cry.

"Cort always tells me that I forget, you're not *like* the other members of the Circle, and until you know how to establish your own," she groped for the word, "perimeter, as it were, proven yourself, there is no doubt, none whatsoever, that those you are close to and those close to them are in danger."

My skin tingled when Fran's agitation bled back through me and my stomach tightened when I felt the sharp fear that knifed through her.

Whatever else Elizabeth was about to say fell unheard because I bolted along the same path Fran had taken, her pain tearing through me as if it were my own heart that would break.

I caught myself on the door frame and took a breath, just in time to see Fran place the phone back in its cradle.

Even as she turned to face me with tears streaming down her cheeks I already held her in my arms and I shared her fear and anguish as she clutched at me and sobbed against my neck.

"There was an accident—Gemma—I have to get to Milan—a car will be here in about an hour. My father," she gulped and caught her breath, "arranged it."

"Tell me all about it," I asked softly as I guided her to the settee with me. "Start from the beginning."

The details were a bit sketchy, but from what I could make of it, the family had been enjoying a late-night cappuccino at an outdoor café when a driver apparently lost control of his vehicle and plowed onto the sidewalk, scattering chairs, tables, and a few people along with them. Mrs. DiTomassa had suffered a fractured wrist, but Gemma's skull had been fractured; she was in critical condition in San Rafael Hospital.

"When did this happen?" It was a little after midnight in London.

"About an hour ago, maybe a bit more," she answered. "It's bad enough that Gemma's so hurt—but my father is using this as campaign publicity," she said indignantly as she sat up and wiped her eyes. "He has a press conference scheduled for ten in the morning."

I remembered quite well the man who made a speech at my father's funeral, then had a great photo op next to me and Uncle Cort as I was handed the flag that had been draped over the casket. And as I felt through the image, I could see him, read him, clearly.

He'd been at a loss, hadn't known what to say or do for such a young person, especially one he'd almost literally watched grow, facing something that made him ache for his own children, so he did what he could—he was a politician, and hoped that he could make a difference.

"He's scared, Frankie," I said, "he's scared, and he's doing the thing he knows how to do." I knew he had issues with his son and his daughter being gay, but he did love them in the way he could.

"Wish he'd learn something new," Fran said bitterly.

I didn't blame her for feeling or saying that.

"What time is your flight?" I asked quietly.

"Three thirty. It's a little more than three hours long, and my father said it would give me time to be presentable before his little circus."

A buzz ran through me, the beginning of something more than concern for Fran and her family. I wanted…I wanted to hold her hand when she visited her sister, I wanted to cheer her smiles, hold her like I did now when she was scared, and shield her from anything, everything, that might bring pain to her heart or tears to her eyes. I mutely held her closer and the buzz beat through me, the muted start of warning. "We have to get your things."

She shivered against me and took a deep, shaky breath. "Yes."

I knew one thing: there were no accidents.

Elizabeth had kindly started the job of packing Fran's things, and on top of her suitcase, she'd placed the peacoat Fran always wore. Fran sighed when she saw it. "I can't take that, you know," she said.

"Of course you can," I disagreed then smiled. I put my arms around her, kissed her forehead, kissed her cheek. "It's always looked better on you than me anyway."

"You think so, huh?" she asked as her hands rounded my waist.

"I know so." I hugged her to me. "We don't have a lot of time," I reminded her. "You're going to want to shower, dress, before your flight."

"Oh man, where's my head? Yeah," she agreed and stopped short. I knew what she was wondering about.

"Go, I've got clothes you can wear, don't worry," I assured her as I went to the bureau to get my own things together.

She headed for the door, and hesitated before she stepped through. "Will you be here when I'm done?"

"Yes."

❖

We decided to wait in the library we'd spent so many hours in together until the arrival of the car that would take her to London's Gatwick Airport for her flight to Milan's Linate. If it wasn't for the tearing sensation in my rib cage, my heart would have swollen in gratitude for the crackling fire Uncle Cort had once again taken the time to set up, and for the quick fix of sandwiches and tea that had been laid out on the desk.

"You'll get hungry on the flight," Elizabeth said, encouraging us both to eat something.

Fran gamely tried to take a bite, but quickly put her sandwich down, and Elizabeth took her hand in both of her own.

"Your sister," Elizabeth said, "was willing to fight and move across the ocean to be with her brother—she's a natural warrior. It's okay to be worried," she said gently, "but to give her strength, you'll need your own. Please eat?"

"I'll eat with you," I volunteered and it would of course figure that Elizabeth knew what she was about, since as I swallowed food and tea I felt my own internal tensions ease just the slightest bit.

"You know," Uncle Cort said as he walked into the study and took a seat directly across from us, "that you're always welcome, wherever any of us are, whenever, for however long. We are family."

Fran glanced up at him with an expression that made me want to weep. "Thank you," she said, "I feel the same way."

Elizabeth stepped over then reached down to hug her. "Of course you do," she said as Fran returned her hold. "We're all part of and sealed to the same Circle." She kissed the top of her head. "You've a home here, always, and I'm certain you'll be back before you know it."

She sighed as they released one another. "You've a little while," she said, and glanced over and caught Cort's eye, "so we'll leave you to chat."

He came over and crouched down to look into Fran's eyes, then took her hand in his. "Whatever happens," he said solemnly, "she is Wielder and your chosen Champion, and *nothing* can change that. Courage and faith, Fran, and we'll see you soon."

She nodded as he gave her a quick hug as well and when he stood, he and Elizabeth left us alone to our own good-bye.

Once they were gone, the same sense of wrong came back, was an alarm in my head, had grown from a shake in my gut to a repeated thump that I couldn't ignore, and it combined with the frantic sense that I had to *tell* Fran, tell her that I—

I needed to do something, something tangible to let her know that even if she wasn't with me… Inspired, I fumbled a moment with the clasp behind my neck until I got it loose and I held the ankh in my hands to drape around her.

"Here," I said, "I want you to hold on to this, to have this." I smoothed it along the soft skin where her collar left her neck bare even as her eyes widened at me.

"You, you can't do that—it's yours, part of you and—" she tried to protest.

"It's part of both of us," I corrected her quietly. "It holds both of us."

It was appropriate—the symbol that promised me to life worn by the woman who had grounded me back in it, had willingly bound herself to me and me through her to the Material. The metal lattice not only charged with energy, the pure energy of the Light, translated through me, through her, it also literally carried the essence of us, our *intents*, even our feelings toward each other.

It was a powerful charm and if Fran kept it, not only would she carry a part of me with her, but in a very real way, she'd carry the Light, a shield, a very direct protection that I...I didn't need anymore. I had it melted into my skin.

What I didn't know then, would come to learn later, was that her wearing of it, that symbol and especially that specific charm, older than even I could have guessed at the time, marked her as directly under the watchful eye of the Inner Circle—on every possible level. That had been why Cort had bade me not to take it off before I'd been sealed; it marked and protected me until I was one with the Circle, with the Light, and could take care of myself.

Fran stared at me wordlessly through eyes that threatened to overflow, and I kissed the beginnings of her tears as she cupped my face. "I'm sorry," she said.

"You've got nothing to be sorry for, Frankie," I told her through the salt taste on my lips and held her against me. I could feel her breathe, her heartbeat against my chest. "Everything's going to be fine—go see your sister, and when she's better..."

I couldn't help it; I ran my fingers down her back, across her arms, trying to memorize the feel of her as I covered her lips with mine to lose myself, just for the moment, in us while we still had it, which was insane, because there was no reason to think she wouldn't be back soon.

"Samantha," she said softly, and the sound of my full name from her lips made my eyes smart, "I'm going to miss you—maybe you can come to Milan and—"

"One step at a time," I said, "we'll be okay." I covered the ankh with my palm, felt the fierce thump under my hand. "We're still together, we're always together."

And yet maybe…maybe now was the time, maybe there would never be another… "Frankie," I breathed quietly against her. "I'm… you know that…that I'm in…" The words caught in my throat hard, burning, hurting, as she turned lambent eyes on me, eyes that told me she knew what I felt, what I wanted to say, what she wanted to say, too, and even if I wasn't certain that she could read the same from mine, I hoped she did, even as the warmth of it, the reality of it, wrapped around and filled the spaces between us.

"Don't," she whispered even as she nodded that she did know, and placed gentle fingers against my mouth. "If you say it," she told me, "I will, too—and then I *can't* leave."

She was right, and we both knew it as we wrapped around each other on the settee, holding each other so closely, so tightly, with so much to think and say and yet *almost* everything already said and felt, *known* between us. As the light from the fire flickered on the hearth and we simply listened to each other breathe, waiting for the inevitable, the lines of possibility and probability grew, stretched and shaped before my eyes, flashes of potential, flashes of the future. There was a quick but clear image in my mind, a sending through the Aethyr, a slip of the sphere projection-reality of time that made my pulse jump.

"Promise me something?" I asked softly against the hair I'd buried my face in.

"Anything, Sammer. Everything."

"If your father asks you to go back to the States with him, will you do it?"

She stirred in my arms and kissed my neck. "I want to come back for Christmas, celebrate the Solstice with you."

"I want that too," I answered, "but would you? Please?"

She moved her head to gaze into my eyes even as her fingertips measured along my face, trying to memorize me the way I did her. I didn't know if she could see what I did, but she easily knew what I felt.

"You're scared." It was a statement, not a question and I nodded, knowing it was useless to deny it to her when she lived under my skin too.

"Yes."

"For Gemma?"

I could only bite my lip and shake my head. "For you."

"Okay," she said finally with a soft exhale. "I'm not going to make you ache it out. I love you, I trust you. I will."

"Thank you," I told her and we pulled each other in again, waiting, waiting, for the sound that would make us part.

When Uncle Cort and Elizabeth came to the doorway we knew it was time and he carried her bag down the stairs as we followed behind.

We stepped out into the frigid air and I helped her into the black car her father had sent. "Hey, if your dad asks you what I'm studying," I began in an attempt to be lighthearted, "you can tell him—"

"Alchemy?" she supplied and grinned.

I chuckled. "Yeah. Sure. Something like that."

And then it was time, one last hug, one last kiss, one last feel of the grounding fit of her body against mine along with the mute promise of *soon* as everything I felt burned through my skin, and then she absolutely had to leave. "Call me when you land," I asked. "Don't worry about the time, call collect if you need to, okay?"

"I will," she promised, "as soon as I can, and then right after I've seen Gemma."

"Yes, good."

My chest tore open when the door slammed shut, and when the car pulled away, the pull of some vital part of me with it was a physical ache as I forced myself to watch and wave until I couldn't see it anymore.

My eyes stung as I stared at the semiquiet street, and still I felt the drag, my edges raw, exposed, and empty. Uncle Cort patted my shoulder with bracing roughness. "You'll freeze, come on."

I'd forgotten it was cold. I followed him inside and up the stairs. Neither he nor Elizabeth knew what to say to me and we paused, all facing each other in the silent hallway.

Elizabeth's eyes were large on me and I watched as Uncle Cort noted the charm missing from my neck. "You okay, dear heart?" he asked, gentle gruffness in the last words.

I was relieved to hear it because between the expression Elizabeth wore and the concern they both couldn't help but show, any other tone from him would have probably brought me to tears, and that was something I didn't want.

"Fine, I'm fine," I said and nodded at each of them past the sudden thickness in my throat. "Just gonna clear the library, play a little bass, is all."

"I'll help you," Elizabeth offered.

"Nah, 'sokay," I said and tried to grin. I think I failed. "I got it."

The fire still burned on the hearth while I cleared the detritus of the half-eaten food and as I carried the tray to the door, I paused—there, on that very settee, I'd held her, felt her heart beat against mine, could still feel the embrace of her body everywhere.

My room was even worse, because she lingered there even more strongly in my mind as well as the Aethyr, was a bodily flood of physical and emotional memory, and I pulled out my bass and slung it over my shoulder, hoping the vibration of it through my frame would still the thrumming pain that raced through me, would force me to center and still, to empty my mind. What the hell was wrong with me? I was caught between hurt and a panicky edge that swore to me that more was coming, the green sky threat of twisting, howling winds.

Oh dammit, playing wasn't *working* and I put the instrument down. I couldn't focus, couldn't rid myself of the waves of tingling pressure that rode up and down my skin, nor the ripping that cut through me.

This was ridiculous, I couldn't possibly allow this edgy hurt that scathed and tore and swam, it *had* to *stop*. For the first time since the summer, I rummaged into the bottom of the second drawer of my nightstand until I found it: a pack of double edged razors. I sat on the edge of my bed and pulled one out, contemplated its steel edge.

This can't hurt, I can't hurt like this, this is insane, I thought, and grasped the blade between my thumb and forefinger.

The tremble grew in my body, a bag of worms tumbling under my ribs as I pushed my sleeve up and stared at the unmarked skin above my wrist, the skin I hadn't touched—yet.

This I could control and if it didn't hurt, nothing would, nothing could hurt me more than I could. *I can't cry*, I thought and dispassionately drew a red line diagonally across my forearm. Blood for the lie I'd told, as if that could wash it away, blood for the lie based on the vision I'd had, the lie I sensed Fran knew anyway, and had been good and kind and brave enough to leave alone, blood for the tears, for the words, I couldn't, I *wouldn't* let go.

It didn't hurt at all, not really, anyway. The pain was a distant reality, a sting that had no deeper meaning and I fell into that same distance, from my head, from my body. *Nothing* hurt.

That's so odd, I observed with the same detachment. The blood welled up, but even as it ran, it thickened quickly, turned almost jellylike. I'd noticed that the first time I'd slashed my wrist those months ago. I'd had to repeat and repeat the movement; the initials I'd drawn, the cut across my palm during my sealing, they too had only bled for moments before the blood had thickened in the same way. I wondered what it meant as I brushed at the stuff on my skin and right then I heard pounding at the front door.

The sheer panic that radiated from it made me fly down the stairs, Elizabeth and Cort seconds behind me as I unlocked the door and swung it open without thinking.

Graham. It was Graham, dressed in his shirtsleeves, tears in his eyes, and fear billowing from him like smoke from a fire.

I dragged him in from the cold even as he spoke. "Lyddie," he said, "it's Aunt Lyddie—a neighbor just came to tell me—she's in London Hospital. Can you take me?"

"Yes, of course," I said.

"Come up and get warm, get a jacket before you go," Elizabeth said.

Cort helped me hustle him up the stairs. "What's happened?" he asked.

Graham drew a gulping breath. "Don't know. Alice came by—thank you," he nodded to Elizabeth as she handed him a cup of tea, "said we'd been burgled, heard a shout, then a shot, and now—we've got to hurry." He was desperate.

"We'll get there," Cort assured him as I ran up the stairs to grab another coat. Everything fell into place with the vision I'd had before Fran had left. My father had known something, something definite and so, geographically removed, and more importantly, his connection from the Circle stretched, thinned, he had been vulnerable. I grabbed a jacket and then, inspired, took out a long coat as well.

Whoever these people were, I thought, they believed I knew it too—but they couldn't get me directly. As above, so below...and as below, so above. So long as I was in the Circle...

Something else niggled and tickled at my brain and it seized on Fran and her family, her brother and sister who looked so alike and so like her, so like their mother...

"Fran was named for her mother," I announced as I sped downstairs and Cort's head snapped in my direction. "They're trying to eliminate the Circle and anyone connected to it," I explained as I crossed the floor. Cort nodded grimly

"What've you got in mind?" he asked.

An answer had already occurred to me as I'd covered the last few steps. "Take Graham to London Hospital, take Elizabeth with you," I said as I tossed the jacket to Graham, then slipped my own coat on. "If Lyddie's all right, take them all to Aberdeen—they should be safe there for a while. You and I will meet back here in three days."

Graham and Elizabeth stared at me as Cort nodded agreement. "And what will you do?"

The path was so very clear before me, I couldn't help but smile. It shone with a chill clarity, the clean, sharp whisper of a razor, the bright reflection of burnished steel, and the perfect, pointed cool logic of numbers as the ice ran through me, filled me, became the oh-so-welcome cold burn that made me want to dare the black wave to come and claim me—*if* it could. "I'm going to find Old Ralph Jones—it's time we chatted."

I let myself out and into the shop, took my weapon of choice, then got on my Vespa. I had a date with the devil and I knew how to dance.

AMERICAN GOTH

Yea, though I walk through the valley of the shadow of death,
I will fear no evil:
for I am the toughest motherfucker in the valley.
—Americanized Psalm 23

He was just outside the door of Spit, lounging against the brick. "Out for a spin?" he asked, nodding his chin toward me.

"*Je vous cherche,*" I seek you, I mocked as I walked toward him.

"*Vous êtes seul,*" he said in the dry voice that sounded like nettles blowing in the wind.

"Yes," I agreed, "I'm alone."

"But you're armed—I can sense it from here."

"I don't need a weapon for you," I said as I walked toward him.

He straightened from his perch and smoothed out his coat, a black that hung to his ankles. "Like the new threads?" he smirked as he ran his hands along his chest, then brushed at imaginary lint. "Ah, cashmere— not like the rough wool of a peacoat." His smirk grew wider.

But the tables had been turned since we'd last met, and it was time he knew it. This time I moved faster than he expected and pinned him to the wall. "Do you like breathing?" I asked him as I stared into glittering black eyes. His shoulder was surprisingly bony under my hand, and even on this level, his skin still carried a grayish waxy tint.

He cocked his head and gazed at me from under half-closed lashes. "You can't kill me—I'm part of the order of things, the way of the worlds, the Ex—arp!" he breathed harshly as my hand closed around his throat. That. Felt. Good.

"The Circle, you've betrayed them." The words were jagged as they ripped from my throat. "They allow your maggot existence, and you've sold them out. You've told someone who, where, Lyddie is, you've set them after Fran. Who else have you given up? Who did you tell?" I released him and he fell back hard against the brick, his breath harsh little puffs of steam in the air between us.

"You're smarter than the others," he said, attempting to recover his grin as he rubbed his throat. "A bit rougher too. I like that."

"I don't have to kill you, you know," I told him casually. "I know how the sword works—I just have to...let in a little light. I can do *that* on the Astral. Besides," I added, "it might...hurt...in other ways. You might grow a conscience."

"There's nothing wrong with a friendly little cash exchange," he said, the menace he'd had weeks before and the mockery from just moments ago all gone. "And they get what they ask for—no more, no less."

I let my hand drift to my side, and he swallowed as he watched where it landed. "So who asked you?"

"Uh-uh, it doesn't work that way," he shook his head as he took a step back and regained some of his earlier composure. "You offer me something, or I offer you something—that's the way it goes, the balance kept. I *do* like this coat. I should probably get new shoes to go with it."

I pretended to consider for about half a second. "Here's my offer. I don't rip you down to the nothing you deserve to dissolve into, your energy not even a memory trace on any level, and you tell me what I need to know."

He moistened thin lips with the tip of his tongue. "I could help you—tell you who the Dark Master is that's so close to you, so close and you're so blind, and then you'll owe me twice—I've already done you a favor."

I knew by now how Ralph worked—he never offered anything that wouldn't happen of its own accord, in its own time. He told the truth, but it was a truth to be examined from every angle—his deceptions were based on that.

"I owe *you* nothing," I said and wrapped my hand around the leather-wrapped hilt at my side. "Now you're useless *and* you're boring me—let's end it, and I'll figure it out from there." I moved on him again as I half drew.

"Wait—don't be so hasty—we can come to some sort of agreement!" he said, his voice a higher pitch as he held up his hands and backed away.

I advanced on him anyway until he was wedged in the corner of the outer vestibule. The brick wouldn't help or protect him.

"They just wanted a name—the name of the person who held you grounded. You did know Francesca is named for her mother, didn't you?" The words tumbled out, almost tripping over each other as he spoke. "Yeah," he said, nodding, "easy to find—politicians are very public figures—and they found what they were looking for. I give the goods, *and* I did you a solid—they didn't find *her*, right?"

My breath steamed out between us in little clouds as the full import of what he said sank in and I relaxed my grip. Holy shit. My instincts—my *seeing*—had been good, but not good enough—and Fran was even now on her way to Milan. Shit. Shit. Shit.

"Shame 'bout Lyddie, though. Got that on their own." He gazed at the ground and shook his head with seeming regret. "Well, then again, she's served the Light forever, probably time to—*rawk!*"

I again caught him by the throat. "I don't want to hear your speculations. I want the name of whoever paid for that coat, the identity of the next target, and anything else you can tell me." I shook him before I let him go, and he rested back against the wall, again rubbing his neck, resentment in the squint he gave me.

I pinned his eyes with mine. "I don't want your version of the truth—I want exacts. Fuck with me," I told him very precisely, "and I *won't* kill you."

"You won't?" he asked, obviously surprised.

"No." I shook my head and smiled with the same emotion I'd left the shop with thrilling through me—cold flame. "I will hunt you on every level and I *will* find you. I promise, I will break, and I will take you—piece by piece—and you won't know when I'm coming to claim them—Rafael."

It was a hunch, to call him by his true name. Names had power, and since his was never used, I wondered if it held power over him, power that might compel him.

"I *hate* that name," he muttered as he scratched the back of his neck. "You drive a hard bargain, but I accept your terms. Just keep that pointy thing away from me," he said, jamming a thumb toward what we both knew hung from my side. "Pure Light—ugh!" He shuddered dramatically. "Like drinking warm milk."

"Names, Rafael. Give me the names and the information I asked for."

He straightened once more, and energy flowed from him, an electric haze that popped with the real power he commanded. His voice changed, took on an echoing resonance. "Elizabeth. Elizabeth is the next target—and as above, so below. Don't assume the threat is purely Material," he warned.

I nodded as I accepted that—I'd have to get back before everyone left London. "Who contacted you?"

"I can't tell you."

"You can't, or you won't?"

He shook his head. "You've called me by name, I must tell you. But this was only a hound, probably several steps below the adept who commanded her. But I know what you seek," he said softly. "Find that adept—and find Judas."

I was young, I was still very new to the role I'd inherited, and the shocks had come thick and fast this night. But that one punched through my ice, and I couldn't completely hide my surprise. "That's a legend!"

"It is now," he agreed and shuddered, whether with memory or the very cold of the night I couldn't tell, "but your father knew differently."

I left Old Jones shivering in the dark while I took off and raced to London Hospital, questions and answers burning in my head as I rode down silent streets.

I understood now what my father had meant about possibilities and probabilities. Possibilities were infinite, probabilities were not—they were shaped by the circumstances that surrounded them, leading always, *always* to one and only one answer—and I was my father's daughter: I was Wielder.

The scratches on my arm and the burn scar above them throbbed as I rode, the reminder of my first failure to live up to my charge. It didn't matter that I hadn't known my role at the time—I had known the circumstances and had done nothing to change them. That would *never* happen again, I vowed as I neared the hospital.

I parked safely, then cut the engine and as I strode to the entrance I knew who I was and what I had to do—it was my *sworn* duty: to change the circumstances, to ensure the answer was right, for all time.

About the Author

JD Glass lives in the city of her choice and birth, New York, with her beloved partner. When she's not writing, she's the lead singer (as well as alternately guitarist and bassist) in Life Underwater, which also keeps her pretty busy.

JD spent three years writing the semimonthly *Vintage News*, a journal about all sorts of neat collectible guitars, basses, and other fretted string instruments, and also wrote and illustrated *Water, Water Everywhere*, an illustrated text and guide about water in the human body, for the famous Children's Museum Water Exhibit. When not creating something (she swears she's way too busy to ever be bored), she sleeps. Right.

Works in progress include *X*.

Further information can be found at www.boldstrokesbooks.com and at www.myspace.com/jdglass, where you can check out the daily music plays, blogs, reviews of all sorts of fun things, and the occasional flash of wit.

Books Available From Bold Strokes Books

Branded Ann by Merry Shannon. Pirate Branded Ann raids a merchant vessel to obtain a treasure map and gets more than she bargained for with the widow Violet. (978-1-60282-003-6)

American Goth by JD Glass. Trapped by an unsuspected inheritance and guided only by the guardian who holds the secret to her future, Samantha Cray fights to fulfill her destiny. (978-1-60282-002-9)

Learning Curve by Rachel Spangler. Ashton Clarke is perfectly content with her life until she meets the intriguing Professor Carrie Fletcher, who isn't looking for a relationship with anyone. (978-1-60282-001-2)

Place of Exile by Rose Beecham. Sheriff's detective Jude Devine struggles with ghosts of her past and an ex-lover who still haunts her dreams. (978-1-933110-98-1)

Fully Involved by Erin Dutton. A love that has smoldered for years ignites when two women and one little boy come together in the aftermath of tragedy. (978-1-933110-99-8)

Heart 2 Heart by Julie Cannon. Suffering from a devastating personal loss, Kyle Bain meets Lane Connor, and the chance for happiness suddenly seems possible. (978-1-60282-000-5)

Queens of Tristaine by Cate Culpepper. When a deadly plague stalks the Amazons of Tristaine, two warrior lovers must return to the place of their nightmares to find a cure. (978-1-933110-97-4)

The Crown of Valencia by Catherine Friend. Ex-lovers can really mess up your life…even, as Kate discovers, if they've traveled back to the eleventh century! (978-1-933110-96-7)

Mine by Georgia Beers. What happens when you've already given your heart and love finds you again? Courtney McAllister is about to find out. (978-1-933110-95-0)

House of Clouds by KI Thompson. A sweeping saga of an impassioned romance between a Northern spy and a Southern sympathizer, set amidst the upheaval of a nation under siege. (978-1-933110-94-3)

Winds of Fortune by Radclyffe. Provincetown local Deo Camara agrees to rehab Dr. Bonita Burgoyne's historic home, but she never said anything about mending her heart. (978-1-933110-93-6)

Focus of Desire by Kim Baldwin. Isabel Sterling is surprised when she wins a photography contest, but no more than photographer Natasha Kashnikova. Their promo tour becomes a ticket to romance. (978-1-933110-92-9)

Blind Leap by Diane and Jacob Anderson-Minshall. A Golden Gate Bridge suicide becomes suspect when a filmmaker's camera shows a different story. Yoshi Yakamota and the Blind Eye Detective Agency uncover evidence that could be worth killing for. (978-1-933110-91-2)

Wall of Silence, 2nd ed. by Gabrielle Goldsby. Life takes a dangerous turn when jaded police detective Foster Everett meets Riley Medeiros, a woman who isn't afraid to discover the truth no matter the cost. (978-1-933110-90-5)

Mistress of the Runes by Andrews & Austin. Passion ignites between two women with ties to ancient secrets, contemporary mysteries, and a shared quest for the meaning of life. (978-1-933110-89-9)

Sheridan's Fate by Gun Brooke. A dynamic, erotic romance between physiotherapist Lark Mitchell and businesswoman Sheridan Ward set in the scorching hot days and humid, steamy nights of San Antonio. (978-1-933110-88-2)

Vulture's Kiss by Justine Saracen. Archeologist Valerie Foret, heir to a terrifying task, returns in a powerful desert adventure set in Egypt and Jerusalem. (978-1-933110-87-5)

Rising Storm by JLee Meyer. The sequel to *First Instinct* takes our heroines on a dangerous journey instead of the honeymoon they'd planned. (978-1-933110-86-8)

Not Single Enough by Grace Lennox. A funny, sexy modern romance about two lonely women who bond over the unexpected and fall in love along the way. (978-1-933110-85-1)

Such a Pretty Face by Gabrielle Goldsby. A sexy, sometimes humorous, sometimes biting contemporary romance that gently exposes the damage to heart and soul when we fail to look beneath the surface for what truly matters. (978-1-933110-84-4)

Second Season by Ali Vali. A romance set in New Orleans amidst betrayal, Hurricane Katrina, and the new beginnings hardship and heartbreak sometimes make possible. (978-1-933110-83-7)

Hearts Aflame by Ronica Black. A poignant, erotic romance between a hard-driving businesswoman and a solitary vet. Packed with adventure and set in the harsh beauty of the Arizona countryside. (978-1-933110-82-0)

Red Light by JD Glass. Tori forges her path as an EMT in the New York City 911 system while discovering what matters most to herself and the woman she loves. (978-1-933110-81-3)

Honor Under Siege by Radclyffe. Secret Service agent Cameron Roberts struggles to protect her lover while searching for a traitor who just may be another woman with a claim on her heart. (978-1-933110-80-6)

Dark Valentine by Jennifer Fulton. Danger and desire fuel a high-stakes cat-and-mouse game when an attorney and an endangered witness team up to thwart a killer. (978-1-933110-79-0)

Sequestered Hearts by Erin Dutton. A popular artist suddenly goes into seclusion, a reluctant reporter wants to know why, and a heart locked away yearns to be set free. (978-1-933110-78-3)

Erotic Interludes 5: Road Games, ed. by Radclyffe and Stacia Seaman. Adventure, "sport," and sex on the road—hot stories of travel adventures and games of seduction. (978-1-933110-77-6)

The Spanish Pearl by Catherine Friend. On a trip to Spain, Kate Vincent is accidentally transported back in time—an epic saga spiced with humor, lust, and danger. (978-1-933110-76-9)

Lady Knight by L-J Baker. Loyalty and honor clash with love and ambition in a medieval world of magic when female knight Riannon meets Lady Eleanor. (978-1-933110-75-2)

Dark Dreamer by Jennifer Fulton. Best-selling horror author Rowe Devlin falls under the spell of psychic Phoebe Temple. A Dark Vista romance. (978-1-933110-74-5)

Come and Get Me by Julie Cannon. Elliott Foster isn't used to pursuing women, but alluring attorney Lauren Collier makes her change her mind. (978-1-933110-73-8)

Blind Curves by Diane and Jacob Anderson-Minshall. Private eye Yoshi Yakamota comes to the aid of her ex-lover Velvet Erickson in the first Blind Eye mystery. (978-1-933110-72-1)

Dynasty of Rogues by Jane Fletcher. It's hate at first sight for Ranger Riki Sadiq and her new patrol corporal, Tanya Coppelli—except for their undeniable attraction. (978-1-933110-71-4)

Running With the Wind by Nell Stark. Sailing instructor Corrie Marsten has signed off on love until she meets Quinn Davies—one woman she can't ignore. (978-1-933110-70-7)

Punk and Zen by JD Glass. Angst, sex, love, rock. Trace, Candace, Francesca…Samantha. Losing control—and finding the truth within. BSB Victory Editions. (1-933110-66-X)

Punk Like Me by JD Glass. Twenty-one-year-old Nina writes lyrics and plays guitar in the rock band Adam's Rib, and she doesn't always play by the rules. And oh yeah—she has a way with the girls. (1-933110-40-6)